"What do you want to do at the new house?"

She laughed and tugged at her haphazard bun. "So much. A complete overhaul." When she looked up, he was staring at her with a look akin to awe.

"Santo? Are you okay?"

He nodded. "Uh…yes." His gaze moved over her face and then settled on her hair. "I've just never known a contractor with such beautiful hair."

A blush moved down Davina's neck. Great. Now she'd get the blotchies, as her sister Tilly always called them. A flush that only showed off her freckles. Maybe he wouldn't notice.

He kept staring at her.

"Santo, the house?"

"Oh, yes, the house," he said with a wry smile. "I need to focus on the house."

Frantic now, she searched her notes. What was happening to her anyway? She never acted like a ninny with clients.

With over seventy books published and millions in print, **Lenora Worth** writes award-winning romance and romantic suspense. Three of her books finaled in the ACFW Carol Awards, and her Love Inspired Suspense novel *Body of Evidence* became a *New York Times* bestseller. Her novella in *Mistletoe Kisses* made her a *USA TODAY* bestselling author. Lenora goes on adventures with her retired husband, Don, and enjoys reading, baking and shopping... especially shoe shopping.

Books by Lenora Worth

Love Inspired

Men of Millbrook Lake

Lakeside Hero
Lakeside Sweetheart
Her Lakeside Family

Texas Hearts

A Certain Hope
A Perfect Love
A Leap of Faith

Sunset Island

The Carpenter's Wife
Heart of Stone
A Tender Touch

Love Inspired Supense

Men of Millbrook Lake

Her Holiday Protector
Lakeside Peril

Visit the Author Profile page at Harlequin.com for more titles.

Her
Lakeside Family

Lenora Worth

HARLEQUIN® LOVE INSPIRED®

Recycling programs
for this product may
not exist in your area.

LOVE INSPIRED BOOKS

ISBN-13: 978-0-373-62257-3

Her Lakeside Family

Copyright © 2017 by Lenora H. Nazworth

www.Harlequin.com

Printed in U.S.A.

Therefore with joy shall ye draw water
out of the wells of salvation.
—*Isaiah* 12:3

To my family, always.

Chapter One

"Lucia, stop aggravating your sister! Adriana, hurry and get your backpack. Daddy's late for work. And where did your brother go?"

A screaming cyclone whizzed by, all dark curls and giggles.

Nate.

Santo Alvanetti grabbed his two-year-old son and tried for the third time to get his shoes on. But Nate wasn't in the mood to get dressed so he kept running away, taking off an article of clothing each time. Now he was down to his little blue jeans and one shoe.

"Daddy, the school bus is coming," Lucia—the oldest, who'd just turned nine—screamed from the floor-to-ceiling front windows. "I'm gonna miss it again."

Santo sent her a pleading glance. "It's okay, honey. I'll drop you off at school."

The school was in town, near Millbrook Lake. Completely out of his way but he was already late. Thirty more minutes wouldn't hurt. His cell rang, indicating his being late had already cost him money. Alvanetti Imports moved at a fast pace. He needed to do the same, but these days every morning had become a challenge and a race against time.

Adriana stomped a booted foot. "I can't find my purse, Daddy."

"She has a purse?" he asked Lucia. His middle child was only seven. But then, her late mother had loved expensive purses.

Lucia's dark eyes opened wide. "Duh. We both do. Mom bought them for us a long time ago, before…" Her eyes went dull. "We need Mom back here. She knows how to find purses."

Santo wasn't sure how to answer that. His wife Althea was dead. She'd died a horrible death about a year ago, in a showdown with his sister Rikki and a police detective. While Santo both mourned her and resented her for betraying him, her children still missed her. Althea had tried to be a good mother but something had gone so wrong in their marriage.

Raising three children and trying to run a business made Santo too tired and stressed to try to figure out what had happened to bring his life crashing down around him. He thought of happier times with Althea, when they were younger and she still loved him. He'd pushed away his anger and pain for a while now, but his children had been acting out. They all needed help.

Nate started crying.

Santo wanted to cry right along with him but he couldn't do that. He had to be strong. He had to get to work. He needed every ounce of strength just to make it through each day. The import business the Alvanetti family had been running for decades was legitimate now and finally back in the black.

Because he'd put every waking hour into making it work.

So he grabbed Nate again and managed to get him dressed, but the boy didn't want to go to the day care.

"I want Mommy," the little boy cried, kicking to get out of Santo's arms.

Nate probably didn't remember Althea all that much but he always echoed whatever his older sisters said. The counselor had warned Santo to let his children talk about their mother but each time they mentioned her, his heart hurt with a pain that rivaled a jagged cut. It was a tear that would never heal. Promising himself he'd never go through that kind of pain again, Santo gritted his teeth and focused on his children.

The doorbell rang, the chimes echoing over the fifteen-foot-high ceiling and the modern, wood-and-steel open staircase. Outside the spring sunshine glistened on the infinity pool and the bay below the bluffs. Santo had a stunning view thanks to the wall of glass across from the living room and kitchen.

There had been a wall of glass between him and Althea, too.

But he didn't even notice the view anymore and the guilt he'd felt at not knocking down that wall between them had long dissipated like a morning mist over the water. He'd be so glad to get out of this house. Too many bad memories for him and too many memories of her for his children. They all needed a fresh start.

"Daddy, the bus!"

"Daddy, the doorbell!"

"I want Mommy."

He prayed the new nanny—one of many his sister, Rikki, had hired since Althea's death—had arrived. He hadn't met the woman but Rikki and Blain had vetted and cleared her, stating she had impeccable credentials. Santo hurried to the door and opened it while he held Nate's squirming, screaming little body against his heart.

The woman standing there didn't look like the typical nanny. She had strawberry-blond hair that shot out in chunky layers around her face and chin. Her eyes were an ethereal green, like the bay waters in the early morning. She wore a plaid button-up shirt, worn jeans and…work boots.

"Hello," the woman said. "I'm—"

"I'm so glad you're here, Mrs. Brownlee," Santo interrupted, shoving Nate into her arms. "The instructions are on the counter in the kitchen. The girls go to Millbrook Elementary and they usually catch the bus or ride home with a neighbor. I'll take them to school and call the neighbor to pick them up this afternoon. Nate has day care but now that you're here, let's just keep him home today."

He kissed his sobbing son. "C'mon, girls."

Nate started crying all over again. But the woman standing there marched right on in and said something soothing in his son's ear. Nate hiccupped and stopped crying, his misty brown eyes glued on the woman holding him.

She smiled over at Santo. "I'm sorry but—"

"I want my purse," Adriana said on a scream, her long brown curls falling over her purple tunic and matching leggings. She looked at the surprised woman. "I can't leave without my purse."

The pretty nanny looked at Adriana with sympathetic eyes. "Of course not. I never leave home without my—"

"Found it," Lucia said, shoving the shiny purple

shoulder bag at her little sister. "Now can I please get to school?"

Santo let out a sigh and nodded to the woman. "You don't have to apologize but please try to be on time from now on, okay?"

The woman's green eyes flared with something akin to mirth. "Mr. Alvanetti, I don't think you understand. I'm not—"

"I'm here." A shrill, laughing voice came from the open door. "And not a moment too soon from the looks of things."

Confused, Santo turned to find a plump, smiling woman with short auburn hair and black-framed, crystal-encrusted glasses standing on the threshold. "I'm Virginia Brownlee. I'm your nanny."

Santo looked from the smiling woman at the door to the bemused woman still holding his son. "Then who are you?"

"I've been trying to tell you that for the last five minutes," she said, passing Nate back to him. "I'm Davina Connell. I'm here to help you get this house in shape to sell. I'm the contractor."

Davina almost felt sorry for him.

Santo Alvanetti exuded power and assurance, his tailor-made suit, his hair crisp and dark and falling in touchable curls around his face and neck much in the same way as his son's. But right now, the man's expression filled with realization and panic, his onyx gaze darkening even more.

"I am so sorry," he said, obviously rewinding his thoughts so he could assess the situation. "It's been one of those mornings and I was expecting Mrs. Brownlee and I must have gotten the time wrong and…I completely forgot you would be coming by today."

Even as he explained, one of the beautiful little girls let out a yelp and his son started crying again. While his cell buzzed over and over.

"Give me the boy," Mrs. Brownlee said in a manner that made them all stop what they were doing. "I'll put him in his car seat and I'll get the girls to school. You did alert the school that I have permission to drop them off and pick them up, of course."

His gaze moved from the prim woman to Davina. "Not yet, but I'll put that on my list."

"Well, let's get on with it then," Mrs. Brownlee said, her big glasses and boot-cut jeans made her look much too hip to be a nanny.

"Look, I'll drop the girls at school," he replied. "And I'll get it all straightened out. If you can just handle Nate."

"Nate and I will be fine," Mrs. Brownlee replied. "When you get home tonight, I'll go over the terms of my employment. For now, we're all going to be okay."

He looked from her to Davina again as if caught in a trap. Again, Davina felt empathy and sympathy for him, her heart doing a little tug that made her much too aware of how handsome the man was. "Would you walk me to my car?" he asked. "So we can discuss what needs to be done with the house?"

"Sure." Davina smiled at Mrs. Brownlee, her heart hammering an erratic beat against her insides. "I'll be back to look over the house and do some calculating, if that's okay with both of you."

Mrs. Brownlee nodded. "Won't bother me a bit." Giving them both an impish grin, she added, "I'll be doing the same."

"Let's go, girls," he said, prodding the two dark-haired children toward his sleek sedan. After he had the chattering, fussing girls inside the car with their seat belts on, he left the driver's door open and turned to Davina. "I'm so sorry I didn't know who you were. I thought my sister said David…somebody…would be coming by. I wasn't expecting—"

"A woman?" she finished. "I've never been called David but my dad calls me Dani." She spelled out the nickname for him. "I prefer Davina, however."

"Davina," he said, his dark eyes pouring over her like liquid chocolate. "I think I'll remember your name from now on."

"It's okay," she said to hide the sizzle of something richer and darker than even his chocolate eyes. "I was hoping we could do a walk-through on the house."

His cell buzzed with an annoying hum. "Work," he explained, checking it and shutting it down. "I'm late for a meeting."

And by the way he was fidgeting, he wanted out of here.

"Well, I'm burning daylight," she said in her firm voice that usually made surprised, unsure men sit up and take notice. "What do you want me to do?"

"Rikki trusts you so I guess I will, too," he replied, already getting into the car. "Look it over and call me with an estimate. Maybe we can meet here again later."

"Maybe." She wasn't going to hold her breath on that. "My time is just as valuable as yours, so that's your choice."

He stared up at her again, causing Davina to shiver

even while the early springtime sun was warm on her skin. "My sister says you come highly recommended," he said. "She just neglected to explain that you're a woman."

"Does that matter?" Davina asked, used to this type of conversation. "I work harder than any man you could hire." She handed him her business card.

"It matters," he said, his tone low and gravelly. Tucking the card in his pocket, he added, "But not in the way you might think."

Then he cranked the car and backed out of the driveway, leaving Davina to wonder why her being here should matter to him at all.

Chapter Two

Davina moved around the modern, sleek living room of the house on the bay, reminding herself she was taking on this job and the renovation of the other house this man had also purchased because her friend Rikki Alvanetti Kent had handpicked her. She'd known Rikki since college and they'd kept up with each other since they both worked in the same field.

Rikki was an interior designer, so they threw each other work here and there. And this was a big chunk of work.

Davina needed this project on her résumé since she was trying to establish her budding construction company as a leading player in the ever-changing Southern real estate market. But she'd heard the rumors that swirled with all the flickering evasiveness of fireflies around the quaint town of Millbrook Lake, Florida.

Santo Alvanetti came from a gangster family. A Mafia lord. His wife murdered two people close to Rikki Alvanetti and tried to kill her, too. Althea Alvanetti died in a shoot-out at an old warehouse. Detective Blain Kent killed her to save the woman he loved. The whole mess involved a diamond-and-emerald necklace that belonged to Santo's mother, Sonia.

Everyone says they've changed and that they aren't doing anything illegal now, but you need to stay away from that family.

Although she and Rikki hadn't talked in detail about the tragedy that had happened over a year ago, Rikki had told her if she didn't feel comfortable taking the job, they'd all understand. But Davina had a policy that had always served her well. Ignore the rumors and get to the truth. And in renovating houses, the truth always lay in the bones. This house was a showpiece, no doubt. But the bones were sorely lacking.

Something was missing.

"I don't feel the love," Mrs. Brownlee said as she came back into the big open area with the majestic windows that highlighted the pool and the water beyond. "I just don't feel it at all."

Davina turned toward the older woman. "Me either. There's a sadness shadowing this brilliant room."

"I think it's called neglect," Mrs. Brownlee replied, running her finger over a dusty table, her earrings swaying. "It lacks warmth."

"Yes, I agree," Davina said. She liked Virginia Brownlee. "Even with the stunning view and all the glass that brings in the sunshine, it's still a bit cold."

"Call me Virginia," the other woman said. "What do you aim to do to make this place worthy of love again?"

Davina grinned and grabbed the leather tool pouch her daddy had given her for her twenty-fifth birthday. Da had always understood her need to hammer and build since he'd once owned his own construction company. A company where she'd worked after school and on weekends just to learn the business. Until her daddy had booted her out and sent her on her way once she'd finished college.

Now, she turned to study Virginia Brownlee. "You're awfully blunt. I like that."

"I don't pull any punches," Virginia replied, her brown eyes turning melancholy. "This family is in crisis. But I knew that coming in. Such a tragedy."

Davina wasn't going to gossip.

"But it's not my place to discuss Mr. Alvanetti's personal life with anyone," Virginia replied, confirming that she didn't intend to do that either. Lowering her voice, she added, "My focus is on the children. I'm going to check on little Nathan. I think he might be coming down with something."

"Have you always been a nanny?" Davina asked, making conversation since they'd be around each other a lot during the next few weeks.

"No." Her new friend started up the open stairs and unlocked the safety gate at the top.

Okay, a bit cryptic but maybe the woman didn't like nosy questions. Davina was known for asking a lot of questions, however. Curiosity could get her into trouble.

"I'll be measuring and taking notes," Davina replied in a loud retort. "I'll also have my crew come back with me later to show them what needs to be done. I think I can bring this place up to speed to sell but it'll be a challenge."

"And bring the light back into this home," Virginia said with a smile, her hoop earrings jangling. Then she toddled off on her cushioned wedge loafers, her funky glasses sparkling in the sun.

Mary Poppins with Bohemian earrings is in the

house, Davina thought. But this house needed someone to shake it up if Santo expected to get top dollar when he put it on the market. Davina moved around the wide rectangular kitchen, ideas popping into her head. The planes and angles of this place were sharp and jagged, made of wood, stone and granite. Icy. Cold. Unyielding.

Like the man who owned it?

His eyes weren't icy. They were rich and warm and chocolate. She loved chocolate. Especially dark chocolate. But his onyx gaze also held a hint of regret and a longing for redemption.

Stop that, she cautioned. *Out of your league. Out of your range. Not your type at all.*

Davina wasn't sure what her type was anyway, since she went through what her younger sister, Tilly, called *possibles* as fast as she went through nails. She didn't have time to date, let alone think about a client in romantic terms. Her chaotic family back in Bayou Fontaine, a sleepy river town near New Orleans, needed her help.

Her brother Darren, a hothead who thought he should be ahead of his baby sister in the construction field, always teased her about her pointed views and blunt ways.

"You can't be mushy and sentimental about building houses, Davina. You'll never survive."

She'd not only survived. She'd thrived. She didn't build houses. She rebuilt them. Her daddy had forced her out of the company, telling her she needed to make her own way. Now her overconfident brother wasn't speaking to her but that was okay. As long as Darren took care of what was left of Connell Construction, she'd do her part by helping with the family finances.

So she ignored how Santo Alvanetti made her stomach lift and crash like a confused wave and started taking notes on what needed to be done to breathe some life into this stunning house.

Two hours later, the front door opened and Davina jumped and whirled around to find Santo standing there staring at her.

"I shouldn't have left like that," he said. "I hurried through my meeting so I could get back to you. I mean, back to this." He lifted a hand toward the high ceilings. "I need to get away from this house and I've put off doing it long enough. My children need a new start in a more modest, child-friendly home. Whatever you can do to make that happen, I'm all for it."

Davina went to her tote bag and pulled out a cupcake centered in a clear plastic container. "Breakfast," she said with a shrug. "But I'm willing to share. I never make decisions on an empty stomach and I got so involved in work, I forgot I had this in my bag."

Glancing at her cupcake, he said, "I know where you bought that and I sure *hope* you're willing to share it."

"Let's go over my plans for this place and then... I might let you have half. That is if you agree to my stipulations."

"You're tough, aren't you?"

Davina wasn't all that tough. Right now, she felt weak, her knees trembled and her sturdy boots were the only thing holding her up. Santo Alvanetti seemed to be flirting with her. Probably trying to make up for that false start, which was still kind of sweet since she got to hold that adorable little boy.

"Don't look so glum," she said, trying to show him she could be fair. "I'll try to make this as painless as possible."

He actually smiled. And her insides turned as mushy

as the center of this Peaches-and-Cream cupcake she'd bought earlier.

Mushy doesn't cut it, Davina.

The challenging echo of her brother's words made her spine stiffen. And made her want to demo something.

"From Marla's place?" Santo asked, hopefulness cresting in his expression when he pointed to the cupcake.

"Don't you know it," she retorted, trying to calm her suddenly jittery nerves. "We'll nibble while we walk and talk. I have a lot of ideas."

An hour later, Santo felt sick to his stomach, the sweet bite of cupcake weighing heavily against his gut. "This is your estimation?" Staring at the figures on her list of needed updates, he said, "I thought some paint and a few new rugs would do the trick."

"Then you don't know your house," she retorted, her black pen tapping the paper. "One of your toilets has a loose handle and really, the whole thing has seen better days. You need something with less water-flow. More economical."

"Toilets? I hadn't even thought of toilets."

"My point exactly."

"Okay, so you also listed new hardwood flooring to replace the tile in here?"

"Yes. To warm things up and make the floors more family-friendly for the next owners. This marble in the entryway from the pool is dangerous for children with wet feet. We can put a sturdy rug there to keep the skids to a minimum."

"And adults, too," he admitted. "I've slipped there myself, several times." Althea used to laugh at him when he'd wipe out. Of course, his deceased wife always walked around in stilettos.

"Then I think engineered wooden floors with heavy rugs at all the entryways will help with that. Now, in the bedrooms we can go with a strong, durable allergy-free carpet for the kids' rooms and maybe hardwood in the master." She paused. "Oh, and your master shower is outdated and kind of pretentious."

He nodded and winced. "I've never liked it. I don't need a waterfall inside a terrarium running 24/7 near my shower."

"Good. Because this is a house, not a jungle," she said on a smile. Then she went on to explain several more problems that he'd either ignored or hadn't even been aware of. "We can fix all of it with a few tweaks and some sweat equity."

"I wish it could be a home again," he replied. "I'll write you a check for the renovations."

"I'm sorry for what you've had to deal with," she said on a low tone.

His radar went up and the trust stirring between them disappeared. "What have you heard?"

Davina's soft green gaze held his, strong and steady. "Enough," she said. "But I don't gossip and I don't judge. I'm just sorry for your loss and everything you and Rikki have been through. She told me a little but...it seemed hard for her to talk about so I didn't pressure her."

Santo exhaled a breath. No, he didn't like to talk about this and furthermore she was an outsider who had no reason to be involved in the horror of his past. But maybe he could trust her.

"I lost more than my wife," he admitted. "Getting out of this house seems like the right thing to do. To start a new phase of my life with my children. I tried to make it work but instead of getting better, things are getting worse. It's not healthy. They need a different kind of home now." He leaned against the counter. "And I need to be away from this place."

"Well, that's where I come in," Davina replied, her tone thankfully neutral. "I'll fix this one up to sell and then we'll tackle the one you bought on the lake. Now that is going to be a charmer."

He wanted to tell her she was a charmer. She made him smile and Santo had forgotten how to do that. But he couldn't go on just a smile. He needed her to get this done so they could all get on with their lives. "I suppose it will be worth giving my children something new and hopeful to focus on. I'll cover the expenses. So do whatever you need to do. Just do it fast."

"It might take as long as three weeks here and at least that many months on the lake house. So my crew and I will be around for a while."

Santo wasn't sure he wanted to hear that, either. Strangers moving through his home at all hours. "Okay. I'll make arrangements to keep the kids out of your hair."

"I'll coordinate that with Mrs. Brownlee," she said. "I'll bring in a couple of crew members and we'll work around your routine."

Santo realized he was letting other people control his life these days but he didn't know how to get it back on track without a little help. His sister, Rikki, had taken over a lot of the responsibilities around here. Santo needed to get himself together so Rikki could enjoy her married life.

"Whatever you have to do to make this quick and

painless, I'd appreciate," he said to Davina. "I'll be at work most of the time but I'll check in on things."

She stood across the counter, her gaze danced over him and then back to what remained her of the once-giant cupcake. "Okay, now we can work out the details about who gets the rest of that cupcake."

Santo laughed in spite of the heaviness that had burdened him for months now. "You've been eyeing that thing the whole time, haven't you?"

"I sure have," she said, grabbing the cupcake holder. Then she launched back into her grand plan for his house.

Santo listened, watching as she nibbled on the cupcake without losing a crumb. In awe, he couldn't remember the last time he'd felt this relaxed, money and remodeling aside.

When she whirled around to face him, they almost crashed together but he caught her and then stood back, the second of contact jolting through him like an electric shock.

But Davina didn't miss a beat even if her eyes did widen. "And wait until you hear what I have in mind for the lake house. We'll have a whole cake to soften that blow when I go over the details."

Santo decided he could handle that. Davina was smart and talented and determined. And she loved her work. His sister had put him in good hands. But then, Rikki knew him so well and she'd been through this awful ordeal, too. He was glad she'd moved back here and he had grudgingly accepted her husband, Blain Kent, as a trusted friend. They'd both been a comfort to Santo over these last long months and truth be told, they'd suffered just as much as he had. Blain still had nightmares about having to shoot Santo's wife in order to save Rikki. But they had each other and Blain loved Rikki. Santo wished he and Althea could have had that kind of solid foundation.

Maybe this house had been built on sinking sand.

He had no one, and his children, while a joy, weren't old enough to understand what he was dealing with. Not yet, but Lucia had asked a lot of questions.

He'd have to make good on his side of this bargain, Santo decided. He'd have to invest some sweat equity of his own.

And watching Davina now with anticipation lighting up her pretty face, he didn't think that would be such a hardship. She'd breathed new life into this house.

Maybe being around her could bring him back to life, too.

Chapter Three

Two days later, Davina stood in the galley kitchen of the garage apartment Rikki had suggested she rent for the spring. Since she'd be here in Millbrook Lake for months, Davina had readily agreed after seeing the neat little one-bedroom apartment located on the church grounds. It had a massive picture window with a great view of the lake, and she could walk to church and just about anywhere else. She loved walking around the lake every evening. Tonight would be a good time. Lovely, warm and with a gentle breeze.

But her cell rang before she could go put on her sneakers.

Mom.

"Hello," Davina said, waiting for the usual questions of "How are you? Are you working too hard? Are you seeing anyone?"

She got those and more, but she only told her mom what she wanted her to know. Coming from a big, noisy and nosy family had shaped Davina's entire personality. She liked being independent and out on her own, even if she did miss her family all the time. But she wasn't about to tell her mother about Santo Alvanetti.

"When are you gonna settle down?" Nancy asked each time she went home to Bayou Fontaine.

"I'm settled, Ma," Davina would always reply. "Settled into my work. I love what I do and one day, I'll finally get our house back the way it should be."

Ma always laughed and kissed her on the cheek. "Look at you, worrying about this old money trap when you need to be having babies and cooking meals."

She didn't want babies and meals. She wanted rooms to paint and trim and she wanted walls to tear down and rebuild. Her daddy had once been in charge of a growing construction company but his bad health and some equally bad decisions during the lean housing market had caused him to almost lose everything. She and Darren had done what they could, but Da was still working part-time and still struggling.

He'd forced Davina to leave the nest, telling her she had a lot of talent that she shouldn't waste following him around.

But she'd always wondered if maybe her dad had sent her away because she was a woman and he believed she'd never be good at construction.

She'd show all of them. She wanted to help her family so she needed to get her crew settled in nearby apartments and hotels since they'd be here for the long haul.

Santo and his adorable children came to mind.

He had a family. A family in need of a good home. A loving home. But he also had walls that needed rebuilding. Or moving.

"You'll certainly have a challenge with *him*," she mumbled.

Santo Alvanetti had a solid wall around himself.

An invisible wall that he didn't even see and a wall he obviously couldn't see through, either. Davina always summed up a home owner while she was measuring and calculating. It didn't take much to sum up Santo Alvanetti. Widowed, tragic and stressed to the max. Unavailable. Unwilling to risk anything. With anyone.

Her focus was on getting his place in shape to sell so she could get to the really good project. The old rambling house he'd bought on the lake in town. That house had not only good bones. It had a real heart. It would be the one house that could showcase her talents on a regional and maybe even a national level.

Davina would focus on the houses and not their owner because her goal had always been on rebuilding and renovating.

Virginia would focus on the children.

But Davina had to wonder who was focusing on helping Santo Alvanetti to heal from his wife's betrayal.

"I can't seem to focus."

Santo didn't like admitting that but he had to talk to someone and the man sitting across from him was the only person he could trust not to spread any more rumors about him.

Rory Sanderson's blue eyes remained calm and blank. He was a good minister and Santo liked him a lot. But Rikki and her friends had brought him kicking and screaming to visit with the man who preached each Sunday at the Millbrook Lake Church in town. Today for the sake of privacy, Rory had driven the few miles north of town to the offices and warehouse at Alvanetti Imports to counsel Santo. While he looked more like a beach bum or maybe a surfer than a minister, Rory was kind and compassionate and he withheld judgment. He listened a lot more than he advised. Which scored points with Santo. He was so tired of unsolicited, unmanageable advice.

"Why can't I just snap out this?" he asked Rory now, his gaze moving to the business card on his desk that stated in a bold, black scroll—*Davina Connell Construction, Bayou Fontaine, Louisiana.* "I have a new nanny and she's great with the kids and Davina Connell is working day and night to update the house. It's beginning to look like a different place, a better place. She's doing things I would have never thought of doing. I should be able to relax a little and concentrate on what's important. I've never had trouble balancing things, even when Althea neglected the entire family. I made it work but now… I don't have any energy. I need to keep things going for my children and for this business."

"It takes time," Rory said. "Grief can take a toll and it shows up in many forms and it comes at the most unexpected times. It can exhaust you completely. You and the children might all experience outbursts, impatience, lack of focus, lack of appetite, lack of sleep."

"All of the above," Santo admitted. "I see the outbursts in my children but I know I lose my patience even more now than I did before."

"So you've never been a patient man?" Rory asked with a wry smile.

"Not very good at it, no." Santo thought back over the last year or so. "It's been a while since…Althea died. I thought I'd be able to get on with my life by now but I can see how this was building up when she was still alive. My children are still suffering and I don't know how to help them."

"You can help them by *learning* to be patient. But more importantly, you need to be in the moment with them. I know that might sound cliché, but it works," Rory replied on a gentle note. "Hold them. Talk to them. Sit with them. Read to them. And when they ask about their mother, let them talk and try to answer their questions."

"How can I explain what happened to my wife?" Santo asked, that old dread burning through his stomach. "I can't tell them the truth. It's hard enough for me to accept but to explain that she died because she was trying to steal from our family and she became a murderer—trying to explain that to my children is downright impossible."

"You don't need to give them the brutal details," Rory replied. "Not yet. But Lucia is old enough to hear things at school or even at church and you've mentioned she's already asked some questions. Other children can be cruel. You don't have to tell her anything but if she comes home upset, let her explain and then work from there. You can tell her that her mommy went through a bad time and made some bad choices and that you're sad she got into trouble. If your children ask for the truth, you have to keep reminding them that Althea loved them and that it's not their fault any of this happened."

Santo leaned over his desk, a hand going to his forehead. "I don't want that day to come, Rory. My heart can't take seeing my children hurting any more than they already are. That's why I decided to move. She came home crying one day because a friend teased her about not having a mom anymore."

"No one's heart is safe when it comes to their children," Rory said. "Parents hurt when their children hurt. But you have to be strong for them."

"I'm tired," Santo said. "Too tired."

"Have you thought about taking some time off?"

He let out a sigh and picked up a pen that had the Alvanetti logo on it. "I can't."

Rory didn't push him. "Well, maybe leave a little early once or twice a week. Surely you have someone here you can trust to run this place in your absence." Then Rory added an enticing tidbit of a suggestion. "Why don't you do what you said you'd do and help Davina and her crew with the renovations on the lake house?"

Santo thought about that. Was he afraid to turn over the reins to anyone else? Probably since his trust meter was broken these days. He'd certainly become more controlling since his wife's betrayal and death. "I did tell her I'd put in some sweat equity," he said. "But I'd probably get in the way."

"Davina's good at showing home owners how to become handymen," Rory said. "She was gentle with Vanessa and me when we renovated Vanessa's house. A word of warning, however. Davina believes in authenticity. The house is a Craftsman style and she made sure we both honored that."

Santo grinned and bobbed his head. "Yes, over the last couple of weeks, I've heard all about my mid-century modern and how I should have been true to that style while updating as needed. The woman is a tough taskmaster but she delivers her lectures with such a pretty smile, I hardly know I'm being fussed at."

"Oh, it's like that?" Rory asked with his own grin.

Santo held up his hand. "Oh, no. It's not like that. We're existing in the same space at times. I see her when

I get home each night and early each morning before I leave for work. Sometimes we talk on the phone, too. She's good at keeping me updated on how she's spending my money."

Maybe it *was* like that, he realized since he'd begun to enjoy those quick visits and her detailed updates. In fact, they had a meeting scheduled tonight at her apartment for a change.

"I'll think about what you've suggested," he told Rory. "I'm still trying to make amends for getting her confused with the nanny. Won't make that mistake again."

Two very different women and both of them trying to help him. He wondered what they'd thought, what they'd talked about once he'd left the house that first day. Still surprised at how attractive Davina Connell had turned out to be, he had to smile.

Rory picked up on that. "Well, you're looking more rested and it's good to see you smiling. I know Davina is not what you expected, but that could be a good thing."

Santo didn't comment. He wasn't ready to delve into his mixed feelings regarding his pretty contractor.

After Rory said a prayer with him and left to go back to town, Santo sat and stared out at the river beyond the docks, wondering how he'd ever get over the horror of what had happened in his family.

The tall pines and old twisted oaks swayed in the spring breeze and the brownish-green water, filled with tannins and covered with a brackish sheen, moved in a steady flow to meet up with the bay. Everything moved, except him.

Once they were over the initial shock of Althea and Victor's betrayal and the scandal had died down, his parents had become even closer and surprisingly, more faithful to God. Rikki and Blain had gotten married just a few months after they'd confronted Althea in a cold, dank warehouse not far from here but they still had bad days, too. His brother, Victor, was sitting in prison, waiting for his sentence to be up so he could get back to gallivanting and spending more of the family funds. But Victor kept telling Santo he'd changed. He wanted to help out now.

Santo couldn't trust his brother on that yet. Victor would have to prove that he'd truly become a new man.

But Santo was here, unable to move. Paralyzed by a grief that he found both revolting and necessary. He grieved a woman he'd stopped loving long before she'd died and the guilt of that admission floored him and held him captive. His children deserved better and he needed to give everything he had to them. Not every material thing, but everything of himself.

How did he reconcile all the anger and bitterness inside his soul and go on with life even while he tried to raise his children shielded from the awful truth?

Santo sat there in the quiet of his office listening to the hum and flow coming from the warehouse. Shipments moved, employees went about their business and things got done.

He prayed for God to show him a way to make it all work together. A way to show his children that he loved them and would always protect them.

Preacher Rory had suggested he needed to be patient and he also needed to spend more time with his children. Thinking about Davina Connell and their meeting tonight, Santo decided it might time for him to make some changes, too.

Chapter Four

Davina eyed the I-Need-Chocolate-STAT cupcake she'd picked up at Marla's Marvelous Desserts and thought about how she was going to eat it while watching a movie she'd recorded two nights ago. One of the many nights she'd spent alone since she'd arrived here, which was perfectly fine with her. She loved to sketch ideas and jot down notes during her quiet time. She also loved to eat decadent chocolate desserts for dinner.

But her cell buzzed before she could make it across the space from the tiny den to the rectangular galley-style kitchen, where her prized cupcake set on the counter.

The caller ID lit up. Santo Alvanetti.

"Seriously," she said, glaring at the name and number. Now he was calling her at night?

Davina hit Accept on her cell and reminded herself she was doing this to increase exposure for her fledgling construction company. And because she loved the old lake house Santo had purchased. Not quite Victorian and not quite Craftsman, the rambling white house with its deep porches and sturdy staircases begged for a new life and a good family. She'd be the one to give it new life and Santo could supply the family, but she planned to showcase this project big-time to increase awareness of the skills she and her employees could provide.

"Hello," she said into the phone, her eyes on that tempting cupcake with the marshmallow icing.

"Uh, hi. It's Santo. Did you still want to meet to go over the details of the renovations for the lake house?"

Davina groaned and glanced at the clock. "Uh…yes. I am so sorry. I forgot we agreed to meet tonight."

How could she have missed that important detail? Maybe because she'd been so busy all day, she'd agreed to this meeting in passing and didn't type it into her phone's calendar with a reminder.

She heard him inhale. "You weren't there when I got home, so we didn't verify."

Had he missed her?

Smiling, she said, "No, I left early to meet Rikki at the lake house. We went over the whole house and I think we have a good plan. I just forgot about you coming here. I'm so sorry."

"It's okay, but I'd love to hear all about it," he said. "Mrs. Brownlee is available to stay with the children." He took a long breath. "And she made this amazing shrimp dish. I could bring some over."

This sounded almost like dinner, together. A date?

Davina didn't want to panic, but she felt that fluttering in her heart. It wasn't a good idea to get involved with a client. But then, she'd never had a client like this one. No wonder she'd pushed their meeting out of her head. She had to, to get him out of her head.

When she didn't answer, he rushed on. "I did come home early but I wanted to visit with the children and help them with their homework."

Davina had to admit that was sweet and impressive after the confusion and chaos she'd seen at his house a week ago. She was tired and she needed that cupcake. But she'd also agreed to meet him here so they could have some quiet time to discuss the lake house. And she really wanted to discuss that project in full.

"Do we need to reschedule?" he asked, the hesitation showing her a crack in his moody demeanor. At least he was coming around on being involved in the day-to-day decisions of renovating a house.

"Of course not," she said. "I'm here and I'm ready."

She ended the call and stared at her chocolate dinner. "You're going to have to wait," she decided, not wanting to gulp down her cupcake right before she met with him.

Grabbing a banana instead, she ate it and then fluffed her hair and put on some lip gloss and mascara.

She wouldn't change out of her leggings and tunic, however.

Davina had an early day tomorrow so she planned on staying casual and comfortable tonight. In spite of her rapidly beating heart.

She invited him in and plopped a huge chocolate cupcake on the counter. "I haven't had anything to eat since breakfast," Davina announced. "I'm starving and I'm going to eat this before I go to bed or someone is going to pay."

Santo actually chuckled and felt something like a jolt of heat moving through his heart. "And hello to you, too."

"Sorry." Her green eyes reminded him of a lush tropical forest. "I've had a long day and I'm mortified that

I completely forgot this meeting. That's not how I conduct business."

Santo should have insisted they cancel but he'd been looking forward to this all day long. But obviously, Davina had a lot more on her mind than spending a couple of hours with him. Which should have been okay, only he had to admit he felt a bit disappointed. But he'd get past that because she wasn't here to sit around with him. She had a lot of work to do yet.

Since he was here now, he carried on. "I've had some of the best shrimp fettuccine I've ever eaten for dinner," he said, handing her a warm plate covered with foil. "Miss Virginia is an amazing cook and she insisted I bring this over to you."

Davina's eyes lit up, causing yet another aftershock to charge through him. The woman was like an exotic chameleon, ever-changing. Then she said, "Are you going to feed me?"

He liked the way she asked that with a bit of a dare. "Yes, I am," he said. "Because I've had a long day, too, and…I want to make some changes in my life. That's one reason I wanted to talk to you alone tonight, without any interruptions from my wonderful children or their equally wonderful nanny."

She eyed him as if he'd turned into a sea monster. "You mean changes such as being on time and being a little more organized? Or maybe being more available?"

"Ouch." Did he look like a total loser to her? "Yeah, those things and more." Watching as she sank onto a bar stool and dug into the shrimp dish with gusto, he said, "I guess I need to work on a lot of things." Then he glanced around the little beach-themed apartment.

"At least Miss Virginia got the children to bed on time. She's a keeper."

"I'm sorry," she said between bites. "I shouldn't have implied you're not organized and involved with these projects. It's obvious you're doing the best you can. And yes, Mrs. Brownlee is a jewel."

Santo stayed across from her, the kitchen island separating them. He needed a buffer to remind him he'd hired her to help him, not so he could stand here and stare at her. "No, you have every right to be a little put out with me. First, I mistook you for the nanny and shoved one of my screaming children at you and then I left you and the real nanny standing in the middle of my den. And tonight, I didn't call until it was almost too late to have a business meeting. We could do this some other time."

"No, no," she said, waving her hand. "You're here now and I shouldn't judge you. I don't have children but I grew up in a big, crazy family. My mom, bless her, was always running behind. It drove me nuts but now I'm beginning to appreciate her efforts a whole lot more." She shrugged. "I have four siblings, so growing up, I watched several train wrecks and a whole lot of drama being played out. All my life, I only wanted some peace and quiet and to be my own person. I became a nomad of sorts, just to be by myself."

"So you don't get along with your family?"

"We get along," she explained. "Well, my older brother is also in construction and he resents me a tad but I ignore him. My younger brother is in the army so I don't get to see him much. But my sisters Tilly and Alana and I are close. We butt heads but we love each other."

She saw the darkness in his eyes, the searching glance.

"Do you ever get lonely?" he asked, the ache of his own loneliness echoing out around them.

"All the time," she admitted. "It's hard being a woman in construction but…I've always loved old houses and I want to fix up the one I grew up in one day. It's a beauty but it's falling apart. I want to do that for my parents if they'll allow me. We are a proud clan." She went on to tell him about her father's health and struggles. "I want to do what I can to keep them afloat since they've supported all of us through thick and thin."

Santo could see the remorse and the pride in her expression and in her eyes. Her amazing green eyes. "A big family, huh? That explains why you didn't complain when I threw Nate at you. You're probably used to that kind of messy morning."

She smiled at that. A pretty smile that seemed to make this tiny space shrink even more and go at least twenty degrees warmer. "Yes. I'm the middle one. Irish to the core, too. So you can only imagine fighting over the last slice of pizza or who got dibs on my mom's car on Saturday night."

"I'm thinking you won in both cases."

She laughed and dug into the shrimp again. Then she tore off a piece of the chunky French bread he'd included in the meal. "You'd better believe it. Being caught in the middle kept me out of the fray on either side. I got away with a lot."

Santo relaxed, his face muscles going slack, the constant ache in his neck loosing up the vise grip it had held on him for so long now. Glancing at her cupcake, he said the same thing he'd said about the Peaches-and-Cream cupcake they'd shared a few days ago. "I know where you bought that and I sure hope you're willing to share it."

"Let's go over my plans for the lake house and then we can fight over the cupcake. But I seem to remember I won last time."

"Can we negotiate?" he asked, realizing he just might be flirting with his house contractor. He'd forgotten how, but this felt dangerously close. Too close. It also felt refreshing and good. Too good. He'd made a vow to never open up his heart to a woman again. Santo had loved his wife but his love couldn't save their marriage or her. He'd been blinded by ambition and a need to please her, no matter the cost. Why would he want to risk that again? No, he'd go into this with his eyes wide open and his children as his first priority. Why would he put his children through any more trauma?

"Of course we can negotiate," Davina said, bringing him out of his anxious reevaluation. She opened her battered canvas tool bag and pulled out a notebook. "Everything is negotiable, right?"

"Right." But Santo decided this woman would be a tough adversary. And she probably always came out a winner. At least she'd keep him on his toes.

"Are you ready?" she asked, a bright glee in her eyes. "Let me show you what I have in mind to make your next home look like the showpiece it's supposed to be. Once I'm finished, you should be able to move your children into it knowing it's the best house it can be. I'll keep the historical integrity while updating the kitchens and baths, and adding charm to the living areas and bedrooms."

"You sound like those guys on that home network show that my mother used to watch all the time."

"I'm trying to sell you on the idea, so I practiced that speech."

"You're very convincing, so I'm ready," Santo replied, a new kind of excitement coursing through him. But he wasn't ready, really. He didn't have a clue about his old house or his new house or her or why he was so intent on moving. Maybe he wasn't trying to start a new life for his children. Maybe he was just running from the memories and the guilt associated with the showy, ostentatious house that had only brought him misery.

Chapter Five

Davina pulled out the sketches she'd made and then placed the original house plans she'd gotten from the former owner onto the counter. "Can you see?" she asked Santo, well aware of the hint of spice in his aftershave.

"I'll come around," he replied.

Both afraid of that and doing a happy dance in her head in spite of her fears, Davina reminded herself that she had to maintain a professional persona or she could very well mess up this project. So she took a calming breath and ran a hand over the plans and the photos she'd taken and printed out.

"This is an interesting house," she said, her excitement building with each word. "I can't wait to get started on it."

"And when will that be?" he asked over her shoulder, the warmth radiating off of him like a welcome wind.

"In a week or so," she replied. "We've done a lot at the bay house since Mrs. Brownlee manages to get the kids out of the house while the construction crew is there."

"Yes, they've been going over to my parents' place a lot," he said. "My parents are on a cruise right now, but the kids love it there anyway. And our housekeeper still lives here, so she's a help with them, too."

Rikki had told Davina that their parents lived in a big house on the bay not far from Santo's house. The Alvanetti compound was off the road and secluded and had a large horse stable and pasture attached. A perfect place for kids to play. A place that used to have armed guards, according to the gossip she picked up on here and there.

"Well, I'm glad they have somewhere to hang out after school," she said. "Anyway, we're almost done with the floors and the walls have been painted and freshened and the furniture edited down a bit. Rikki and I picked out some lovely rugs and vases from your store earlier this week."

"You were in the store?" he asked, surprise in his dark eyes. "You should have come back to the warehouse and office. I would have given you a tour."

"We were in a hurry," she said. "And I didn't want to bother you."

No need to visit the man at work unless she had something really important to discuss with him. Which could happen one day since she'd have a million decisions to make during renovations.

"That can only mean my sister went over budget on whatever she bought, even with the family discount."

"*Because* of the family discount," Davina replied with a grin. "But the bay house is coming along. What do you think about it so far?"

He studied the plans in front of them and then looked up at her with admiration. "You've done an amazing job. I couldn't see it before but you've brought out the integrity of the place. Now I know what a mid-century modern is supposed to look like, at least."

Davina wanted to hug him for complimenting her work. But even more wonderful, he understood what she'd try to accomplish with his swank waterfront property. The big house still had its industrial planes and angles but she'd added color and fire and brightness that brought the outside in and merged the house with the bluffs and the bay beyond.

"I'm glad you're pleased," she said. "It should be ready for you to list soon." She poured him a glass of water and then refilled her glass. Then she named the estimated selling price.

"Wow, that much?"

She laughed at the shock on his face. "Yes, that much. I did a good job."

"I think you did." He tapped a finger on the plans. "On to the new house. What do you want to do there?"

She laughed and tugged at her haphazard bun. "So much. A complete overhaul." When she looked up, he was staring at her with a look akin to awe and longing.

"Santo? Are you okay?"

He nodded. "Uh…yes." His gaze moved over her face and then settled on her hair. "I've just never known a contractor with such beautiful hair."

A hot blush moved down Davina's neck. Great. Now she'd get the blotchies, as her sister Tilly always called them. A flush that only showed off her freckles. Maybe he wouldn't notice.

He kept staring at her.

"Santo, the house?"

"Oh, yes, the house," he said with a wry smile. "I need to focus on the house."

Frantic now, she searched her notes. What was happening to her, anyway? She never acted like a ninny with clients. But then she'd never had a client who'd commented on her hair in such an intimate way. The room grew warm, the air stifling.

"It's a lovely house," she said, regaining her footing while she didn't make eye contact. "Only one owner for the last fifty years or so and with a big family that's scattered now. He's in an assisted living home up in Milton."

She took a breath and stared at the house plan. "I went and visited with Mr. Floyd so I could get a feel for the place. He told me all about his wife, Katie, and their four boys. Kind of reminded me of my family back in Louisiana. They lovingly took care of the home but no one has lived in it for a couple of years and it needs some updates. The kitchen is quaint but outdated and, of course, the bathrooms need major overhauls."

He laughed and nodded, his smile radiating even more heat. "Of course."

Davina had to swallow. Grabbing her water, she gulped it too fast and started coughing.

"Are you okay?" Santo asked, those all-seeing eyes moving over her again.

"Yes." She hacked another round and prayed the blotchies were gone by now. "Just…not very ladylike."

He smiled and pointed to her notes. "So I think I'm beginning to see how you operate. You redo the current house to sell and you redo the new house before anyone can move in. You've got quite a racket going here, don't you?"

Seeing the mirth in his eyes, Davina nodded. "Of course. I make money on both ends of the deal. My mama raised me right."

"Smart." He leaned close and she became transported to some exotic spot where herbs and spices were rich and sweet and enticing. The man smelled like something unique and fresh and forbidden. An outdoor market, a quiet alfresco café, a moonlit night in some faraway place.

Get over it, Davina.

"So not only are you smart but you're also pretty and you can outwork any man I've ever met. You're amazing."

"You haven't seen the final bill yet," she quipped, only because she was about to hyperventilate. "Anyway, so we have the first floor. We'll start with sprucing up the entire outside, of course. Fresh white paint and new shutters in keeping with all of the designs around the lake."

"Yes, we need to keep up with appearances," he said.

"Historical features," she corrected. "You know Lake Street is a prestigious and unique oval road that runs all along the lake."

"Yes, I know that. That's why I decided to buy there. The kids love it when we go to Alec Caldwell's house."

"Oh, the big Victorian with the turret on top. I love that house. A perfect example of preserving the historical features while bringing a home into this century. Just gorgeous."

"My sister loves it, too."

"Alec and Marla are so nice," Davina said, glad to be on a safe subject. "And I've gained five pounds because I seem to go by her café just about every day."

Santo eyed the chocolate cupcake. "Yes, you do travel with one of those hidden in your big bag at all times, right?"

"Right."

"Let's get on with this so I can sample your treat."

His gaze wasn't on that cupcake.

He was staring at her lips.

Davina swallowed again but refrained from grabbing her water. "So we have the downstairs master with a lovely sitting area. I know you wanted some office space—"

"You do?"

He looked so surprised, she laughed. "Yes, because your sister told me. Thank goodness she knows what you'd like to happen with this house."

"I haven't talked to her in a while."

"Well, then, she's making decisions for you. Good ones, though."

Santo ran a hand through his hair and tugged at it as if he wanted to pull it all out by the roots. "I need to become more involved in this, don't I?"

Davina motioned to the sofa. "Let's talk."

He sat down with her and gave her a helpless glance. "My wife always took care of any repairs or updates on our house. But I didn't always agree with her taste."

Having witnessed Rikki's gaudy taste, Davina could agree with that.

"If you don't get involved, you can't complain," she said. "Why don't you tell me what you want in a new home, Santo?"

He leaned forward and templed his fingers over his knees. "Everyone keeps asking me that," he said. "They ask me why I'm leaving such a stunning house and that amazing view."

"And what do you tell them? Or what is it you're not telling them?"

He kept staring at his hands. "I tell them I'm ready

for a change, that the kids need something different and more kid-friendly."

"That's all true," Davina replied. "But I need to know more. I need to know your heart. Because when I renovate a home for someone new to move into, I want to show that family's heart in everything I do. I don't know your heart."

"You don't want to know my heart," he said, getting up, his mood dark now. "And me coming here was a bad idea. Just remodel the place and make it livable, Davina. That's what I'm paying you for."

Davina couldn't give up in spite of the glaring warning in his eyes. "What else are you willing to pay for?"

"What does that mean?"

"I'm worried that you're moving for all the wrong reasons."

"Do you want me to find another contractor?"

"No," she said, her determination giving her the courage to face him. "I want this job. I need this job. But I also want to understand you…so I can make you a home that you'll appreciate and be happy in."

"I don't know if I'll ever be completely happy again," he said, his hands on his hips, his eyes full of a raging torment. "But…I want my children to be happy. I want them to have a tree house and swings and I want them to go fishing on the pier by the lake. I want to take long walks with them and read to them and hold them when they're afraid. I want to stop their nightmares and show them that we're going to be all right."

He halted, his eyes filling with dread and apprehension. "I don't like talking about this. Just do what you need to do, and leave me out of the details."

He turned to go.

But she moved in front of him. "I'm sorry. I shouldn't have pushed. But, Santo, what you just told me gives me a whole different perspective."

"I'm sure it does," he said, anger coloring the words. "Now you feel pity for me and my poor children, right?"

"No. Not pity. I admire you for what you're trying to do. Why don't you cut yourself some slack and become part of the process. There's healing in renovating things, especially houses. They can tell a story."

"And what does my current home tell you?"

"That you're lonely and full of guilt."

He stood at the door, his head turned toward the wide window that showcased the old live oaks and palm trees and the lake beyond. "I came here thinking I was ready to dive in and help you, put in some physical labor. But I don't think I can do this, Davina. All I know is my own work and it consumes me because I had to bring my family out of a disaster. I stay busy and I try to get home and spend time with my children. I try to sleep."

"But you don't sleep, do you?"

He shook his head and stayed silent.

"You've been through something horrific and traumatic," she said. "I don't expect you to share all the details with me."

Whirling, he dropped his arms to his sides. "But you've heard the details. It made the national news. The whole world knows what happened to my family, to my children. To my wife and me. No wonder my parents decided to leave the country."

Then Davina saw it in his eyes. The shame, the despair, the regret, the guilt. "It wasn't your fault."

He shook his head. "Doesn't matter. I'm the one who's

still here. I'm the one who has to protect my children and show them that we have to get on with our lives."

"And you're doing that," she said, moving closer to him. "This house will be sunny and bright and full of joy. I'll see to that. But Santo, you'll have to do your part, too."

He gave her a twisted smirk. "And how do I do that? I've been dealing with this for over a year now. The first few months, I was too numb to feel anything. But my children needed me so I had to find a way to keep moving. So what part do I play now? What can I do to make this right again? How can I do anything more?"

"By forgiving your wife," she replied. "And yourself."

"Stop it, please," he replied on a quiet tone. "I didn't hire you to be my spiritual counselor. Your work is good, Davina. Let's leave it at that."

"Okay. I'm sorry I overstepped," she said, her heart breaking for this man. "I've never been through anything like what you've had to deal with. I came from a loving, happy, chaotic family but we didn't have a lot of money. So I'm driven to prove myself and sometimes in my zest to make a house perfect, I ask too many personal questions. It won't happen again."

Lifting his head, he almost spoke but stopped himself. After a brief silence that told her exactly how he felt, he said, "I'll check in with you again soon."

"Okay. Thank you for the dinner." She glanced at the cupcake they'd never shared, her stomach roiling in protest, her nerves tangled tighter than electrical cords. "I'll make sure you get the official reports on both houses."

"I appreciate that," he said.

And then he turned and walked out the door.

Davina watched him get into his car and zoom away.

And then she sank down on the couch and started praying.

Dear Lord, help this man to heal. Watch over him and his precious children. And please guide me in renovating this home for them.

Because she knew in her heart that it would take a lot more than hammers and nails to mend this broken family.

Chapter Six

Davina couldn't get the conversation she'd had with Santo last night out of her mind. Not that she hadn't stayed busy. She'd finished up the last details on the bay house today and planned to spend most of the afternoon over at the fixer-upper lake house. Since Santo had told her to do what she needed to get the place in order, she had the go-ahead, such as it was. But she'd really hoped he'd change his mind and decide to get more involved in this project. He needed to see the skeleton of the house, test its bones, learn its structure and explore every nook and cranny because that was exactly what his children would do.

How could anyone not want to do that with a house?

Maybe Santo wasn't wired like her. Tilly and Alana teased her about loving houses more than she loved wanting a home of her own.

Her sisters had a point. Houses were easy to love, easy to shape and mold and change. People, not so much. Davina wasn't good at building relationships, probably because she'd always been right smack in the middle of her family's sometimes tempestuous relationships with each other. But no matter now. Santo had made it clear he wasn't good at that either. Or so he thought.

Since Davina didn't want that lovely old home to become cold and rigid like the bay house, she'd keep her mind centered on making it spectacular again. Glad she was finished here, she did like how the modern beauty was coming along nicely. But working around the children had been a challenge.

Thinking about Santo's beautiful children made her smile in spite of the intensity of their words last night. She'd miss these kids once she was done completely. She'd miss this community, too.

"I think I'll be a carpenter like you when I grow up," nine-year-old Lucia announced this morning when Davina walked through the door. "It's a lot of fun. I like hammering things the way you do. And you're always laughing and smiling."

The dark-haired beauty with eyes so like her father's hadn't witnessed Davina screaming at plumbers or discussing with the tile man why the counters didn't fit. That was because when the children were around, Davina tried to make the whole reconstruction fun and interesting as long as they stayed clear of any danger. She'd even found each of them bright yellow hard hats to wear. Which earned her points with the kids and Mrs. Brownlee and brought a scowl from their dad.

She wouldn't tell him she'd also let them hammer some nails into old boards, with both Mrs. Brownlee and herself supervising. Her parents had been protective but also lenient when letting their children explore and learn things. She hoped if she ever had any children, she'd be the same. But watching Santo's children run around this treacherously beautiful house had brought out all of the maternal instincts she didn't even know she had.

"This is a fun job," she told Lucia now with a big grin. "You would be very good at it since you've had practice bossing your brother and sister around. And taking care of them," she added, because Lucia did help with her younger siblings.

"I have to be the boss," Lucia replied with a stern expression, her eyes growing even bigger. "I'm the oldest and we don't have a mom anymore." Then she'd lowered her voice. "She went to heaven."

Davina squatted and took Lucia's hand, wishing she hadn't teased so much. "I know and I'm so sorry about that. You're a great big sister. And your daddy is so proud of you."

"He acts mad all the time."

Davina could vouch for that. Her heart tumbled over itself, seeing the serious concern in Lucia's eyes. What must this child think about the horrible thing that had happened in her life?

Putting on her best reassuring face, Davina shook her head. "No, no, he's just got so much to take care of. He works hard so he can provide for all of you. He loves you."

"He tells us that," Lucia said in a matter-of-fact voice. "Sometimes I wish he'd just stay home with us. Saturday is supposed to be fun day and this Saturday, there's a festival on the lake but he won't remember. Mommy used to say that Daddy only remembered work and nothing else. But I don't think he forgets on purpose. I wish he'd go with us, though."

Before Davina could respond to the little anxious girl,

her sister, Adriana, ran by and screamed, "Nate's hiding. And he's not wearing his hard hat."

After that, a game of cat and mouse had ensued and soon, Davina and Mrs. Brownlee were both highly involved. They'd found the little boy in the corner of the master bedroom, hiding behind a big rocking chair that Davina had just placed by the locked doors out onto a cedar terrace.

"I like this chair," Nate said, a finger to his mouth. "Can you rock me?"

Davina looked at Mrs. Brownlee and nodded. "I certainly can." So while Virginia took the girls to the kitchen for a snack, Davina rocked Nate to sleep, her mind going back and forth with the cadence of the heavy wood hitting the plush carpet.

A girl could get used to that kind of cadence.

The little boy had lifted his head and smiled at her. "Da-danina."

"Davina," she'd said, grinning down at him.

Nate shook his head. "Danina." Then he snuggled closer, burrowing into her arms. And into her heart.

As he drifted off, Davina had whispered close, "Dani. I'm Dani."

A soft giggle had erupted against her heartbeat.

The sweetness of that moment had stayed with her all day. Now she was finished. The crew would come back and clean things up and do a run-through and then, she'd do a final walk-through with Santo and see if they'd missed anything. Not that he would notice or care.

She'd purposely been late this morning. Yes, she was avoiding him. It was for the best. The man was in a world of hurt and she'd pushed him too far, too soon, last night.

"Mind your own business," her mother always told

her children. They never did, of course. Nor did Ma. Ma was a caring, loving soul who could spot a hurting heart from a mile away, human or animal. She'd be over the moon with these three Alvanetti children and she'd immediately insist they needed a big dog to follow them around.

"Are you really all done?" Mrs. Brownlee asked through a sigh, her hands held together over the apron that stated Free Hugs with Each Cookie.

"I am," Davina said. "And in record time. This job would normally take at least a month but when you have an unlimited budget, you can get things done pretty quickly. Three weeks for a general overhaul is my personal best now."

"Yes, you did seem to hurry this into overdrive," her new friend pointed out, sparkly red earrings warring with her auburn curls. "I take it you and Santo don't always see eye to eye."

"He's tough to read," Davina replied, glad to be able to have a confidante. "Some walls can't be torn down because there's no support beam."

"He needs to find his faith again," Mrs. Brownlee said. "And no, you can't do that for the poor man." She shrugged and stared out at the water. "We each have to walk our own faith path and it can be fraught with detours."

Davina gathered her things to leave, wondering about Virginia's detours. "I'll arrange the walk-through after the workers have cleaned up. I'll get together with Santo on that and then we can list the house."

"I can keep the children occupied for you."

"Thank you," Davina said. "I guess they don't need to see the final version of the house they're leaving."

Mrs. Brownlee glanced at the glistening bay beyond the small bluff. "They're already excited about moving to the lake." She pointed outside. "That water down there is out of reach for them, but the lake has always been the center of this town. It will do them good to fish in the shallows and ride their bikes along the trails. They're isolated here in this cold tower. There, they'll meet friends and have neighbors all around."

"I hope so," Davina said, turning to head for the door before Virginia picked up on how much she'd miss the children. She'd just put her hand on it when it flew open and Santo stood there, blocking the light. Stepping back before she got banged, Davina held on to the tidal wave of feelings surging around her.

"You're home early," Mrs. Brownlee said, pointing out the obvious.

"Am I?" he asked, his eyes on Davina. "Where are you going?"

"To the lake house to meet with Rikki," she replied. "I'm done here."

"So soon?" He glanced at his watch.

"I've been telling you for days that I would be finished by the end of the week." She shrugged. "It's the end of the week."

He rubbed his head as if to get answers. "What about the final…look?"

Davina shot Virginia a glance and looked back at him. "The workers have to clean out any debris and tools and then we can do that later. Maybe Monday, after you're done with work?"

"How about now?"

Davina waffled between telling him yes or no.

"Nate's asleep," Mrs. Brownlee said. "And the girls are in the game room watching an animated movie."

Santo paced a foot or so. "So it's not a good time?"

"It would be better if we do that on Monday," Davina said, steeling herself for his reaction.

A curt nod. "Okay, then I'll walk you to your car."

Did he want to talk to her?

"All right." She moved to leave.

"Daddy!"

Lucia rushed up to him and Santo took her into his arms. Adriana followed and soon both girls were giggling into Santo's ears.

He looked at Davina, a smile cresting on his face. "You two are certainly in a good mood."

Lucia bobbed her head, her dark curls whirling around her face and shoulders like inky swatches of silk. "That's 'cause we have the best idea ever."

"Oh? And what's that?" Santo asked, still smiling even if his eyes had gone dark again.

"The Millbrook Lake Art Festival," Lucia said through another giggle. "It's tomorrow, Daddy. And we want to go. With you and Miss Davina."

Santo's grin went slack.

Davina's heart went bump.

And Virginia Brownlee chuckled and watched the whole scene with a little too much mirth in her eyes.

"I'll explain to her later," Santo said once he'd told Lucia he'd have to consider her request.

"I'll probably be at the festival anyway," Davina said. "Vanessa told me about it. Lots of local art and good fresh seafood and the weather's supposed to be nice." She hesitated and then went on. "I could take the kids."

Surprised, Santo shook his head. "Oh, no. You don't know what you're offering. They'd all take off in three different directions and you'd spend the whole day rounding them back up."

"I can handle them," she said, her tone firm. "Lucia is set on going and…she mentioned you'd probably forget."

Wow, straight to the heart. His pretty contractor could sling more than a hammer. "She said that to you?"

"Yes. But I'm sure Virginia would love to go, too. Together, we should be able to keep your children corralled."

"You seem a bit aggravated," he pointed out.

"You seem a bit surprised," she retorted.

"I'm sorry," he finally said. "I was rude to you last night and I didn't mean to be. I'd still like to be more involved in the new house, if you still want me to be."

"It's not what I want," Davina said, thinking right now she wanted a lot of things. "It's what you need to do. Most people who buy a house want to check it out and study it and walk through it several times. You have an amazing yard and one of the best views of the lake. Or do you even remember those things?"

He had to stop and think. "Rikki was with me during the final walk-through and she did the looking. I had to get back to a meeting."

Davina's pained expression told him she wasn't impressed with him. "So you don't know anything about the house you bought?"

He stared up the street, watching as a row of palm trees danced in the wind. "No, I guess I don't. I looked at it once by myself and told Rikki to handle the details. I didn't really give it my full attention the day we closed."

"Then I'll handle my details with your sister," Davina said. "I have to go. I'm supposed to meet her there anyway."

"I could come along," he said, wishing he'd been better prepared for this woman.

"That is up to you, of course."

But he saw the flare of hope in her expressive eyes.

"You go ahead and after I visit with the kids awhile, I'll meet you there."

"Right." She didn't sound sure.

But then, neither was he.

Chapter Seven

"Your brother should be here to help with these decisions," Davina told Rikki once she arrived at the lake
house. Still reeling from his moods and his recent abrupt
change of heart, she added, "This place needs a major
overhaul but I want to talk to him and show him what I
plan before I get started. He said he'd be here later but
I'm not going to count on that."

"Oh, no," Rikki said. "Did he upset you again?"

"How do you know he's ever upset me?" Davina
asked, appalled that it showed.

"Because my brother makes everyone mad sooner or
later. He has that knack. It took Blain many months to
get used to Santo and his quick mood swings."

"Months?" Davina didn't have months to work out
the kinks in her relationship with the man footing the
bills. "I just want him to care about this for a few days
at least." She moved through the empty house, the echo
of her frustrations following her. "Maybe two or three
months on this one, actually. I want to take my time and
give this graceful old lady a proper makeover."

Rikki's dark eyes, so like her brother's, filled with an

apologetic darkness. "Santo is always busy. He trusts us to do what we have to do so it'll be his fault if he doesn't like the end result. But honestly, I don't think he'll care. He just wants to get his children out of the bay house. I think the memories finally got to him. Instead of going away, they starting crowding around him. And I know Lucia has had some nightmares and some of her friends have made cruel comments about her mother. The children have talked to counselors but what happened has been hard on my family." She shook her head. "Blain and I talk about it still. He had to kill Althea, but…it's just been so hard on all of us."

"I'm sorry," Davina said, her aggravation with Santo overshadowing the fact that Rikki had been targeted and almost murdered by her own sister-in-law. "I'm so sorry for you and Blain. And Santo, too. I don't mean to sound insensitive. I get so caught up in the job I for- get everything else. You went through this, along with your whole family. I mean, you could have been killed. But you seem to be handling it a lot better than Santo."

Rikki's grim expression softened. "If I didn't have Blain, I'd have nightmares all the time, too. I lost my best friend and my ex-boyfriend. Althea killed both of them and my brother, Victor, had to go to prison. He was so involved with her he didn't see until it was too late that she'd gone off the deep end. None of us did."

She stopped and took a breath. "I think that's the main thing eating at Santo. That he didn't know his own wife and that his children could have been in real danger. He and Althea had an intense relationship from the beginning but it burned out in a very bad way. She only wanted the money and what she thought he could give her. He tried so hard to please her, but Althea was beyond pleasing. She always wanted more."

Davina thought about Santo and his moods. "It must be horrible, having to carry that burden. Maybe I need to stop pushing him on this and just get the work done."

"No, he needs someone besides family to help him see past his grief," Rikki replied, her expression full of encouragement. "And I think you might be the perfect person for that."

"I met him barreling through the door as I was leaving to come here," Davina said. "Intense does not even describe the man." She hesitated and then said, "He told me a little bit about what he's been through. He's a proud man, Rikki. But he loves those children so much."

"Yes, anyone can see that," Rikki said. "He's trying to spend more time with them."

"Well, he had his hands full with your adorable nieces this afternoon." She made notes on the hardwood floors. A good buffing could bring some new luster to them. "I'll try to be gentle with him but I so want him to help with this, for his own sake."

Rikki's expression changed to worry. "He can't seem to keep a good nanny but Virginia is hanging in there. I worked hard finding someone I thought could tough it out. She's perfect. A widow but still young at heart. Of course, it's only been three weeks." She laughed. "That's a long run for Santo and his kids."

"I think that problem's been solved," Davina replied. She went on to tell Rikki about Virginia's many outstanding qualities. "She takes his gruffness right in stride."

"He's always had an edge about him," Rikki replied, her long dark ponytail falling across one shoulder while she measured the old Formica countertops. "Brooding and moody. That describes Santo. Now Victor on the other hand—all fun and games and...currently sitting in prison for five years."

Wishing she hadn't said anything, Davina tried again. "Don't worry. I can handle Santo. I'll do what I need to do and send him the bill. But I want you to be my witness and help me go over some of my concerns here. The bay house is done and it looks a lot better. I think it will go quickly, so I need to get kicking on this one."

"I'll help where I can," Rikki replied. "And Santo will get my bill, too."

"How's your house coming?" Davina asked, to change the subject. Rikki and her husband, Blain Kent, a detective with the Millbrook police, had bought a bungalow not far from here. But it had already been updated by the previous owners so Rikki was adding some finishing touches to make it more personal. The one-level house was cozy and colorful and filled with a coastal cottage decor.

"It's great," she said. "I'm going through each room at a time and having fun doing it. I can't wait to shop for art and knickknacks at the festival tomorrow."

"The kids want to come to that festival," Davina said. "I'm not so sure your brother will bring them." She didn't add the part about being invited to come along with them. Rikki didn't need to hear that. No one needed to hear that.

Rikki took a few photos of the beadboard walls in the big, rambling kitchen. Davina planned to clean up the white subway tiles along the backsplash and maybe salvage the black-and-white-tiled floors, too. With sturdy rugs scattered here and there.

"Santo doesn't like crowds," Rikki said. "He's really more of an introvert."

"I can tell," Davina replied, jotting notes and measuring yet again to get a feel for fresh new white cabinets and shimmering marble countertops. The breakfast room was square and sunny, with a big paned window that showed off the long back porch and the fenced-in yard. Good place for the kids to play away from the water across the narrow Lake Street in front of the house.

But the lake side was even better. A big, deep porch that begged for a light blue ceiling in keeping with the Southern tradition of fooling insects into thinking the ceiling was part of the sky, and fresh gray planked floors to hide dirt and feel cool on bare feet. She'd update the sturdy columns and refurbish the wide front door with the exquisite stained glass panels. Those would stay. The porch needed red geraniums and flowing ferns, rocking chairs and settees, a big swing for the children.

The house had an unobstructed view of the center of the big lake. Even now, she could see a red-and-white sailboat gliding along on the silent wind. The old, moss-covered oaks and deeply rooted camellia bushes and azaleas only added to the charm. The smell of jasmine and magnolias lingered throughout the rooms since she and Rikki had opened the doors wide to bring in the fresh air.

"I love this house. I want your brother to love it, too."

Davina could see it all. And for the first time in her career, she wanted to stick around to see beyond the finished project. She wanted this to work, to be a safe haven for Santo and his children.

An image of herself inserted in that picture caused her to inhale a breath. She'd prayed for this little family but now her heart had rearranged itself for them. She had to make this right. With the Lord's guidance, she knew she could create a safe haven in this old house.

"Are you okay?" Rikki asked from the massive dining room.

"Yes, just so many ideas."

"You'll make this place a showcase," Rikki called. "I can't wait to see what you do with it. I'm excited about helping you decorate it."

"Because you know I'm going to do what's right and because you'll know how to fill in the blanks for me," Davina said as they met in the wide central hallway. "I'm going to make this house shine so Santo can bring his children into a sunny, bright, happy home. A real home."

"That's exactly why I hired you," Rikki said. "You're the best at what you do and I need someone who can get around Santo and his issues to make this work. He'd never listen to me and he'd try to force me to keep the cost down. Those children need a safe, calm environment that's comfortable and childproof. Not some showplace that looks like it needs to be in a magazine. They need a home. A real home. You can give them that, Davina."

"I'd like to hear how she plans on doing that."

They both turned to the open French doors leading to the back porch and found Santo standing there in a button-up shirt and jeans, his hands stuffed into his pants pockets, and his eyes on Davina.

"We were just discussing how I'm going to do that," Davina said, determined to be strong and stand up to his black moods.

"Show me your plans," he said. "I want to hear about all of it."

Rikki gave Davina a steady stare, her dark eyes full of surprise and awareness. "Well, okay then."

Davina couldn't speak, had barely squeaked out a quick response at seeing him there. Unusual but then, Santo made her whole system short-circuit.

"You do still want me involved, don't you?" he asked, giving her a daring once-over.

"Of course." Only now, she wasn't so sure that was a good idea after all.

The way the man was looking at her had nothing to do with renovating a house. But it had everything to do with destroying her heart.

Santo didn't know what had come over him.

"I…uh…wanted to see this house again. To make sure I made the right decision."

Rikki glanced at her watch. "I only have a few minutes before I meet Blain for dinner. I'm going upstairs to take pictures and stare at blank walls."

His sister took off so fast her sneakers barely hit the stairs as she scurried up and away.

Santo kept his gaze on Davina and hoped she was still speaking to him. "Can you show me the house?"

"Do you really want to do this?" she asked, her green eyes wild with distrust and something he didn't want to recognize. Compassion? Pity? Understanding? She must have a war going on inside that pretty head, and if so, he was pretty sure he'd cast himself as the enemy she was trying to fight.

He walked up the empty hallway, the old planks croaking and groaning against the weight of his steps. "Yes. I want you to guide me through this renovation."

"No, I mean do you really want to leave the bay house?"

"Of course I do," he said. But even while he said the words, his heart lurched at the thought of changing his life so completely. He owed Davina the truth on that, at least. Closing his eyes for a second, he took a long breath. "This is going to be hard. Uprooting my children could cause them to go off on a tailspin again. They need stability and security."

"They'll find it here," she said. "Once Rikki and I are finished, this place will look like a big playhouse."

"They need a home, not a playhouse."

Discouragement took the bright glow out of her eyes. "What do you want me to do, Santo? You say one thing, but then I feel as if you mean something else entirely. I don't need mixed signals. I need decisiveness and con- sistency."

The woman didn't back down. He'd give her that. And she was right.

"I'm sorry. I shouldn't have said that. I'm a wreck about this move. Months ago when I decided to do this, it felt like it was for the best. I'd lost yet another nanny and the kids were acting out. I thought it was just be- cause of the hectic Christmas break, but it was because they missed having Christmas with their mother. She died right before Christmas the year before last. So after yet another sad holiday, I started early in the year look- ing for something different. It became an obsession and then I saw a for-sale sign on this place and…I bought it after one walk-through."

Moving another step closer, he looked into Davina's eyes. "I don't normally act so impulsively but some- thing grabbed at me that day because Lucia had been harassed at school. I talked with her teachers and her counselors and we addressed the problem, but I needed to do something more. I had this need to find a fresh start. A need to see my children in a big backyard with a secure fence. The water across the street, nearby instead of right there and down below a dangerous bluff. The porches and the beautiful wide staircase made me think of how happy my children could be here. This place seemed like what I'd been longing for. Can you understand what I'm saying?"

Davina's whole expression changed, softened, mellowed. Holding his gaze, she moved close. No islands or counters stood between them here in the big, wide heart of this house. They were in open territory. The house stilled, almost as if a sigh had moved through the walls. Rikki's sneakered feet walking around upstairs didn't even touch them here in this cocoon.

"I understand," she said. "More than you will ever know. It's a lovely house, Santo. I can picture you and your children here. This house needs a good family. Houses, just like humans, tend to wither up and fade away if they aren't cared for and lived in."

Santo swallowed the pain that cut through his vocal cords like a whipping anchor rope. "I felt like that, yes. As if I was slowly fading away, dying inside. This house changed all of that."

"And now?"

"And now, I'm afraid I made a big mistake. I walk around the bay house and…I hurt all over again. I'm taking my children from the only home they've ever known. I remember good times there. Althea was very convincing. She pretended to care. She tried to be a good mother but she wanted more than any of us were willing to give." Putting two fingers to his forehead, he rubbed the spot that pounded like a storm surge. "What if my children aren't happy here either?"

Davina touched a hand to his arm. "Santo, your children will be happy with *you*, no matter where you are. Show them all the love you tried to show their mother. Show them how to be strong and how to recover from this. Help me build you a new home with new memories and let them be involved in this project so they feel ownership, too."

Santo's heart beat too fast. He'd never been scared of anything or anyone in his life but he'd had a good life, a pampered, privileged, protected life up until that fatal day when Althea had been killed. Now, he couldn't breathe. And he prayed he wouldn't humiliate himself and have a panic attack in front of Davina.

As if sensing his need to turn and leave, Davina took his hand in hers. Her hand was strong and soft, calloused but gentle, warm and firm and sure, her fingers tightening against his in what felt like a varnish of protection.

"I'll be right here," she said. "But I need you to be here with me. I think that once we get going on this, you'll be able to work through some of this anxiety and concern. You can take ownership, a real ownership of your new home."

"And will this help me work through my nightmares?" he asked, holding his emotions in a tightly coiled entanglement.

"I believe so," she said, her gaze caught in his, her green eyes giving him the peace of a cool summer forest.

When they heard Rikki coming down the wooden stairs, their gazes slammed together and then they broke apart, both physically and emotionally. But Santo still felt the warmth from Davina's touch.

Now his heart pulsed a new kind of beat. One that had a lifeline.

"What's up?" his sister asked, suspicion and surprise in the question.

"I'm going to help," he said. "Starting next week."

"Okay," Rikki replied, clearly sensing the static that crackled through the empty room. "I'm glad you two worked that out."

Santo nodded and finally smiled, a great rush of relief pouring over him. "Because tomorrow we have plans."

"What kind of plans?" Rikki asked while Davina kept watching him.

"The kids and I will be attending the Millbrook Lake Art Festival. And I have strict orders to bring Davina with us."

He hadn't planned on blurting that out. He hadn't planned on including the pretty contractor in their outing. But now, he wanted her with him. He needed the comfort she seemed to bring to his tattered soul.

"Are you interested?" he asked, waiting.

"I…uh…" She glanced from him to Rikki.

Rikki crossed her arms and gave Davina a knowing nod followed by a look of awe aimed toward him.

"I'd love to attend the festival with you and your children," Davina said. "Sounds like it'll be a good day."

Santo nodded and then whirled around. "Okay, so now I can see my house."

Chapter Eight

Davina wasn't sure where to begin. She wasn't even sure what had just happened between them. Rikki made a few suggestions and left, moving faster than Davina had ever seen before.

She'd talk to Rikki later. Right now, she intended to give Santo her best pitch on how to renovate and restore this rambling house.

"Let's start with the kitchen," she said. Then she went on to explain how she'd tear out the old walnut cabinets and put in fresh white wood. "With white marble countertops but with curved edges. More childproof."

"Do you see how the kitchen and breakfast room flow right into the big living room?" she asked, already creating a new space in her head. "I want to knock out this wall between the kitchen and the living area to open up this space. So when Virginia is in the kitchen, she can easily see the kids in the living area. I plan to build them a play area upstairs but for here, they'll have a corner nook for reading and homework, complete with their own television—for approved movies and shows."

She lifted her hand to indicate the corner by the back

porch that would be perfect for their study nook. "And the fireplace will be cleaned and updated with new tiles and maybe I can find some repurposed wood to update the mantel."

"Wood can be repurposed?" he asked, his dark eyes shiny with interest.

"Anything can be repurposed," she said, nodding. "I know a place over in Alabama that specializes in old wood. Doors, window frame, boarding from walls. You'd be amazed at what people throw out or give away."

"I am amazed," he said, his tone quiet. "I have a lot to learn."

"You could add wood to your business," she suggested. "Have a spot in your warehouse where people can come and shop for exotic or hard-to-find wood products and pieces."

He laughed at that. "Wow, slow down. Let's get the house finished before you take over my business."

Davina reeled in her enthusiasm. "Well, Rikki tells me you're expanding. You have the store now for retail, right?"

"Yes." He walked around the big rectangular kitchen and leaned forward to glance out the big, tall windows. "Alvanetti Imports is now selling retail straight from the warehouse. So far, we're doing pretty well. We sell to a lot of the condo developers and to people building or renovating private homes."

"So you could use some beautiful wood and wood products?"

"Stop it," he said, wagging a finger at her. "You're a bad influence."

"I've never heard that one before," she admitted. "I was always the good daughter."

"Tell me about your family," he said as they moved around the living room and then on to the formal dining room.

"Not much to tell. My parents are hardworking and simple. I have two sisters and two brothers—an older one and younger one of each. I'm the middle child. My mother was a teacher but she's retired now. My father owned and sold his own construction company but he's still a contractor. I got my love of building things from him. My older brother works with Da and my younger other one is in the army. My younger sister, Tilly, and I are very close, but my other sister, Alana, is single and she lives in New Orleans. We don't see her much because she's mad at the world these days because the man she's loved since high school ran off with another woman right before their wedding."

"You and I have that in common," Santo said. "Big families with lots of issues."

"I couldn't get away fast enough," she admitted.

She took him into the big master bedroom down a short hallway from the living area. "Now in here, you have your room and bath with a great view on either side—the yard and the lake." She pointed to the bay window across from the wall where she and Rikki had agreed the bed should go. "You needed dedicated space for your home office. I think this could be it. A desk in front of those windows and a nice view of the porch and the yard beyond. And you have a French door right off to the side in case you need a break."

"I need a break right now," he replied. "On my shrinking wallet."

"I'll try to keep the cost down," she said, glad he was tuning in to her ideas. "But if we do this, it has to be done right the first time. This house deserves our best efforts."

"The things you say," he replied. "Doing it right the first time. Our best efforts. You truly are that kind of woman."

"What kind of woman is that?" she asked, confused.

"The kind who won't betray anyone."

With that he turned and marched back into the big central hallway. "Let's go upstairs."

Davina needed a drink of water. Did he distrust her so badly that he didn't even want to be around her? That would explain why he'd pushed her away when she only wanted to do the best job possible. *Business,* she told herself. *This is strictly business.* This man was so bruised and battered, she was surprised he could even function.

But he had to function. He had to keep moving.

And so did she. This house could give her the kind of professional recognition that most contractors only dreamed about. Then she and her crew could go from being a small-time company to becoming Davina Connell Renovations—her name for her one-day full-fledged company. Da would be so proud.

Her father had always believed he'd failed his family when his company went under several years ago. But if she made a name for herself, Davina could help him bring it back to life and get her brother Darren involved, too. If he'd quit being so stubborn about things. Darren worked hard to help Da, but he'd sure resented her going out on her own five years ago.

She'd wanted Darren to be her partner, but at the time her brother hadn't been ready for that. He'd been too caught up in his own heartbreak. Darren didn't believe that their father had suggested she strike out and find her own way. He thought she'd betrayed them all by leaving the fold. He still believed that.

What would Santo think if she told him that story?

Pushing her tumbling thoughts away, she followed Santo upstairs. He stopped on the wide landing. "I like this spot," he said, turning with hands on his hips in that Santo way.

"I thought I'd put another, smaller den and sitting area up here since the children will need some privacy as they grow older."

"Good idea." He moved down the hallway and they talked about the three bedrooms. "This one near the stairs will be good for Nate. We'll have to put up a child-proof gate on the stairs, of course."

"Of course. If you're worried, we could take that extra room off the kitchen and make it his bedroom for now. It's technically a sitting room but since you rarely sit…"

"That might work," Santo said, giving her a wry smile. "I worry he'll fall down the stairs. He's come close several times at the bay house but we did finally find a gate we could secure the last time it happened."

"I'll do some sketching," she said, making a note. "Meantime, we'll make sure his future bedroom is ready and waiting. You can use it for guests for now."

"Or Mrs. Brownlee," he said. "She has an apartment here in town but I might persuade her to move in. If things continue to go well with her."

"Yes." Davina smiled at that. "She doesn't talk about her past a lot but I do know she went to nanny school in England. I can't get her to say what she did before that, however. She's a very private person."

"There's a nanny school?"

"Yes. Do you know anything about her besides what you checked on when you hired her?"

"I only made sure she was fully vetted and would be good with my children. Rikki and Blain made sure of that but we didn't get a lot of details. She had excellent recommendations from past employers." He shook his head. "I've got to get into the game, don't I? Just saying that out loud makes me sound like an arrogant, distant father. I don't want to be that kind of man."

"You're not that kind of man," Davina said, joy bursting through her. "But yes, you might want to get to know the woman who's taking care of your children."

"I think you're right. We usually pass in the hallway or talk about instructions and schedules rather than personal things." He gave Davina a direct glance. "You and I talk more about personal things. Or at least, you drag it out of me."

"I'm not prying," she said in her defense. "I'm trying to get a handle on you so I can create a house that works for you."

"It's working so far," he said, his expression sheepish and surprised. "Amazingly."

Santo was beginning to see the whole picture. Her heart seemed to turn on her as the image of his family being happy here came to mind. That would make this a perfect home.

"I'm glad," she said. "I want this to work."

Davina would have to move on, but oh, the daydream of staying to witness that was way too tempting. The daydream of being a part of that threw her completely. Way too tempting. It couldn't happen.

"I'd better go," she finally said. "I've got lots to think about."

They went back downstairs and talked about landscaping and furnishings and several other aspects of renovation. Santo listened and asked all the right questions. She hated to leave now that they were finally communicating.

Thirty minutes later she'd stalled long enough and was headed out the door when Santo called her back. "Do you want to go grab a bite to eat?"

"You and me?" she asked, caught off guard.

"Yes, you and me," he replied. "The kids and Mrs. Brownlee are going to an early movie."

"Oh, well, then. I do need to eat. I don't have any cupcakes in my bag."

"I wondered when you'd whip one out," he said, his gaze moving over her face.

Davina's head told her to decline. But her heart was dancing around in a happy jig. "I…uh…"

"If you'd rather not."

"I am hungry," she said. "I only had—"

"A cupcake for breakfast and another for lunch."

She grinned at that. "I had a banana and some walnuts for lunch, thank you very much."

"That's not a meal."

"It is when you're too busy to eat anything else."

"So?"

"So, let me run by my place and freshen up and I can meet you somewhere."

"No. I'll go with you and wait out by the lake. We can walk to one of the cafes nearby."

"All right," she said, thinking about how strange it would be to come down from her little apartment and see him waiting for her. And then thinking about how she must look and wishing she had time to tidy up.

But he'd seen her worse than this. She wouldn't put on airs or mascara for this man. She couldn't let her heart overrule her head. She needed to get this job done and move on.

But one quick meal wouldn't hurt, would it?

Just another part of that daydream that she shouldn't be dreaming. One meal and then she'd get through tomorrow for the kids' sake. But come Monday, back to business.

Or at least she told herself that while she hurried to clean up and look presentable for a man who didn't have the heart to see beyond her carpentry skills long enough to even notice her as a woman.

Chapter Nine

Santo watched as she came back down the stairs. He'd stood here for all of ten minutes, looking up at the white church steeple silhouetted against the end of dusk and the beginning of night. Beyond the starkness of the steeple's spire, one by one, all the stars took their cue from the evening star and began to twinkle and wink down at the dark waters of the lake. The crescent moon lifted up into the night like a delicate sliver of gold, shimmering and unreachable.

In spite of all of that, he'd come close to leaving.

But he was tired of running from the things he didn't think he could handle and he was tired of running from the strong pull of Davina Connell and her tool belt. He had to do this. He had to help her restore the house he wanted to spend his life in, with his children. The letting go was hard for him but the freshness of being around her was intoxicating and enticing.

She'd lured him into believing he could make this work and he wanted to follow her and see it through to the end.

When he turned and saw Davina coming down the

stairs, his heart, hard and bruised and shut off for so long, began that strange, exhilarating beat again. She looked the same and yet she looked different. She wore clean jeans and a lightweight blue open sweater over a white blouse. She'd taken her hair down from the usual haphazard bun. It hung in loose, riotous curls and waves around her face and shoulders.

And she smelled so good. Like a cluster of pure white magnolias hanging heavy from an old limb, like a spray of tiny jasmine blossoms floating on the night breeze. He'd never smelled any scent so sweet. It cleared his senses and made him breathe again, really breathe.

"I'm ready," she said, her tone timid, her eyes on him steady and searching. That statement seemed to become a challenge between them.

"It's a good night to walk," he said, not needing to fill the silence, but needing to affirm that they were actually doing this.

"Yes. One of those rare late spring nights where the humidity has lifted. Clear and crisp." She looked up as the stars. "And that sky. I wish I could capture this time where the sun is settling down and the moon is taking over. I'd put it on a wall so I could see it every night."

Santo cataloged her request and decided he'd search for a painting that came close to what she wanted. It had been a while since he'd bought a gift for anyone other than his children.

"Where would you like to eat?" he asked, keeping a few inches of air between them.

"I don't know. Maybe something near the marina. I love seeing the boats coming home for the night."

They strolled along the boardwalk, speaking to strangers and people they recognized. When Santo spotted the quaint Lakeside Café, he motioned toward it. "French and discreet. Good food without being pretentious."

"Do you come here a lot?" she asked, those green eyes questioning.

"No, not much. I've had lunch with my parents here and I've brought a few clients here but I've never brought anyone here for dinner."

"I'm not dressed," she said as if to ward off the intimacy of his admission.

"You're fine," he replied. "It's casual. Look at the place. It's the oldest restaurant in town and it's on the marina. People come for the ambiance and the view."

She smiled up at him. "Okay. Now I'm craving French food."

Santo guided her underneath the blue-and-white arched awning leading to the restaurant doors. Several white wooden benches flanked by pots of saucy red geraniums lined each side, patrons gathered on some of them.

After he gave the hostess his name, he noticed the young girl's curious expression. "We'll be the talk of the town," he whispered to Davina as they sat down on one of the benches.

"Why?" she asked, glancing around.

"I'm an Alvanetti," he said, rethinking this whole dinner plan and wishing he had gone on home.

She shrugged and turned to stare down a few curious people.

"And I'm a Connell. It's none of their business."

"They make it their business," he said, wanting to shield her from the brutality he and his children had gone through.

She leaned close. "We can choose to ignore all that. Tell me what's good on the menu."

Santo shook his head. "Does anything ever get to you?"

"Many things. All the time. I hate it when people neglect things or throw away perfectly good furniture. I like neat lines and a minimalist kind of decorating. I'm not good with clutter."

He absorbed that and then said, "Sometimes when you're talking about houses, I think you're not really talking about houses."

She gave him that secretive smile again. "And sometimes when you're talking about protecting your children, I think you're not really talking about protecting *just* them."

"You think I need protecting?" he asked, the quietness of being near her a nice contrast to the curiosity all around them.

"Yes, I do," she said. "From yourself."

The pager buzzed in his hand, its blinking red lights bringing them apart.

"This is going to be an interesting dinner," he said. But he was looking forward to talking to her, really talking to her. He needed to talk to people more. And starting with Davina seemed like the nicest way to form that habit.

Davina couldn't remember when she'd had a more relaxing meal. They'd dined on citrus chicken salad, crusty bread and a lemon-basil soufflé that melted in her mouth.

"That was incredible," she told Santo after she'd scraped away the last of the soufflé.

"It was a good meal," he replied. Then his lips turned

up in a half smile. "I've never known a woman like you. You don't hold back on anything, including eating a good meal."

Davina put a hand to her mouth. "Oh, no. I'm not very ladylike. My mother tried to teach me manners but I do enjoy good food."

"No, you did nothing wrong and your manners are impeccable," he said. "I'm giving you a compliment. My wife, she ate like a bird. She liked being skinny."

Davina could see the old hurt in his dark eyes. "Skinny is not in my vocabulary," she said, hoping to keep things light.

"You don't need to be skinny," he said, his gaze touching on her and moving on. "You have curves."

"You've noticed?"

"I notice a lot of things," he replied, his smile simmering down into a daring but friendly smirk.

"Hmm. I'll have to remember that. You are observant but you don't share your observations."

"I learn things when I'm quiet."

She had to ask. "What have you learned about me, other than I can pack away food?"

"You're thoughtful," he said, giving her another thorough stare. "You have a sweet tooth."

"Yes." She pointed to the empty soufflé dish.

"You like children but I think you're not ready for your own."

That shocked her. "Why do you think that?"

"Because you came from a big family. You like the freedom of being independent. You don't want to be tied down."

That last part was wrapped in a tone of disappointment that caught at her like a tattered curtain. But she wouldn't tell him about how hard it had been when her father told her she needed to strike out on her own. "I have a lot I want to accomplish," she said, "but one day I'd love to have children."

She thought about his three. About holding Nate and rocking him to sleep. The little boy had captured her heart from the time Santo had thrust the crying toddler into her arms.

"I want children," she said on a somber note. "When the time is right."

"I'm glad to hear that," he replied. "I didn't mean to upset you."

"I'm not upset. You're right. But what I want right now is to continue renovating and rebuilding houses. I watched the house I grew up in slowly fall apart and I wondered why my dad, one of the best in the business, did nothing to keep it updated and working." Staring out at the water beyond the fancy sailboats and yachts lining the marina, she went on. "Later, when I was old enough to understand and after I'd made a nasty comment in front of my mother, she told me that my daddy was out there making everyone else's dreams come true because he couldn't make enough money to keep our dreams going."

"The cobbler with no shoes," Santo said, nodding.

"Yes. But he tried so hard to make it all work. I'm determined to keep working hard so I can repay him for teaching me my love for building, especially rebuilding. And one day, I hope to be able to renovate the home we all love."

Santo reached across the white linen tablecloth and took her hand. "I hope you can make that happen. I have dreams for Alvanetti Imports, too. Dreams that come by honest work and doing what's right. My wife didn't share those dreams. She didn't care if my family had a suspicious background or went about breaking the law. And I loved her too much to see her flaws."

"But you've worked to make it all right," she reminded him, not wanting to ruin their night. "I can see the good in you, Santo."

Pulling his hand away, he said, "Can you?"

"If you can see all you've mentioned in me, isn't it my turn to tell you what I see in you?"

"I don't want to hear what you see about me."

"Why do you dismiss your own good?"

"I don't want to talk about me. Up until now, this has been all about me. My houses, my children, my nanny, my family. I want to know more about you."

"You know enough," she said, leaning back in her chair, one finger moving over the gold etching on her coffee cup. "I love what I do and I'm trying to find my place in the world. In what is predominantly a man's world. I want to help my family, too." She wanted to make them proud.

"We share the same values when it comes to family. I'm trying to help my entire family get back on the right path, the good path."

"I can see that," she said, trying again. "I watch you with your children and you're a good father."

"You've only seen me recently," he said. "I haven't always been this attentive."

"We all learn from the past and work hard for the future," she replied. "I know you're doing that. So will you do me a favor?"

He gave her a look that told her she might be asking for too much. "What?"

"Don't be so hard on yourself. Remember, this can be the redo you need in your life. Go with it."

"So you want me to pretend when I'm still confused and grieving?"

"No, I want you to give up some of that control you hold so dear." Then she shook her head. "Let's just see how things go next week. Tonight, I want to enjoy that moon and those stars on the walk back to my place."

"Is that my signal to take you home?"

She tilted her head and shook out her hair. "I am tired. I've been up since five."

"Do you sleep?" he asked.

"Like a log. Most nights. But then, that's changed since I met you."

That brought a dazzling smile to his face. "Oh, so I keep you up at night?"

"Renovating your homes keeps me up at night," she amended so he wouldn't get the wrong idea.

Although, thoughts of this man did seem to find their way into her dreams.

He grinned and, thankfully, didn't pressure her on that.

They made their way outside and strolled along the boardwalk. Davina was full and content but her mind was in turmoil. Most of her clients were older and married, or younger and wanting a new house to start their lives. Happy people who wanted to create warm, cozy homes.

This man was different.

Tormented and brooding. Stubborn and proud. Lonely and distrustful. He was every romantic hero her sister Tilly had ever raved about. That alone should be enough to warn Davina away from him.

They walked in silence and spotted a blue heron

standing still underneath a dock light. She pointed so Santo could see. "He's waiting for his supper. He can spot the fish in the shallows thanks to that light."

Santo watched the lanky, graceful bird. "I guess we all need a guiding light to spot sustenance, right?"

Davina pointed to the soft spotlight shining on the church steeple. "Yes, we sure do."

When they reached her little apartment, he insisted on walking her to the door. And there they stood, staring at each other, too much left unsaid between them.

"Thank you for going to dinner with me," he said, taking her hand in his. "I didn't want to go home to an empty house."

"I enjoyed it," she replied. "I guess I'll see you tomorrow."

"Oh, that." He looked as if he wished he'd never asked her to go to the festival with his family. "Bright and early. The girls will see to that."

"I get up early," she said. "Especially here where the light comes through the fan windows in the wee hours to wake me up."

His expression changed, intensified, brightened. "I'd think you must be beautiful in the early morning light."

Davina lost her breath. That image of waking up to a house full of running feet and dogs barking and life pulsing in pure joy around her caught her in a net of sweet imprisonment. She saw it there in his eyes, the same need, the same longing.

But before he could lean down and kiss her, she blurted, "You'd think wrong. I'm grumpy and unpleasant first thing in the morning. In any light."

For a moment, she held her breath and wished he'd

just kiss her and get on with this. And he looked as if he felt the same way. His eyes went dark. Too dark.

Neither of them were ready for this.

"Good night, Santo," she said on a shuddering of breath.

And then she turned and hurried inside and leaned back against the solidity of the heavy wooden door, not daring to breathe until she heard his footsteps echoing away from her.

Chapter Ten

"Why haven't you called?"

Davina glared at her cell for waking her up so early on a Saturday morning. "Tilly, it's six a.m."

"You never sleep late," her spunky younger sister said through a heavy chuckle. "Are you ill?"

"I *do* sleep late on the only day off I've had in three weeks," Davina replied through an irritated growl while she went in search of the coffeepot. "Or at least I'd planned to. Why are you up so early?"

"I miss you," her sister said on an exaggerated whine. "Da and Darren work all the time and Ma has been baby-sitting and dog-sitting to bring in some extra income. This big old house is lonely."

"Ma is dog-sitting now?" That was new. Nancy Connell had always loved animals but Davina had never known her mother to take on extra dogs for pay. "Doesn't that make the house a little overcrowded since we already have two dogs and a cat?"

"No. She goes to some of the fancy homes in the Garden District and actually stays with the animals."

"Wow, that sounds interesting," Davina said, wide awake now. "How's Da?"

Tilly's voice changed from frivolous to serious. "He's working too hard. I worry about him. He and Ma seem at odds these days, too."

Davina had never known her parents to fight much. They were lovable and cuddly most days. "Is that why she's getting out of the house more?"

"Maybe," Tilly said. "I stay at my apartment most days but we all show up at the house when we want. But we miss you. That's why I'm worried about Da."

"Because of me?"

"Because of everything. You're part of it. He's a proud man and he doesn't like his daughter secretly sending money to his wife."

"He knows?"

"I think so."

Davina inhaled the smell of fresh-brewed coffee filling the air. "Well, I'm not going to stop but I'll figure out how to handle our father. I'm going to be here for a while so I can't deal with this right now. Three more months at least, but I'll send a check next week when I get paid for the first project. We finished the bay house yesterday."

"And how is it going, working for this mysterious Italian with three children?"

"That's a long story," Davina said. "And I haven't had enough coffee to tell it."

"Oh, this sounds good," Tilly replied, her tone full of questions. "I can wait for you to drain your cup."

"I'll have to call you later," Davina said. "I do have plans for this morning. Not this early but in a couple of hours. There's an art festival on the lake and I want to go. I'm going to buy Ma something nice for her birthday."

"Hey, I have a birthday, too," Tilly reminded her.

"I'm sure I'll find a trinket or two for you, too." Then she asked, "So what kind of mood is Alana in these days?"

"A dark one, as always," Tilly retorted. "She's never gonna get over breaking up with Lewis."

Davina's older sister Alana had always been moody and hard to read. But she'd dated the same man since high school and had big plans to marry him once he was through medical school. But once he was done, he'd suddenly called off the wedding and moved away with another woman. Now Alana, an RN, rarely came to family events and kept herself busy with work at one of the big medical centers in New Orleans.

"Well, they did date for seven years. He promised her the moon and left her in the dead of night."

"For another nurse," Tilly redundantly pointed out. "I can't reach her. You need to call her."

"She never picks up or returns my calls," Davina said. "But I'll keep trying. Have you heard anything from Quinn?"

"No. Deeply embedded somewhere in a dangerous place that I don't even want to think about."

"I'll say an extra prayer for him."

They talked almost an hour. Davina glanced at the clock and took one last nibble of the toast she'd popped into the toaster. "I have to go and get dressed. Santo and the children will be here at eight thirty."

"Wait? What did you say?"

Davina winced, realizing her mistake. "I said I have to go."

"No, the part after that. So it's Santo now, is it? And with the kids, too. Are you going on a family outing with your client?"

Davina muttered under her breath. Tilly was like a dog with a bone. She wouldn't let go. "It's just the festival. He needs someone to help him keep them all together."

"Didn't you tell me he hired a nanny for that?"

"It's her day off."

"Right. You never date, Davina. Especially not with a client."

"It's not a date. It's a day in the park."

"That's a date in my book."

"Speaking of your book, are you still sweet on Axel?"

"Don't change the subject," Tilly said, her tone a little put off. "I want to hear all of it."

"I have to go," Davina said, again. "We'll talk later."

"Good. You'll have more to tell after spending the day with all of them."

Her sister ended the call. But Davina knew she wouldn't hear the end of this conversation. Tilly was right, however. She'd never before broken her strict rule of not getting involved with a client.

After last night, Davina wondered if she was doing the right thing by going to the festival with Santo. Would it send him the wrong message? She didn't even know what the message was anyway.

Or did she want to send him a distinctively different message than what her head was telling her. Could he sense that she was attracted to him?

Nervous and fidgety, she took a shower and dressed in denim capris and a sleeveless button-up blouse with a vivid wildflower print. After tying her navy sneakers, she tugged her hair into a loose ponytail and put on some lipstick and blush.

"This is crazy," she told her reflection in the bathroom mirror.

She kept talking to herself as she watered the plants and tidied up the little den. Out beyond the porch, the lake glistened and sparkled like a dazzling blue blanket. She could already hear the chatter moving between the vendors as they set up their tents along the shoreline. The smell of funnel cakes and barbecue merged to make her stomach beg to be fed again. The dry toast hadn't satisfied her but she didn't have time to go buy a muffin or cupcake.

By the time she heard a knock at her door, Davina had finished off three cups of coffee, two pieces of buttered toast and two small pieces of chocolate.

She was ready.

Santo wasn't sure how this was supposed to work so he'd sent Lucia and Adriana up to the door to get Davina.

But he watched with his breath held as the door swung open.

Surprise. She looked down to find his daughters standing there in their shorts and T-shirts, excitement making them dance and sway.

Confusion. She glanced down to where he stood with Nate, her eyes holding his in a silent question. Santo waved. Nate giggled and pointed. "Daddy, Dani."

Dani. She'd told him only her father called her that. How had Nate figured out her nickname? Or had his son found a way to say her name, toddler-style?

"Davina," he corrected with a gentle tone.

"Dani." Nate stuck to his guns with a pouting bottom lip.

Maybe he'd heard Davina and Mrs. Brownlee talking about their families. Those two did talk a lot.

He wondered what they'd said about him.

Too late to worry about that now. Davina and the girls were coming down the stairs. She looked prim and proper in her bright blouse and cute pants.

"Hi," he said, searching for a smile that he hoped would cover all of his insecurities.

"Good morning." She smiled back, hesitation in her words.

"It's a gorgeous day."

"Yes, it is."

"Daddy, can we ride the ponies?"

Lucia's question brought Santo out of the shell he was trying to stay inside. Like a tortoise, he lifted his head and stared around them.

The festival was in full swing.

Food trucks and drink wagons, booths displaying paintings and sculptures, jewelry and knickknacks. Some full of funky beach-inspired clothing and accessories and some full of books and photographs. Ice cream wagons and clowns and balloons and…life. This place was full of life.

Santo had forgotten what that was like.

Adriana squealed and pointed to the kiddie rides. "I want to ride all of them!"

Nate followed his sisters, squealing and pointing and asking for everything in sight.

Davina laughed and hurried to keep up. "They're wired."

"Yes," Santo said, watching the children and warning them to stay close. "They got me up early."

"My sister woke me with a phone call," she said, laughing.

"Do you talk to your family a lot?"

"As often as possible," she said. "She was checking up on me. She keeps me posted about everyone."

"Rikki does that for me," he said. "By the way, we've been invited over to Alec and Marla's house this afternoon after we've had enough of the festival. They're grilling and Rikki and Blain will be there, along with Preacher Rory and Vanessa. And maybe even Hunter Lawson and his new wife. They got married this spring."

"I've heard Marla mention all of those people," she said. "I haven't met Hunter and Chloe yet, though."

"Well, you might get that chance today."

"Do you want to go?" she asked, her question full of resistance.

"I didn't at first, no." He could admit that now. But he had to be honest with her. "I was an outsider around here for a long time but most of the people I know have been kind since everything fell apart. Rory has helped me a lot. I talk to him at least once a week. I'm teaching him how to play golf."

She glanced over at him. "And what is he teaching you?"

"How to find grace."

She looked pleased with that. "I've talked to him a lot, too, since I'm renting my apartment from the church. He's a good man."

"Yes." Santo wanted someone to say that about *him*. "Anyway, I can go to Alec's by myself or we can just hang out."

Another hesitant glance. "You don't have to drag me along. Are the children going?"

"Yes. Marla insisted. My girls play with her daughter, Gabby, a lot." Shrugging, he finally said, "We'll see how the kids are in a couple of hours. We might all need a nap."

Davina chuckled. "I'm thinking that chasing these three around is harder than putting up drywall."

They moved with the children, stopping for rides, face-painting and hot dogs, cotton candy and lemonade. Davina saw several pieces of art she liked and bought a few things for relatives and friends. By the time they'd gone through the whole thing twice, her tote bag was brimming with treasures and she'd made connections with several antiques dealers and art vendors.

They finally sat down at a picnic table by the water. Nate watched the boats coming and going while the girls fiddled with their new jewelry and some books Santo had bought.

Lucia got up to throw away some napkins.

"Stay close," Santo warned, pointing to a nearby trash can.

Then he turned to Davina and exhaled a long breath. "I'd forgotten what spending an entire day with these kids does to me. I'm both exhausted and rejuvenated."

"That's what children are for," Davina replied. "You have three precious ones, Santo."

"I know," he said. He finally looked her fully in the eyes. "I really enjoyed today. And last night."

She held his gaze and then dropped her head. "What exactly are we doing here?"

He lowered his head and looked up at her. "Eating too much junk food?"

She shook her head at his feeble attempt to dodge the real question. "You know what I mean."

Time to lay it all on the table. "I know what you're asking but I don't know the answer," he admitted. "I haven't thought of dating anyone since…since a long time. It wasn't on my agenda."

"Are we dating?"

"Do you want to go out with me again?"

"I don't normally get involved with my clients," she replied. "Never a good idea."

"Are we involved?" he asked, his head filling with what that could mean.

"Not yet," she said. "But if we're not careful, we could be headed that way."

"I can't explain," he replied. "Let's enjoy today and come Monday, we'll get back to work."

Her eyes filled with a bit of relief and a bit of disappointment. He shouldn't have blurted that out. But before he could explain, Adriana grabbed his arm.

"Daddy, Lucia's fighting!"

Santo stood and searched for Lucia. When he saw her a few feet away rolling on the ground with a little girl, he turned to Davina. "Watch Nate."

"Go," she said. "I've got him."

Santo lifted Lucia up and away from the angry blonde with the short bob. "What's going on here?"

Lucia was crying, sobbing and gulping, her face dirty and red. "She called Mommy a…a murderer. Tell her that's not true, Daddy."

"It is true," the other little girl shouted through her own sobs. "My mama told me not to play with you. Your mama was a bad person."

Santo held his daughter close and prayed for the right

words. This was the same little girl who'd been taunting Lucia on the playground at school. He thought they'd cleared this up. But the other girl's mother rushed up to them before he could speak.

"What did your daughter do to my Beatrice?"

"I don't know what happened," Santo said, trying to explain without blurting out what the little girl had said. "They got into an argument."

"I know who you are," the woman shouted. "You had the principal call me to school because of your little brat there. You keep your children away from mine, you hear?"

Santo didn't respond. Instead, he held Lucia tight against him and searched for an escape from the crowd that had gathered.

And then he felt a hand on his arm. Davina, holding Nate in one arm and clinging to Adriana with her other hand. "Rory is here, Santo. He's taking us across the street to Alec's house."

Santo nodded and followed the preacher and Davina out of the park and across the street. He didn't stop or look back until he was inside the cool hallway of Alec and Marla's spacious Victorian house. But when he did turn, Davina was right there with him, his other two children still safe in her arms.

Chapter Eleven

Davina stayed seated in a comfortable side chair tucked away in the cozy open den, Nate asleep in her arms and a border collie named Angus curled up in a protective blob at her feet. She watched as Alec and Marla made sure everyone was okay. Marla gave the girls water and crackers and soothed them with soft words, her wheat-colored hair falling softly around her face. Her daughter, Gabby, and a cute white poodle named Roxie followed Marla around, helping.

The little dog wore a red vest indicating he was a service dog. He'd helped Gabby get over a traumatic event in her life, and now he was helping Lucia and her sister to forget what had just happened across the street.

But Davina couldn't forget it. Her stomach lurked and churned, her cheeks burned red with anger. She'd never liked bullies. Her parents had taught her to be tough but kind.

No matter what had transpired in the past, Santo and his family needed some kindness in their lives, and here in this house they were receiving it.

Rory and his wife, Vanessa, manned the grill outside

and talked quietly to each other. Vanessa came inside with a platter of charred hamburgers and then turned to Davina. "Are you all right?"

"I'm fine," Davina said. "I just can't get that scene out of my head. It was horrible."

Vanessa sat down beside her. "Rory had a talk with Lucia. Only to reassure her that her parents love her and that her daddy won't let anything bad happen to her. She seems to think someone will harm her family." Lowering her voice, she added, "Apparently, this isn't the first time Beatrice has attacked Lucia. And her mother doesn't do a thing about stopping it."

"What did Santo say to Lucia?" Davina asked, a yearning to soothe him overcoming her.

"He told her that her mommy had gone through a difficult time and it had made her change into an unhappy person, but he assured Lucia that her mommy loved her and wouldn't want her to be sad."

And yet, the real question remained. How could he ever truly answer it?

Davina wanted to find that woman and child and have a good talk with them, but the woman would probably ignore her pleas. How could a grown woman be so cruel in front of a child?

Vanessa stood again. "Do you need anything? I'm going to check on the side dishes."

"No. I have some water." Davina indicated a tall crystal glass full of lemon, mint and ice.

Alec's aunt Hattie washed faces and placed the children's treasures away for safekeeping. She sent Davina encouraging smiles now and then, her pearls dazzling and her hair as shimmering gray-white as her jewelry.

"Can I get you anything, Davina?" she asked now,

leaning over to touch a hand to Nate's forehead. "What a beautiful child."

"No, I'm fine," Davina said. "Maybe a place to let him sleep?"

"Of course," Aunt Hattie said. "Alec's office is across the hallway. The couch there is apparently quite comfortable, since I find him napping on it a lot."

Davina rose up, careful to hold Nate close, but before she could make a move, Santo, who'd been out on the back porch with Alec and Rory, came through the door and walked toward her. Then he gently took Nate from her, his tormented eyes locking on her. "I've got him."

"I was going to take him into the office and put him on the couch," she said, pointing across the house.

The look he gave her told her everything. A blank, empty stare that held a world of hurt and resolve. "I'm taking him home."

He turned and called to the girls. "Lucia, Adriana, let's go."

"Daddy, we don't want to leave," Adriana said. "Gabby says we can play with water balloons."

Lucia stood and gave him a look full of fear and determination. "I'm okay now, Daddy. If you want to stay." Her dark eyes grew big and misty. "I'm sorry."

"You didn't do anything wrong," he said. "But it's getting late and we should get home. Your brother is exhausted."

Davina glanced at him. "I can go with you—"

"No need."

With that, he took his children and walked out the back door to the side garden, obviously planning to take the back way to get to his car still parked at her apartment.

Hurt and hurting for him, Davina almost went after him. Instead, she turned to Marla. "What should I do?"

Marla looked toward Alec, sympathy clear in her eyes.

"Let him go," Alec said. "He has to absorb this in his own way. He thought this had ended the last time it happened at school. And he wants to have a private talk with Lucia."

Marla sank down on the couch. "Lucia will be okay but sooner or later, he's going to have to explain to her what that girl was saying."

"Where are Rikki and Blain?" Aunt Hattie asked. "He needs his sister with him."

"Waiting for him at the bay house," Rory said, his tone quiet. "I've already called them."

Vanessa took his hand, smiling over at him.

Davina decided she needed to go home. No point in hanging around now. Santo didn't need or want her help and she was at a loss as to what she should do. Then she thought of the lake house and suddenly felt energized. She'd go there and work.

That was always a good way to find a solution to her problems. She'd take it out on old drywall and dingy carpet.

"I'm leaving, too," she said, smiling at the group gathered in the big room. "Thank you all for inviting me."

"Are you sure you won't stay?" Marla asked. "My parents are coming and my dad really wants to meet you. I think my mom's been bugging him about remodeling."

Davina laughed at that when she wanted to run away. "Tell him I'd be glad to talk to him another time. I'm wiped out right now."

Marla nodded, an understanding in her eyes. "I will. Maybe when you're finished with the Alvanetti project."

The Alvanetti project was an understatement, Davina decided.

She said her goodbyes and walked home with a covered plate of food. But for once, Davina wasn't very hungry.

Santo had been better today—laughing, talking to her and opening up in a casual way that allowed her to get to know him in a new light. The kids had fun, too. They'd played, ridden fun kiddie rides and had done what kids needed to do, spend time with a parent.

Then, that terrible moment when the little girl's shrill accusations had echoed out over the crowd. She'd never forget the expression on Santo's face. Anger, despair and humiliation all caught up in a stony glare that dared anyone to touch his child again. It must have taken all of his efforts to keep from telling that woman to shut up.

He'd been dealing with this for so long now. No wonder he needed a change. But he might need to consider if moving to the lake would keep this from happening. Surprised he hadn't just packed up and taken his kids far away, Davina put the food in the refrigerator and changed into her clean but old work jeans and a paint-spotted button-up work shirt and then she buckled on her tool belt.

Since she'd already had some of the crew drop off the other tools at the renovation house, she could easily walk around the lake, away from the festival, to get to the house. And she needed that walk to clear her head.

By the time she'd made it to the house, she could see the remains of the day across the water. The festival had died down and the few vendors left were loading up their wares. A gentle spring breeze danced through the palm trees as she crossed over by the rambling Tudor-style Millbrook Inn, where rumor had it that last summer Hunter Lawson had helped Chloe Conrad escape from two hit men who'd been hired to kill her.

So many people passing through her life had survived all sorts of life crises and had now fallen in love right here in this quaint waterside town not far from the Gulf of Mexico. She thought of Santo as she stood on the porch and stared out at the big lake.

And she knew in her heart, she didn't have a chance with him. Since she wasn't sure about her own feelings, she could handle that. What she couldn't abide was the pain and torment she'd seen in his eyes when his sweet little girl had begged him to tell her it wasn't true. That her mother wasn't a murderer.

He couldn't say that to his child. He wouldn't lie but he didn't know how to explain the truth.

And she didn't know how to help him. Except in the way she knew best. She could create a home that protected and shielded his children from the cruelty of the world. At least when they were within these old walls.

So she turned from the tranquil beauty of the sunset cascading out over the lake like spilled gold and concentrated on demolishing old walls and creating new open, tranquil spaces.

When she finally glanced up it was fully dark outside and… Santo was standing in the hallway staring at her with such a look of need that she dropped her sledgehammer and immediately rushed to take him into her arms.

He held her and breathed in the essence of her. Dust and a mustiness that spoke of aged walls and decades of footsteps, sweet florals and good, honest sweat that spoke of her commitment to this project. Santo didn't speak. He didn't have to with Davina. He held her and he let her hold him, their bodies tucked close to create a shield of warmth that made him feel safe, so safe.

Finally, he pulled away and looked down at her because he needed to look into her eyes. "You have smudges all over."

Reaching his hand to her skin, he gently traced the construction dust and wiped it away, his fingers finding the softness beneath the grit. "I'm sorry," he said. "I shouldn't have left you there earlier."

"It's okay." She put some space between them and wiped at her clothes. "Your children needed you."

"I needed my children." He glanced around and came back to her. "And I guess you needed to destroy some walls."

"Don't we all?" Then she asked, "How is Lucia?"

"Asleep," he replied. "Rikki and Blain are with them. And Mrs. Brownlee showed up and announced she's moving in."

"Good idea."

He felt the lump growing in his throat, swallowed, prayed he wouldn't break down. "People care about us, Davina. Good people care about my family."

She moved close again, one hand holding his bare arm in what felt like his only link to reality. "Then remember that. Remember that you stayed here for your family, to rebuild the business so your children would have a good legacy instead of that one defining memory."

"But what if that one moment does define them? I can't always protect them."

"These people who care about you, they can define

and protect your children. They will be with you all the way. Your parents will return soon and they love you and the kids. They'll help you. Rikki and Blain and now Virginia Brownlee will make sure your children are never alone. And Santo, I care, too. You have to see that."

He broke away before his emotions broke apart. "My children see that. Do you know that Nate calls you Dani?"

She gasped, tears forming in her eyes. "I rocked him to sleep the other day in…your room. He'd hidden there and when we found him, he got into my arms and asked me to rock him. Then he tried to say my name and I tried to teach him. But…he couldn't grasp it. He was drifting off when I told him to call me Dani. I didn't think he heard me."

"He heard," Santo said, his throat raw, his head hurting. "And he remembered."

She pushed at her haphazard hair and wiped at her eyes. "He's such a sweet little boy."

"I'm blessed," Santo said. "I wanted to keep them here but maybe I should leave Millbrook Lake."

"Are you thinking of doing that?"

He could see the disappointment and regret in her eyes. "I should have done it before things got too far out of hand. Before my children were exposed to the ugliness of it all." Then he shrugged. "But I think this will follow us no matter where we go."

She stood, looking like a fragile doll in the center of the big, empty room. But her gaze held a determined strength that no artificial doll could pull off. "Did you come here to tell me to quit?"

He shook his head, his heart gripped in a battle. "No, I came here after my children were asleep to look at what will soon be our new home." He paced again, staring up at the tall ceilings and the ornate chandeliers. "I came here to…pray. I asked God to give me a sign. Should I leave or should I finish what I started."

Walking back to where she stood, he touched a hand to her hair. "And then I saw a light on and I saw you, here alone, tearing things apart."

She moved closer, her fingers grabbing at his shirt, her eyes asking him to be honest. "And?"

"And I took that as a good sign. I'm staying."

Then he pulled her into his arms and kissed her, the taste of dust and decay mixing with the taste of sweetness and light.

He knew that sweetness and light would win out if he kept her near him.

Davina pulled away, surprise and what looked like awe in her glistening eyes. "Santo?"

"Give me that sledgehammer," he said. "I want to learn all about how to do a restoration."

Chapter Twelve

They worked into the night, talking some, not talking a lot. But getting to know more about this house and each other.

Around midnight, Santo's cell rang.

"Hello, Rikki."

He winked at Davina while he assured his sister that he was okay. "I'm with Davina at the other house. We're taking the first step. Demo."

Davina hid a smile, a sense of accomplishment and relief washing over her. After he'd kissed her, and after she'd recovered from the shock of need that had jolted through her at that kiss, she'd explained "demo" to him while his gaze had moved over her with a new awareness, while her heart had beat itself into that new awareness. Then they'd worked in silence, taking little breaks to discuss their plan for the house.

His plan.

Davina had to remind herself that this was Santo's home, not hers.

No. His plan.

God's plan, of course. This was out of her hands. She

had to turn the future over to God and if that mean walking away, then she'd have to do that.

But when she heard Santo's soft tone, she prayed God would give her a sign, too. Glad that he'd calmed down, she knew nothing had been solved. He still needed to find a way out of his grief and pain and his children needed some sort of understanding of things.

He ended the call and looked at his watch. "I think we've done enough for tonight."

Had reality kicked in on him? Made him see he still didn't want to be here after all?

Davina ignored the disappointment of that possibility. "Is Rikki still at your house?"

"No. They left the children asleep and Mrs. Brownlee snoozing in a recliner. My sister was just worried about me. But when I told her I was with you, she seemed relieved."

That spoke volumes, Davina thought. Rikki's trust in her meant a lot to her. But she needed to process all that had happened today. "It *is* late and my muscles are screaming."

"How did you get here?" he asked. "I didn't see your truck."

"I walked," she said. "Never considered I'd have to also walk back this late at night."

"Nonsense, I'll give you a ride."

She brushed her hands off and then looked at her dirty clothes. "I'm a mess."

He tugged her close, his hand around her waist. "You look beautiful."

Davina smiled up at him and distanced herself from that attractive and rare happy look on his face. "Okay, we got a lot accomplished. Tomorrow we rest and then

Monday morning my crew and I will get started on the big stuff." Pointing to the sturdy load-bearing column she'd left in place after they'd taken out the wall, she said, "We have to put up a support beam to make sure this open area is secure and once that's done I can take this column out. Then new drywall, updated fireplaces, all new doors and windows to hurricane-strength code."

Santo put a finger to her lips. "Stop. I'm so tired and you are making me even more tired. Let's go."

Davina pretended to pout but her chatter had defused the situation enough that she could resist his tempting kisses.

But when they got to his car, she shook her head. "I should have known."

A fancy sports car with the top down.

"I rarely drive it," he said with a sheepish shrug. "Rikki told me to get in it and put the top down to clear my head."

"And did it clear your head?" Davina asked, admiring the sleek black car.

"No, but being with you did."

He opened the car door for her, his dark gaze holding hers, a challenge in his expression.

Davina didn't speak. But she got in the car.

Sunday morning, a gentle rain fell as Davina walked the short distance to church, her umbrella forgotten back inside her apartment. Her muscles ached and she needed a good nap, but excitement coursed through her when she glanced across the way.

She could see the lake house located around the bend. The house that Santo and she had worked on last night.

Davina had worked on a lot of houses, mostly doing

grunt work for construction foremen and before that, following her daddy around and asking too many annoying questions. Then she'd worked her way up the ranks until finally she'd bought her first flip three years ago with a loan from a small bank back in Bayou Fontaine. After a lot of sweat and angst and physical work from her daddy and her reluctant brother Darren, that house had sold and she'd made a tidy profit. Since then, she'd bought, renovated and resold four more houses. But this house, the lake house, would be her biggest challenge.

Her whole future was banking on making the lake house a true gem. Unless she got sidetracked by the handsome man who'd kissed her there in the demolished kitchen last night.

And kissed her again at the door of her apartment.

Can I do this? she wondered as she made her way up the slippery church steps. *Can I love the house and leave the man?*

"Whoa."

Davina looked up in time to see the preacher standing on the steps above her. "Oh, I'm so sorry," she said. "I need to watch where I'm going."

"I got you," Rory said, offering his hand to help her. "But you did seem somewhere far away just now."

"Not that far away," she replied on a wry note.

"Just across the lake maybe," he said with a knowing smile.

"You're too smart for your own good," she retorted. "Yesterday was a strange day, full of all kinds of emotions."

"How did it end?" he asked, his expression serene.

"On a good note." She knew she could trust Rory. "Santo and I worked on the house until late into the night. Which explains why I need more coffee this morning."

"You know where the coffee is," he said, thankfully not asking for any more details. "And I think Marla dropped off breakfast cookies, too. You know, the ones that are supposed to be good for you, with oatmeal and less sugar and all kinds of healthy stuff but still worth the effort."

Davina knew the ones. "Thank you."

"Hey," he said as she was walking away, "I'm glad your night ended well."

"Me, too. Now I have just a few more weeks of praying every workday will end like that," she called back.

Davina made her way past the sanctuary and toward the kitchen at the end of the fellowship hall. But when she reached the open kitchen door, she heard a familiar voice.

"And that little brat had my Bea down on the ground, pounding at her. It scared me so bad, I'm still shaking."

The mother with the little girl from yesterday at the festival.

"I heard about it," another woman said. "But if Beatrice said those things—"

"Can you believe that? That little heathen is just like her mama, attacking Beatrice right there in front of everyone."

Another voice echoed out through the partially closed divider between the kitchen and the dining hall. "Well, maybe the child was upset."

"Why? Beatrice was telling the truth. Everyone knows what that woman did. It's horrible. I'm surprised those children haven't been taken away from that man."

Anger moved through Davina like a steamroller.

Dear Reader,

IT'S A FACT: if you answer 4 quick questions, we'll send you 4 FREE REWARDS!

I'm not kidding you. As a leading publisher of women's fiction, we value your opinions… and your time. That's why we are prepared to **reward** you handsomely for completing our mini-survey. In fact, we have 4 Free Rewards for you, including 2 free books and 2 free gifts.

As you may have guessed, that's why our mini-survey is called **"4 for 4".** Answer 4 questions and get 4 Free Rewards. It's that simple!

Thank you for participating in our survey,

Pam Powers

To get your 4 FREE REWARDS:
Complete the survey below and return the insert today to receive 2 FREE BOOKS and 2 FREE GIFTS guaranteed!

"4 for 4" MINI-SURVEY

1 Is reading one of your favorite hobbies?
☐ YES ☐ NO

2 Do you prefer to read instead of watch TV?
☐ YES ☐ NO

3 Do you read newspapers and magazines?
☐ YES ☐ NO

4 Do you enjoy trying new book series with FREE BOOKS?
☐ YES ☐ NO

YES! I have completed the above Mini-Survey. Please send me my 4 FREE REWARDS (worth over $20 retail). I understand that I am under no obligation to buy anything, as explained on the back of this card.

❏ I prefer the regular-print edition 105/305 IDL GLPN

❏ I prefer the larger-print edition 122/322 IDL GLPN

FIRST NAME   LAST NAME

ADDRESS

APT.#   CITY

STATE/PROV.   ZIP/POSTAL CODE

Offer limited to one per household and not applicable to series that subscriber is currently receiving.
Your Privacy—The Reader Service is committed to protecting your privacy. Our Privacy Policy is available online at www.ReaderService.com or upon request from the Reader Service. We make a portion of our mailing list available to reputable third parties that offer products we believe may interest you. If you prefer that we not exchange your name with third parties, or if you wish to clarify or modify your communication preferences, please visit us at www.ReaderService.com/consumerchoice or write to us at Reader Service Preference Service, P.O. Box 9062, Buffalo, NY 14240-9062. Include your complete name and address.

LI-217-MSH17

She hurried through the door and glared at the woman and her two shocked friends. "You don't know me," she said, "but I was with the Alvanetti family at the festival yesterday and I heard what you said to Santo Alvanetti."

"It's none of your business," the red-faced woman said on a huff, her tone not so smug now. "And why would you want to be with a man like him?"

"He's a good man and he's my friend," Davina replied. "And his children have been through a lot more than most. He's trying to put his life back together. Could you please consider how fragile those children are? How it's not your place to shout out something like that in a public venue? Your daughter isn't to blame here since she obviously repeated what she'd heard an adult talking about, right?"

"My daughter is most definitely not to blame," the woman said, her hands on her hips.

The other women had moved away, clearly embarrassed. Davina knew she should leave it at that, but she had to defend Santo. "I'm only asking you to consider how your words not only affect his daughter but your daughter, too. It's not really your place, is it, to judge this family. What if you'd been through something like this? Would you want someone saying that to your child?"

"I'd never—" The woman stopped and looked behind Davina. "Well, that just figures. Now he's coming to church to find redemption."

The woman turned and hurried away, her skin beet-red. But Davina had seen a flash of regret in the woman's eyes, too.

Davina looked around to find Santo standing there with that tormented darkness back in his eyes.

* * *

Santo's stomach clenched. The coffee he'd had earlier now burned hot against his gut. Davina had defended him. And it made him even angrier than ever. She shouldn't have to do that.

Not here, of all places.

She hurried toward him. "I'm sorry, but someone needed to tell that woman to back off."

"You shouldn't have done that," he said, the good feeling he'd carried home last night now gone. "It's not your job to fight my battles."

She didn't even blink. "It is when someone like that doesn't see what her words can do to people."

"Let it go, Davina."

He saw the hurt in her eyes. And the determination. "So now you're angry at me?"

"I'm angry that you even have to defend me."

"I don't mind that, Santo. Let me decide that for myself."

"And let me take care of my own issues," he retorted. "You shouldn't get involved in this."

"I'm going to church," Davina said, her eyes downcast. "To pray for understanding. Because I'll never understand you."

Santo needed her to understand that he didn't want her good name to become tainted because of him. "Davina, wait."

But she was gone in a swish of skirt, her sandals clicking on the tiled hallway floor. Santo stood alone in the empty kitchen, wondering why he'd thought this was a good idea. He'd purposely left the children at home with Virginia to protect them, but now he had the added burden of keeping Davina out of the fray.

So he turned to leave, thinking he'd go home and tell Virginia to take the day off since she had a few more things to move to the spare bedroom, where she'd become an official squatter.

But his brother-in-law Blain Kent was standing at the other end of the big fellowship hall.

"Hey," Blain said, passing him by to grab some coffee. "What are you doing?"

Santo didn't want to explain. "I'm about to go home. Changed my mind. The woman who upset Lucia yesterday just got into it with Davina, too."

Blain's steady gaze didn't waver. "You're gonna let some misguided woman with an unchristian attitude keep you away from the service?"

"I had to keep my children away so why should I be here?"

Blain gave him that hard detective glance he'd seen so many times. "This is the best place for you to be," he said. "Hold your head up and I mean up, bro. Look to Him for your strength and your answers. The woman who has it in for you, she's dealing with her own issues. Without going into detail, I can tell you she's divorced and she has a teenage son who's acting out. His little sister is probably following his lead. That woman is frustrated and scared and she shields her own issues by gossiping about others. Right now, she's thankful that you're on the hot seat because that can deflect the spotlight off of her troubles."

Santo absorbed that information and then asked, "So that's supposed to make me feel better about what she and her daughter did to Lucia yesterday?"

"Nope," Blain said. "It's supposed to make you see that we've all got something. But He's got us all." He shrugged and gave Santo a hard stare. "I see it all when I close my eyes at night, Santo. I see your wife coming for Rikki and I hear the gun go off and I sit up in bed, my breath caught in my lungs. I have to live with taking your children's mother. And we'll have to deal with that for the rest of our lives. But He's got us. He will see us through. It won't be easy but we've got to stand firm on this."

Santo wanted to walk away. But Blain's blue-eyed gaze dared him to do that. He's been so caught up in his own pain, he sometimes forgot Rikki and Blain and how they'd discovered the truth about Althea and Victor and their criminal intent.

"C'mon," Blain said, his expression shifting. "Rikki will be glad to see you."

Santo shook his head and stared at Blain. "I really don't want to like you, you know."

"Same here," Blain said with a wry smile. "But like it or not, we're family now. And family sticks together."

Santo couldn't argue with that. Blain had been a good brother-in-law considering how he'd met Rikki and how he'd felt about the whole family before. Santo followed Blain into the sanctuary and held his head high. And when he went to sit down next to his sister, he saw Davina sitting there with her.

Their eyes met and she smiled at him, a tentative smile that asked a lot of questions.

"I'm sorry," he mouthed, hoping she'd forgive him.

She didn't speak. Her eyes said what he needed to know.

Davina was better at forgiving people than he was.

And once they were alone together again, he'd also thank her for standing up for his family.

Yet another quality about her that he admired.

Chapter Thirteen

Monday morning.

Davina took a deep breath as she and her five-person crew entered the lake house. "This is it, guys," she said, turning to face the four men and one woman who followed her all over the place these days. After they'd finished the bay house, she'd told them all to take a long weekend. Some had headed home and some had headed to the nearby beaches.

"You already started?" her right-hand man Kurt Martin asked, his eagle eyes moving over what had once been a wall.

Kurt didn't like to miss out on demo. He'd gone back to Alabama to see his wife and two boys for the weekend so now he was anxious to get started.

"Yes. I had some time Saturday night so I went to work."

"You worked on a Saturday night, boss?" Kurt liked to tease Davina about her nonexistent love life. "That's just not right."

"Yes, and I enjoyed every minute of it."

Too much, she wanted to add. One brooding, confusing man and two wonderful kisses too much.

"Well, you sure got a lot done," Josh, the college kid who was working with them until the end of summer, said. "Who were you mad at this time?"

Did they all know her that well?

"Nobody in particular," she retorted. "Just needed to burn off some energy."

"She missed us," Becky said, grinning.

"I did," Davina admitted. Becky was older than her and divorced but the woman knew how to swing a hammer. And she was an Amazon woman so none of the boys messed with her.

That left Adam and Howie, two brothers who wanted to work with her forever, according to what they told her after each job. They were in their early twenties and both had business degrees but they'd rather be in construction than sitting behind desks. They had aspirations of being on one of those home shows on television one day.

"So we need to get that support beam up and these columns down," Kurt said, already anticipating what needed to be done.

"Yes." Davina went to the old counter. "Here's the new plan. You've all seen it before but just as a reference."

"An amazing house," Becky said, coming to view Davina's blueprints. "You'll do great, boss."

"So do I look that worried?"

"Something's bugging you," Becky said, her short blond hair curling in the humidity. "Or someone."

"I'm fine," Davina said. "I should have taken the weekend off myself but I didn't. If I go home, I get caught up in the family drama too much and usually wind up getting back to the job late. Didn't want to risk that chance with this one."

"Maybe you can go home Memorial Day weekend," Becky suggested with a knowing smile. "Get away from that burr in your bonnet."

"Maybe."

Davina hoped she wasn't blotching everywhere but the burn of kissing her handsome, troubled client on Saturday night and then making him extremely mad on Sunday had certainly stayed with her all weekend. She also hoped that Santo would stay away today. She was still confused about what had happened yesterday at church. Sure, he'd told her he was sorry for being so harsh with her after she'd confronted that woman. And yes, they'd sat together in church. But he'd left so fast after that, she had to wonder if the man would ever be able to look her in the eye again.

Too many mixed signals and she had too many other things to worry about anyway. So Davina did what she'd always done whenever she needed to work through a problem. She kept tearing away walls.

By the end of the day, they'd cleared out the kitchen and dining area, secured the new open space between them with a massive support beam and widened the opening to the big room across the hall that would soon be a family room. The house looked younger already, as if the letting go of some of the burden had lightened it.

"Okay, go get showers and dinner," she told her tired crew. "And rest. Tomorrow, we start on the stairs and the bedrooms."

They all left for their rooms at the Millbrook Inn, teasing each other, daring each other, their laughter moving through the breeze off the lake in sweet echoes.

Davina stayed behind to go over the details one last time, her mind filling with images of what the finished project would become. Her mind filling with images of three dark-haired children running down the stairs to greet their dad at the stained-glass front door.

"I see you had a lot of help today."

She whirled from the spot where the old sink had been and saw Santo across the hallway. Blinking to clear her head, she said, "My entire crew is back. I couldn't do this without them and the locals we'll bring in to help us."

"A lot goes into this," he said, making it a statement, not a question. "You even manage to create temporary jobs for people here."

"Yes, well, we need carpenters, plumbers and all sorts of journeymen." She wasn't in the mood to convince him again tonight. She'd plied her case, told him her plans and laid this gem of a house at his feet, hoping to give him hope, hoping to win him over so that he'd become a part of this in an all-inclusive way. But he still balked and walked out when he didn't like the situation and he was probably still fuming because she'd stepped into a battle that he considered his alone.

He moved across the space, his shoes hitting against the old floors with a purposeful stride. "I came to apologize."

She pretended to be studying the massive support beam. "For what?"

"You know what," he said, spinning her around, his hands on her arms. "For what happened in church. You were standing up for my children and me and I shouldn't have snapped at you. I didn't handle it very well."

Davina moved away and whirled. "I'm becoming used to your snappish ways, Santo."

"That's not good."

"No, but good to know, at least."

Frustration sparked in his eyes. "I told you in church I was sorry and you seemed to accept it. Are you going to make me suffer and beg for forgiveness or will you accept my apology?"

Davina couldn't put him through any more suffering. "I could do that, but I'm not that kind of person. Consider it forgotten. And consider me a ninny for interfering where I'm not wanted."

He didn't speak but his eyes told her she was wanted in a way that took her breath right out of her lungs.

"I'm sorry, too, Santo. And I forgive you but you have every right to be a little upset with me."

Relief washed through his eyes. "Well, you'll be glad to know I didn't sleep at all. I wanted to talk to you after church but I had an emergency at work and spent the rest of the day trying to put out administrative fires."

"I guess I'll have to accept that excuse," she said. Then she added, "I didn't sleep much either. I shouldn't have butted into your business. It won't happen again."

She tried to leave. Needed to leave. This man was infuriating and complex and troubled and…so kissable. Too much of a temptation.

But he held her arm. "I'm sorry. Blain had a talk with me and made me see reason and a whole lot of other things. The woman's name is Annette Pickett. Her daughter is Beatrice and she has a fifteen-year-old son who's having some issues and causing her a lot of problems. She's afraid he'll turn to a life of crime. She's going through a bad divorce. Blain didn't give me all the details but after he told me some of her problems, I found out who she was and where she lives."

Davina's eyes went wide. "Are you going to confront her?"

Santo let go of her arm, his eyes filling with surprise and disappointment. "Do you think I've hired a hit man or that I just might scare the woman? Shake her down a bit?"

"I didn't mean that," Davina said, realizing how her question sounded. "Santo, honestly, I didn't mean it that way."

"But you thought it, right?"

"No. Maybe. You were telling me you'd found out about this woman and you had all of her information. I jumped to the wrong conclusion." Then she put a hand to her mouth. "That's it, isn't it? You purposely didn't confront her at the festival because you knew people would jump to the wrong conclusion. And that's why you were aggravated with me yesterday?"

She leaned into the now-hollow counter support. "I never considered how that could cause a ripple effect."

His reaction made her see how much restraint he'd been using. Anger, followed by disappointment, a minute of staring at her and then…a long exhale. He'd been fighting this, too. Learning to control his anger so people wouldn't continue to judge him wrongly. She had to wonder how many times he'd turned the other cheek for the sake of his children.

"I can see how you'd get the wrong impression," he said. "And you know something? I can't blame you or anyone else. I can't even blame Annette Pickett or her little girl. I think the shadow of my family's reputation will always be over me, no matter what."

"No. Not if you keep doing what you need to do to

make it right," Davina said. "So what are you going to say to this woman when you contact her?"

"I'm not planning on saying anything to her," he explained. "But I know she's looking for a better-paying job and I have several openings at the store and in the warehouse."

Davina didn't hide her surprise. "A good idea, but she might spit in your face."

"I won't be the one offering," he said. "Rory's going to mention it to her."

"And if she says no and spits in his face?"

"Then I've done all I can do."

"And what about Beatrice and Lucia? They have to go to school together."

"I talked to the school officials today and Lucia and Beatrice aren't in the same classes so they rarely see each other and they have different recesses now. I think Beatrice heard her mother talking about us at the festival and said something to Lucia only because it was fresh in her mind. Her teachers are aware of the situation, but it will be up to her mother to change this."

"How is Lucia?"

"Better. We had a long talk when I got home yesterday afternoon, just she and I." He paced the floor and touched on the exposed walls. "I told her that Mommy got confused and made some decisions that caused her to get in trouble and she hurt a lot of people but that none of that is Lucia's fault. I tried to explain that Althea's death was a tragic event and that none of us wanted it to happen. I also told her that she and I are going to talk to someone who can guide us through this. A new counselor Rory suggested."

Davina wanted to hug him tight. She could see the

fatigue circling his eyes like a dark aura. "I'm glad to hear that. I can't imagine how hard this has been for all of you."

"It will always be hard," he said. "One day, they'll all know the truth and then Rikki and Blain will have to deal with it even more. It won't end, Davina. Ever."

She didn't miss the warning in that statement. "Is that why you keep pushing me away?"

"Do you think I'm pushing you away? I mean, you have a life and you have plans. Why should you want to get involved with someone like me?"

"Maybe you don't want to get involved with anyone at all," she replied. "You didn't like me coming to your defense and you're still mad about it, even after both of us apologized."

He gave her one of those doleful, dark stares that said everything but told her nothing. "I'm mad about life in general but you will never understand how it felt to see you rush to my defense. No one besides my family has done that. Not in such a bold way."

"I can be bold," she said, walking up to him. "I fight for what I believe in and I believe in you."

"Why?"

"Because I've seen you in action, Santo. You have integrity and grit and you want to do what's right. You'd do the same for me."

"But these days I have to walk away. I can't fight. It would only set things back."

"Or set them straight," she countered.

He pressed his hands against the skeleton of what used to be cabinets. "I came by to tell you how sorry I am for taking my frustrations out on you yesterday.

And I wanted to let you know that I'm taking a couple of weeks off from work to help with this project."

Davina shook her head. She was tired and she needed a shower but all she wanted to do right this minute was hug Santo close. "You are full of surprises."

He laughed, a low growl of a sound because technically, he never did really laugh. "Is that okay? Me hanging around with a hammer?"

"Depends," she said, walking toward the back door. "I'll have to see your skills."

"Oh, I have skills. I'm only just beginning to show you my skills."

"Right." She checked the empty, echoing room, her mood decidedly better now. "Let's go. I need to get cleaned up and find some dinner."

"Okay. I'll wait for you at your place."

"You don't have to do that. I wasn't fishing for us to eat dinner together."

"Yes, I do. Virginia wants you to come over to our house for a proper meal."

Davina thought about that. "How thoughtful of Virginia."

"Yes, isn't it, though?"

"But you don't need to wait. I can meet Virginia at your house."

"No, I will take you and drive you home."

"Did Virginia suggest that?"

"No, that's all my idea. My plan is to have you alone for at least fifteen minutes each way."

"Sports car? Top down?"

"Yes. It's a nice evening out."

"In that case, give me about twenty minutes."

He nodded, clearly relieved and pleased with himself. "I'll go visit Rory and Vanessa while I'm waiting. How's that?"

"Good idea." Because she'd be a wreck knowing he was sitting in her living room or hanging out on her porch.

"Let's go then. I'll follow you to your place and give you exactly twenty minutes before I come looking for you."

Davina knew he meant that. And she had a feeling they'd just turned a very important, very intimate corner.

But she sure couldn't predict what they might encounter down the road. Only prayer and God's grace could reveal the future. She'd have to trust Him to show her which road to take.

Chapter Fourteen

"Hello, Davina."

"Hello, Virginia."

Santo watched as the two new women in his life exchanged pleasant greetings, their expressions as serene as the water down in the bay.

"Thank you for inviting me to dinner," Davina said, her gaze moving over the house she'd renovated. "You've got the place looking good."

Santo followed her gaze. Color shined brightly in the glow of the new light fixtures she'd had installed along the big oval hop-up bar that occupied a huge space between the kitchen and the den. More color brightened the spacious den in pictures, drapery and rugs. A still life of sailboats in the bay hung over the massive fireplace, mirroring the real bay outside.

Warmth. This home now had a warmth that had been missing before. One wall in a discreet corner held black-and-white photos of the children, laughing and running, right along with colorful portraits of each one in a more formal setting.

Althea had never bothered to display them. She'd kept

them hidden away in a box in a storage closet, always saying she would let Rikki do something with them one day.

That day had never come.

But he was here now, with Davina.

She had certainly brought more than just warmth into this house. She'd breathed a new life into his whole family. He'd miss her when she was gone.

"Daddy!"

The sweetness of his children hurrying toward him brought Santo the kind of peace that made him thankful for each breath he took. "Hello!" He grabbed up Nate and tickled his tummy and kissed his cheek. Then he did the same with Adriana. "How did your day go?"

"Good," Adriana said, bobbing her head. "Miss Virginia let us swim and she showed Nate how to hold his breath."

Nate demonstrated with puffy cheeks and mischievous eyes.

Lucia stood to the side. "I'm learning how to do a flip, Daddy."

"That's great," Santo said, nodding at Virginia. "Our new nanny is a woman of many talents."

"I was a champion swimmer in college," Virginia stated in a matter-of-fact way. "I'll have them all acting like little fish before summer is over."

Davina turned to Santo and took Nate out of his arms. "I've missed all of you so much."

Nate giggled and poked her in the cheek. "Dani."

"Dani," she said, nodding, her gaze meeting up with Santo's.

Lucia tugged at Davina's crisp white blouse. "We just

saw you on Saturday. That means you missed us for almost two whole days."

"I sure did," Davina replied with a grin. "Two whole days of not seeing you."

"Seems longer," Santo interjected and then wished he hadn't when Virginia grinned.

"I missed you a million-gazillion," Davina retorted with a wink to Nate. She put him down and turned to Virginia. "What can I do to help with dinner?"

"Not a thing," Virginia said. "The children and I have it well in hand."

Davina looked surprised and pleased. Santo met up with her near the glass wall out to the pool. "I guess you saw the for-sale sign in the yard. Rikki listed it today."

"I did notice that," she said, giving him a focused stare. "How do you feel about that?"

Remembering his earlier conversation with Rory and Vanessa, he said, "Good. Like I'm finally coming out of a dark fog." He told her that Rory had set up a meeting with Annette Pickett to counsel her. He hoped Santo and Annette could meet in the next week or so and resolve this issue with their girls. "That's part of why I wanted to talk to Rory. We can't start over if Lucia is still being harassed and bullied."

He shook his head. "I told him when I watched Rikki put up the sign, I almost stopped her. But then I thought of you and the new house and how hard your crew worked both here and now there. Change isn't easy, is it?"

"No. I've seen a lot of people during this kind of transition process. There's so much emotion that goes with a for-sale sign. Each one has a story behind it, sometimes good and sometimes not so good."

"You're not like any contractor I've ever known before," he told her. "I've never looked at houses in that way. All wrapped up in emotions and tough decisions. I just always saw the housing market as a sign of progress. Now I see things so differently."

"Buying something that takes a lot of attention and income is always an emotional and stressful endeavor," she replied. "But I love being a part of the process."

His eyes met hers. "You picked the right profession."

She glanced around when the children started laughing and talking and saw Virginia demonstrating with exaggerated clarity how to butter bread. "Seems like she did, too. She clearly adores your children."

He let out a sigh. "Yes, I have to admit the morning you both walked into my life has changed our world."

"It's just beginning," she said. "This is a beautiful place but change can be good."

"I'm seeing that," he said, a soft smile on his face.

Virginia motioned to them. "Dinner in five minutes."

"It smells so good," Davina called out. "I'm starving."

"Chicken pot pie and salad, with lemon bars for dessert," Virginia said. "And the children helped with everything."

Davina walked into the kitchen and grinned at the girls and ran her hand through Nate's always-messy hair. "I'm impressed."

Santo guided her into the dining room where the changes she'd made seemed to bring the tropical yard right into the room. Parlor ferns and bird-of-paradise plants sitting in the corners and a bright, floral rug underneath the teakwood table. A comical portrait of a parrot sitting in a jungle on the wall.

Before this room had been sterile and unwelcoming,

with the bare table and some sort of twisted sculpture clinging to the wall like an old vine.

The children loved this room now. He did, too.

As they sat down to dinner and joined hands to say grace, something Virginia had incorporated into each meal, he thanked God for these two remarkable women.

He prayed that Virginia would never leave and he prayed that he'd be able to let Davina leave.

Later, Davina insisted on helping Virginia with the dishes.

"You're a good cook," she said, wondering about Virginia's past. "Where did you learn?"

Virginia gave her that Mona Lisa smile. "Here and there. I worked a lot of odd jobs before I settled on taking care of the wee ones."

"How long have you been a nanny?"

Virginia's smile seemed to slip. "Close to twenty years now."

Davina didn't press for any more information on the past. Instead, she looked toward the future. "So you're living here now?"

"Yes." Virginia dried the baking dish she'd used to cook the pot pie. "When I heard what had happened at the festival, I thought they might need me more than just seven-to-seven. I'm alone and I don't mind. Just made sense."

"It does make sense. Are you moving into the lake house with them?"

"I hope," Virginia replied, her gaze searching for the children across the way. "The little stinkers have embedded themselves into my heart."

"Good," Davina said. "I have the perfect suite of

rooms for you. Near the kitchen and near a room where Santo wants to put Nate until he's older."

Virginia didn't speak but the glistening mist in her eyes showed Davina that she needed this family as much as they needed her.

"I had a nice time," Davina told Santo after he'd pulled the sleek sports car into the tiny gravel drive up to the garage apartment. "Virginia is an interesting woman."

Santo stared at the dark lake waters. "Yes, but she won't talk about her past. It's strange but I trust her. Which is unusual for me."

"Rikki had Blain did a background check, right?"

"Yes. I asked Rikki about that the other day since I didn't get all the details before. Virginia passed the check with flying colors. She went to nanny school in England, just as you told me." Then he turned to face her. "But…do you really want to spend our last few minutes together tonight talking about Nanny Mod-Squad?"

She had to giggle at that. "She does remind me of someone out of a seventies' sitcom."

"Another bright spot in a house that had lost its luster."

Davina's heart seemed to be casting out a line but she wasn't sure she was ready to grab this catch. "Santo, are you okay? I mean really okay?"

He held to the steering wheel and stared up at the full moon hovering like a lost beach ball in the sky. "I'm getting there, yes." Then he slanted his body so he could see her better. "Are you afraid of me?"

Davina's mouth dropped open. "Afraid of you? Why would you think that?"

"You seem unsure about me."

"I am unsure, about a lot of things. I've never done this before."

His eyes turned onyx. "What? Sit and look at the moon on a beautiful night?"

She slapped at his arm and he grabbed her hand. "I've looked at the moon a lot, but never with someone like you," she admitted. "I'm not sure what to make of you."

"Do you have a boyfriend? I should have asked you that a long time ago, huh?"

"I've dated off and on," she replied, the warmth and strength in his hand holding her steady. "Work tends to get in the way of anything lasting."

"I could use that same line on you," he retorted. "So that excuse won't work on me."

"I don't have any excuses. Just concerns."

"And I ask again—are you scared of me?"

"I'm scared of how you make me feel," she said, the touch of his fingers against her sure and secure even while her heart was racing in a frenzied confusion. "I told you, I've never done this before. Of course, most of my clients are either retirees or young couples. Sometimes, big families needing more space."

"I'm different that way."

She glanced over at him and saw the smile in his eyes.

"That's different," she said.

"What?"

"You've changed since the first time we met. You've lightened up."

"Oh, so you've noticed. How else have I changed?"

"Your eyes didn't smile before. Now when you look at me, your eyes seem bright and aware."

"I am very aware of you, I can tell you that."

She basked in that admission. "I mean, you're more

aware of everything—what needs to be done, your children, the nanny. Me."

He laid his head back against the headrest. "I guess I'd forgotten how to really smile. So that scares you?"

"No. That's a good thing."

"But?"

"But I don't know how this will end." She turned to stare over at him. "Before, it's been simple. I come in and renovate and spruce things up and then I hand over the keys, get my check and leave. But with you, I can't be sure of the end."

"I'm not so sure of the end of this either," he replied. "But for now, can we just go with what's happening in the moment?"

Turning the tables, she asked, "Are you scared of me?"

"Absolutely," he said. "Completely."

Then he kissed her, his arms wrapped around her. "You terrify me," he said after he'd sat back to look at her. "There are so many reasons I shouldn't be here with you."

"Yes, I agree."

"So we agree we shouldn't be doing this and yet we can't seem to stop doing this."

"It's a problem."

He kissed her again. "But I have three very good reasons to want to keep you near."

"Only three?"

"Yes. Lucia, Adriana and Nate. They seem to like you a lot."

His words touched her so deeply, she had to take a breath. "I like them, too. A lot."

She loved his children but if she mentioned that word, things could take a definite twisting turn.

"Do you like me? A little?"

"Yes," she said. "I do."

"So for now will you please stop being scared of me and let me be a part of renovating the lake house?"

"Are you kidding me? I want you to help there. You know that."

"Yes, but you want me for professional reasons. I want to be there for personal reasons."

She leaned close and whispered, "I told you this would get emotional. It's all about personal reasons."

"It got emotional the day I handed Nate over to you."

Davina kissed him this time, turning yet another corner, taking a detour that had warning signs all over it.

"I'll see you bright and early tomorrow morning, Santo," she said. Then she hurried to get out of the car. "If you think I'm scary now, wait until you've been through a whole day of renovations with me."

He laughed at that but she heard the edge in that laugh.

He truly was terrified of change. And that meant they might have to end this before it ever really got started. This attraction could only carry them so far before they'd have to get to the bones of this budding relationship. The whole thing could cave in on them if they weren't careful.

Chapter Fifteen

"I'm yours for at least the next two weeks," Santo told Davina the next morning.

Tilting her head, she gave him one of those questioning glances. "You might live to regret that."

The sun was up, bright and sure. The day held little humidity but already, he could tell it would be warm.

Each time he glanced at Davina he turned warm. "I'm not completely helpless in the handyman department," he said. "We're always hammering and fixing things around the warehouse."

"That's cute," she said with a mischievous grin.

Santo wondered if he truly would live to regret this. Being around her day in, day out could prove to be his undoing.

These foreign feelings had kept him up last night and given him time to reflect on his life and what he wanted from here on out.

His children. His family. A quiet life. An honest life. Honest work. And someone like Davina in that life.

And yet, he didn't feel he had the right to tug her into the jarring spotlight of being around the mighty Alvanetti clan. So he'd decided he needed to back off on the top-down drives and the over-the-top kisses. The woman should be able to do her job without worrying about him all the time. She had big plans for her future. He could give her exactly what she wanted. He'd give her a glowing recommendation and a great review. He'd refer his few remaining friends to her.

Davina would make it big in the real estate and construction market. And he could try to forget her and get on with his own life.

"Are you ready for this?" she asked, passing him a cup of coffee.

"I'm not sure. What do you want me to do?"

"Mainly, stay out of the way," Kurt said in passing, a grin on his face. Then he shook Santo's hand. "Good to have you here, Mr. Alvanetti."

The brothers Adam and Howie whizzed by, nodding a sleepy-eyed hello.

Becky came in and looked around, her hands on her hips. "Oh, good. A rookie. Always love me a rookie on the work site."

"I detect sarcasm," Santo said with a smile.

"You detect right," Becky answered. "But I promise I won't nail you to the wall."

"She knows how," Josh said, shaking his head. "Watch that one, Mr. Alvanetti."

After they'd all gone on to get started, Santo glanced around and then back to Davina. "Do they all know… about me?"

She gave him a direct stare. "They only know that we don't discuss clients or their personal lives on the job. We do our work, consult each other when we have problems and keep moving. You don't have to worry about any of them harassing or annoying you."

"Refreshing," he said, already feeling out of place but also impressed with her no-nonsense work ethic. "I'll ask again. What do you want me to do?"

"We're going to pull up carpet and see if we can salvage the wooden floors," she said. "Just follow my lead."

"I can do that," Santo replied. "I think."

Three days later, he hurt all over. But Santo had to admit, showing up here every day and being a part of this tearing down and rebuilding did have a therapeutic effect on him. Rory had told him physical labor was good for the body and the soul.

Or maybe being around Davina had a lot to do with his new attitude.

"It's lunchtime," Davina called. He followed her to where they all washed up with a water hose attached to a spigot near the back porch. "I think Kurt is looking for a nearby place to order takeout since we're so dirty and sweaty."

Santo was definitely dirty and sweaty. Sitting down on an overturned bucket by the old chair she'd pulled up near the front porch railing, he said, "I haven't been this tired or dirty since I used to work in the warehouse after school. Mandatory labor, according to my father."

"Tell me about your family," she said, grabbing an apple and a cold bottle of water.

They talked a lot on the brief lunch break, but usually it was about the crew or the work or her family back in Louisiana. She'd never pestered him much for information.

"You know a lot already," he replied. Then he gave her the quick version of how far the Alvanettis had come. "I run a clean operation. And from everything we can tell, so did my father once he turned his life over to God. Blain's father was a big influence on him."

"And Blain's been the same with you, it seems," she said with a soft smile.

"Well, when your brother-in-law is a detective…"

"Hey," Kurt called out. "We're ordering catfish from that place out on the main highway. You want in?"

"I'll take a single filet plate," she replied. "Santo?"

"The same," Santo said. Then he stood up. "Hey, Kurt, let me buy today, okay?"

Kurt glanced at Davina. She nodded. Santo pulled out several twenties and handed them to Kurt.

"Be back in a few," Kurt called with a wave. He and the brothers hopped into his big truck. Becky and Josh stayed behind to toss old carpet and other debris into the Dumpster they'd rented for the duration.

"Ready to throw down your hammer?" Davina asked, grinning at him. "I'm impressed that you keep coming back for more."

She had no idea. "No. But I need two pain pills."

"We have plenty of the over-the-counter stuff around."

"I'll take one after lunch." He drank his water and stared out at the lake. "This really is a nice spot. I hope the kids will make new friends here."

"I'm sure they will. Gabby is right down the street. She's a sweet little girl."

"Yes, she is. And her stepfather has a lot of influence in this town."

"Do you hope to cash in on that?"

So she still wasn't sure about him. "I hope he'll continue to be my friend."

His cell rang and he stood to dig it out of his pocket. "Time for my daily check-in with my manager at work. I'd better take this."

Davina checked her messages. One from Ma. Two from Tilly. And one from Alana. Hmm. Alana never called.

She hit her older sister's number and waited for her to answer. "What's up, Alana?"

"I'm worried about Da," Alana said without preamble.

"Why? What's wrong? I talked to Ma two days ago and everything seems fine."

"He's not doing well. He and Darren are struggling. They've been at odds for months now, and you're off doing your own thing as usual."

"Alana, what are you talking about?"

"Dad won't ask you to come home, but he needs you. You should know that."

"I'm calling Ma," Davina said before ending the call. Her absent sister had some nerve since she was mad at the world in general but took it out on her family. But if Alana was correct, Davina would have to go home immediately.

"What's wrong?" Santo said, obviously seeing the worry in her eyes.

"One of my sisters. She says my dad is sick and needs me."

Santo touched a hand to her arm. "You should go."

"I will, once I get the whole story." She moved away. "I have to call Tilly. She'll tell me the truth."

"Hey," he said, rushing after her. "Don't worry about this. Can your crew work without you?"

"If they have to, to get it done."

"And will they mind if I help out?"

"Not if I tell them to work with you."

"Then you do what you need to do and we'll take care of the rest."

Davina nodded and hurried away to call Tilly, her prayers now centered on her family back in Bayou Fontaine.

Santo sat with the crew, their food barely touched, and waited for Davina to come back from the far end of the yard.

He'd watched her pacing back and forth for a half hour now. When she finally ended the phone call and headed toward them, he could tell she'd been crying.

"He's in the hospital," she said, holding up a hand. "They took him this morning but he wouldn't let anyone call me. Not even Ma. I'm so angry I could kick something."

Kurt sent a bucket her way. "Go ahead."

Her eyes flared and she sent a booted foot straight into the hard plastic. The bright blue bucket went flying across the yard.

"Feel better?" Kurt asked, gentleness in his tone.

"A little." Davina let out a sigh. "I'm going to drive over there as soon as I can get cleaned up."

"You shouldn't go alone," Becky said. "I can go with you."

"No, I need you all here," Davina replied. "Now that we're down to the bare bones, you can get going on the trim work and painting. The paint is waiting at the hardware store. Kurt, you have all the information."

"We'll be fine," Kurt said. "You've laid out the plans. We know what to do. And I'll call you if we're not sure." Then he put his hands on his hips and gave her a fatherly smile. "Darlin', this ain't our first rodeo."

"*You* could go with her," Becky said, pinning Santo with a level stare.

Had her crew picked up on things between them already?

Davina shook her head. "Oh, no. I don't need anyone with me." Giving Santo a warning glance, she said, "No."

Santo would be glad to drive her up to see her folks, but it didn't look as if she'd agree to that. "I don't mind," he said. "But only if she wants me with her."

Davina looked over at him, worry and fear in her eyes. "It's four hours. I've driven it alone lots of times. Besides, I thought you wanted to stay here and work."

"I'll do whatever you need me to do," he replied. "I can drive you over to New Orleans and I can hop a flight home so you can stay. Then you'll have a car there."

"Good plan," Kurt said. "Then Mr. Alvanetti can come on back if everything's okay and help us here."

"Call me Santo," Santo said, a sense of relief settling over him with Kurt's approval. "Davina, how do you feel about that plan?"

"I don't need a babysitter," she retorted, anger clear in the declaration. "I'll be fine."

"No," he said, his hands on her arms. "You need a friend."

Davina glanced around and then back to him, a

surrender softening her eyes. "Okay, you can go with me. But you're not staying."

Davina didn't know what to do or say.

"You'll have to leave your children," she told Santo after she'd come back to her senses later that day. "I can take care of myself. I've driven this route so many times I can do it in my sleep."

"The kids will be fine," he said. "Virginia knows what's going on and she agrees. Rikki is nearby and Marla has offered her help. Rory is praying for your family and he's coming by the house tonight to visit with the kids. We've got it all under control."

"Why are you doing this?" she asked, tossing an overnight bag into the covered toolbox in the back of her truck. Because she'd refused to take his sleek sedan or that too-obvious sports car.

"I told you," he replied, his tone firm. "You need a friend right now."

"I could get Vanessa or Rikki to go with me."

"They're both busy. I have two weeks off."

"To work on your house."

"I've worked for three full days now. And I'll take the red-eye back tomorrow and get in some more sweat equity. We both have to learn to trust other people, Davina."

"I do trust people. You're the one with that issue."

"It seems I'm not the only one," he pointed out as she backed out of the churchyard and headed toward I-10.

Davina let out a breath and watched the late afternoon traffic. "I trust my team. I'm worried about my dad. I'm upset that they didn't call me right away."

"They didn't want to scare you."

"No, Alana and Darren are angry at me. They think I've abandoned the family for my own ambitions."

"Do they know you send money home?"

"How do you know that?"

"I was guessing based on some of your comments," he said, looking sheepish. "You do what you can. You said your dad always encouraged you to strike out and follow your dreams. It sounds like he encouraged all of you to do that. You can't change how your siblings feel about things. Rikki stayed away from our family for years because she thought we'd caused her first husband's death. He was driving drunk and had a wreck. But she didn't know that. My father didn't want to cause her more pain but he finally told her the truth."

"Do you think there's something more to what's going on with my family?" she asked, her mind whirling in turmoil. "I should have gone home last weekend."

"I think you feel guilty but you shouldn't. You're not that far away at any given time. Your sister is going through her own thing, just like the woman who was so rude to Lucia and me at the festival."

"Have you talked to her yet?" Davina asked, to take her mind off her worries.

"No, but Rory is counseling her and he's mentioned me. I don't think she's ready to come around yet."

"People can be so stubborn." She stared at the road, her hands tight on the wheel.

After they'd gone a few miles, Santo pointed. "Stop here."

"You need a rest stop already?" she asked. "At this rate it'll take us till midnight to get to New Orleans."

"Pull into the parking lot, Davina," he said, his tone commanding.

She did as he said, thinking he wasn't a very good traveler. But Santo surprised her yet again after she'd parked the truck. "Now get out and come around and let me drive."

"What? No. I'm fine."

"You're not fine. Let me drive. I'll get you there so you can see your dad for yourself. But you need to rest and calm down."

"Bossy," she said, finally giving in to the fatigue and apprehension clogging up her head.

Santo let her get in and then shut the passenger-side door. Then he came around and took over the wheel. "Rest," he said. "We'll get a bite to eat later."

"Not hungry," she replied. She wanted to pout and cry and have a fit but she had to be strong. Why hadn't Tilly mentioned any of this in all their daily calls? Why hadn't Ma told her that her daddy wasn't feeling well? Why had she left them all there alone to fend for themselves?

Why was she so glad that Santo was with her?

Why was she falling for him?

That was her last thought before she drifted off to sleep, her head shoved against the seat and caught against the window. When she woke with a gasp, she saw the exit sign for New Orleans up ahead. Her daddy was in a hospital there but Bayou Fontaine was only about twenty miles south of New Orleans and like that famous city, her hometown was centered around the Mississippi River.

A shard of homesickness hit her full force as they bypassed the sign to the right. "That's where I grew up," she said, her voice raw and husky. "Bayou Fontaine."

"You'll have to give me the tour one day."

"That wouldn't take long. Only one main street through town. River Drive."

"How are you?" he asked, his gaze touching on her.

"Better. I didn't realize how tired I was."

"We should be at the hospital in about fifteen minutes. Are you hungry?"

"No." She watched the traffic as they neared the city. "And Santo?"

"Hmm?"

"Thank you."

Chapter Sixteen

"Who is he?"

Davina turned from staring at the vending machine to find her older sister Alana's piercing deep blue eyes on her.

Not in the mood for a confrontation, she went blank. "Who is who?"

"That strange man you brought with you," Alana said, a hand tugging at her long dark hair. "Mr. Tall, Dark and Italian. I mean, he's good-looking but...kind of broody."

"He's a friend," Davina replied. "Santo. I introduced him to everyone but you were in with Da."

Alana's eyes brightened and then darkened. "Santo, as in Alvanetti?"

"Yes. My current client."

Alana actually smiled. "You brought a client home with you? And a nice-looking one at that."

"He's not staying," Davina retorted, her appetite gone. "He insisted on coming with me but he'll take a flight home now that I'm here. I told him I could drive by myself but my crew went all mutiny on me and kind of forced him into escorting me."

"Hmm. Interesting."

Davina shook her head and changed the subject. "What do you think, I mean, really think about Da?"

Alana's invisible nurse hat went on even though she was off duty tonight. "He's not taking care of himself. It's stress and worry and he doesn't eat right. You know Da loves his food but he needs to cut back and eat healthy. His blood pressure was off the charts when Ma called me this morning."

"She called you first?"

Alana nodded. "Yes. He didn't want any doctors. So I hurried over and I knew even before checking his vital signs that he needed to come to the hospital."

"Why didn't you call me immediately?"

"We called you when we had something to tell you," Alana said. "And I'm sorry I blamed you. It's nobody's fault. Da is who he is. Proud and stubborn."

"I should check in more, but Ma and Tilly always assure me he's doing okay. Besides, he tells me to keep doing what I'm doing."

"It's okay," Alana said. "I was so upset and worried when I called, I took it out on you. I'm trying to do better about things like that. But...this is Da."

Relaxing a little bit, Davina nodded. "Those two traits—proud and stubborn, seem to run strong in our family."

"Tell me," Alana replied, her tone less confrontational now. "I was scared, Davina. I wanted you home."

"I'm here now," Davina said. And her eyes were wide open. She'd have to readjust her schedule to include more trips home.

Alana didn't speak but the sheen of tears in her eyes

told Davina that her sister was still hurting from being jilted at the altar. Alana deserved better than that.

Davina thought back to Santo and Annette Pickett, the woman who'd verbally attacked him at the festival. How many people were walking around crushed and broken in this world, fear and hurt hidden behind their bitterness and anger?

She closed her eyes and said a prayer for everyone. For all of them. But mostly for her daddy.

When she looked up, Santo's gaze held hers. Seeing him here, with her family all-around, brought her peace but also added to her angst. He didn't look out of place and that scared her because she wasn't ready for him to be in place yet. He'd talked to her brother Darren and they seemed to be getting along. He'd charmed Tilly and brought her coffee before she left to make a run home to check on things and bring back supplies for Ma. And she was pretty sure he'd win over Alana if her sister would quit being so standoffish. But she couldn't see Santo in her world on a permanent basis.

They were from different worlds.

They both came from big, confusing families and they both brought a lot of baggage with them but he was a widower with three children and she was a nomad who needed to keep moving. Santo was wealthy and settled into a routine with his children while she liked moving from one work site to the next. Could the two worlds merge?

She wasn't so sure. She shouldn't have let him come here with her. Everyone would jump to the wrong conclusion and assume too much. Her life would be one constant tease-fest.

Ma walked out of Da's room and reached out a hand.

Davina took her mother's hand and then she hugged her close. "How is he?"

"Tired. But he's resting." Ma's green eyes were misty with tears, her dark cropped hair haloing around her face. "They think he might have suffered a mild heart attack."

"I want to see him," Davina said.

"He'd like that," Ma replied. "He's been asking for you." She looked over Davina's shoulder. "For all of you." Then she lifted her head and said, "I want you to visit him but you are not to mention any of your worries or your observations or anything that you think has gone wrong in your lives. Your da carries the weight of the world for all of us. It's too much. We each have to share the responsibility of getting him well. Do I make myself clear?"

"Yes, Ma," Darren said, his reddish-brown shaggy mane hiding his solemn expression. He'd told Davina earlier that he and Da had been arguing when Da went pale and almost passed out.

The others echoed in agreement after their mother's stern warning.

Davina was about to go in, but Ma took her hand again and walked with her over to where Santo stood off to the side. "While you visit your daddy, Davina, I'll let Santo tell me all about the house you two are renovating."

Davina shot Santo an apologetic glance. "Of course, Ma. It's a real beauty."

"Go and see your father," Nancy Connell said, her tone serene. "I'll keep Santo company while you're gone."

* * *

Davina silently opened the door to her father's hospital room. She'd been in earlier but he'd been sleeping. Now he opened his eyes and smiled at her, his vivid blue eyes so like Darren's, his once thick reddish-brown hair now thinning and gray-streaked.

"Dani."

"It's me, Da."

"I must be pretty bad off for them to call you home."

"Not so bad. I just wanted to see you. You have some fancy machines hooked up to you so don't wiggle too much."

"Don't need machines. I'm fine. Just needed a little sleep."

"But you have to take care of yourself," she said, holding back tears. "I can come back and help Darren—"

"No."

The monitor beeped and the lines moving across it spiked.

"We'll talk about that later," she said, her own pulse quickening. "Just rest, okay?"

"You should get back to work, girl. So proud of you."

"Thank you, but aren't you proud of all of your children?"

"Of course. I tell 'em that all the time. Darren needs to find his place again."

"He will."

"Alana needs to love someone."

"I hope she can."

"Tilly…ah, my Tilly is such a joy."

"She's the best."

"Quinn isn't coming home, is he? 'Cause I'd know I'm bad off if you're bringing him home."

"No. We're keeping him posted. That is when we can get through to him. You know how that works."

"He's serving our country."

"Yes. My hero." Davina missed her younger brother Quinn so much, since they were close in age and they'd always had a special bond. Quinn would hug her and tell her it would be all better soon.

When her dad started drifting off again, she stood but he grabbed her hand. "Don't you worry about me, girl. You keep doing what you've been doing. I'm not blind, you know. You've been a good daughter, sneaking money to your ma."

Davina let out a sigh. "So does everyone know I've been doing that?"

"Of course. Can't keep a secret in this family."

He held her there, his smile softening as his medication kicked in and he drifted back to sleep. Davina held on until he was breathing peacefully and then she turned and left the room.

When she entered the waiting room, Santo stood and came to her. "How is he?"

"As aware and shrewd as ever," she said. "But he looks pale and tired. I think he's exhausted. Just completely exhausted."

"He's in a good place," Santo said. "The best doctors."

"Yes." She glanced around. "Tilly should have been back by now."

Her sister had gone home to get their mother a fresh change of clothes and some other necessities.

"You don't have to stay," she told Santo. "I'm with family now."

His expression filled with understanding and what

looked like disappointment. "Of course. I'll grab a cab to the airport and catch a flight back to Florida."

"I shouldn't have let you do this," she said, her mind whirling with complications and concerns.

"I didn't mind," he said, his tone low. "You got some rest on the way so that's a good thing, right?"

"Right."

"I can stay."

"No." She looked over at him, trying to find the strength to smile. "You go home and help my crew finish your house."

He took his time in responding, his eyes holding hers. "I guess that is for the best."

"I think so," she replied, wondering if this was some sort of ending to their budding relationship. Maybe he'd seen enough of her big family to decide he didn't want to be a part of it. Who could blame him? She'd sure seen enough to know she had no business longing for something she couldn't have right now.

She'd taken off on her own to prove herself but at what sacrifice to her family?

Santo's eyes held hers, so much unsaid between them. "I'll just go and tell your mother goodbye. She was really interested in the details of the house."

And other details, Davina was sure.

She watched as he shook hands and talked quietly to her mother. Then he came back to her. "I've called a taxi. I'll wait for it outside."

"Santo?"

"Yes?"

"I do appreciate you riding over here with me even if I did fall asleep on you."

"I liked watching you sleep," he said, his dark eyes centered on her. "I'll see you when you get back."

And with that, he was gone.

Davina stood against the cold hospital wall and watched him leave, her mind accepting that she was needed here more than she was needed back in Millbrook Lake.

She'd finish his house for him and then she would come home and take care of her family. No reason she couldn't work from Louisiana. She'd started out here and she could make a good living here.

But her heart wanted her to go out into the night and follow Santo home. Only her buzzing cell kept her from doing just that.

"Tilly, where are you?"

"Still at the house," Tilly said. "We've got a problem. The water heater is busted and the whole lower floor is flooded."

"I'm on my way," Davina said, ending the call.

"What's wrong?" Darren said, his head coming up.

Davina grimaced and motioned to him. "Busted water heater at home. Let's go."

Her brother didn't hesitate. "Ma, we'll be back as soon as we can."

Their mother nodded her head and held her hands together, a dejected expression on her face. "I'll be here."

Chapter Seventeen

Santo pulled his sedan up to the lake house and got out.

It was early. The sun peeked through the old oaks and towering pines across the lake in bold, creamy rays. The morning air was damp with dew and humidity, a frisky breeze awakening the fronds on the palm trees surrounding the house.

He stared at this new home and marveled at the changes taking place before his eyes. His heart had rearranged itself in the last few weeks. It had softened and stretched and…opened to the possibility of hope again. In some ways, he felt like this sunrise. New and fresh and warm. Almost happy again.

Now, standing here with this lemon-colored morning light shining on the bright white house with the new black shutters, Santo could imagine his children running across the gray-planked porch with the sky blue ceiling. He could see himself out on the lake in a sailboat, drifting, just drifting for the pure pleasure of it.

He could see Davina smiling and laughing with his children.

Whoa. That image stopped him in his tracks.

Did he dare hope? Did he give in to these new feelings that had him both excited and fearful?

"Are you gonna stand there all day?"

Santo whirled to find Rory and Blain staring at him from the curb. They'd obviously walked over to his house. "What are you two doing here?"

"We heard you might be in over your head," Blain said, grinning. "We came to rescue you."

Frowning, Santo shrugged. "I don't need rescuing."

"But you need to get this house finished, right?" Blain asked.

"Uh…yes, but—"

When Alec and Hunter showed up in Alec's fancy black truck, Santo wondered if this was an ambush or an intervention.

"What is going on?"

Hunter, who rarely spoke, explained. "We're gonna help you and the crew finish this house. So get over it and let's get it done."

Touched, even by such a blunt offering, Santo could only nod. "Davina will be happy."

"Well, we hope so," Rory said, chuckling. "Let's see if we can actually hammer nails and cut tile and then we'll see if she's happy."

"We have a crew, you know," Santo went on to say as they all walked toward the house.

"We heard," Blain said. "I called Kurt Martin and got the all-clear but we won't bother Davina with the details. He said Davina's blueprints and instructions leave little room for error. And besides, we'll only do basic stuff like buffing floors, laying carpet and changing out windows. Easy-peasy."

"Famous last words," Hunter said on an early-morning growl.

The rest of the crew came driving up and soon Kurt had all of them going at it. Santo had to stop every now and then and just watch the activity. Blain and his friends didn't have to be here on a beautiful Saturday morning. But friends did such things for people.

This house was becoming a real home.

And he was finally finding his way back to becoming a real father again.

He thought of Davina and wondered what she was doing and when she'd come back and for the first time in a long time, Santo said a prayer. For Davina and her family, for these men who showed him the example of forgiveness and friendship, and for himself and his children.

Then he went back to work.

Davina thought of the lake house.

Kurt had texted her and called her as needed over the last three days but it sounded like everything was on schedule there. Thankful that she was a little obsessive about having the best-laid plans on every project, she relaxed against the back of the waiting room chair and tried to make notes for Rikki on the interior of the house.

They'd need new furniture and artwork, a mixture of antiques and modern furnishings. Rikki could handle that part.

Davina hated missing out, hated not being there but she had to be here right now. She and Darren had declared the water heater as DOA, so that had been a new expense but they'd both paid half and now the old house by the river had immediate hot water. A luxury after years of hit-and-miss warm showers over the last decade or so.

They'd worked together seamlessly after picking up the new water heater early this morning, sometimes in silence and sometimes discussing what they should do next regarding their aging parents.

"Da isn't ready to throw in the towel," Darren told her. "But he can't keep this up much longer."

"I can come back and help," she offered. "We could try to work together, be partners."

Her brother gave her a long, measured stare. "Equal partners?"

"What else?"

"You created your own company and I've never seen a spot for me in that company," Darren replied.

"You resent me."

"Some, yeah," he admitted. "But I also admire you."

"And yet, you can't work with me?"

"I can't work *for* you. Dumb male pride."

"Stupid male pride. Do you and Alana think any of this has been easy for me?"

"No, we're aware of what you've done and what you've accomplished. But sibling rivalry is alive and well around here."

"Get over that," she suggested. "And when you do, call me and we'll figure out how to merge Da's company with mine, with you as my partner."

"I have one question," Darren said. "What made you strike out on your own anyway? You could have accomplished pretty much the same thing working with Da and me."

She finally told him the truth. "Da told me to do it. He thought he'd be holding me back. He knew I had a bad case of wanderlust so he suggested I start small and work my way up to creating my own company. And that's it. I went with his blessings but… I also went thinking he booted me out because I'm a woman. I never could tell any of you that."

"He's never once said that to me," Darren retorted, the old bitterness clear in his words. "I might not have been so tough on you if he'd explained it in that way. Or if you'd been honest with me."

"I didn't want to accuse Da," she said. "I could be wrong but I'm glad he sent me packing. I've learned a lot and I'm stronger for it."

"Does that make me stronger because you left then?"

"You could have done the same," she said, understanding his frustrations. "Would you have done it if he had given you his blessings and urged you to go?"

"I don't know," he admitted. "He always wanted me here to take over and yet, he won't let me take over. I stayed anyway, because I think I kept waiting—"

"For Lara?" Darren had been in love but it didn't work out.

"I don't know," he said again. "But I'm here and I'm not leaving. It's too late for me to leave."

"But you could be based here and still work with me."

He nodded, his eyes as dark as blue velvet. "I'll think about it…but not until Da is better."

They'd left it at that, but the more Davina thought about things, the more it made sense to partner up with Darren. He was as good at this as she was, since Da had trained them both.

Now if he could put his dumb male pride aside, they might get something going.

She glanced up when Tilly came out of Da's room.

"He's awake and feeling better," Tilly said, her grin sweet but not her usual perky full-blown one. "The doctor is going to update Ma when he makes rounds. And Nurse Alana the Hun is back on the case so she'll update us soon enough."

"You shouldn't call our sister names," Davina replied with a snort of laughter.

"You've seen her in action," Tilly whispered. "Makes Nurse Ratched look like a choir marm."

Alana walked out of their dad's room, her blue scrubs clean and neat, her stethoscope slung around her neck in a precise curve, her wild curly hair caught up in a controlled chignon. When she cast a piercing look toward her sisters, Davina hid a giggle.

"Okay, I get it about the nickname," she said under her breath.

"Told you," Tilly said.

"What are you two mumbling about?" Alana asked after marching straight toward them in her bright pink floral orthopedic sneakers.

"Oh, this and that," Tilly said with a twisted grin. "How is Da? Tell us straight."

"His vitals are good," she said, suspicion still in her eyes. "We think he's had angina for weeks now but he didn't mention it to anyone. Just kept right on going." Glancing back, she lowered her voice. "Ma doesn't know the half of it yet. He's probably had a couple of mild heart attacks already. If we don't get this under control now, the next one could be fatal."

She went on explaining in medical terms but Davina followed enough to understand more tests were needed and he'd go home to a completely new lifestyle. More EKGs, more scans, more instructions. More medicine to avoid blood clots. He wouldn't be an invalid but he'd have to be careful and slowly build up his strength.

Knowing Da, this would not go over very well.

"Can he ever go back to work?" Tilly asked, tears in her eyes. "Because if he can't, he'll surely die."

Alana's stern expression changed as she sank down by her sister. Taking Tilly's hand in hers, she said, "Yes, he can go back to work. With stipulations. We have to get him on a proper diet and the right medications. Exercise is important, too. He works hard but that doesn't necessarily constitute the right kind of exertion to make him healthy."

"We'll all be here to make sure he does what he needs to do," Davina said.

"All of us?"

Alana's question hung in the air like a thin thread of twine.

"All of us," Davina replied without an explanation.

She still had to absorb what this could mean for her. All of her life, she'd only wanted to be away from Bayou Fontaine. Now she might wind up right back here. But what else could she do?

Her cell buzzed. Santo.

"Excuse me," she said to her curious sisters.

Then she got up and found the atrium overlooking a nice quiet courtyard around the corner. Staring out at the banana tree fronds and the elephant's ear plants, she spoke into the phone.

"Hi," he said. "How are you?"

"I'm okay." She gave him the latest update. "How are things there?"

"Steady." He told her what they'd accomplished in

the three days since she'd been gone. "It's coming along. Today, we're retiling the new master bath."

"I hope you like how I redesigned it."

"I've always wanted a soaking tub."

"Ha. I put that in for future use."

"Future use?"

"In case you ever marry again…or sell to someone else. I also added that nice walk-in closet for more storage, too."

He went silent for a minute and then said, "You're always thinking ahead."

Was he upset that she had to consider every woman's dream—a big tub and a big closet?

"Part of my job but I can change it if you don't approve."

"I'm sure the kids will love the big tub."

"I hope so."

They talked about the house and her family and how Virginia had hung strange artwork all over the room she'd taken at the bay house.

"It's eclectic and expensive artwork, at least," he said with a chuckle. "Nicely placed with an eye for detail. And the kids love it."

"They love her," Davina said, missing him and the kids and Virginia. "She probably made her room colorful and interesting so they'd be more comfortable with her."

"Then I guess we'd better consider that when we move."

"Done."

"I miss you," he said on what seemed like a final note.

"I miss you, too," she admitted, knowing it would have to do for now.

"When you get back, we need to talk."

Oh, mercy. They were going to do this in person with the-we-need-to-talk speech? She wasn't sure she could do that, not with Santo. "All right," she said, thinking this was not all right at all.

But it has to be done, she reminded herself. She'd never planned on getting a crush on her client. She'd never planned on that crush turning into something more.

When she hung up, her sisters were standing a few feet away, staring at her with such intensity she burst out laughing. "You both look ridiculous."

"We want to hear all about you and Santo," Tilly said without even flinching. "There's something brewing there. Even Ma noticed it."

"Ma thinks every man I meet has something brewing with me," Davina said, hoping that would shut them up.

It did not.

"Ma is very astute that way," Alana replied as they started back toward the waiting room. "I think Dani's finally met her match. And I think we will get the truth from her sooner or later."

"And I think you need your head examined," Davina retorted, squirming to get away.

"We'll get the details," Tilly announced with assurance. "All of them."

Another nurse walked up to them with a big white box. "Special delivery for Davina Connell."

"What is that?" Tilly asked, her eyes bright.

Davina saw the return address. "Marla's Marvelous Desserts. One of my favorite places in Millbrook Lake."

"Food?" Both of her sisters squealed like hungry piglets.

"Not just any food," Davina said, awe in her words. "Cupcakes. And the best in the world."

She tore open the shipping box and then the container to find a variety of her favorites from Chocolate-Pecan-Praline-Paradise to Lemon-Bar-None to Coconut-Crazy-Caramel and Really-Red-Velvet.

"I might cry," she said while nosy Alana read the card. "I can't thank Marla enough for sending this."

"Don't thank Marla," Alana said on a smug note. "Thank Mr. Santo Alvanetti. The very man you refuse to talk about." Poking Tilly to show her the card, she added, "And he signed it. 'Thinking of you and missing you.'"

Grabbing a cupcake, she said with a bright smile, "If he went to the trouble to send these and sign that card in that way, then you need to tell us more. Lots more."

Davina couldn't speak. Her heart filled with little torn pieces of joy. There was so much more going on than she wanted to tell right now. Mostly how she wasn't sure she'd ever be able to get over Santo Alvanetti.

Chapter Eighteen

Santo's palms were sweaty.

"I'm not so sure this is a good idea," he said for the tenth time.

Blain rolled his eyes.

Alec chuckled.

Rory said a prayer.

Hunter grunted.

"I don't think she'll like being surprised this way."

"Look, man," Hunter finally said. "You just need to go with this. Trust us. It works." He waved his hand in the air. "Every one of us brought a woman here...and every one of us married said woman."

Santo got up and went out on the big deck of AWOL, the camp house out on the bay where these four apparently sat around playing matchmaking games when they weren't fishing or hunting or watching the sports channel.

"Why did y'all target me?" he asked, uncomfortable under the intensity of their interrogating stares. "I'm not that guy. I'm not ready for a real relationship again."

Then he hastily added, "No matter what you think about Davina and me."

"Right," Alec said. "Just keep telling yourself that."

Santo decided he had to make them understand. "Look, it's nice that you brought me out here for some R & R, but I don't belong here. I didn't serve my country the way all of you did."

"No, but we found a way around that," Rory explained. "You get in by default because Blain is now your brother-in-law."

"And because your family donated that million-dollar piece of jewelry to the Alexander and Vivian Caldwell Service Dog Association Training Facility, which brought in a lot of money at our silent auction last year," Alec added.

"And because you learned to say all of *that* without flubbing it the way I do," Hunter said on a droll note.

Rory slapped Santo on the back. "And because you're trying to make some changes in your life and you need a wingman or two or three."

Santo grabbed a soda out of the ice chest. "I've never had a lot of friends."

"We know," Blain said, grinning. "Don't worry. You'll get used to it."

"I need to thank all of you," he said, trying again. "The house looks great. When Davina gets back, we can finish up and I'll be able to move in."

"With her?"

"I don't know. We've only known each other a few weeks."

"Things happen fast around here, bro," Blain said.

"I need to take this slow," Santo replied. "You know

what I've been through. I don't want to make another mistake."

Rory took a sip of his drink, his expression serious. "Davina is a good person, Santo. Nothing bad will happen if you fall in love again."

"Maybe not. But then, I didn't expect that the first time and look how that turned out."

Rory didn't speak for a couple of moments. "I can't promise things will be perfect...but sometimes when you see a second chance right there in front of you, you have to take a leap of faith and go for it."

"I don't know yet," he said, pacing back and forth. "I want to take that next step with Davina but I'm not sure how."

"Like we said, you bring her here for a nice, romantic dinner," Alec said in his best sappy voice. When Santo balked again at their suggestion, he added, "Hey, don't blame us. Our wives thought up this plan."

"Based on?" Santo asked.

"Based on the way you and Davina seem to be skirting around the issue," Alec replied. "Who knows how women figure things out but they always do."

"It's a trap, man," Hunter said. "But it's a nice kind of trap."

Santo knew all of their stories. Fascinating stories of survival and faith and strength and danger and everything else you could throw in there. "What if I don't get that kind of ending," he said. "I don't know if Davina is ready for this. Ready for me."

"Well, since you're not so sure yourself maybe we shouldn't be pushing you," Rory said, giving him a clear out.

He turned to view the bay. It was late in the day and

Davina would be home tomorrow. Home. No, not home. She'd be back here tomorrow to finish what she'd started. But they had to have that talk. The one where he told her he wasn't sure he could do this and he didn't expect anything from her. Or the one where she told him this had been nice but she had to keep moving on.

"I need some time to think," he admitted. "This is a great place. I never knew it was here."

"Most people don't," Alec said. "Just a couple of bad guys here and there but we took care of them."

"Is that a warning?" Santo asked with soft grin.

"If you hurt Davina, yeah," Blain said. "But it won't be us hunting you down. It'll be our wives. They all want her nearby for remodeling purposes."

"Oh, so they have an ulterior motive?"

"Of course." Rory laughed and flipped the juicy steaks he had on the grill. "The rule used to be—no girls allowed."

"Until we all broke it," Alec said.

"I didn't like that rule anyway," Blain retorted.

"I liked it and wanted to keep it," Hunter insisted. "But you know how that goes. I'll be glad when Chloe gets back from Oklahoma." He stood and put his hands in his jeans pockets. "Chloe and I made it against all the odds, man. You can, too."

Santo had met Hunter's wife, Chloe. She was pretty and smart. They'd overcome a lot to be together and now Chloe was finishing up getting her PI license so they could work together to bring down corrupt people.

Santo turned and faced all of them. "You know, Davina and I don't have a history. Nothing to overcome except my background and her need to prove herself. I'm trapped in the shadow of my family's indiscretions and she doesn't want to settle down. Her company is growing. She needs to move on."

"Are you kidding me right now?" Hunter asked, giving Santo a firm eye roll.

"I'm serious."

"Excuses," Rory said. "Vanessa and I didn't have a history but we both sure had a past."

Santo gave up. "Okay, so I'd like to get to know Davina more and I'd like to keep her around. But that will have to be her decision and right now, it's not looking good. She might have to go back to Louisiana to help her family."

"It's not that far," Rory pointed out.

"No, it's not," Santo agreed. "But it's far enough."

"So what are you going to do?" Alec asked him.

Santo glanced around again. "I guess for starters, I'm going to plan a romantic dinner here tomorrow night."

"Good plan," Alec said. "Marla's already got the cupcakes ready."

Santo thought it would take more than cupcakes to bring him and Davina together. But he couldn't let her go without trying to convince her to stay.

Davina parked her truck and stared up at the little apartment that had been her home for weeks now. Taking a deep breath, she checked her watch. Just enough time before dark to go by the lake house and check on things. She couldn't wait to see what Santo and the crew had done.

She stepped out of the truck and her cell rang.

Santo?

Did the man have a built-in radar that told him when she pulled into town?

"Hi," she said. "I just got back."

"I know. Rory called me."

"Well, that was thoughtful of him. Do you have people spying on me with some sort of coconut telegraph?"

"Yes. Stay right there. I'm coming to get you."

"But I'm tired and I need to freshen up. I want to go by the house."

"No, don't go by the house. Stay right there. Please?"

"Okay." She was too exhausted to argue. Maybe he was bringing one of Virginia's home-cooked meals. Her stomach jumped and rumbled at that since she hadn't eaten much since breakfast.

Davina checked her cell once again. No news from home.

She'd left reluctantly now that her dad had been home for a couple of days and situated into his new routine. He was doing great but she still worried about him.

"I could stay another week," she'd suggested this morning.

"I'll give you daily reports," Alana had promised her.

"I'll call you every night," Tilly said.

"I promise we'll let you know if he sneezes wrong," Ma had told her. "Now go and do your work. Your da wants you to do that. Knowing you're happy and back at work will do him good. He wants all of you to get on with your lives and stop treating him like an invalid."

"But I'm coming back, Ma," she'd insisted. "I'll be back as soon as I'm done with this project."

"Okay, honey," Ma had said with a secretive smile. "Okay."

So here she was, torn between duty and need. And so much more. Because finishing this house would be bittersweet on so many levels. It would be her first big job. And her last, until she could help Darren get Connell Construction up and running again. Maybe together, they could create the kind of homes that would put Connell Construction back on the map again.

She hurried and freshened up, combing her hair and putting on a clean blouse and jeans. When she heard a car outside, she was surprised to find a shiny blue pickup pulling up to her house.

A pickup driven by Santo and full of dark-haired children.

Davina couldn't stop the squeal that emitted from her lungs. Tears pierced her eyes.

"Oh, I've missed them so much," she said as she opened the door and rushed down the stairs.

So very much.

"Hello," she said, grabbing Nate up in her arms. "It's so good to see you."

"Dani," Nate said, poking at her shoulder with his chubby finger, his smile bright, his hair wild around his cute face.

"We made you things," Lucia said, her hands widening to show big things. "But it's a surprise."

Adriana bobbed her head. "Miss Virginia baked all day and Miss Marla sent us cupcakes for dessert."

"I'm hungry," Davina admitted, her eyes catching on Santo. He looked even better than she remembered. Tanned, buff, less stressed, less fatigued. "So…let's eat?"

He moved close and took Nate and stood him down on the ground. "We're having a picnic," he explained. "But it's at a surprise location."

"Oh, okay. And to think, I almost put on my ball gown."

"You're silly," Adriana said, giggling as she took Davina's hand. "You can't wear a ball gown where we're going."

"I see you went shopping for a new car," Davina said once they were on their way, the children safe in the backseat of the big double-cabbed monster.

"Yes. Tearing down walls and renovating bathrooms made me feel manly."

He was already way too manly, she thought.

"I like it. Good for hauling things."

"We like it, too," Lucia said. "It's a truck but like a car. I feel safe in it."

"Like it, like it," Nate echoed.

"Where are we going?" she finally asked, too shocked and content to protest much.

Santo only smiled, his dark eyes full of something she recognized as hope. But she needed to tell him this couldn't be happening. She couldn't stay here.

Tomorrow or the day after, she thought. *Or a month or two from now. I'll tell him when the house is finally done.*

Santo pulled the big truck into a long and winding shell-covered road that seemed to lead to nowhere. She looked ahead and saw the bay shimmering beyond a big square house built high up on pilings.

"Where are we?" she asked, surprised yet again.

"We've gone AWOL," he said. "This is a special place where Alec, Blain, Rory and Hunter hang out a lot. It belongs to them but tonight we have it to ourselves."

Davina's heart tried to escape the joy and pain that merged like a great wave of water in the center of her soul and turned into a full-blown undertow. "Wow. I don't know what to say."

"You don't need to say anything," he told her. "Just for tonight, Davina, let's forget everything that's standing between us and enjoy being together."

She glanced from his hopeful face to the excited faces of his beautiful children. "I can do that," she said, her heart heavy with something so solid, she felt grounded for the first time in her life. "I'll be happy to do that."

So they all unloaded, baskets and boxes filled with surprises going with them to the front yard of the big house where the palmettos and magnolia trees and old oaks opened wide to the white sand of the bay.

"We're having a picnic," Santo told her again. "And then we're going to watch the sunset. I've heard it's really a good view of it from here."

"It's beautiful," she said, her gaze holding his.

She never wanted to leave. But she'd already promised her family back in Bayou Fontaine that she'd do just that.

Chapter Nineteen

The children frolicked and played in the water and got sprayed down with bug repellant and sunscreen several times. Virginia had thought of everything, Santo thought.

"Is it cupcake time yet?" Adriana asked, her dark eyes gleaming.

"Are you hungry already? You had two chicken legs," Davina said, grinning.

"Yes, and they were good but I want a cupcake," Adriana replied, her hand on her hip and her long hair falling loose from the once-neat ponytail she'd arrived with.

Santo went to the big basket they'd carted down to the beach. The sun was on its final stroll over the water and soon it would be full dark.

"Maybe we should let them eat dessert inside," Davina said. "The bugs are hungry, too."

"Good idea." He turned from the basket and whistled out toward the shallows. "Cupcakes inside."

"Why?" Lucia called, a sand bucket in her hand.

"Why?" Nate echoed from where he sat in the sand, making a crooked sandcastle.

"It's getting late," Santo explained. "C'mon now. We'll play inside games."

After they'd rounded up all three, the kids washed up and settled on a blanket in front of the massive television.

"Are we at a movie?" Nate asked, pointing.

"No, honey, we're in a man cave," Davina said, smiling over at Santo.

"Man cave, man cave," Nate chanted, giggling.

"I don't think children have ever entered these doors before," Santo told her as they fell in exhaustion onto the big, comfy man couch.

"How did you finagle this?" she asked, her heart content, her tummy full and her mind in turmoil.

"That's a funny story." Santo turned to her, his dark eyes solemn. "The guys brought me out here one night after I'd worked on the house. Actually, they helped with the house all weekend."

"The guys?" Davina knew which guys without even asking. She was just so surprised. "They joined you and the crew?"

"Yes and don't look so panicked. They were great. Even when we found the termites underneath the old master bathroom tub."

"Termites underneath the tub?"

"Yeah, a small colony. That delayed things for a couple of days."

"Yes, I know all about termites and what has to be done to get rid of them. I'm wondering why Kurt didn't call me about that."

"Because he didn't want to worry you and because I'm footing the bill and I was standing right there."

"That makes sense."

"I'm glad you see the logic. Anyway, the guys kind

of forced me to come out here and then…told me that their wives think we should…continue in the same vein. You and me. Not them and me."

"You're cute when you're trying to explain something."

"I can't explain this," he said, a helpless look in his eyes. "I was told to come up with a romantic dinner but I panicked and brought the kids as a shield."

She let that admission soak in, knowing the truth was wrapped up in there somewhere. "I'm glad you brought your children. I love your children. They need time with *you*. I don't mind spending time with *them*."

"And me?" he asked, a new vulnerability in his eyes. "Do you like spending time with me?"

"More than I want to admit," she said, giving him a sincere smile.

"So you don't want to spend time with me?"

"Yes, Santo. I enjoy being with you. And that's a big problem. I've broken my ironclad rule against becoming involved with a client."

"We can break some other rules," he said on a whisper. But he didn't touch her. His eyes said enough.

"I think one or two should be enough for now. As you said, let's forget everything else for a little while. I'm glad you brought the kids. I've missed all of you."

His gaze gentled as he glanced to his children and then back to her. "Well, that's all good and well, but I'm still not sure what's happening here."

"For tonight, we're having fun, right?"

"Right. Lots of fun."

"We can worry about the rest later," she said, deciding that was best for now. She had to stay here and finish the house and get him settled. Then…she'd go home.

But he didn't need to know the details. He'd probably already figured out the details. It didn't take much to see where this was headed.

"Okay, I agree," he said. "I'm pretty sure I suggested that all on my own. But Marla and those other very forceful wives and my interfering nanny came up with everything else."

"You mean even the artwork from the children?"

"Even that." They both peeked over at the framed drawings the kids had presented to her. The lake, shimmering in watercolor blues, from Lucia. The house, white and stark and with palm trees all around, created by Adriana. And a cupcake, bright and rich and definitely done in I'll-Miss-You-Chocolate from Nate.

"I love these masterpieces," she'd declared after they'd eaten grilled chicken and pasta salad and potato chips and peanut-butter-and-jelly sliders.

"Any other surprises?" she asked now, bracing herself. "Besides this place and cupcakes?"

"We found a snake at the lake house, living in one of the drainpipes."

"*No*, you didn't."

"He was tiny. A garden snake."

"I don't need details. Did you find him a good home?"

"Yes. Near the water. He has a great view now."

Santo leaned close. "I'd really like to kiss you right now."

Davina could go for that kiss. Right now.

"Cupcakes!"

Nate's loud squeal brought them apart.

"Hold that thought," she said, happy and relaxed for the first time in a week. "Let's eat dessert."

They shared a whole batch of Marla's latest culinary

creations. Just-Kidding-Around-Creamy-Vanilla and Home-Is-Where-The-Heart-Is-Caramel-Apple.

"Marla is sending mixed signals," Davina pointed out, caramel icing on her finger.

"She thinks I might be doing that, too," Santo replied.

"Are you?"

"I think I am. It's confusing, being around you. One day, I'm all in with running away with you and the next, I'm back to being the stoic, angry man everyone tries to avoid."

She drew back to look at him. "Do you think *I'm* sending mixed signals?"

"I think you're trying to do what's right for yourself and your family."

"And so are you," she reminded him.

He gave her a soft smile and wiped the caramel off her cheek. "Somehow, we need to figure out a way to make things right for us."

Ready to get back to work, Davina rose early the next morning. The warm memories of last night stayed with her enough to ward off her fears and worries. If Santo was trying to win her over, he'd done a good job by bringing those children along as bait. How could anyone resent those three?

Santo could only work on the house a few more days and then he'd have to get back to work. She wanted to make the most of their time together. But she also wanted to reassure him that he could do this. He could be happy here with his children once she was gone.

"The boss is back," Kurt called, grabbing her to hug her tight.

"Thank goodness," Becky said, patting Davina on the head. "I kept 'em straight while you were gone, boss."

"Good. I've heard some tall tales, but I can't wait to see what you've done with the place."

After the others joined them and she gave them a full update on her dad, they all walked into the house and Davina stopped to take in the progress. The walls were back up, sturdy and painted a shimmering white called Sea Wind that had a hint of blue in it. The floors had been buffed and stained a rich burnished brown that highlighted the grain of the hand-scraped walnut. Covered with drop cloths while they worked, the new floors would be protected to the bitter end.

The dough box she'd found at a nearby antiques shop would have a place of prominence in the kitchen. Virginia had almost wept with joy when Davina had informed her of finding it.

"I can make bread from scratch," the nanny had declared, her expression dreamy. "Or at least pretend to, without actually having to use the dough box. Maybe we can use that for storage but I can sure use the surface for a lot of baking."

Virginia knew immediately that she'd found the family for her. Why couldn't Davina give in so easily to her feelings?

"The kitchen is coming along," Becky pointed out, her eyes gleaming with pride. "The new cabinets are perfect. Rikki worked hard with the builder to make them look old."

"They are exactly how I imagined," Davina said, moving her hand over the clean white wood and the ornate brass knobs and pulls on the cabinets and drawers.

"The cornices add that extra richness. I'll have to send the cabinet builder a thank-you."

"Oh, he'll be thanked enough when you send him that big check," Kurt said with a deadpan expression.

The countertops were coming this week and she couldn't wait to run her hands over the white marble for the walled counters. They'd decided against marble for the island since the kids would use it for doing homework and helping with the cooking. There, they'd use a bacteria- and toxin-resistant bamboo to give a bit of pop to the center of the kitchen and to be more efficient and eco-friendly.

"It looks good," she said, wondering where Santo was. He'd told her he'd see her bright and early.

"We haven't made it upstairs yet," Kurt told her. "But the master bedroom is just about finished. We've primed it and now we'll go back and paint it that dreamy green you like so much."

"Distant Horizon," she said, remembering the names of every paint for every room.

"It's going to be so peaceful and welcoming," Becky said, a worried expression on her face. "Hey, boss, you okay?"

"I'm fine," Davina said. "Tired and still concerned about things back home."

"Well, everything here is okay and on track," Kurt replied. "You know you can count on us."

"I heard about the termites," she said, giving them a mock frown.

"And just who exactly told you about that?" Becky asked, her eyebrows lifting to meet her bangs.

"Santo," Davina admitted. "Since he had to pay for the treatments."

"Ah, Santo." Her crew members started teasing her.

"We think Santo has it bad for the boss," Josh said, walking by with a grin.

"We're friends," she retorted. If she said that enough maybe she'd believe it, too.

They got to work and things settled back into a routine.

But when Santo hadn't shown up at noon, she started to think maybe he wasn't as serious about this as she'd thought.

Finally, she got a text from him while she was nibbling on a pack of crackers.

Work emergency. Missing shipment. Sorry. I had to go to the office.

Davina went back to work, wishing she didn't miss Santo but glad for some breathing room while she got into the routine of work again. He was a distraction she shouldn't want around. But she did want him around. And that scared her.

But when she got a phone call later in the day from Virginia, Davina dropped her tools and informed her team she was leaving.

"Nate's in trouble," Virginia said. "He had an accident at preschool. Santo's with him. We're at the ER."

"I'll be there as soon as I can," she told Virginia before offering up a prayer. Santo had been with her when she'd gone to see her father. She'd be with him to see him through now.

That's what friends did for each other.

Chapter Twenty

"A broken wrist." Virginia shook her head. "But that's the nature of the thing. Kids go and go and then…something happens that you just didn't see coming."

"Do you know how it happened?" Davina asked, memories of broken bones and sprained ankles when she and siblings were growing up came back to the surface of her mind. "He's a pretty active little man."

"Tripped over a tree root walking in from the playground and fell right on his left wrist," Virginia explained. "It can happen so quickly."

"Are you sure he'll be okay?" Davina asked.

Virginia didn't speak. She seemed to be lost in her own thoughts. "Virginia?"

Virginia blinked and focused on Davina. "Oh, I'm sorry. What did you say?"

"You look tired," Davina said. "I can sit and wait until Santo comes out of the ER."

Santo was with Nate while they temporarily set his wrist to allow the swelling to go down. He'd have to have a small cast put on in a few days. Not easy for a boy his age.

"That might be a good idea. He told me to take the girls to his parents' house and leave them with the house-keeper because, of course, he can't leave Nathan. And I didn't want to leave either of them. I'll go pick up the girls in a little while."

Her eyes went blank again.

"Virginia, are you okay, really?"

"I'm fine," the older woman said. "I don't like hospitals."

Davina didn't pester the woman, but Virginia was usually the calm during the storm. Maybe Nate's accident had shaken her more than she wanted to let on.

Santo walked through the ER doors with Nate in his arms. The fresh tear streaks on Nate's face tore through Davina's heart. Nate saw her and burst into tears again.

"Dani."

She took him in her arms and kissed his forehead. "Hey, buddy. You had a bad day, huh?"

Nate gulped back tears. "Uh-huh." He touched his arm. "Off."

Santo let out a fatigued sigh. "He doesn't like his temporary cast."

"I don't blame him," Davina said. She glanced at Virginia. The woman had gone pale. Davina turned to Santo. "I can follow you two home while Virginia goes and picks up the girls."

Virginia snapped to. "Yes, good idea. I'll see you back at the house."

"She seems to be taking this hard," Davina told Santo as they walked out of the hospital together.

"I noticed that. She was certainly concerned when I called her. Insisted on coming here to be with us."

"She cares about all of you. We both do."

When they got to her car, she waited for Santo to take Nate. But the little boy refused to leave her arms.

"I'll ride with you," she told Santo. "We can get my car later."

They got Nate settled in his car seat and Davina got in beside him, her hand on his hurt arm. The trusting little boy kept his gaze on Davina until he started drifting off to sleep on the short ride home.

But Davina knew something for certain now.

She not only loved Santo's children. She was beginning to care about him in a big way, too.

The house was settled and quiet now.

Santo padded down the stairs in his socks, hoping no one would wake up again.

But he stopped at the bottom of the stairs and took his time looking at Davina. She sat in a chair she'd brought into the house to brighten things up. It had become the reading chair, as the kids loved to call it. She had her head against the broad, cushioned back, her eyes closed. Her hair fell in soft curls against the primary colors of the big floral chair.

She was beautiful and she looked right at home here.

He imagined her in the new house, puttering around the kitchen, straightening cushions, fussing over his children. She'd done all of those things and more tonight. Along with Virginia, she'd made sure his children were fed and bathed, done their homework and, finally, tucked into bed.

She'd kissed Nate good-night and told him she'd see him soon. Nate could see what Santo had been denying for weeks now, maybe from the very first day.

Santo's heart caught against a tangle of emotions.

He was falling in love with Davina.

"What are you doing?"

Santo whirled to find Virginia standing in the hallway underneath the open stairs in her bright red robe. "I don't know," he replied.

"Can I talk to you?" the nanny asked, her hands together in front of her in a tight grip.

"Yes." He came into the den and met her by the fireplace. "Would you like to talk in private?"

"No. I want Davina to hear this, too," Virginia said through a deep breath.

Davina sat up in the chair, her eyes bleary with sleep. "What's going on?"

Virginia marched over and sat down on an ottoman near Davina. "I need to make a confession."

Santo sank down on the couch. "I'm not so sure I *want* to hear this."

"No, you both need to listen and understand what I'm about to say."

Wide awake now, Davina leaned forward. "Go ahead," she told Virginia.

Virginia looked at Santo. "I love your children—"

"You're quitting?" he asked, panic in the question, his gut churning.

"No." Virginia held up her hand to shush him. "I don't want to quit. That's just it. I don't want you to fire me either."

"Then what is the problem?" he asked, his mind exploding with too many things at once.

"I need to tell you both where I came from," Virginia said.

"Oh, boy." Santo got up and paced the floor.

Davina reached out her hand. "Santo, sit down and let her explain."

He did, taking another breath, Davina's hand in his bringing on a calm he didn't feel. "Go ahead, Virginia."

"I was married once," Virginia said, her voice shaky. "It didn't go very well."

"You're divorced?" Davina asked, wishing she could help the poor woman. She'd never seen Virginia so afraid to speak.

"Yes. I left him after…after a terrible thing happened in our lives."

"What kind of thing?" Santo asked, his hand gripping Davina's. If somebody didn't explain soon, he was going to explode. No, no, he wasn't that man anymore. He took a deep breath. "Tell us, Virginia."

"I had two children."

Davina's gaze slammed into Santo's. "Okay," she said. "Go ahead."

"He took them from me," Virginia replied, her voice low now. "Took them right out from under me and tried to smuggle them away."

"You mean, kidnapped them?" Santo asked, his heart stopping.

"Yes. The divorce was ugly. He beat me a lot and I got custody of the children. He could only have supervised visits. So to punish me, he watched the house and I went inside just to get some snacks. They were playing in the yard where I could see them. But he got them when I turned away and took them. The police were chasing him and he had a horrible wreck. We lived in California then. So far away. He took my babies and me away from everyone."

Santo couldn't speak now. "Virginia, what happened?"

"They all died," she said on a long sob of a breath. "All gone in an instant."

Davina tried to stand but Virginia held up a hand. "Let me finish. I was a mess. Lost my job, almost lost my mind. Gave up on life. I had no one, no reason to live anymore. That was well over twenty-five years ago. But then about three years after it had happened, I heard in church about a course you could take to become a nanny. I thought after all the jobs I'd left or been fired from since I'd lost my babies, this one might work. So I sold my house and belongings and I went to England and I learned how to be a good nanny. It wasn't easy. I had this history, a past. But I didn't have a criminal record. And I passed all the necessary tests. But I never told anyone what I'd been through. I couldn't speak about it. I knew it would horrify people and I might not be able to work with children simply because people are afraid of grief and what it can do to a person."

Santo couldn't say a word. He looked at Davina for help. Virginia had hit on his personal fears and regrets in a way that jarred him.

"I'm so sorry, Virginia," Davina said. "I would have never thought—"

"No, no one would," Virginia explained. "I came back to the States and went into a panic. I lived in my car for two weeks because I was afraid to find work. But I finally saw an ad in the local paper. A single mom trying to make ends meet. I went for the interview and the poor woman was at her wit's end. I knew that feeling. I raised her little boy until he went to high school. Since then, I've roamed around and worked at two more homes, both good, solid homes." She stopped, gaining some of her old spunk. "Then I decided to come to Florida, to retire. I had relatives here. But my cousin showed me your ad and I called and talked to Rikki and, well, you know the rest." She gave Santo a steady glance. "You needed me and I hope you'll keep needing me, even if…if you get married again." Wiping at her eyes, she added, "You're all caught up now."

Santo shook his head. "We didn't know. Virginia, are you all right? I mean, I'm so sorry. Here you've helped me through a very bad time and…you're still grieving."

"We never stop grieving," Virginia said, her tone firm and clear. "But I'm okay. Your children are safe with me. I hope you'll let me stay with them until they go off to high school, too."

"Of course," Santo said. "I wouldn't have it any other way."

Davina finally stood and went to Virginia. Falling on her knees, she touched her hands to Virginia's arms. "When Nate got hurt, you had a flashback of all that happened, right?"

Virginia nodded, tears forming in her eyes. "The school called me and I hurried right away. When I walked into the ER, it all came rushing back. I'm sorry. I can usually handle this type of situation but…this was little Nate. He's the youngest I've ever taken care of and he's a year younger than my daughter. I had a daughter who was three and my son was seven. Janie and Frederick. I kept remembering them all day. I didn't want to scare either of you, but I had to tell you. In case I had a nightmare like I used to. I didn't want to upset the children or make you think I was some sort of weird nanny."

Davina hugged Virginia close. "I'm so glad you're

here and that you told us this. I'll feel better when I'm gone, knowing you'll take care of Santo and his children."

Virginia searched Santo's face. The look she gave him begged him to do what needed to be done. She didn't want Davina to leave either, but Davina had just announced she'd be doing that very thing, no matter what.

Santo took Davina to get her car, his mind reeling with the acceptance of what she'd said to Virginia. He'd have to let her go. She wasn't the kind to do this even if she did have a way of soothing him and his children. Davina had a whole bright future ahead of her. He'd already had one bad marriage, which made his future shaky in the love department. But he couldn't blame its failure completely on his misguided, sick wife. He'd neglected his marriage because of work and he'd almost done the same thing with his children.

He wouldn't risk putting Davina through that and he couldn't risk falling for her while she was so wrapped up in her own career and her family's needs. He had to let her go.

"Thank you for helping out tonight," he said. "Sometimes I feel inadequate as a dad and I think I should be able to handle things on my own. But it's not easy."

She settled against the seat and let out a sigh. "No, it's not. I have experience since I have such a large family. Our parents taught us to pitch in, to help out as needed and to dive in with both feet. I sometimes overstep in that area."

"I like the way you overstep," he said when they'd reached her car. He turned off the truck's engine and turned to her. "Can you believe what Virginia must have gone through?"

"More than a person should have to endure but it explains how cryptic she's been about her past at times. No wonder she seemed so distant and pale today."

"I think she's afraid I'll fire her."

"Promise me you won't."

"I promise."

"I guess I should get going. Don't worry about coming to work at the lake house tomorrow. Nate will want his daddy."

"I'll see how things go," he told her, wishing he could say more. "Maybe I'll ride over later and see how far you and the crew have advanced."

"Okay." She touched her hand to his. "Get some rest."

Santo stared into her eyes and then against his better judgement, he tugged her close and kissed her. Then he sat back. "You, too."

Davina's eyes darkened and glistened underneath the parking lot security lights. "Good night."

Then she got out of the truck and hurried to her own.

Santo sat there with his hands on the steering wheel, watching until her vehicle disappeared into the night.

Chapter Twenty-One

The next few weeks moved at a rapid pace. Davina and the crew worked from early morning to sundown, going from room to room and remodeling. New walls and windows, shiny new floors and carpet, updated cabinets and closet space and a clean crisp freshness all over the house, all of these occupied her time.

Santo occupied her mind, however.

He'd pulled away after Nate's accident. He worked with the crew here and there, but he spent the last few days of his time off with his children. Davina and he still talked and laughed and she hung out with the kids when she had down time. But Virginia was usually the one there. Not Santo.

He worked all day and devoted his spare time to his family. He brought the children to the lake house at times, to let them see the updates and to show them their rooms. He'd helped out on the weekends for a few hours, but he avoided Davina and concentrated on following Kurt's orders.

"I can't wait to move in here," Lucia told Davina just yesterday. "This is the best new house ever." She skipped to one of the big windows. "Daddy's gonna put up a swing on that big oak tree. He said."

"I'm sure he'll do just that," Davina replied. "I'll be glad to help him."

The bay house had several showings and according to Rikki seemed to be on several buyers' radars.

"I think by the time school ends, we'll have a buyer," she told Davina.

Tonight, Davina came home to her little apartment and took a long shower. It had been a warm day and they'd all worked up a sticky sweat, the humidity feeling like glue against their clothes and skin. Santo hadn't come by, but he'd called her to get a status check.

"We have some buyers who are coming back for a second look," he said.

"Maybe they'll be the ones."

She hadn't heard back from him. They seemed to be at an impasse. A place where they'd both decided to get through this and move on. A place where they'd just ignore their feelings for each other. Davina didn't like that place.

She'd just put on black leggings and a white linen tunic and was about to call and check on her dad when her doorbell rang. Surprised, Davina squinted into the peephole.

Rikki stood there, her dark hair pulled up in a loose bun.

Davina opened the door and smiled. "Hi, what brings you by tonight?"

Rikki pushed her way in and motioned behind her. "We came to rescue you."

Davina looked beyond Rikki to find Marla, Vanessa and Chloe marching up the planked steps to the tiny porch, all dressed as casual as she was. "What's going on?"

"Spa night," Marla declared, holding a basket that held all kinds of creams, lotions and polish. Along with some serious primping equipment.

"I don't recall asking for a spa night," Davina said, her mouth falling open when Chloe, all girl-next-door fresh and looking chic as always in a floral tunic and bright leggings, her tawny hair down around her shoulders, carried in bags of good-smelling food.

"It's a surprise," Vanessa said, laughing. She held drinks and what looked like dessert. "You've been working hard and since you're all alone here and your family has been dealing with a lot, we decided we'd do a girls' night in."

"Yes," Marla said. "We wanted to hold this fun-fest at AWOL, but the guys are all there and for now, they've reestablished the no-girls-allowed policy."

"They confiscated my stubborn brother," Rikki said. "Santo needs a break, too. He's been working hard but he's spent more time with the girls and Nate lately, so even he needs some downtime."

Vanessa dumped her packages on the counter. "Besides, he has a lot to celebrate."

"Why is that?" Davina asked in a controlled voice.

"The house sold today," Rikki said. "Didn't he call you?"

Davina's stomach knotted. "No, he told me he had some serious return lookers but when I didn't hear from him, I thought maybe nothing happened." She watched as Marla and Chloe unloaded all the loot. "That means he'll need to move soon, right? I'll have to speed up things on the lake house."

"He has a month," Rikki told her, understanding in her eyes. "Meantime, we'll hold a garage sale and start packing up what little he'll be keeping."

"This is really happening," Davina muttered, both happy and sad. "He'll finally get to start his new life."

The other four women stood around the tiny counter and stared over at her.

"We all hope you'll be a part of that life," Marla said.

Davina shook her head. "I don't think so."

Rikki put a hand on the counter. "Do you want to be with Santo?"

"I…I don't know. He's become so distant lately. I think he has to decide if he's ready to have another woman in his life."

"He's trying to do the right thing," Rikki said. "He knows you want to go back to Bayou Fontaine to be with your family. I think he's afraid of holding you back." She sighed. "And my brother still has a bad case of cold feet in the relationship department. Be patient with him, okay?"

"I am patient," Davina admitted. "I can tell he's not ready to make any type of commitment and I've accepted that, but then I'm not so sure about our relationship either. You're right. I do need to go home and I can't predict what will happen when I get there."

"It's not that far," Vanessa said. "Rory and I managed a long-distance relationship when I still lived in New Orleans and we made it through while I came back and forth before the wedding."

"But you two knew you were in love," Davina said. She'd heard their story and it hadn't been easy.

"I fought it," Vanessa said. "Fought against loving him and now I can't imagine my life with anyone else."

Davina couldn't imagine her life without Santo and his children in it but how was she supposed to be in two places at once? Those kids needed stability, not someone who came and went in their lives. And she'd have to do that until her family was solid again and her dad's health was better.

"What's going on between you two?" Marla asked as they spread out the food. Chicken salad and crackers, cheese and fruit.

"Have you ever noticed that we eat all the time?" Davina asked to stall the questions.

"Yes, now tell us how you feel," Chloe said with a soft grin. "We didn't just come here for manicures. We want the scoop on the most talked-about couple in town."

"Are people gossiping?" Davina asked, not surprised.

"Oh, people always talk," Marla said, a carrot in her hand. "Annette Pickett seems to be spreading rumors and even letting people who look at the bay house know what went on there. That woman is a piece of work."

"I thought Rory had talked to her," Davina said.

"He has talked to her and he mentioned Santo's job offer but she said it was insulting so she refuses to meet with Santo to discuss anything. She's bitter and that's understandable but…it's affecting her children, too."

Davina dipped a carrot into some hummus. "Maybe that's why Santo's cooled his jets. He's protecting his children."

"And he's shielding you from that kind of unfortunate stuff," Chloe said. "But all that aside, talk to us. We only gossip about the good stuff."

Davina smiled at that. "I feel as if I've found an old wall and discovered a treasure hidden behind it," Davina said. "I've torn down walls all my life but Santo has been a challenge. He's strong and unwilling to bend at times, but at other times he's tender and sweet. I can't decide what he's thinking."

"Keep tearing away," Rikki said, between bites of fresh Alabama strawberries. "My brother needs someone good in his life. And besides, his kids adore you."

Touched that they all liked her enough to cheer her on, Davina wasn't so sure Santo was ready or willing to make the next move.

"There is a lot to consider," she said.

"Okay, enough," Marla ordered. "It's time for facials and pedicures and polished nails." Pointing to the dessert bag, she said, "And praline cheesecake."

"Can we just skip to the cheesecake?" Chloe asked.

"Spa and then dessert."

"You're tough," Vanessa told Marla.

"I hope our men will be just as tough on Santo," Marla quipped. "Somebody needs to talk some sense into that man."

They all laughed and soon, they had Davina in a chair with her feet soaking in lavender oil and wonderfully hot water and her nails glowing with a light pink polish that Rikki called "Pinky Power."

"You know I'll ruin these first thing tomorrow, don't you?" Davina asked.

"Enjoy them tonight then," Marla suggested.

They took turns doing each other's nails, giving each other neck massages and laughing as they plastered smelly masks on their faces and took selfies.

The night went on and Davina relaxed and had a good time. They ate cheesecake, danced like schoolgirls and laughed while they discussed the men in their lives.

When the clock struck midnight, Marla announced it

was time to go but Davina knew she'd made friends for life. "I haven't done this in a long time," she admitted. "My sisters and I used to be so close and now we're all caught up in our own lives and just trying to stay afloat. Thank you for coming to see me."

"We had fun," Marla said. "We love our men but, hey, every woman needs some girl time, right?"

"Right," came the echo as they cleaned up and left, hugging and laughing and promising they'd do it all again soon.

Davina's apartment went silent again.

Then her cell rang.

"Da's back in the hospital," Tilly said, her voice shaky. "I think you need to get home as soon as you can."

Sleepy and still wondering why his four new friends had come close to throttling him because he hadn't made any progress with Davina, Santo walked through the warehouse the next morning in a dour mood. That mood only got worse when he had to go over shipment orders and send out emails demanding answers for problem areas. The Alvanetti Imports store had been open for six months now and they were finally beginning to see a small profit, but lost orders and damaged goods were always a problem.

He really did need an assistant. Someone who could shadow him and get things done. His secretary was great at making his daily schedule bearable but she didn't know the ins and outs of running a wholesale commercial business.

Santo thought about Annette Pickett. She'd refused to consider his job offer. Rory had talked to her, urged her to reconsider and meet with Santo, but she wouldn't bulge. She didn't want any part of the Alvanetti family.

Why? Pulling out his phone, Santo found the number Rory had given him. Annette Pickett's number. Did he dare call the woman?

The Alvanetti name was becoming synonymous with high quality furnishings and a lot of the builders were using them exclusively. That meant big volume shipments for the continuous stream of condos and luxury homes that were going up all across the state. So business could only increase over the next few years. He had to show the world that this was a solid, by-the-book, legal operation.

His sister had certainly utilized the family store in both of his houses. Now the bay house was sold. He'd be able to move into the lake house in a few weeks.

Davina.

He hadn't called her about the house selling and he wasn't going to have time to go by and see her today. After talking to one of his warehouse foremen about some broken vases that had been shipped from Italy, he headed back to the office to call Davina. He owed her that news at least. As for the rest, he'd pointedly told his buddies to back off. This was between him and Davina.

That hadn't fazed them, of course. They wanted an update later in the week. He'd better call Davina or she'd hear all kinds of things from their bossy wives, too.

But his cell rang before he could make the call.

"Rikki? Hi."

"Hi," his sister said. "Listen, Davina had to go to New Orleans. Her father is back in the hospital and it's not looking good."

"Really?" She hadn't called him. "When did this happen?"

"Late last night after we'd left her house. She got dressed and took off as soon as she heard. Drove all night to get there, from what Rory told me."

Santo held two fingers between his eyes and rubbed the throbbing beat there. "So this is bad?"

"Yes. He had a massive heart attack. They don't think he's going to make it."

"Can you help Virginia with the kids?"

"Of course. Go."

Santo didn't waste any time. He called in his top people, explained the situation and then called Virginia. "I'll be home to give the kids a kiss and grab some clothes. Will you be okay with them for a few days?"

"Of course. Give Davina my love."

He was on his way to New Orleans an hour later.

Chapter Twenty-Two

Davina stood huddled with her sisters.

Ma stood with Darren by their daddy's bed.

The room was cold but she shook mostly because she couldn't believe her sweet, hardworking daddy wasn't going to make it.

"This can't be real," she said, wishing she'd stayed here over the last couple of weeks. "I thought he was better."

"He tried to get better but…he's so tired," Tilly said, her hand on Davina's arm. "This one just hit him out of the blue. And in his sleep at that."

Alana wiped at her eyes. "He's only alive because of sheer grit. Just be prepared. He could go to sleep and not wake up."

"Is Quinn coming home?" Davina asked, praying her brother would be able to make it in time.

"We're still trying to reach him."

Ma motioned to her. "He wants to speak to you, Dani."

He was speaking to his children, one by one.

Dani didn't want to have this talk. Not at all.

Ma never called her by her nickname. She wouldn't break down. Not now, when Da was trying to tell them goodbye. Wondering what he'd said to Darren, she glanced at her brother's stoic face. But Darren didn't even look at Davina. He marched out into the waiting room without a word.

Alana and Tilly held on to each other, knowing their turn was coming. She wished Quinn were here.

Davina went to her daddy and took his hand. He opened his eyes wide and gave her a weak smile. "Did good."

She knew what he was trying to say but she didn't care right now. "Why did you send me away? I could have helped right here."

"Did help. Did fine."

"I should have stayed. I'm not leaving Ma again."

"Shhh. Live your life. Live, you hear."

"I can't, Da. Not without you here."

"Yes, you can. Strongest of all."

She shook her head and kissed him. "Rest. I love you."

"I love you, my good girl. Keep at it but find some love out there, okay."

Davina thought about Santo. "I will, Da. I promise."

Then he motioned. "Alana."

Davina reluctantly let go of his hand and turned toward her sister. "Alana."

Alana gulped a sob as she walked by their mother. Davina moved away and went into her mother's arms. "We have to do something."

Nancy looked into her eyes. "It's not ours to fix, honey. He's going home to God."

"I don't want God to have him."

"Of course you don't. But your da is ready and he'll be all fresh and new when he gets there."

Davina wiped at her eyes and pulled away. She needed some air. Tilly hovered in the corner, afraid. Davina wanted to run away from this room and this hospital but she had to be strong for Tilly. She could see it now. She'd always been strong and determined and impulsive and independent. Caught in the middle, she'd been torn between all of them. Da had seen it—the stifling of her creativity, with everyone around her telling her what to do and how to act. With her trying to take care of everyone and failing.

He'd needed Darren to stay. So he'd sent her away.

Alana passed her, crying. Tilly shook her head. "I can't do this."

"Yes, you can," Ma said, urging her forward. "You'll do this for him, understand?"

Tilly bent her head and hurried to their daddy's bedside, bobbing her head as he looked up at her with those vivid dark blue eyes.

After Tilly came back, they both went outside.

"He's waiting for Quinn to get here," Tilly said through her tears. "He'll hold out till that."

Davina knew that was true. Quinn would want to be here in Da's last hours.

She held on to Tilly, comforting her little sister while her own heart shattered like chipped tile pieces all around her. Tilly's head came up and she gasped, causing Davina to whirl to see if Quinn was finally here.

But her baby brother wasn't standing there by the wide door to the cardiac care unit.

Santo was. He took one look at her and held out his arms.

Davina went straight into his warm embrace and held him close, her tears misting against his crisp white shirt.

She never wanted to let go.

"What are you doing here?" she asked later when she could breathe again.

"I came as soon as I heard," Santo said. "You can't go through this alone."

Wiping at her eyes, she said, "I'm not alone but I have to admit seeing you standing there made me feel a whole lot better."

All around them, friends and relatives were talking quietly. Dawn was popping up outside in muted pinks and yellows that looked like cotton candy floating over the trees and buildings. Davina's bones were so weary that she thought she'd collapse if she tried to stand.

"It's been a long night," she said. "We're waiting for Quinn. He tried to get leave when we finally got word to him that Da had the first heart attack but we don't know if he's on his way or if he'll make it."

Santo listened and held her hand, his gaze on her. "Is there any hope?"

She shook her head. "Surgery would kill him and there's nothing else they can do at this point. Alana says he has coronary heart disease and no one caught it in time, mainly because he refused to go to a doctor. I want to be so mad at him for that, but I can't. I just can't."

"I'm so sorry." His fingers tightened on hers. "Rory and Vanessa are coming later. I'm sure they'll be a comfort to you."

"They don't have to do that."

"They want to do that," he replied. "You have new friends now, Davina. We'll help you get through this."

She couldn't speak. Thoughts of Millbrook Lake and his beautiful house went to the back of her mind. All she could think about was how she'd abandoned her family. She should have put her foot down and explained to her parents that she needed to stay. They all needed to stay. Even Alana, who still lived and worked in New Orleans, had pulled away from them in the last few years and now guilt was eating at her, too. Darren had stayed but he'd resented every minute of it. And Tilly just wanted everyone to be happy, but how could she make that happen now?

Santo came because he knew all about that gnawing, all-consuming kind of guilt.

"You don't have to stay," she kept telling him.

"I'm not leaving you," he replied. "I didn't have a whole lot of people on my side when Althea…died. It was a horrible time. Blain couldn't even look at me because he had to shoot my wife in order to save Rikki. He wouldn't leave Rikki's side either. We almost lost her so I don't blame him for watching over her even after the case had been solved. And I wonder sometimes, if things had gone the other way and if Rikki had been killed, how would I have felt about Althea then? How would my children cope with that? It was just a horrible time and… I think that's why I've held back on…everything."

On them. He didn't have to say the words to tell Davina why he'd been avoiding her lately. They'd grown too close for comfort because they'd both been through so many things that had shaped them and molded them.

"Did you feel torn?" she asked, needing to understand.

He nodded. "In about fifty different directions. Torn between my loyalty to my father and my siblings and torn between the truth and the lies. Torn because my children lost their mother and destroyed because I couldn't explain why. I hated myself because I was so blind, so clueless, that my own wife tricked my entire family right underneath my nose. I don't know if I'll ever recover but…I'm trying."

"Santo, I'm so sorry. Losing my daddy is going to be the hardest thing in my life but what you've been through is the worst."

He shook his head, tears in his eyes. "When you lose a loved one, good or bad, close or not so close, it's always hard to deal with. My mother has such a strong faith. She told me that we're only on this earth a short time. She wants me to embrace life while I'm still here. And you've helped me to do that."

Davina didn't know what to say. So she said the only thing she could. "Thank you for coming. It means the world to me."

Before Santo could reply, Tilly came rushing up to her.

"Quinn's on his way. He was already on his way before this happened, thankfully. He should be here by nightfall."

Davina hugged her sister close. "That's good news."

Santo stood to the side and out of their way but her eyes met his over Tilly's shoulder. She couldn't explain how much having him here meant to her. And she couldn't explain how much it meant that he'd shared some of his own pain with her.

They might not be able to come to terms on being together but she knew one thing for sure. Santo would always have a place in her heart and he'd be her friend for life.

She might have to accept that as her only comfort for now and thank God for the blessing of having Santo as a friend.

Chapter Twenty-Three

"Shhh. She's coming."

Santo held his hand up to all the people he'd smuggled into his new home, signaling that Davina had arrived. This impromptu housewarming party had been the brainchild of his sister and her well-meaning friends, but he hoped Davina wouldn't take it the wrong way.

It had been a month since her father died and she'd been back and forth between finishing this house and doing what she could to help her family. Each time she left, he lost a little bit of her. Davina had promised to come back one last time, to see him and the children finally in the house with everything in place. One last evening together.

Then, she'd be out of his life forever.

"Unless we throw a big party and show her how much we want her to stay," Rikki had suggested. "We can do it over Memorial Day weekend."

Now Santo wished he'd stuck to his original plan and kept things low-key, just the two of them and the children.

Too late for that. She was standing on the curb, looking up at the house with awe in her eyes and a soft smile on her pretty face. She looked small, her features hollowed out. She'd lost weight. But she was still beautiful. Her long floral dress wrapped against her calves in soft folds, the wind lifting it out like flowers on a breeze. Her hair fell around her cheeks in a rustle of reds and coppers. It was hard to read her expression but she looked sad and afraid, a distant longing settling over her features.

He almost went to her.

"Here she comes," Rikki said, excitement in her voice.

Davina had helped his sister to heal, too.

Okay, Lord, help me make this right. I'm in love with this woman but I'm so afraid of telling her how I feel.

He hoped his feeble prayer had been heard. Rory always said the Lord heard prayers even when you didn't know you were praying them.

The children started squirming and giggling when the doorbell rang. "Shhh," he said with a grin.

Then he opened the door. "Hi. It's good to see you."

She stared at him and then looked inside. "Why is it so dark in there? I know I put lights in the best places to show off the—"

He pulled her inside and hugged her close. "I'm sorry for this but—"

"Surprise!"

About twenty adults and three very eager children came rushing at them. He held Davina back and gave her an apologetic gaze. "It wasn't my idea."

She stared up at him, blinked away tears, and then peeked over his shoulder at the room full of people waiting for her.

And then she turned and ran back down the front steps.

* * *

"Dani!"

Not even Nate calling after her could make Davina go back inside that house. Tears flowing down her face, she kept walking until she was out of breath. When she looked up, she was at the church. She almost went inside the apartment that she'd come here to shut down for good. But instead she walked into the small prayer garden Rory had been working on all spring.

Davina sank down on a Monet bench made out of eucalyptus wood that he'd ordered on her recommendation. She touched her fingers to the beautiful golden-brown grain. Why did she always feel so safe around old wood?

The wind off the lake tickled at the fan palms centered on one side of the tiny rectangular garden and frolicked over the chimes Vanessa had hung on a crape myrtle tree. The smell of gardenias and jasmine lifted into the dewy early evening air. Somewhere off in the distance, a child's laughter floated through the trees and a dog barked a playful, frisky answer. Somewhere, the smell of wood smoke indicated that someone was cooking on a grill.

Davina closed her eyes and thanked God for bringing her to this small, quaint little town. She'd never forget her time here. While she'd stayed busy and her personal life had changed dramatically, this place had given her a sense of peace.

"I wish you could see this, Da," she whispered on the wind. "That house is so amazing. They'll be so happy there. I promise I'm going to make our house that special again one day. For you."

When she opened her eyes, Santo was standing

underneath the jasmine-covered pergola, his hands in the pockets of his jeans.

Wiping at her eyes, she croaked, "Did you hear all of that?"

"Yes," he said. "And you're right. He would be proud."

She smiled and let out a sob of a breath. "I wish I could stay, Santo."

"I'm so sorry," he said, moving closer, hesitating. "I tried to tell them you might not be ready…"

"It's not that," she said, wiping at her eyes. "It's not that at all. Seeing everyone there just took me by surprise because you've all been so welcoming to me and…this just added to that. I didn't mean to be so rude."

"They understand. I told them to stay put so I could talk to you in private. But with one call, they'll all be gone if you don't want to see them."

"That's the problem," she said, motioning for him to join her on the bench. "I do want to see them. But I'm such a mess these days. My crew was there, right?"

He nodded. "They came back to surprise you. And spend some time on the water during Memorial Day, of course."

She laughed at that. "Yes, I think Kurt has developed a strong fishing addiction."

"Nothing wrong with that. I think the AWOL crowd is going to do some deep-sea fishing next weekend. I've never had good friends before. I don't know why I waited so long."

"They are good friends," she said. "I'll miss all of you."

"So…you're leaving us?"

"I don't see any other way. Darren is taking over the company but he needs my help. Ma wants to move out of the house but Darren is going to move in with her and try to fix it up. And Tilly's living there for now." She shrugged. "I want to help with that. My mother deserves a nice place to spend the rest of her years."

"Yes, she does. How's she doing?"

"She's strong and her faith is solid, but we find her crying alone in the little sitting room, where they always watched television together. One chair is always empty now and none of us can bring ourselves to sit in it."

Santo put an arm around her and tugged her close. "I know that kind of emptiness. Even after everything Althea did, I would still look up expecting to see her coming down the stairs." Taking a deep sigh, he added, "But you know what? Now, in the lake house, I look expecting to see someone else coming toward me."

Davina started crying all over again. "Me?"

"No," he said to make her laugh. "Becky. I've got this crush on her."

Davina slapped at his arm. "Right."

"Of course you, always you," he said. "I won't force you to make a choice since I've learned lately about the importance of family. But I want you to know something."

"What's that?"

"I will be here, waiting for you to come back to me."

"But I—"

"I mean it," he said. "I love you. I fell for you the day you walked into my house wearing that cute tool belt. When you took my son into your arms and comforted him, my heart began to heal. You have to come back to me, okay?"

"I can't promise—"

"Try."

"I'll try," she said. "It's just all so confusing right now."

"I'm willing to give you some time."

"Okay."

"And we can visit now and then, right?"

"Right."

"You don't seem so sure."

"I don't know what's going to happen. All I know is work."

"You should remember what that'll get you."

"I do. But for the next few months at least."

Santo felt her slipping away again. "I love you," he said. Then he kissed her to show her he was ready. She kissed him back and smiled up at him but he could see it in her eyes.

She'd already made her decision. She hadn't told him that she loved him, too.

Then she surprised him. "I'm starving. I think I'm ready to go back to the house now. I want to see the children. So I'll have some good memories to take with me."

A month later, Davina and her brother Darren were busy in what they'd turned into a downstairs bed and bath in her parents' house. They were giving their mom her own apartment, downstairs near the kitchen but with a sitting room and galley-style kitchen on one wall and a nice bedroom with a private bath. A camera crew was following them around. Just a local team from the evening news that wanted to highlight remodeling older homes in Bayou Fontaine. Tilly had sent in a picture of Santo's lake house, citing Davina's skills.

Things were turning around but she couldn't leave until she and Darren had an ironclad agreement regarding the company, starting with getting this house completely overhauled.

Santo called her a lot. They talked about getting together but just as she knew would happen, they were both too busy. The Fourth of July was coming up. He wanted her to come to Millbrook Lake for the weekend.

But she wasn't sure that could happen.

Finally, Ma came into the big bedroom, her eyes glistening with pride. "Your Da would think we were living in the Garden District," she stated, tears forming. "I don't deserve such luxury."

"Yes, you do," both Davina and Darren said.

They were equal partners now. Working together, they'd discovered all kinds of ways to streamline the business and make things more efficient.

"You don't have to be here 24/7," he told her while their mother listened and nodded. "We've got a system now. You can do the regional work and I'll hold down the local construction projects. We're well-known thanks to your latest remodel down in Florida."

"I'll say," Ma added. "A film crew and talk of a reality show."

"I'm not doing a reality show unless it's all about preservation and renovation," Davina stated. "But yes… I might just go back to Florida for a while."

"For the rest of your life," Ma said. "Go on with you. You're in love and I'm tired of seeing you walking around, pining away for that good-looking Italian."

"Do you think I should?" she asked Ma and Darren.

"Yes," they both said.

"Yes." Tilly's reply came from the kitchen.

Then her brother Quinn, who was now officially done with his tour of duty, walked in, his blue eyes bright, his dark hair a little longer now, and said, "Yes, please." Tugging someone else into the room, he said, "'Cause if you don't go to Florida, I think we might have a house-guest for a long, long time."

Davina dropped her hammer. "Santo?"

"I came to help," he said with a shrug. "And I brought a few of my friends with me."

She watched in awe as Alec, Blain, Rory and Hunter all stalked in. "We're reporting for work, boss."

Davina's gaze met Santo's. He was carrying a fa-miliar box.

"I know where you got those and I hope you're willing to share," she said, eyeing the cupcake emblem.

"That depends," Santo said. "I have stipulations."

"I'm pretty sure this man loves you," Tilly said. "That's his stipulation. What are you waiting for?"

Davina gulped in a breath and rushed into Santo's arms. "I love him, too," she said. "I do. I love this man." Then she snatched the box away from him with a grin.

"It's about time," Darren said, pride in the words. "And yes, we could use some help here."

Davina shooed her brother away while she kissed the man she loved. "I don't know what I was thinking, try-ing to stay away from you."

"You were trying to be a good daughter," he said. "But I need you to be my wife. Our children are wait-ing for you."

"I like the sound of that," she replied. "Help me here and feed me a cupcake and I promise I will follow you home."

"That sounds like a plan," he said. Then he kissed her while their fascinated audience clapped and whooped.

* * *

"C'mon, it's almost time for the Fourth of July fireworks," Gabby called out, her great-aunt Hattie's hand in hers.

"We have plenty of time," Marla said, grinning over at her husband. "Before we watch the show, I'd like to thank Santo and Davina for hosting this party. Santo, your new home is so lovely. Welcome to the neighborhood."

Santo smiled and lifted his cup of soda. "Glad to be here. And I should be able to spend more time here since I have a very capable new assistant to help me at work."

Annette Pickett had finally showed up at his office one day and told him how sorry she was about making things harder for him. "I heard about what you'd been through with your children and how you wanted to start a new life and I just ignored all that and I judged you way too harshly. But after talking to Preacher Rory and some other friends, I realized I'd been so wrong to judge you. I want to start over, too. Preacher Rory has helped me and now my son has found a great place to teach him and show him the right path and…well, I'm blessed. I want to stop all of this so it won't be too late for Beatrice. I need a good job. I'm willing to give it a try if you are."

Santo had agreed. Best decision he'd ever made. Other than asking Davina to marry him. "Thank you all for coming," he said as he glanced around. "I'm blessed to have all of you in my life." He winked at Rikki.

Marla and Alec held each other and smiled. Roxie sat at Gabby's feet, waiting for a treat, and Angus lay on a rug in the corner, snoozing. Blain and Rikki were happy in their new cottage on the lake. Rory and Vanessa traveled back and forth to the girls' home she'd opened in Alabama and helped hundreds of troubled teens find hope again. Kandi Jordan, the foster teen Vanessa had first mentored, planned to work there after college. Hunter and Chloe led a life of mystery and danger, solving corporate crimes. And Santo and Davina were going to get married this Christmas and make their hectic schedule work since they'd soon have offices side-by-side at Alvanetti Imports. He was content at last.

"So…we have an announcement," he said, smiling at Davina. Her whole family was here also and Nancy Connell gave him a thumbs-up. "We're going to get married."

"We've already figured that one out," Alec said on a droll note. But everyone congratulated them and hugged them anyway.

Then Alec held up his hand again. "Marla and I have one more announcement and then it's on to fireworks."

"What?" Gabby asked, looking between them. "Y'all are already married."

"Yes, we are," Alec replied. "Thank goodness."

"We're going to have a baby," Marla said, bending down to smile at Gabby. "How would you like that?"

Gabby clapped her hands. "You mean, a brother or sister, all for me?"

"Yes, all for you," Marla said, tears in her eyes. "For all of us."

Santo hugged Davina close while everyone celebrated. "This is amazing," he said. "I've lived here all my life but right now in this very minute, I finally feel as if I belong."

"You do belong," she said, touching a hand to his face. "To me. And now you have my family and all of these other people in your life."

"And us."

They turned to find his mother and father standing there. After hugs and introductions, Franco Alvanetti stated, "We're tired of traveling." He hugged his grandchildren tight. "We missed all of you."

"We're home for good," Sonia said, hugging Rikki and Santo and giving her grandchildren kisses. "And we want details on all of this."

"Yes, you've got a lot of explaining to do," Franco Alvanetti said in his gruff voice, his dark eyes full of pride.

"Yes, I do," Santo admitted. "I'll tell you all about it after the fireworks."

His father chuckled and patted him on the back. "I love this house, son."

"So do I," Santo replied. "And I love the woman who restored both this house and me."

Franco inclined his head toward Davina. "So I hear."

Taking Davina by the hand, Santo said, "Let's go watch the fireworks."

"Good idea." She kissed his cheek. "But I have a feeling they're just beginning."

* * * * *

Dear Reader,

I hope you enjoyed this last installment of the Men of Millbrook Lake. I had not expected to write a fifth book, but after Santo showed up in Book Two (*Her Holiday Protector*), I knew he had to have his own book. I wanted this solemn, stoic man to have his own happily-ever-after. There are a lot of hurting people in the world who deal with loved ones who've taken the wrong path. Sometimes that path leads to tragedy. Santo's story is about how to deal with the worst kind of tragedy—betrayal and death.

He needed a woman like Davina who could show him the true meaning of family. While they come from different backgrounds, they had that love of family in common. We can all learn a lesson from their issues.

I will miss my Men of Millbrook Lake but I hope you will continue to follow them and tell your friends about them. They will always hold a special place in my heart because they kept me busy while I adjusted to a new life in the beautiful state of Florida.

Until next time,
May the angels watch over you. Always.
Lenora

REQUEST YOUR FREE BOOKS!

2 FREE INSPIRATIONAL NOVELS
PLUS 2
FREE
MYSTERY GIFTS

Love Inspired®

LI15

"We all know Teacher Lillian is a terrible cook, don't we,
children?"

Lillian Keim's students erupted into giggles and some
outright laughter. She crossed her arms and pressed her
lips together to hold back a smile.

Timothy Bowman winked at her to take any sting out
of his comment, but she wasn't offended. They had been
friends for ages and were members of the same Amish
community in Bowmans Crossing, Ohio. She knew he
enjoyed a good joke as well as the next fellow, but he
was deadly serious about his job today and so was she.
The lessons they were presenting might one day prevent
a tragedy.

He stood in front of her class on the infield of the softball
diamond behind the one-room Amish schoolhouse where
she taught all eight grades. Dressed in full fireman's
turnout gear, Timothy made an impressive figure. The
coat and pants added bulk to his slender frame, but he
carried the additional weight with ease. His curly brown

hair was hidden under a yellow helmet instead of his usual straw hat, but his hazel eyes sparkled with mirth. A smile lifted one side of his mouth and deepened the dimples in his tanned cheeks. Timothy smiled a lot. It was one reason she liked him.

His bulky fire coat and pants with bright fluorescent yellow banding weren't Plain clothing, but their Amish church district approved their use because the church elders and the bishop recognized the need for Amish volunteers to help fill the ranks of the local non-Amish fire company. The county fire marshal understood the necessity of special education in the Amish community, where open flames and gas lanterns were used regularly. The Amish didn't allow electricity in their homes. Biannual fire-safety classes were held at all the local Amish schools. This was Timothy's first time giving the class. With Lillian's permission, he was deviating from the normal script with a demonstration outside. Timothy wanted to make an impression on the children. She admired that.

Don't miss
HIS AMISH TEACHER by Patricia Davids,
available March 2017 wherever
Love Inspired® books and ebooks are sold.

www.LoveInspired.com

"I'm your mail-order bride."

"What?" Philip wished he could cover the shock in his voice, but he couldn't.

"I answered your advertisement for a mail-order bride." Bella's cheeks flushed and her gaze darted to the little boys on the couch.

Philip didn't know what to think. She didn't appear to be lying, but he hadn't placed an ad for marriage in any newspaper. "I have no idea what you are talking about. I didn't place a mail-order-bride ad in any newspaper."

She frowned and stood. "Hold on a moment." Bella dug in her bag and handed him a small piece of newspaper.

His gaze fell upon the writing.

November 1860

Wanted: Wife as soon as possible. Must be willing to live at a pony express relay station. Must be between the ages of eighteen to twenty-five. Looks are not important. Write to: Philip Young, Dove Creek, Wyoming, Pony Express Relay Station.

Philip looked up at her. He hadn't placed the ad, but he had a sinking feeling he knew who did. "Did you send a letter to this address?"

Bella shook her head. "No, I didn't have the extra money to spare for postage. I just hoped I'd make it to Dove Creek before another woman. I did, didn't I?"

"Well, since this is the first I've heard of the advertisement—" he shook the paper in his hand "—I'd say your chances of being first are good. But this is dated back in November and it is now January so I'm curious as to what took you so long to get here."

"Well, I didn't actually see the advertisement until a few weeks ago. My sister and her husband had recently passed and I was going through their belongings when I stumbled upon the paper. Your ad leaped out at me as if it was from God." Once more she looked to the two boys playing on the couch.

Philip's gaze moved to the boys, too. "Are they your boys?"

"They are now."

Sadness flooded her eyes. Since she'd just mentioned her sister's death, Philip didn't think it was too much of a stretch to assume that the boys had belonged to Bella's sister. "They are your nephews?"

"Yes. I'm all the family they have left. The oldest boy is Caleb and the younger Mark." Her soulful eyes met his. "And you are our last hope to stay together."

Also by Peter Abrahams

A PERFECT CRIME
THE FAN
LIGHTS OUT
REVOLUTION #9
PRESSURE DROP
HARD RAIN
RED MESSAGE
TONGUES OF FIRE
THE FURY OF RACHEL MONETTE

CRYING WOLF

Peter Abrahams

FAWCETT BOOKS • NEW YORK

A Fawcett Book
Published by The Ballantine Publishing Group
Copyright © 2000 by Pas de Deux Corp.

All rights reserved under International and Pan-American Copyright Conventions. Published in the United States by The Ballantine Publishing Group, a division of Random House, Inc., New York, and simultaneously in Canada by Random House of Canada Limited, Toronto.

Fawcett is a registered trademark and the Fawcett colophon is a trademark of Random House, Inc.

www.randomhouse.com/BB/

Library of Congress Catalog Card Number: 2001116242

ISBN 0-345-43503-6

Manufactured in the United States of America

First Hardcover Edition: March 2001
First Paperback Edition: May 2001

10 9 8 7 6 5 4 3 2 1

To Dr. Alejandro Berenstein and his staff at the Center for Endovascular Surgery, Beth Israel Medical Center, Singer Division, New York.

1

One should not avoid one's tests, although they are per-haps the most dangerous game one could play and are in the end tests which are taken before ourselves and be-fore no other judge. (Beyond Good and Evil, *section 41*)
—Introduction to the syllabus for Philosophy 322,
   Superman and Man: Nietzsche and Cobain
   (Professor Uzig)

A rolled-up newspaper spun through the air, defining place. What kind of place? The kind of place often described as leafy or even idyllic, where a boy on a bicycle still tossed the paper onto lawns and porches, sometimes over actual picket fences, where the newspaper still brought news.

"Nat," called a voice inside one of the houses, a simple 1950s roofed box, much like all the others.

"What is it, Mom?"

"Come quick."

"This couldn't be happening to a better boy," said Mrs. Smith, the guidance counselor at Clear Creek High. "Or should I say young man?"

She raised her hand, pink and stubby. Was Mrs. Smith going to pinch his cheek? Nat tried not to flinch; he owed her a lot. At the last second, her hand veered away and settled for an upper-arm squeeze instead.

"What a question!" said Miss Brown, the school principal,

regarding Mrs. Smith with annoyance. "Young man, of course, as should be perfectly obvious to anyone." Mrs. Smith and Miss Brown were identical twin sisters, although easily distinguished: Miss Brown had hair the color of shiny pennies, Mrs. Smith's was gray; Mrs. Smith shook when she laughed, Miss Brown didn't shake, seldom laughed.

Hiss and pop: fatty juices dripped on open flames. Miss Brown turned to Nat's mom, who was laying another row of patties on the grill. "And of all the young men I've encountered in my thirty-two years of education, some of them very fine young men indeed, this one is the—well, I won't say it, comparisons—"

"—being odious," said Mrs. Smith.

"I'll finish my own sentences, if it's all the same to you," said Miss Brown in a low voice, but not so low that Nat didn't hear.

Even though the comparison hadn't been made, to Nat's relief, and even though he suspected that the adage they'd used might be obscure to his mom, her face, already pink from the heat of midday and the glowing coals, went pinker still. "Thank you," she said, wiping aside a damp wisp of hair—almost as gray now as Mrs. Smith's, as Nat could see in the bright sunlight, despite her being so much younger—with the back of her wrist. Then she blinked, that single slow blink she always made when she was feeling shy but believed something was required from her anyway; at least, that was Nat's interpretation. People didn't understand how brave she was. "I'm obliged to the both of you," she said, "for getting him into such a place."

"Don't thank us," said Miss Brown.

"He earned it," said Mrs. Smith.

"This golden opportunity," said Miss Brown.

"And everything that's going to come from it," said Mrs. Smith. "His own doing, from A to Z." For proof, she held up the *County Register*—the Fourth of July special edition, with the red-white-and-blue banner at the top of page one and the winning essay in the DAR's $2,000 "What I Owe America" contest, open to graduating high-school seniors across the state, printed beneath it in fourteen-point letters. Old Glory, the prize essay, and a picture of the winner: Nat, in his yearbook photo, wearing a blazer borrowed from Mr. Beaman, his mom's boss, tight across the shoulders. Mrs. Smith brandished the paper against the sky—like a weapon, Nat thought, as though defying an enemy.

But what enemy? There were no enemies here in this tiny backyard on the western edge of their little town, with the land stretching flat into the distance. The distance: where on some days, in some lights—like this day, this Fourth of July, in this light—the summits of the Rockies floated white and baseless in the sky, reminding him of . . . what? Some metaphor that didn't quite come to mind.

Mr. Beaman himself arrived. Tugging off her apron, Nat's mom hurried to him, drew him toward Nat. Mr. Beaman was a lawyer, the only one in town other than Mr. Beaman senior. Nat's mom was his receptionist.

He shook Nat's hand. "I hear congratulations are in order."

"Well, I—" said Nat.

"Quite a sum of money," said Mr. Beaman, giving Nat's hand a good hard squeeze before letting go.

"A tidy sum," said Miss Brown.

"Two big ones, Junior," said Mrs. Smith. "Makes all the difference."

The difference it made: at Mrs. Smith's direction, Nat had applied to three colleges—Harvard, because it was number one on the *U.S. News and World Report* ranking of universities; Inverness, because it was number one on their list of small colleges; and Arapaho State, thirty miles away, in case something went wrong.

The results: admission to Harvard, making Nat the first student ever taken from Clear Creek High, and possibly from the whole county. But Harvard hadn't offered enough money, not close. Admission to Inverness, also a first, with more money, but still not enough. Arapaho would pay the full shot. That was that: Arapaho. Until this morning. Now, with the $2,000 added to a home equity loan, the savings Nat would accumulate that summer at the mill, and an on-campus job at Inverness, they could swing it. Just. Nat and his mom had each done the figures, figures that covered two sheets of yellow-pad paper still lying on the kitchen table.

Mr. Beaman produced a bottle of pink wine. A ray of sunlight made it glow like a magic potion. A pink day: the wine, Mom's face, Mrs. Smith's hands. Pink—the color that separated girls from boys. Inverness was far away. "Glasses, Evie?" said Mr. Beaman.

The long slow blink. "Wineglasses, are you saying?"

"Whatever you've got, Evie. Paper cups will do."

Mr. Beaman unscrewed the bottle, filled five cups. Nat knew almost nothing about wine, but suddenly had a strange thought: *I might have to know, from now on.* He checked the label, saw *pink zinfandel* in big letters, also read the serving suggestions—*cold, on the rocks, with soda water, with a twist.*

"To the big bucks," said Mr. Beaman. His eyes met Nat's. Nat couldn't help recalling that his mother had asked for a raise—from $8.50 to $9.00 an hour—after the Inverness financial aid package had arrived, and been turned down. Mr. Beaman's eyes slid away.

"To Nat," said Miss Brown.

"To Nat," said everyone.

"And four great years at Inverness."

They drank. The wine was cold and sweet. Nat had tasted wine a few times before, but nothing as good as this. He memorized the name of the winery.

"So," said Mr. Beaman, "what's the story with this famous place? Tell you the truth, I'd never heard of it."

"No?" said Nat's mom; a little wine slopped over the side of her cup.

"Bosh," said Mrs. Smith. She dug a copy of *U.S. News and*

World Report from her purse, flipped through, thrust the relevant page under his nose. "See?" she said. "Inverness first, Williams second, Haverford third."

"Elite," said Miss Brown.

"Crème de la crème," said Mrs. Smith. "Imagine the people he's going to meet."

"Just odd I hadn't heard of it, that's all," said Mr. Beaman.

Miss Brown and Mrs. Smith both pursed their lips, as though keeping something inside. Miss Brown succeeded, Mrs. Smith did not. "You weren't a bad student, Junior."

"Not bad?" he said with irritation. "I graduated ninth in my class."

"As high as that?" said Mrs. Smith. "Nat was first this year, as I probably needn't mention."

"But it's not just a matter of grades and test scores nowadays," said Miss Brown. "Nat had his basketball, and his coaching Little League, and the job at the mill."

"The mill? That counts?"

"It all adds up," said Miss Brown. "We're talking about—"

"—the whole package," said Mrs. Smith. Miss Brown narrowed her eyes at Mrs. Smith but said nothing.

Mr. Beaman drained his cup, studying Nat over its rim. It was very quiet for a moment, one of those small-town moments, with no sound at all but that of a jet plane, almost inaudible. Nat caught his mom studying him too, as though she were trying to figure out some stranger. He grinned at her and she grinned back. Her upper left front tooth was slightly chipped, just like his.

"Why don't you fetch the brochure to show Mr. Beaman, Nat?" she said.

Nat went into the house, one of the neighbors patting him on the back as he mounted the porch stairs. "Go get 'em."

The Inverness brochure lay on the kitchen table beside the sheets of calculations. The picture on the front showed well-dressed students and a professor sitting under a red-leafed tree. Nat gazed at it, a beautiful photograph, very clear. The professor had tassels on his loafers and so did two of the boys and one girl. He heard Mrs. Smith through the window screen: ". . . best boy ever came out of this town." Nat left the brochure on the table, went out of the house by the front door.

He stood at the foul line in the driveway. The foul line itself was invisible, had faded away years ago, but his feet went to the right spot; the same way he could walk around the house in the dark. He picked up the ball, eyed the back of the rim hanging on the backboard over the garage door, shot. Missed. Bounced the ball a couple of times. Shot. Missed. Nat took one hundred free throws a day, every day. Shot. Missed. Even the day his father left. Shot. Missed. He had a good shot if open, and was not bad at getting open. He'd been the shooting guard for Clear Creek High since sophomore year. Shot. Hit. And made second-team all-star in the Tri-County League this year, and honorable mention in the region. Shot. Missed. Good enough to play for Arapaho State—the coach had already called. Probably good enough to play for Inverness as well: it was only Division III. He bounced the ball a few times; not looking at it, not really bouncing it anymore. The ball more or less bounced itself, almost shuttling on its own between his hand and the pavement. Now when Nat looked up, he was aware of an invisible current of air, tube-shaped, flowing up from his hand to the basket. All he had to do was bend his knees and boost the ball up into that current. Shoot. Hit. Shoot. Hit. Shoot. Hit. He was an 81 percent foul shooter in competition, and here in the driveway he had once made a hundred straight. Forgetting the cookout, the brochure, the essay, aware only of the invisible air current and the ball that had to be tossed into it, Nat hit shot after shot. *Unconscious* was what they called it. He became a cog in a machine consisting of ball, himself, air current, basket. The other parts of the machine did most of the work, leaving his mind free to wander. It wandered back to those baseless mountaintops in the sky, and suddenly he had his metaphor: they were like sails of ships whose hulls had sunk beneath the horizon. Not that Nat had ever seen sailing ships on the horizon—he'd laid eyes on the ocean only once, from a plane, when his mom's sister, who lived in San Bernardino, was in the hospital—but he remembered a description of that effect from his reading.

Nat made twenty-five free throws in a row before emerging prematurely from unconsciousness, emerging the moment he remembered he wouldn't be playing at Inverness even if he could make the team: he'd have to work after class. He missed the next six, then hit a few, missed one, hit some more, missed some more. The invisible current of air was gone, or flowing elsewhere. He made sixty-eight out of a hundred, the lowest in years, maybe ever. As he put up the last shot a quotation drifted into his mind: *Ambition should be made of sterner stuff.* Antony's speech at Caesar's funeral, act 3, scene 2. The ball rattled off the rim. Behind him a car door slammed.

He turned to the street, and there was Patti, climbing out of her father's pickup. Her father beeped and drove away. Nat saw they already had an Arapaho State sticker on the back window; Patti was starting there in the fall. The ball rolled toward her down the driveway. She let it go, which wasn't like her at all, maybe didn't even see it; normally she'd have picked it up and tried to dribble around him.

Patti had the paper in her hand. She raised it, but only a little. It flapped back down at her side, as though very heavy. "Nat?"

"Hi."

"You're in the paper."

"Yeah."

"Cool."

"Thanks."

"You always were a good writer."

"I don't know about that."

Nat heard Mrs. Smith laughing in the backyard. Patti's face paled several shades.

"A good everything."

"Hey, come on."

"Sorry," she said. Pause. "Nat?"

"Yeah?"

"Does . . . does this mean . . . ?"

"It looks like it," Nat said.

Patti nodded. "Con . . . congra—" She started crying before she got the full word out.

Nat went to her, put his arms around her. "It'll be all right," he said.

She shook in his arms. "No, it won't. You'll forget all about me."

"That will never happen."

Patti cried. Over the top of her head, Nat saw the paperboy, now off duty, bicycling up the street, baseball glove hanging on the handlebar. Nat knew him, the second baseman on his Little League team, the smallest player and the best. The kid grinned, started to wave; then saw what was happening, looked alarmed, and pedaled off quickly, head down.

"You'll meet all kinds of girls, prettier than me."

"No."

"Prettier and smarter."

Nat shook his head. Patti wet his shirt with tears. "And richer," she said. "I hate Mrs. Smith."

Nat held her close. His mind fed him a view from high above: he and Patti in the driveway, the basketball on the grass, the folks in the backyard, the town mostly hidden by its trees, everything tiny. He didn't know what to say to her.

That night Patti went to bed with him for the first time. They'd come close before but she'd always held out, not quite ready. After—in her bedroom, her dad in Denver at his brother's—she didn't cry at all. She said: "What were we waiting on?" Nat almost told her he loved her then. It was probably the right thing to do, but he still wasn't sure he really did. He ended up holding her tight instead.

There were plenty of tears in the weeks that followed.

* * *

One funny thing about that mental bird's-eye view. At the end of the summer, when Nat flew out of Denver—second time on a plane—he looked out the window and saw his town, just as he'd imagined it on the Fourth of July. The mill, the high-school fields, the main street, even his street, even his house and the tiny backyard: he saw it all. No one in the backyard, of course. His mom, Patti, and Mrs. Smith would barely be out of the airport parking lot. Nat was thinking about what that drive would be like when, far below, a lake went by. There was no lake in his town. He'd been looking at someplace else.

2

All journeys fall into one of two categories, to home or from home, each unsatisfactory in its own way.
—From Professor Uzig's welcoming remarks,
  Philosophy 322

Freedy heard a man's voice from inside the house: "Better put your bathing suit on. The pool boy's out back."

Freedy stared up at the house, saw nothing but his own reflection in the glass sliders. He looked buff, ripped, diesel, a fuckin' animal (except for the intelligence in his face, not visible in the distant reflection, but he knew it was there). The intelligence in his face—according to his mother, he had eyes like the actor, name escaped him at the moment, who played Sherlock Holmes in old black-and-white movies—that intelligence was what separated him from all the other fuckin' animals out there and made him more of a lady's man. Women liked brains, no getting around it. Brains meant sensitivity. For example, floating in the water near the filter was a little furry thing. *Poor little fella,* you could say to some woman who happened to come by the pool. That was all it took: sensitivity.

Combine that with the ripped part, the buff part, the diesel part, so obvious in the window—that bare-chested dude, wearing cutoffs and work boots, the skimmer held loose in his hands, was he himself, after all—and what did you have? The kind of dude women went crazy for, absolutely no

10

denying that. Freedy squeezed the skimmer handle a little and a vein popped up in the reflection of his forearm. Amazing. He was an amazing person. But *pool boy*. He didn't like that, not one bit. Would they say it if he was black? Not a chance. That would be racist, and none of these people in their big houses in the hills over the Pacific ever spoke a racist word. They were politically correct. Well, on the panel of the van he drove it said: *A-1 Pool Design, Engineering, and Maintenance*. So that made *pool engineer* the correct term, didn't it? *The pool engineer's out back*. That's what he should have said, the asshole inside the house, Dr. Goldstein or Goldberg or whatever his name was. Freedy swept the little furry thing into the skimmer and tossed it over the ridge.

Thong. He turned back to the house and there was Mrs. Goldstein, Goldberg, whatever, walking across the patio in one of those thong bikinis. What a great invention! About forty, maybe even older, what with that sharp face and turned-down mouth, but the body: all these people with their pools, houses, cars, worked out like crazy, probably harder than he did. Except they didn't have a bottle of andro in their pocket. Or maybe they did. Nothing surprised him anymore. That was one thing he'd learned almost as soon as he'd come to California, three or four years before, the precise number momentarily unavailable. He'd been in a bar down in Venice when a cigar-smoking guy beside him answered his cell phone, listened for a while, and then said: "Nothing surprises me anymore." Right on the money. Freedy'd used the expression for the first time himself that very day.

The woman in the thong was talking to him.

"Excuse me?" he said.

She raised her hands to shade her eyes, bringing her breasts into play. "I said, are you new?"

New? What? He'd been doing this pool for six months. Three, anyway. "No," he said.

"Sorry, I didn't recognize you. Aren't you a little early?"

"Columbus Day. Traffic was light."

She nodded. "What's your name again?"

"Freedy."

"Nice to meet you, Freedy. This is when I normally do my laps."

In a thong? You swim your laps in a thong? Then he got it: *Put on your bathing suit.* She swam them in the nude.

"Want me to come back some other time?" Pause. "Mrs. . . ."

"Sherman. Bliss Sherman." From the front of the house came the sound of a car door closing, a car driving off. Had to be hubbie off to work in the Porsche; the Benz didn't make that throaty sound.

"Nice to meet you too, Bliss." But Sherman? That was nothing like Goldberg or Goldstein. Freedy dug the schedule out of his pocket: Goldman, 9:00 A.M. He glanced around, noticed a familiar-looking pool house on the next hilltop, about a ten-minute drive away. The Goldmans. He'd come to the wrong house. These Shermans weren't on the sheet at all. Had he ever been here before? He didn't think so. They weren't even clients. Some kind of mistake.

"How long will it take?"

"Take?"

She gave him a closer look; saw the body at last. Now was the moment to hit her with the sensitivity. Freedy checked the pool for more dead rodents, found none.

"To finish up," said Bliss.

"The pool?"

"Exactly."

He shrugged, a nice slow shrug to show her those delts, in case she'd missed them. "Fifteen, twenty minutes."

"I suppose I'll have to wait till you're done." She turned and went back into the house, closing the slider. Freedy watched until she was out of sight: how could you not watch a woman like that in a bathing suit like that? Then he went to work, skimming, checking the pH, adding chlorine, oiling the pump. The whole time, his mind toyed with the image of her butt as she walked away; not quite the whole time—once or twice it occupied itself with the furry thing, spinning over the ridge. He didn't like that *exactly*, didn't like that *I suppose I'll have to wait.*

Freedy gathered up the vacuum, skimmer, supply box, knocked on the slider. "All set," he called. He listened for a reply, heard nothing. He knocked again, called, "Finito," and walked around to the front of the house. *Finito,* being some other language, went with the sensitivity.

The van was parked beside the Benz in the driveway. He opened the side door, stowed the gear. While he was doing that, he glanced into the Benz and happened to see some money lying on the seat. That was them. He'd be the same way one day, with his intelligence. He'd own A-1 Pool Design, Maintenance, and Engineering himself. Or maybe a whole chain of pool companies, up and down the coast. Pools and California, they went together. Back where he came from, he didn't remember a single pool in the whole town— excepting the one up at the college, which didn't count. What opportunity was there for a person like him in a place like that? None. He knew that oh so well.

But here. Another story. He slammed the van door shut, took out the andro, popped one dry. He was going to be rich, so rich he'd never settle for a lousy 300-series Benz like this one. Was it unlocked? He tried the door. Yup. Unbelievable.

And these Shermans weren't even on the sheet. He'd cleaned their goddamn pool for nothing, even finishing after he'd figured it out, like some kind of saint, or Martin Luther King Jr. Cleaned their pool like Martin Luther King Jr., while that bare-assed bitch had said *exactly.* Not even on the sheet. In a funny way, that meant none of this was really happening. What an awesome thought: it reminded him of *The X-Files.* None of this was really happening. That meant it was like a free play in football, where they throw a flag against the defense while the quarterback's still dropping back, giving him a chance to throw the bomb with no risk. A free play. He wasn't even there. The Shermans didn't even exist, not in terms of A-1. Freedy reached into the Benz and grabbed the money.

Throw the bomb. It was that easy. He felt better than he had in months, better maybe than any time since the first few days after he'd come to California. Here on this hilltop under a huge blue sky, he felt huge too, the way he'd felt back then, before his crummy walk-up on Lincoln, the clunker that wouldn't fucking start half the time, the rent he owed, the advances on his pay he'd already got, all the way to Thanksgiving. On the hilltop with the Valley on one side and the ocean on the other, he knew what it was like to have been one of those conquistadors who'd discovered the place; Spaniards—not the spics he had to work with, even work for, now.

As for the money, he'd earned it, if you wanted to be technical; he'd done the work. Freedy shoved it into the pocket of his cutoffs, down there with the andro. He took a deep breath, felt great. Sober, unstoned, and great. When was the last time that combo had turned up? And how sharp his senses were all of a sudden, even sharper than usual. He smelled a nice plant smell he couldn't identify, saw a high-flying bird of some kind, heard a distant splash.

Maybe not so distant. Maybe from the other side of the house, where someone might be swimming her laps, back and forth, in a zone and possibly daydreaming about the so-called pool boy the whole time.

The so-called pool boy crept back around the house.

This was what was going to happen. He would take off his work boots, his socks, his cutoffs, cross the patio while she was swimming the other way, lower himself in the pool, and just stand there in the shallow end, waiting for her to bump into him on her way back. Surprise. But a nice surprise. She'd look up, eyes wide, mouth opening, then see who it was. The expression on her face would change in some exciting way, and she'd say, "I was just thinking about you," or maybe something subtler, like "What a coincidence." Yeah, that would be it: she was subtle, educated, rich. Freedy remembered the money in his pocket and felt a little badly. No reason he couldn't toss it back in the Benz later.

Freedy reached the corner of the house and stopped. He heard rhythmic splashing sounds, and one soft, female grunt. He peeked around the edge of the wall. Just as he'd imagined. Bliss—right name, in terms of what was going to happen . . . not *psychic* but some word about the future like that—naked in the pool, swimming her laps, tan all over. This was happening. It was just like porn, except he was in it. Freedy started to get hard right away, really hard, andro hard. He had an important thought: this is going to be the best experience of my life, so far. That meant he should make it last, appreciate it, savor it. *Savor:* what a perfect word, a word most people wouldn't have come up with at a time like this, but he knew it well, from the cooking channel. He was intelligent. He had eyes like whatever his name was who had played Sherlock Holmes, according to his mother.

His mother would be five or ten years older than Bliss Sherman. Had she ever had a body like that? Not even on her best day. But enough about her. What the hell was he doing thinking about his mother right now? His mother's face, Bliss Sherman's butt, the spinning furry thing: he shook his head to clear away all that confusion and moved silently across the patio. Silent, not to scare her or anything; he just didn't want to spoil the surprise.

Freedy slipped into the shallow end. The water was cool and clean, made him tingle all over. Of course it was clean: he'd cleaned it himself. He'd made his bed, in other words, and now he got to lie in it—an expression one of his high-school teachers had liked using on him. *Look at me now, teach.*

He stood in the shallow end, up to his waist, eyes on Bliss Sherman's ass, curving up out of the water as she touched the far end, turned. He saw she was wearing goggles; he hadn't imagined goggles, but they made it better somehow, like high heels on a stripper. Another sign of his intelligence, to make that connection. And now, with Bliss almost upon him, just two or three strokes away, he recalled a fragment of a strange cartoon he'd seen on TV, late-night Mexican TV and him maybe tweaked a bit on crystal meth, which was probably why it was no more than a fragment. Some cartoon animal, a duck or a cat, was swimming in a pool like this one, when all of a sudden from the filter outlet came slithering the arm of a giant squid, wrapping round the little critter in coils that left nothing but the webbed feet sticking out. Must have been a duck, then.

Freedy put his hands on his hips. Bliss took one last stroke, then touched. But she didn't feel that cold tile at the end of the pool, oh no. Her fingertips brushed his dick instead. Couldn't have been more perfect. Life was full of fascinating shit, if you just made a little effort. Forget about porn. This was better than any porn he'd ever seen: and he was in it!

Her head jerked up then, and as he'd imagined, her eyes, behind the goggles, opened wide, and her mouth opened wide too, and her face went through exciting changes. Everything as he'd foreseen. Freedy started to smile, a friendly, manly smile, as though they were sharing some mutual joke. Like: *hey, you were in the middle of daydreaming about ol' Mr. Dick here, and now—abracadabra*. That kind of joke. Sophisticated.

But she forgot to say *what a coincidence*, or even the less stylish *I was just thinking about you*. Instead she sprang back quickly into deeper water, deep enough so that her breasts floated on the surface, and sounded almost annoyed or something when she said, "What the hell do you think you're doing?"

"Sharing your dreams, babe." Now if that wasn't smooth, if that wasn't cool, what was? Freedy knew very well it was the kind of remark that made women melt. He had said something like it to Estrella on their date last week, and she had melted, by God.

But Bliss didn't melt, at least not in any way he knew about. She raised her voice, not a pleasant voice to begin with, he now realized, and said: "Get the fuck off my property."

Women were crazy and men were stupid—where had he heard that? *Hard Copy,* maybe. There was some truth in it, but not all men were stupid. Some were just the opposite, some knew that female craziness could be controlled by the use of the right physical . . . something. He couldn't come up with the right word, but he knew the right physical something to use in this case. Besides, he liked when women said *fuck.*

Bliss had moved back quickly, but it wasn't what would be called quick in terms of what someone like Freedy could do. He was quick on a big-league scale, quick like one of those NBA guards. And he was a man, after all—with andro and crystal meth in reserve—and men were plain quicker than women in the first place, weren't they?

They were. Or at least this man was quicker than this woman. Before she knew it, even before he knew it, to tell the truth, Freedy had closed the distance between them and grabbed one of those floating breasts. Not *grabbed.* Wrong word—it was much gentler than that, more like the kind of semirough stuff that drove Estrella, for example, wild.

At first Freedy thought it was having the same effect on Bliss, from the way she was screaming. That was the freaky thing about Estrella, or that other girl from Riverside, her name escaping him at the moment. They flat-out screamed with pleasure. But this scream, Bliss's scream, went on a little too long, and there was nothing pleasant about it. She really had an irritating voice. And what was this? She'd bit his arm or something? Bit him? Not a sex kind of bite, but a hurting bite. Like she was resisting. Like she hadn't been dreaming the dream.

And also this funny taste. Blood in his mouth? Meaning he'd bitten her back? Yes, her tit was bleeding, but not much, not much more than Estrella's when they were having a little fun that night after the Marilyn Manson pay-per-view.

But this woman, this woman with the name that didn't fit, was no Estrella, and that screaming was horrible. Freedy did what the hero always had to do to stop hysteria, swatting her a crisp one across the face.

Didn't work. Bliss kept screaming, higher and higher, making him want to shut her off immediately, the way he would if he'd been flicking the remote and come across one of those opera singers with the screeching voices. Freedy reared back to give her another one, and would have, but someone yelled, "Stop."

A third person. Woman, also with an irritating voice. Freedy looked around, spotted her on the second-floor balcony of the house, a younger woman, his own age or even a few years less, wearing boxers and a sleeveless T-shirt. Dynamite bod, better than Bliss's but a lot like it at the same time. Hair all rumpled, like she'd just got out of bed. And the part that didn't fit: a gun in her hand. Not a little toy, either, but a fucking monster. What was wrong with these people? His hard-on, which had been throbbing underwater like some kind of pumped-up eel, failed completely.

"Stop," said the woman on the balcony again. Her gun hand was shaking, but the gun was on him, more or less.

Freedy put his hands in the air, not high, but visible. "Everything's cool," he said. "Just a consensual misunderstanding."

Bliss, crying, or sobbing, climbed out of the pool, her naked body all exposed as she hoisted herself over the side, but not a turn-on at all, maybe even the opposite, in a funny way like those naked Auschwitz people.

"What should I do, Mom?" said the woman on the balcony.

"Don't let him move," she said, her voice now up in opera territory. Hysterical, no doubt about it. "Don't let the pervert move. I'm calling the police." And she stumbled across the patio and into the house.

Freedy looked up at Bliss's daughter. "This is way overblown."

"You're moving," she said. "Don't. I took marksmanship at camp."

Freedy nodded, kept moving, angling toward the corner of the pool nearest the house. At that end of the patio stood a table shaded by a big umbrella. If he could get out of the water, get behind the umbrella, at least she wouldn't be able to see him. Then somehow to cross the open space between the umbrella and the corner of the house. Okay: that was the strategy.

"You're moving," said the girl.

Freedy held his hands higher now, palms open. He gave her his best smile: he had big white teeth, a dazzling smile, like a movie star, but all natural. "I'm not. Honest." He kept moving.

The gun went off; Freedy couldn't believe she'd actually fired it on purpose. Something smacked the water right beside him at the same moment. Then he was on the patio, running low behind the umbrella. A stupid time to get stung by a bee, but he felt it in his thigh. Then he saw the rip in the umbrella, heard the pop of the gun. Or maybe he'd got it in the wrong order. Didn't matter; in a few strides he was around the house, had scooped up his boots and his cutoffs, jumped in the van, goosed it. And zoom.

Ten minutes later he was bumper-to-bumper on the PCH, like any other citizen, except he wasn't wearing anything and his right outer thigh was bleeding, front and back. But not heavily, more of a seeping than bleeding, and front and back had to be good, had to mean the slug had gone right through. No biggie. In fact, the whole little adventure didn't amount to much. A misunderstanding, like he'd said. And since they weren't even on the schedule, it hadn't really happened, at least not in terms of anything that counted, such as A-1 and his job. Freedy narrowed his eyes, thought hard. Bliss had assumed he was from their regular pool company. Had she seen the van? No. So any investigation would lead to a dead end. And since no real crime had been committed, it would stop there. Plenty of real crimes for the cops to solve. This was LA. Like his mother often said, especially when she was a little stoned: "If a tree falls in the forest and there's no one there to hear it, does it make a sound?" She was a sucker for philosophical puzzles like that. The Shermans weren't on the schedule. That meant no one in the forest, and no sound.

So it was a normal day. Except for that word *pervert:* what a disgusting thing to say.

Freedy turned into a Rite-Aid, pulled on his cutoffs, gently, although he was barely bleeding now, and checked the schedule. The Goldmans—maybe best to skip them this week—and then some other people up Las Flores. He was five minutes away, would be early, if anything. Nothing to do now but buy bandages, tape himself up, a normal worker on a normal day. Elementary, my dear Watson. Smiling to himself, Freedy had put on his boots and was opening the door when his beeper went off.

His leg began to throb at once, from hip to toe, with an intensity that made him say, "Oh, fuck," out loud. A woman loading groceries into a Saab convertible glanced back at him. He closed the door.

Freedy checked the number on the beeper: the office. He sat in the van, taking deep breaths, balling his hands tight, trying to control the pain. Then he remembered the meth, less than a teaspoonful probably, in a twist of foil under the seat. Or in the glove box. Or under the other fucking seat. In his rage, he punched something, hard. The cover popped off the ashtray and there was the meth. Abracadabra. A pinch in each nostril, snort snort, zipped an energy dart up his nose into his brain, through his whole body.

Much better. He corrected that rage thing right away. He hadn't been in a rage, more like frustration. Rage wasn't cool. Freedy went to a pay phone and called in.

"A-1," said one of the office girls.

"Hi there," said Freedy. "Freedy."

"Oh. A moment."

Freedy heard some muffled talking back at the office, but he wasn't really listening. Instead he stared at the sky, a beautiful blue sky with a lone airplane in it, towing a Marlboro-man banner.

"Freedy?" The boss—not the manager, but the boss. A spic too, but he spoke good English, almost like an American.

"Yup," said Freedy.

"Where are you at this moment, Freedy?" said the boss. He pronounced it *Friddy,* one of the only giveaways that he was a spic.

"At a pay phone."

"Where is the pay phone?"

"You mean with some precision?" Freedy said, just to show him what a real American could do with the language.

"I do."

"Hard to say," said Freedy, "since I'm kind of en route at the moment."

"From where?"

"Wherever the schedule says. I'm always on schedule, you know that."

"It says the Goldmans, on Piuma."

"Then it was the Goldmans."

Pause. "There's been a slight schedule change, Freedy."

"Oh yeah?"

"So the best thing would be to return to the office."

"The office?"

"Something's come up. A big job. Bonuses all around if we're done by nightfall."

"So why don't I go right wherever it is and get started?" But Freedy was just playing now. He knew it was bullshit; bonuses never happened.

"Because I want you to take the compressor."

"Right," said Freedy.

"Pardon?"

"I said right. I'm on my way." Freedy hung up.

He got back in the van, took two more hits, had a little think, as his mother used to say. He was thinking very clearly, as he always did on meth: different from his mother, the clearly part. Right away he thought about Las Vegas, where he'd never been and always wanted to go. What better time? First he'd stop by his apartment, where he had three hundred dollars in the freezer and a bag of meth. Then drive as far as Bakersfield, say, before abandoning the van and hopping on a bus to Vegas. There: a plan, simple, like all good plans.

Nothing went wrong with the plan until he turned onto Lincoln, about a block from his place. Freedy had a room over a furniture store on the east side. Parked in front of the furniture store was a cruiser. Two more across the street, and a Paki, that would be the furniture store owner, his landlord, was talking to a cop on the sidewalk. Talking with his fucking hands. That's when it occurred to Freedy that this was a funny kind of speed. Usually he went fast and the world slowed down around him, making it easy to control. This time the world was cranking too.

Freedy spun the wheel, threw the van into a shrieking U-turn, just like the stunt driver whose pool he cleaned on Fridays. In the rearview, he caught a cop glancing up as he floored it. Or maybe not.

But the van—painted the color of the sea, with waves breaking over the fenders—had to go. His own car, his own fucking heap, was in the lot at the office, so that was out. Which left Estrella. She had a Kia, or some shitbox, that she washed and polished twice a week—one of the irritating things about her. Freedy hadn't been seeing Estrella as much lately, had been getting interested in another waitress in the same place, actually, who worked days like he did instead of nights like Estrella. But it was daytime now, and Estrella would be home.

She had a one-bedroom in Reseda, a garden apartment, meaning the entrance was off the alley. The pain was coming back, or at least Freedy thought it might, so he took two more snorts, moderate ones, and popped an andro before getting out of the van. Couldn't hurt. He crossed the alley, heart going pitty-pat, real fast, went through the space where a gate must have been at one time, into the dusty yard.

Across the yard, Estrella stood in her doorway. She rose on her tiptoes to kiss the cheek of a big guy who had his arm around her. A big guy with black hair like Estrella's and copper skin like Estrella's. He wore a white shirt and a black tie, and carried a suitcase. A jolt went through Freedy, as though he'd downshifted at ninety miles an hour. The cause was a combination of things—amazingly, he had that insight into himself even as he took off, but he was an amazing person—and her sleeping with spics was part of it, for sure. He had the grace to admit it.

They looked up. Did Estrella start to smile at the sight of him? He'd got her a good one before he knew. Then the big guy shouted something, "Hey," maybe, and tried to push him away, or hit him or something. Mistake. The top blew off at that point, like one of those oil well gushers, except it was red. Not long after, maybe seconds, the big guy was on the ground and Estrella was kneeling over him, tears, the whole bit.

"Don't expect any sympathy from me, you whore," said Freedy.

She gave him a strange look, although it was hard to tell since her face was already swelling up. "Mi hermano," she cried. "Mi hermano." Or some gibberish like that.

Freedy walked away, silent as Clint Eastwood after a town

square gunfight. Overhead the sky was coppery, much the same as Estrella's skin. The blue sky was on the rich side of town. Freedy had another insight: California sucked.

That night, on a bus to Vegas, Freedy had time to reflect. He felt pretty good, considering. His leg hurt, but nothing he couldn't control. He wore new jeans and a new western-style shirt, bought with Vegas in mind. That wad of money on Bliss Sherman's front seat? Turned out to be $650. Win some, lose some. Not a completely bad day. Call it mixed.

His most important accomplishment had been spiritual, if that was the word. He'd realized that California was not for him. That meant it was time to regroup, to center himself. Spiritual, centering: his mother's lingo. She'd been popping into his mind all day. Was there a reason for that? He thought for the first time of going home. He'd told himself he never would, but how could a week or two hurt? Home cooking, lying up for a while, sleep: what was wrong with that?

In Vegas he picked up a schedule. He'd flown out to California on a coast-to-coast one-way ticket from his mother—high-school graduation present, although a few lost credits kept him from walking with his class. The bus route back wasn't as simple: Vegas to Denver. Denver to Omaha. Omaha to Chicago. Chicago to Cleveland. Cleveland to Buffalo. Buffalo to Albany. Albany to Pittsfield. Pittsfield to Inverness.

Freedy caught the midnight bus to Chicago and soon fell asleep. He awoke to the sound of low voices, speaking Spanish across the aisle.

"Hey," said Freedy.

"Yes?"

"Is there some word, sounds like *hermano*?"

"Si. Hermano."

"What's it mean?"

"Brother."

Had Estrella ever mentioned a brother? Now that he thought

about it, maybe she had; an accountant, or something surprising like that, in Tijuana. In case there'd been a misunderstanding, Freedy decided not to dime her out to the INS, which had been his plan. That was his sensitive side coming into play again.

3

Nietzsche says of the New Testament: "a species of rococo taste in every respect." Using the Christmas story as text, attack or defend in an essay of no more than two double-spaced pages.
—Assignment one, Philosophy 322

The shortest day of the year and therefore the latest dawn, but still it came too soon for Nat. Hunched over his desk in room seventeen on the second floor of Plessey Hall, head almost touching the gooseneck lamp whose similar posture had been mocking him all night, he tried to read faster. The problem was that chapter nine of *Introduction to Macroeconomic Theory: A Post-Keynesian Approach for a Global Polity,* like all the chapters that had gone before it, resisted fast reading. Three times, each slower than the last, he tried and failed to take in "with or without ignoring the realization that a deficit or surplus in the current account cannot be explained or evaluated without simultaneous explanation of an equal surplus or deficit in the capital account." What kind of sentence contained two *withouts*? The words quivered on the page, threatened to change into something else, mere shapes, although interesting ones: he found himself gazing at a *z*. An unreliable letter, threatening in some obscure way, even unforgiving, or was all that merely the result of its comparative rarity, or association with Zorro?

Association with Zorro? Nat sat back in his chair. What

26

was going on in his mind? What was wrong with him? He'd never studied this hard, at the same time never had a shakier grip on the material, never felt his mind wandering so much. If at all, he began, then stopped himself, aware that he was about to wander some more. He rose, rubbing his eyes, and gazed out his window. Dawn, all over the place. He could almost feel the earth spinning him toward that economics exam.

"They're shooting again," he said.

No answer.

Turning, he saw that his roommate had fallen asleep on the couch, chem lab notes stacked high on his stomach. "Wags, wake up."

Wags was silent. Nat went over to him. Wags looked terrible, face unshaven and blotchy, hair wild and oily, eyelids and the pockets under his eyes uniformly dark, as though he'd been using some sort of deathly makeup. But Wags's instructions had been not to let him fall asleep under any circumstances. How long had he been sleeping? Nat didn't know. He touched Wags's shoulder. "Wags."

Nothing. Nat shook his shoulder gently—Wags felt hot—and when gently didn't work, harder.

Wags smiled, a silvery thread of drool escaping from the corner of his mouth. His eyes remain closed, but he spoke. "I was having the sweetest dream."

"What about?"

"Can't remember. Helicopters? It's collapsing in little pieces down the sides of my brain." Wags's concentration on whatever was happening inside his head was so intense that Nat felt his own mind focusing too, without result. Suddenly Wags's eyes snapped open and he sat up abruptly—Nat could smell him—scattering lab notes all over the floor. "My God. What time is it?"

"After seven."

"After seven? In the morning? Then I'm totally fucked."

He plunged to the floor, snatching up lab notes by the handful, pausing once to glare at Nat. "You want me to flunk out, don't you?"

"Right," said Nat. "And then all this will be mine."

All this: the cramped outer room with their desks, computers, the couch, the cigarette-scorched hardwood floor, and off it the two bedrooms barely big enough for the beds. Wags laughed, a single bark, brief and unhappy.

"They're shooting again," Nat told him.

Wags got up, went to the window. "Just getting some establishing shots," he said. It was the fourth or fifth film crew on the quad since September—filmmakers in need of an ideal college campus came to Inverness—and Wags had become an expert on their movements, mixing with the crews when he could and even landing a role as an extra in a made-for-TV movie about a fraternity brother in need of a bone marrow transplant, scheduled for broadcast in the spring. "Wait a minute," he said, leaning closer to the window, leaving another oily nose print on the glass. His voice rose. "Is that Marlo Thomas?"

Nat closed the economics book, shut off the gooseneck lamp, went down the hall to the shower. Wags stayed watching at the window, crumpled lab notes in both hands.

After the exam—it had gone better than he'd expected—Nat went to the gym and took his hundred free throws, hitting ninety-one, despite how drained he was. The best he'd done since coming to the school: no explaining it. As he sank the last one, *swish,* barely disturbing the net, he realized that his answer to the last question had been completely wrong. Monetarism had nothing to do with it, completely irrelevant; they'd wanted all that current and capital account stuff, the two *withouts.* An essay question, worth one-third of the total grade. The mark of Zorro: he'd done not better than he'd expected, but worse, much worse. He hadn't pushed himself, not hard enough, not nearly.

Nat stood at the foul line, bouncing the ball. The workload, the speed, how smart everyone was. He thought of Arapaho State, where Patti was getting straight A's, and where he could be playing on the team instead of entering data in the fund-raising office every afternoon for $5.45 an hour. He thought of the Inverness varsity, whose home games he had watched—they were now one and three—knowing he was good enough to play for them; not start, maybe, but get in for more than garbage time. He thought of his street, his house, the kitchen, his mom.

The sudden feeling that someone was watching him made him turn. Not only was no one watching him, but the gym was empty. He'd never seen it like that before. No one on the court, jogging on the track above, lifting behind the glass walls of the weight room. He went into the lobby, also deserted, looked through the floor-to-ceiling windows at the Olympic-sized pool. Empty too, the water still.

Outside the same thing: not a person on the quad except him, not a sound from the surrounding dorms—no hip-hop, no techno or industrial, no Lilith Fair. For a moment he felt light-headed. Was he coming down with something? Then it hit him. This morning was the last period on the exam schedule. The departure of the students, the teachers, even the film crew, all vanishing at once like characters in a fairy tale, probably happened just this way every Christmas.

The church bell—the top of the chapel tower visible over the gold-domed roof of Goodrich Hall, weathervane pointing north—tolled the hour. At the same time, a cold wind began to blow; from the west, Nat noticed, despite the weathervane. No snow had fallen yet, but everyone said the Inverness Valley was one of the snowiest places in the east. Nat looked up, saw a line of clouds closing over the sky.

He wasn't going anywhere for Christmas. There'd been money for only one trip home that semester, and he'd chosen Thanksgiving, although it was shorter, because Patti's birthday had been the day after. He crossed the quad and went into

Baxter to check his mail. Standing before the rows of brass letter boxes, he realized he was still holding the basketball.

Nat put it down, turned the dial to J3, took out a letter.

Dear Nat

I'm so sorry about that little insident at Julie's party. I don't know what came over me. I'll never drink like that again. For sure. You were so great about it. At least that's what Julie said the next day. Joke. Everythings ok but I miss you so much and not looking forward to Xmas at all.

One ot~~her thing I think I missed my period—but don't worry I may be just got mixed up~~

I love you soooo much.

Patti

ps—my present should be there by now.

Nat reached back into the box, found a small package. He took it back to the dorm. Wags's lab notes still lay all over the floor of the outer room. Nat heard voices in Wags's bedroom, glanced in the open door. No Wags. Clothes trailing over everything, and the TV on. One of those movie channels Wags liked to watch. An actor from the thirties or forties whose name Wags would know at once but Nat didn't stared thoughtfully into his glass while an offscreen actress asked what they were doing that night. Nat smelled coffee, noticed a steaming cup on the windowsill, half full. He left the TV on, went to his own bedroom, put Patti's gift on the bed.

Tacked on the wall was a list of what he wanted to accomplish during the holiday:

clean room
laundry
write home
work out
get to know town and surroundings
→on next semester

That last one being the most important: Nat had registered

for an American novel course that required reading a book a week, and he'd never keep up, would fall behind in everything, without a head start. Book one, *Young Goodman Brown and Other Stories,* already borrowed from the library, was waiting on the orange crate that served as his bedside table.

Nat sat on the bed, picked up the book, but first reread Patti's letter. He tried to see what she'd crossed out, partially distinguishing only one word—*kissed, pissed,* or *missed*—but nothing else. He swung his feet up on the bed, overcame the urge to take off his sneakers. No time for sleep: two hundred pages of *Young Goodman Brown and Other Stories* before dinner was the goal. He read the letter one more time. There, in the center of all those unusual silences—his room, the dorm, the whole campus—he could almost hear Patti's voice. What had happened at Julie's party didn't bother him at all; what bothered him was the spelling. That, and the way she dotted the *i* in her name with a heart. Had she always? If so, it hadn't mattered before. Why should it matter now?

Nat opened *Young Goodman Brown.* The title page showed a woodcut of a young man striding down a country road. Someone had drawn a bottle of beer in his hand and a fat joint in his mouth. Nat turned the page.

Young Goodman Brown came forth at sunset into the street at Salem village. . . .

Nat opened his eyes. It was dark. His gaze went to the window, but there was no window, at least not where he was looking. He'd forgotten he wasn't in his bedroom at home. Rolling over, he checked the clock, read the numbers— 11:37—but before he could make sense of them he heard footsteps in the outer room.

"Wags?" he called, but his throat was thick with sleep; he cleared it and tried again. "Wags?" At that moment he remembered that he'd been leaning out of a helicopter in his dream.

Silence from the other room. Then the door to the hall closed. 11:37 P.M. Wouldn't Wags be home in Pittsburgh by now? Not Pittsburgh exactly, but someplace nearby called Sewickley, as Wags's parents had mentioned a couple of times on the Parents' Day visit in October, the significance lost on Nat at the time. Since then he'd learned that the country hid a network of Sewickleys with names like Greenwich, Chagrin Falls, Dover, Lake Forest, Grosse Pointe; that many students at Inverness came from those places; that Wags knew people they knew, and they knew people he knew.

He sat up. Had the door to the hall simply closed, or had it been something else, more of a slam? Nat rose, switched on the lights, peered into the outer room, saw everything as it had been earlier, Wags's lab notes still strewn on the floor, the screen savers of both computers in motion. He opened the door.

A man was walking away toward the stairs at the far end of the hall, a big man carrying something heavy. Nat took in a ponytail swinging behind his head and an electrical cord trailing between his legs, two dangling things that his half-sleeping mind, still following the logic of dreams, tried to relate. By the time he realized there was no relationship other than the visual one he'd seen at first glance, the man had disappeared down the stairs. Nat went back into Wags's bedroom. Wags's TV was gone.

Nat ran into the hall, yelled, "Hey!" He kept running, fully awake now, down the stairs to the first floor. No one there, but he picked up the sound of descending footsteps. Nat followed, heard the clicking of hard shoes on the old brick floor of the basement corridor. He yelled "Hey" again, took the last flight in one leap, swung around the banister post into the basement corridor. No one there.

Nat went down the corridor, slowing because it ended at a padlocked steel door with the word *Maintenance* stenciled on the front. He walked back the way he had come, passing three other padlocked doors, all of which he knew led to storage lockers for the students, and came to another door, lockless. Nat stood in front of that door. He sensed someone on the other side, tried to think of a way he could summon security and stand guard at the same time. Then came a jolt of adrenaline, and he jerked the door open.

A janitor's closet, full of brooms, mops, buckets, cleansers. Even empty, it wasn't big enough for a man with a television, especially one the size of Wags's. Nat closed the door, went back along the corridor, trying all the padlocks. Fastened, every one.

Nat stayed in the basement corridor for a minute or two, listening for a sound, waiting for something to happen. Nothing did.

He went upstairs, along the first floor to the main entrance of the dorm. Had he imagined those footsteps on the brick floor, or misinterpreted some sound he had heard? It was one or the other. Nat opened the door to the quad. Surprise.

White. White everywhere: snow had fallen while he slept, fallen heavily, although it wasn't snowing now, and the stars shone bright. A foot of snow, maybe more, deep, crisp, even. It bent the branches of the old oaks, gave the statue of Emerson a hulking, steroidal profile, rounded the dorm entry pediments and other architectural features whose names Nat was starting to learn: pure, unmarred whiteness, glowing under the old Victorian lampposts as though lit from below.

Nat called campus security from his room and was told to file a report in the morning. He locked the door to the hall, went into Wags's bedroom, took in the disarray, no worse than before, and the coffee cup on the windowsill, still half full but now cold, satisfied himself that nothing else was missing. Back in the outer room, he picked up Wags's lab notes and piled them neatly on his desk, even trying to arrange them in some sort of order.

Nat sat on the couch that Bloomingdale's had delivered after the visit of Wags's parents and reopened *Young Goodman*

Brown. This time he followed Goodman Brown out of Salem to his meeting in the forest with what Nat supposed was the devil. He paused at the sentence "But he was himself the chief horror of the scene, and shrank not from its other horrors." Nat read it several times and was reaching for his yellow highlighter when he thought: *unmarred*.

Snow unmarred. And therefore? Nat went downstairs, out to the quad. The night was cold and still, the only movement his own rising breath. He circled the dorm, snow up to his knees, sometimes higher. The only footprints were his, a shadow-filled trench he tramped around the building like a moat in miniature. His feet, still in the sneakers he'd slept in, got cold and then cold and wet. Other than that, no result. Back in his room, he called security again.

This time he reached a recording that gave him a choice between voice mail and an emergency number. Was this an emergency? No footprints except his own: didn't that mean the thief was still in the dorm, and had been there before the snowfall? A student, then, some other student still on campus, like him, possibly a resident of the dorm, and therefore a freshman, like him, possibly without money to go home, like him. Better to find him in the morning, get him to return the TV without a fuss, without involving security. Nat hung up the phone.

Were there any freshmen who looked like that, big with ponytails? Nat couldn't recall any, but there were five hundred people in the class, many he still hadn't even seen. He flipped through the freshman directory, useless because he'd had only a back view of the thief. He came to his own picture— the graduation picture, wearing Mr. Beaman's blazer—knew with certainty that he didn't look at all like that anymore. He checked in the mirror and found that he did.

Nat thought of calling Wags in Sewickley, but it was almost one, and he could imagine Wags's mother picking up the phone. He made sure the front door was locked, took off his wet shoes, put them on the radiator to dry, and went to bed.

Nat's mother had a funny story she liked to tell about him. When Nattie was very young, before he could talk, he couldn't bear to go to sleep if any of the dresser drawers in his room were open, even a crack. She didn't always remember to close them, and would sometimes poke her head in the room to find him laboriously climbing out of his crib and crawling across the floor toward the dresser. Nat thought of this story about half an hour later when he gave up on sleep, unlocked the door, and stepped into the hall.

Plessey Hall had three floors, ten rooms on each, most of them doubles, a few triples, and a single for the RA. Nat started at number thirty on the third floor. He checked for light leaking under the door, listened for any sound, knocked, tried the knob. No light, no sound, no answer to his knock, door locked. All the rooms were just like that down to number one, except for seventeen, his own.

Nat went back to bed, first locking the door. He turned his face to the wall and closed his eyes. Once, climbing out of his crib, he'd somehow tangled the back of his Dr. Denton's on the corner of the guardrail and hung there outside the crib, not strangling or anything, but helpless. He'd heard his parents shouting at each other in the next room. That was Nattie's earliest memory.

The next time Nat looked at his bedside clock, it read 10:23. He got out of bed, feeling stiff and sore, as though he'd played some contact sport the previous day, and went to the outer room. Through the window, he saw a morning that could have been painted in a few dull colors: dark gray for the sky and trees, brownish red for the bricks, light gray for the snow, for Emerson, for everything else. One more detail: the footprints. Hard-packed, they caught what little light there was, and shone white. Footprints coming and going at the Plessey entrance, crisscrossing between the dorms, meandering over the quad; footprints everywhere. There were even some ski and snowshoe tracks, also white. Had the quad really been unmarred hours before? Nat went into Wags's bedroom and found the TV still gone. Daytime made it conclusive.

Nat dressed and went outside, headed for the campus security office. A silent campus: as beautiful as in the brochure, but there was more—a sense of gravity, importance, even power—that the brochure, perhaps trying to be friendly, hadn't conveyed. Nat told himself he was glad to have this time alone. He needed to catch up with himself, if that made sense. The workload, the assignments, the expectations of the teachers: all so demanding, but the real pressure came from the kids. So smart; and so cool, some of them, which was very different from home, where smart and cool were almost always opposites. And here the others, the not so cool, could be strange and fascinating—like Wags, for example, with the little shrine he'd built to Alfred Hitchcock, and the way Nat would sometimes hear him late at night, lying in bed and muttering whole scenes of movie dialogue from memory. So even as the sky darkened still more while he crossed the quad, draining what little color there was and lowering the temperature in seconds, Nat told himself this solitary Christmas would be good.

That thought was still in his mind when he saw he wasn't quite alone. Across the quad, the main door to Lanark Hall— the residence opposite Plessey, the nicest, by reputation, although Nat had never been inside—opened. Two girls came out—women's studies majors spoke of women and men, but everyone else on campus said girls and guys—sidestepped down the broad snowy stairs facing each other, carrying something. Nat thought TV at once, because of the mission he was on, and from the way they carried it. The problem was its invisibility. There was nothing to see. Were they pretending to carry something? Was it some sort of pantomime? Nat was about to look around for the film crew when one of the girls lost her footing. He heard a little cry; then the girls were tumbling down the steps, one after the other, a flurry of kicking legs, waving arms, flapping scarves, airborne hats. The object they carried, now free, spun in the air, became visible: an aquarium. It spilled its water in one perfectly shaped wave, a wave topped by a bar of gold.

Everything came crashing down. But no. That was what Nat, moving unconsciously closer as though responding to something gravitational, expected. In fact, only the aquarium crashed. Somehow the two girls landed on their feet, like gymnasts, but without the posturing. He lost sight of the gold object.

The next moment the girls were both on their knees, digging through the snow. Nat reached them in time to hear one say, "Here's the little bastard."

"Gentle," said the other one.

The first girl held up the object in both hands, and Nat saw what it was: a fish. A fish, but unlike any fish, or any living thing, he'd ever seen: a dazzling creature, fat and gold with a wide yellow-lipped mouth, now opening and closing desperately, round yellow eyes, indigo fins, and white polka dots from head to its blue-and-gold tail. A dazzling creature that seemed to contain in its little form all the color lacking in the day.

"Whatever we do better be quick," said the one holding the fish.

The aquarium lay shattered, the water it had contained now a melting depression in the snow.

"Bathtub?" said the second girl.

"Fresh water," said the first girl. "Might as well be poison."

"Then think of something."

"That's my role."

"Not now, Grace, for Christ's sake."

They glanced around, as though seeking help, but didn't seem to see Nat. The fish chose that moment to make a violent flipping motion, flying free. Nat was ready. He caught it in his cupped hands and said: "The bio lab."

Now they saw him. "Where's that?" They said it in unison. Nat didn't reply, partly because the route was complicated, mostly because of how stunned he was by their appearance: one—Grace—light blond, the other darkerhaired, both—he couldn't find the right word, something as absolute as amazing, astonishing, beautiful, but more precise.

He did know where the bio lab was; he was taking a biology course to keep his premed option open. Sticking to the beaten footprint tracks and then the plowed paths, he took off as fast as he could with the fish in his hands—around Lanark, up the hill to the chapel, down the other side past the new science complex, across the old quad to the bio lab building. Nat was a good runner, but one girl passed him on the stairs in time to hold the door open, and the other was right beside him.

Nat ran down the dark-paneled first-floor hall. The bio labs were in the oldest building on campus, originally the entire college, later the science building, now closed off except for the first floor. The labs themselves, lining the hall, had thick wooden doors with windows in them, and he'd peered through them all in the first weeks of the semester.

"Here," he said at the end of the hall, and one of the girls banged the door open. The fish was no longer wriggling in his hands, not moving at all; it was coated in some sort of invisible slime, but Nat could feel the rough scales underneath. He went straight to the dozen numbered tanks on the counter at the back wall, began lowering the fish into the nearest one.

"He can't be with other fish," said one of the girls; the darker-haired one.

"He can't be with other fish?"

"Not ones he doesn't know. They might hurt him."

Nat glanced in the tank, saw three brown fish, half the size of the gaudy one, checked the other tanks, all occupied. "Is that something scientific, or just a feeling?"

"Blah, blah, blah," said the lighter-haired girl, Grace. She leaned over the aquarium, scooped out the three brown fish with her hand, flipped them into the next tank. "Dump him in," she said to Nat. He had never seen eyes like hers in his life.

"Not so fast," said the darker-haired girl, dipping her finger in the water, tasting. She nodded to him, finger still between her lips. Nat saw eyes unlike any he had ever seen until moments ago. The fish slipped from his hands, fell into the tank.

"For God's sake," said Grace.

"Sorry."

"He's sensitive, that's all," said the darker-haired one.

The fish sank down in the water, floated there, but upside down.

"Swim," said the darker-haired one.

But the fish just hung upside down in the tank. Grace reached in, turned him over, swam him vigorously back and forth.

"You're hurting him," said the darker-haired girl.

"Zip it, Izzie," said Grace.

Izzie bit her lip. Grace gave the fish a big push and let go. He drifted forward for a moment, listed to one side, almost capsized. Then one indigo fin began making tentative fanning movements, the blue-and-gold tail flicked to one side, back again, and the fish stabilized itself and swam with increasing strength to the middle of the tank, sending a hazy jet of fecal matter to the bottom.

"You stud, Lorenzo," said Grace.

"The Magnificent," Nat said.

They both turned to him, their eyes somewhat similar in color to Lorenzo's, but toned down.

"How did you know that?" said Izzie.

"It fits."

"I meant how do you know about Lorenzo the Magnificent?"

Nat shrugged; it was just one of those things he knew. Their eyes narrowed on him. "What's your name?" They spoke together, didn't appear to notice the overlap.

Nat told them.

"Well, Nat," said Grace. "I guess we—"

"Thanks," said Izzie.

"Yeah," said Grace. "Thanks."

"He means a lot to us," said Izzie. "We caught him."

"You caught him?"

"Grace did," Izzie said.

"But Izzie kept the sharks at bay."

"The sharks?"

"With her bangstick."

"You're making this up," said Nat.

"Why do you say that?" said Grace. "Sharks are wicked off Bora Bora, common knowledge."

"But thanks, is the point," said Izzie.

"Right," said Grace. "You saved the goddamn day." She reached into the pocket of her jeans, pulled out a wad of bills, removed some without counting or even looking, held them out.

"What's this?" said Nat. He felt his face reddening.

Grace turned to Izzie. "Not enough?" she said in a stage whisper.

Her eyes on Nat, Izzie said: "I think we've made a—"

"—mistake?" said Grace. She turned to Nat. "You're not maintenance or something?"

"I'm a student, actually." That sounded so stiff, but was how he felt.

"Yikes. What year?"

"Freshman."

"Oh, God," said Izzie. "We almost tipped a classmate."

"Not PC," said Grace; and then to Nat: "Well, do you want it?"

They all laughed, Nat as hard as the girls, although he was aware of, and despising, the little part of him that did want the money. He reddened some more. Izzie stopped laughing; then Grace.

"Sorry," Grace said, putting the money back in her pocket.

"Very," said Izzie.

"Hey," said Nat.

An awkward moment. Their gazes all went to Lorenzo, the path of least resistance. He fluttered his fins.

"Will anyone mind if we borrow this one little tank?" Izzie said. "We've got to get Lorenzo home for Christmas."

"I guess not," said Nat, turning to the adjacent tank in time to see the remains of the three brown fish spiraling slowly to the bottom, milky gobbets trailing black nerves and threads of blood. A single pink fish, smaller than what any of the brown ones had been in life, was swimming lazily around the tank. There was a silence.

"Maybe we should leave a note," Nat said.

"Saying what?" said Grace.

Izzie patted his arm. Her hand felt neither warm nor cool, meaning they were at exactly the same temperature, a thought he probably would have had nowhere else but in the bio lab. "We'll bring back some brown ones after vacation," she said.

Nat carried Lorenzo's tank out of the bio lab by himself. "Sure you don't want help?" Izzie said.

"It's not heavy." But it got heavier, and Nat was glad they were walking ahead of him, unaware that although he was carrying it, and would do so for as long as he had to, he wasn't doing it with ease. Glancing down, he caught Lorenzo shitting again.

Grace and Izzie led Nat over the hill, back to the freshman quad, around to the parking lot behind Lanark. There were two cars in the lot; the nearest was one of those second-generation Volkswagen Beetles, a very cool car in Nat's estimation, and he could easily picture them buzzing around in it. He moved toward it, but they kept going.

The second car was something Nat had seen only in movies, the kind of movies with big stars and holes in the plot. Huge and creamy—the color of farmer's cream his mom sometimes brought back from the stand on the edge of town—with the top down, despite the cold, and inside soft red leather and dark gleaming wood.

Grace held open the rear door. Nat started to set the tank on the floor, but she said, "Seat's okay," and so he put it there. The leather didn't feel like any leather he'd ever come in contact with. It was a perfect car for Lorenzo. That was what Nat thought.

But what he said was: "I thought freshmen couldn't have cars on campus." A dumb remark that came out all by itself.

"We don't," Izzie said, tearing off a length of plastic wrap and covering the tank. "We'd been home for two days before we realized we'd forgotten him."

"You had fish for supper?" Nat said.

A pause. They laughed, first Izzie, then Grace.

"Dinner," Grace said.

"But yes, that's exactly what happened," Izzie said.

They looked at him. He looked at them, saw what he probably would have seen right away if it hadn't been for the differing color of their hair: they were twins, identical even to the gold flecks in their blue-green irises, gold flecks that gave their eyes that yellow hue similar to Lorenzo's. He didn't say, *You're twins,* because he knew they must hear it all the time. A silent moment or two went by, as though to allow for the phrase to be said; Nat got the feeling they were waiting for it.

"We'd better get going," Grace said.

"You've been great," Izzie said.

"The hero du jour," Grace said, sliding in behind the wheel. Izzie sat beside her. Nat stepped away from the car, saw the *RR* on the grille. Grace started the car; it made a wonderful sound.

"Where're you headed?" said Izzie.

"Headed?"

"Where do you live? Maybe we could give you a lift."

"Plessey."

"I mean where are you going for Christmas?"

"Nowhere."

"You're a faculty kid?" Grace said.

"No," Nat said, and told them where he was from.

"Yeah?" said Grace. "Do you know Billy Duckworth? He's from around there somewhere."

"No."

"Wait a minute," Izzie said. "Are you saying you're not going home for Christmas?"

Nat nodded.

"How come?"

"It's kind of far."

The girls glanced at each other. "You're not going anywhere?"

"Not that I know of."

"You're staying *here*?" Grace said.

Nat nodded again.

"But that's insane," Izzie said.

The girls glanced at each other again. "Tell you what," Grace said.

"Yeah," said Izzie.

Why not? Nat couldn't think of a reason. True, he hardly knew them, but he hardly knew anyone at Inverness, and what better way to start? He did ask, "Shouldn't you check with your parents?"

And was told: "No problem."

He hurried back to his room—how dreary it seemed now, how much he wanted to get out—to throw a few things in his backpack, collect *Young Goodman Brown* and a few other books, get the money he kept in a shoe in his closet: $70. The list on the wall—*clean room, laundry, write home, work out, get to know town and surroundings, →on next semester*—seemed yellowed with age, but that had to be the effect of the weak light coming through the window.

"Who's this?" Izzie called from the outer room; Grace was driving the car around to the lot behind Plessey.

"My mom." Her picture was on his desk. Patti's picture

was in the bedroom. In the bedroom, out of Izzie's sight: he smothered that thought at birth.

"You look like her," Izzie was saying. "In a Y chromosome kind of way."

He found himself staring at Patti's picture. Was her smile a little forced? He'd never noticed.

"What's this thing?" Izzie called.

"A shrine to Alfred Hitchcock."

"Yeah?"

Something in her tone made him add, "It's my roommate's."

"Who's your roommate?"

Nat told her.

"Is he from Sewickley?"

"Yeah."

"Oh my God."

"Oh my God what?" he said, leaving his bedroom.

"Nothing."

But when they got to the car that was the first thing she told Grace.

"How did he get in here?" said Grace.

"He's brilliant," Nat said. "What are you talking about?"

Izzie got in the front, Nat in the back, beside Lorenzo. Grace drove out of the lot, onto Spring Street, which soon became Route 2. She stepped on the gas. Red-wrapped gifts spilled out from under the front seats.

They floated out of town, or soared, or simply zoomed, but whatever it was had nothing to do with any car ride in Nat's experience.

"How's Lorenzo?" Izzie called back.

Nat checked. Lorenzo was doing what he did, the water in his tank almost motionless. "The same."

"Quel relief."

Except for Thanksgiving, Nat hadn't been out of Inverness since his arrival, had seen little of the countryside. Now it scrolled quickly by, dark and austere, but at the same time there was something he liked about it, maybe just that it seemed so ancient. Snow began falling, tiny flakes that never landed, melted in midair by the silent blast from the many vents of the car's heating system; no one even suggested putting the top up. Nat thought of Mr. Beaman's snow globe collection; then remembered that his mom would be calling on Christmas Day.

He leaned forward into the space between the girls. Tendrils of their hair—Grace's light blond, almost silver, Izzie's darker, almost brown—blown by the wind, brushed his face from both sides. "Could we stop at the next phone booth?" he said. "I forgot to make a call."

Izzie tossed him a cell phone. He'd never used one, but of course there was nothing to it. He checked the time, dialed Mr. Beaman's office. His mom answered. Nat wanted to say, "Guess where I'm calling from?" and almost did. Instead he told her he was going to New York with friends, would call from there.

"New York City?" she said. "That's so exciting. Is it all right with the parents?"

"Yes."

"Be sure to bring them a present. And write a thank-you note after."

"Okay, Mom."

"And Nat?"

"Yes?"

"Be careful."

He heard Mr. Beaman calling her in the background. A very clear connection—Nat could even pick up the impatience in his tone.

The hero du jour. It was like one of those fairy tales where the young adventurer performs a bold deed—in this case, the rescue of Lorenzo the Magnificent—and is brought to the castle. They were crossing the George Washington Bridge, towers by the score rising before them, when Nat thought of the perfect present: a bottle of that pink wine, zinfandel, preferably a big one. Thank God he'd memorized the label.

5

In a city of towers, Nat was ready for elevators, but not this one. No buttons, for one thing; it simply began rising as the doors closed, rising from the underground garage with a speed unprecedented in his limited experience of elevators, so fast it actually scared him. He glanced at Grace and Izzie: they looked bored, the way people were supposed to look in elevators.

No buttons, but there was a Persian rug. And a Persian cat, asleep on a velvet couch that reminded Nat of pictures he'd seen of furniture at Versailles. In one corner, a tall crystal vase full of flowers; in another, a grinning marble faun missing one pointy ear; in front of the couch, a gilded table bearing a bowl of chocolates.

"Bonbon?" said Grace.

Bonbon? Despite his AP standing in French, the word mystified Nat for a second or two. "No, thanks," he said. The speed, of both the elevator and the sensory data streaming in,

48

was making him a little sick. Grace took one of the chocolates, bit off half, popped the rest into Izzie's mouth.

"Yum," said Izzie.

The doors slid open. They stepped out, Grace and Izzie first with the luggage, Nat following with Lorenzo in his tank, the Persian cat, stretching, last. "Hi, everybody," Grace called. "We're home."

Home. The elevator opened not into a corridor but the apartment itself. That was what the girls had called it: they lived with their father in an apartment in Manhattan, they'd said. Nat knew little of apartments—there were only a few apartment buildings in his town, none occupied by his friends—but he didn't associate the word with high ceilings, with a curving staircase leading up to other levels, with vastness. All of this apparent at a glance. And on the wall opposite the elevator, a painted nude, the style instantly recognizable, the signature—Renoir—somehow artistic all on its own. Probably a print—Patti had a Renoir print of two little girls combing their hair hanging in her bedroom—but Nat wasn't sure. As he came to a decision that it was indeed a print, but much better than Patti's and expertly lit, he was also dealing for the first time with the idea that Renoirs could be bought and sold, and that some people could afford them. On his way by, Nat took a close look, spotted individual brushstrokes, layers of paint on the petals of a rose, and in one corner, the texture of canvas showing through.

Grace and Izzie led Nat into a room that seemed big enough to contain his house. Set in one wall—not taking up the entire wall, but most of it—was a slab of thick glass. On the other side, a scuba diver was scrubbing the glass with a long-handled brush, bubbles rising up and out of sight. A little shark swam by in the background. Then another, not so little. Perhaps this was part of a public aquarium, Nat thought, the backstage part that paying customers never saw, some architectural anomaly, built with the cooperation of

Grace and Izzie's father. Or maybe . . . maybe what? He couldn't think of anything else.

Izzie was watching him. "I know just what's on your mind," she said.

"What?"

"But you can forget about it. Not his kind of place. Lorenzo gets the opposite of claustrophobia." She pointed to a tank Nat hadn't noticed, mounted on a pedestal—no, part of the pedestal itself, the whole thing somehow full of water. "In there, Nat."

"Please," said Grace.

Izzie gave Grace a quick look. "Yes, of course, please."

Nat hadn't felt any lack of politeness—he'd heard *please* in Izzie's tone. And she'd used his name for the first time; he didn't know the significance of that, if any, but he'd noted it.

The pedestal tank contained a single fish, a fish of Lorenzo's species, whatever that was. The two fish looked identical. Izzie found a net under the pedestal, scooped up Lorenzo, lowered him into the second tank. The fish eyed each other, defecating in unison.

"How do you know which one's him?" Nat said.

"You can't tell?" said Izzie.

"It's easy," Grace said. "The other one's store-bought. She's Lorenzo's babe."

"You're hoping they'll mate?" Nat said.

"If she's female," said Izzie.

"And if he's male," said Grace. "There's some dispute about both points right now. Dr. Diveboy—" She nodded at the scuba diver behind the glass; he beamed through his mask, waved his brush. "—can't seem to figure it out."

In the tank, Lorenzo's babe drifted behind a chunk of coral. Lorenzo fluttered his fins for a moment, then swam after her. They circled each other, changing places like cards in a close-up trick, before one swam away, which one, Nat didn't know.

"You really can't tell them apart?" Izzie said. "Just by—"

"—how they move, for one thing," said Grace.

But he couldn't.

Did Grace and Izzie, being twins, have some advantage when it came to distinguishing Lorenzo from his babe? Grace and Izzie, identical except for the hair. But there had to be differences: he knew, because he responded to them differently. That was scientific reasoning, and maybe because he'd been so recently in the bio lab, Nat began thinking in terms of an experiment. The observation part, in any case: he could make a mental list of perceived differences. For example, Izzie had a way of raising one eyebrow—the right—when asking a certain type of question, questions like *You really can't tell them apart?* Did Grace do the same thing? He would watch for it.

They climbed a wide staircase to the floor above, walked along a broad hall lined with abstract bronzes. "How about this one?" Grace said, opening a door. "Oops," she said. Nat glimpsed a man sleeping on a bed, dressed in a dinner jacket and one shiny black slipper—pump, was that the name? The other lay on the floor.

"Who's that?" said Izzie as Grace closed the door.

"No idea," said Grace. She tried another room. Empty. "How's this?"

Nat went in. "Fine," he said.

"Make yourself at home. We'll catch you later." And they went off down the hall.

Nat closed the door, laid his backpack on the bed, examined the room, the room where he'd be sleeping over Christmas, his first Christmas away from home. Fine. The room was fine, all right: the finest bedroom he'd ever seen. He pressed his hand on the bed, covered with some sort of quilted material—duvet?—and knew it would be the most comfortable bed he'd ever slept in. Then he turned to the window and saw how high he was. Everything taller in the direction he faced had a name and profile familiar to any movie-going American: the Chrysler Building, the Empire State Building, the World Trade Center. Out in the water, beyond all the towers, lay an island with a foreshortened form rising from it. The Statue of Liberty. So small from where he stood, he almost didn't recognize it. But then he did, and felt goose bumps, just the same.

Nat opened the sliding door, stepped onto the balcony. On the floor below, the first floor of Grace and Izzie's apartment, a tiled deck ran the entire width of the building. He took in small potted trees, wrought-iron furniture, a bar, a telescope, a swimming pool; and a basketball hoop. Condensation rising in thick clouds hid the surface of the pool, but Nat heard the rhythmic splashing of a swimmer beneath. Then a gust of wind tore a hole through the gray and he saw a woman doing the crawl. For a second he thought she was naked—began to step back—then realized she wore a flesh-colored bathing suit. He saw her face as she turned to breathe— a young woman, perhaps an older sister of Grace and Izzie. The clouds re-formed. Nat went inside, sat on the bed, reached for his backpack.

Someone knocked at the door.

"Yes?" Nat said.

A tall man—the kind usually called distinguished because his hair was turning silver at the sides—entered. He wore a white shirt, a dark suit, a bow tie.

Nat rose.

"Welcome to New York," the man said. "I understand you'll be vacationing with us."

"Yes, uh—"

"Excellent. The city's at its best this time of year. Is there anything you need right now?"

"Anything I need?"

"I assume you've found the bathroom? Through that second door. The television and a small fridge are in the armoire, and you can listen to whatever's on the sound system by turning the volume dial over there."

"Oh. Thanks. And thanks for having me. I hope it's all right."

"All right?"

"I mean on such short notice." Or maybe none at all. Nat went forward, held out his hand, introduced himself as he'd been trained.

"Pleased to meet you, Nat." They shook hands. "I'm Albert."

Nat, unused to calling his friends' parents by their first names, and unable to remember the last name, if the girls had told him at all, said: "Pleased to meet you, too, sir. It was very nice of your daughters to invite me."

Albert's eyebrows rose. "My—?" Then he smiled, a smile quickly erased, the mouth part, anyway. "Mr. Zorn is not due till Christmas Eve. I am Mrs. Zorn's personal assistant."

"Oh."

"So if there's anything you need, food, drink, laundry or dry cleaning service, goods from the outside world, just say."

"Thanks."

"Not at all. It's always so exciting when the girls are around. Any special dietary requirements, by the way?"

"Pardon?"

"The kitchen is very flexible."

"Good," Nat said, the first word to pop out. He felt his face grow hot.

Albert backed out of the room. Nat had the feeling the man would burst out laughing the moment the door closed, and to stop that, more than anything, he said: "There is one thing, if it wouldn't be too much trouble."

"No trouble whatever," said Albert, one heel still raised.

"I'd like to buy a bottle of wine."

"Shouldn't be necessary," Albert said. "We have quite a varied selection on the premises, if it's something specific you're interested in."

"As a gift."

"Ah. How thoughtful. Wine is something of a hobby with Mr. Zorn."

Nat wrote the name of Mr. Beaman's wine on a sheet of paper, handed it to Albert with thirty dollars, not knowing much about the cost of good wine, but sure that would be more than enough. Albert took the note only. "Why don't we settle accounts later?" he said.

Nat lay on the bed. He wasn't at all tired, felt lively, even restless, wanted to walk the streets, see the city, do what people do in new places. At the same time, some part of him was a little afraid to leave the room. He had the opposite of claustrophobia, like Lorenzo. Expandrophobia? No, there was a real word; it would come to him.

Nat rose—made himself rise, really—went to the door, put his hand on the knob, paused. Mistaking a personal assistant— was that like a servant of some kind?—for their father. Dumb. And the conversation that followed, also dumb. But he wasn't dumb. He was good at learning things. And what was the point of coming all this way for college if not for new experiences? *Crème de la crème,* Mrs. Smith had said. *Imagine the people he's going to meet.* He was meeting them now. It suddenly occurred to him that Mrs. Smith and Miss Brown, the women most responsible for his presence at Inverness, were twins, like Grace and Izzie. Was there some meaning to this? None that he could come upon by analysis. Still, he couldn't help but suspect that in some way this coincidence was a good thing, an indication that he was on the right course. Nat opened the door.

In the hall, Grace was passing by, trailed by another distinguished-looking man, somewhat younger than the first, deeply tanned, carrying a frothy blue drink in a tall glass. This time Nat made no assumptions.

"Anton, Nat," said Grace. "Nat, Anton. Anton's my stepmom's personal trainer. Nat's a friend from Inverness."

"Cool," said Anton.

Nat laughed.

"What's so funny?" Grace said. She raised an eyebrow, just like Izzie, except it was the left one.

"I was just thinking about Lorenzo."

Grace laughed too, touched his arm, said: "I know what you mean." Her touch: it felt cold, meaning there was a temperature difference, one he hadn't felt with Izzie. There were many possible variables, of course, but he noted it anyway.

He'd told Grace a little lie. It wasn't the thought of Lorenzo that had made him laugh, but the word *cool*, and this guy saying it, and the name Anton, and the frothy blue drink, and personal trainers. Things began to come together in Nat's mind: the drink, for example, was for the woman in the pool and she was not Grace and Izzie's sister, but their stepmother, Mrs. Zorn, despite how young she was. He could keep up. He was going to enjoy himself.

At that moment, too, he remembered the opposite of *claustrophobia*: *agoraphobia*. He didn't have it. Five minutes later he was down in the street by himself, taking in New York, his mind going like never before.

say, and lowered the baton. The change didn't faze that moron; that whole situation on campus was really a mess, perhaps thanks to the faculty. But still. And I love him only in public. Stanislas—. And on the one, too. Don't let that finish him, Ronnie said over and over, and his eyes without showing the same interruption on the bottom. And probably. Funnier times. It's so tough to work on who's most on it. For me. I wouldn't believe this crap. Stanislas. I too would like those only present. He and it had.

"One seeks a midwife for his thoughts, another someone to whom he can be a midwife; thus originates a good conversation." Thus too does Nietzsche describe both the goal and method of Philosophy 322.
—Course description, Inverness College catalog

Living at home wasn't perfect, but at least Freedy could see his old friends, old friends like Ronnie Medeiros.

"Give you twenty bucks for it," Ronnie said, down in his basement.

"Fuck you, Ronnie. It's a Panasonic. Look—picture-in-picture." Ronnie had turned it on to make sure it was working.

"Take it or leave it," Ronnie said.

Freedy took it. What was he going to do? Return the god-damn thing?

They lifted for a while. Ronnie's place was in the flats, not far from Freedy's mom's. Being in the flats was what made the basement so damp, but why was it so cold? "Why's it so goddamn cold?"

"California made you soft, is all."

"Right." Freedy slid another 45 on each end, meaning he was benching 305, the kind of weight Ronnie could pump only in his dreams. Ronnie spotted him, but didn't have to lay a finger on the bar, not even on the last lift of three times ten. Freedy looked Ronnie in the eye on that last one, as if to

say: *Soft, you son of a bitch.* The charge he got from that moment of silent communication gave him the strength to bust
one more.

"What's California like, anyway?" said Ronnie. Freedy
knew what was going on in Ronnie's mind, could follow his
train of thought: California, the fountain of youth, Ponce
whoever he was, Muscle Beach. Freedy had always been
strong—would have been the captain of the football team if
he'd kept up his grades, or maybe just not dropped out—but
never strong like this.

He sat up, rubbed his chest. Ripped. Buff. A fuckin' animal.
Not like Ronnie, who *had* gone soft since high school, with
his pot belly, extra chin, receding hairline, and that stupid
hairy thing hanging under his lower lip: he'd turned into a
Portagee, which was what he was, of course.

"Whole different scene out there, Ronnie."

"Run into any movie stars?"

"Matter fact, yeah."

"Like who?"

Freedy named him. "Kind of an asshole."

"Kind of an asshole? You're joking."

"These people are different in real life, Ronnie."

"You tryin' to tell me you know him personally?"

Freedy nodded. "Customer of mine."

"Huh?"

"Told you already."

"That swimming-pool thing?"

"Business. Not thing. Business. I had a pool business. A-1
Pool Design, Engineering, and Maintenance. Still do, once
the lawyers get through with all their bullshit. Why I'm
taking this little . . . what's the word?"

"Sabbatical?"

"Yeah, sabbatical." They knew words like that, growing up
in a college town.

There was a silence, except for the cartoons on the Panasonic, and water dripping somewhere nearby. On the TV a

shark went snapping after some little critter; recalling to
Freedy's mind that Mexican cartoon of the squid arm snaking
out from the filter outlet. And now he remembered where
he'd seen the cartoon—in a bar in Mexico featuring one
of those live sex shows. An Indian guy and two bleached
blondes. A dark place, except for the TV behind the bar
and the little stage with blue spotlights shining on tits, ass,
and the Indian's enormous dick. Squid arm and Indian dick:
basic psychology, some kind of symbol, like the Eiffel Tower,
precise word for the symbol escaping him at the moment; and
he'd never think of it here, what with Ronnie stroking that
stupid hairy thing under his lower lip and asking dumb
questions.

"Huh?" said Freedy.

"A-1," said Ronnie. "The name of this so-called business."

"What about it?"

"Sounds like one of those outfits that try to get their name
first in the yellow pages."

"So?"

"Not what you'd call, you know, creative."

"Creative?" said Freedy. "You turned into some kind of
fag, or what?" He whipped out his wallet, flashed his business
card at Ronnie. *A-1 Pool Design, Engineering, and Maintenance, Friedrich Knight, Representative.* Maybe Ronnie
wouldn't catch that *representative* bit. That was Freedy's first
thought. His second thought was: maybe the whole A-1 trip
should have been kept out of the conversation. By that time,
Ronnie had the card in his hand.

"Says here *representative*," said Ronnie. "That's like rep,
right?"

Freedy snatched the card back; not snatched, more like
took back swiftly. "Which was before the buyout. The new
cards haven't been delivered. They're so fuckin' useless you
wouldn't believe it."

Ronnie blinked. "Who?"

Freedy slipped the card in his pocket. "Printers, for Christ sake. You not listenin'? And now we're in this Chapter Eleven shit, and everything's on hold."

"Chapter Eleven?"

"Technicality, Ronnie. Ties things up for a while."

"What things?"

Freedy sighed. "Like in football."

"Football?"

"Offsetting penalties."

"Holding and pass interference?"

"That kind of thing."

"I still think of the fucking Hoosac game," Ronnie said. "Remember that pussy?"

"Who fumbled on the one?"

"He was on the goal line, Freedy. I was right there."

"Faculty kid," said Freedy. The college professors' kids usually went away to boarding school, but this one hadn't.

"Cost us the Hoosac game," Ronnie said. "Thanksgiving, what year was that?"

A long time ago, four, five years, Freedy couldn't remember.

"You ever think of that game, Freedy?"

"Nah." Although he did, once or twice—last game he was eligible, junior year—but not because of the score or anything like that. What he remembered was breaking one of the Hoosac player's legs on a blind-side block after a fumble recovery—a clip, actually, but missed by the ref—and the sound it made, a real Thanksgiving sound.

" 'Nother set?" he said.

"Nah." Ronnie's eyes dipped down at him, still sitting on the bench, checked out those muscles, no doubt about it. "So what's this chapter shit?"

"Forget it, Ronnie. I bought out the other guy and now we're waiting on the details. End of story."

"Bought him out with what?"

Money, you asshole. But Freedy didn't say it. Because if he did, then the next thing he knew Ronnie would be saying something like *Why're you selling me your old TV for twenty bucks? Or this old TV that's supposedly yours?* "Listen to me, Ronnie."

"I'm listenin'."

"When they do one of these Chapter Elevens it's like a ref's time-out."

"To discuss the offsetting penalties?"

"You got it."

"And whiles there's a time-out nothing can happen. Bank accounts all frozen, that kind of shit."

Ronnie glanced at the TV. The little critter was trapped inside the shark's mouth, but he had a jar of red-hot pepper in his hand, said *Red Hot Pepper Yiaow* right on it. "All frozen," said Ronnie. "I get it." Water kept dripping, drip drip, from somewhere nearby.

Living at home meant being back in the flats. The flats—at the bottom of the north, cold side of College Hill, sunless most winter afternoons, between the old railroad tracks, where nothing ran anymore except the trash train once a week, and the river—hadn't changed much. It wasn't like he had to get used to anything new. A few more potholes in the streets, the house fronts more dilapidated, another line or two on his mother's face.

She was in the kitchen, pouring lumpy yellow batter into muffin tins. That was what she did: sold her muffins to health stores up and down the valley. Plus cashing her disability checks, welfare, whatever it was, smoking her dope, listening to her music. It was playing right now, and she was swaying to it, there by the counter: Birkenstocks, an Arab kind of robe, thick gray hair almost down to her waist. Freedy disliked all music, but that sixties shit was the worst. He snapped it off.

She turned, not fast. None of her movements was fast. That was part of being centered. "I was enjoying that, Freedy."

"You've heard it a million times."

She looked at him. She had big dark eyes, deeper-set than

they used to be, shadows in shadows. There was also a beauty-mark-sized drop of batter on her chin. "That's what makes it art," she said.

"You call that art?"

She sucked in her lips, one of her most annoying habits. "I'm a bit of an artist myself, Freedy, as I think you're aware."

He avoided glancing at any of her stuff, which wasn't easy. Just in the kitchen: her paintings all over the walls, her pottery on the shelves, her macramé hanging from the ceiling, her embroidered place mats, oven mitts, aprons peeking out from every cupboard. All moons and stars and bare trees and cats and longhaired women in serapes.

"So?" he said.

"So I'm enough of an artist to know an artist when I hear one," she said. "And Cat Stevens is an artist. Of the first water."

Of the first water? What was she talking about? He could hardly understand her half the time, his own mother. They had nothing in common, didn't even look alike. She was a wiry little thing; his size must have come from the father, whoever he was—but that was another story. Freedy didn't even have a name for her: when he was little, he'd called her Hama, some Navajo word for mother. Then she'd wanted him to call her by her first name, like they were friends. Her first name, changed legally, was Starry, had to do with van Gogh, if he was the one who cut off his ear, although Freedy couldn't remember exactly how. She never revealed her real first name; that person no longer existed, was the answer. Starry Knight—it sounded like a joke. Freedy didn't call her anything.

"Why's it so cold in here all time?" Freedy said.

"An old house," she said. "In winter."

She sat down at the table, reached for pen and paper. He knew what she was about to do—try to make up one of her goddamn poems, this one about an old house in winter. She'd made up lots of poems at one time, back when the Glass

Onion, boarded up now for years, had poetry nights. A golden age in her life—she'd actually said that. Freedy went into his bedroom and closed the door, hard, but nothing out of control, not hard enough to break anything.

His childhood bedroom. Freedy had been born right here. She even had a photo album of the birth, with pictures of her with her legs spread, and her hippie friends around her, and the midwife holding up this bloody bawling thing that was him.

He closed the curtains, kept the lights off, made it dark so he wouldn't have to see the wall paintings he'd grown up with—jungles and unicorns and toadstools and rainbows, with a bunch of elves thrown in, some of them smoking long pipes. And the lion—it was meant to be a lion but it looked more like a giant in a lion costume—holding up a poem on a scroll.

Little Boy

> *Soft snow cuddles you*
> *In swaddling clothes*
> *While plastic fantastic planet spins*
> *Its wild, wild way*
> *While away all the groovy ways little boy*
> *In the soft snow arms of mother earth.*

Freedy had no idea what the poem was supposed to mean, but it had scared the shit out of him every night for years; as had the lion man, and the elves, who turned wicked-looking at night, and all the electric blue, her favorite color. He lay on the bed, heard the music back on. That "Winterlude" song by Bob Dylan. She started playing it on the first snowy day and didn't knock off till spring. Freedy hated the song, hated Bob Dylan. He pulled a pillow over his head.

It smelled moldy. The whole house smelled like that. Uneven floors, peeling paint, water marks on the ceiling: it was falling apart. All the kids he'd grown up with lived in houses just the same. Only difference was most of them rented, and the ones that didn't had big mortgages and were always in danger of default, while they—she—had owned their house outright for as long as he could remember. None of these details had interested him back in high school. But now that he knew more of the world, he couldn't help thinking more maturely about things. Like: what was the house worth on the open market? And: did she have a will? With some other softening questions in between those two, naturally.

What with the pillow over his head and fucking Bob Dylan coming through the walls, Freedy didn't hear her knocking, didn't know she was in the room until she touched his shoulder. He sat up, real fast.

She stepped back. "Don't scare me," she said. She handed him the phone and left the room, her eyes drawn for a moment to a red frog on the wall, like she was thinking of some change to make.

"Yeah?" Freedy said into the phone.

"Ever meet my uncle Saul?" said Ronnie.

"You got an uncle named Saul?"

"I never mentioned him?"

"What are you saying—you got some Jewish guy for an uncle?"

"He's not Jewish. It's just a name they have back in the old country."

"So?"

"So he's just, you know, wondering, if you got more extra stuff."

"What extra stuff?"

"Like TVs and shit. Especially HDTVs—you heard of them?"

"Where d'you think they come from, asshole?"

"Huh?"

"HDTVs. California."

"Oh. Right. That's a positive, then. 'Cause my uncle Saul

does a little dealing in high-tech stuff. HDTVs, PowerBooks, digital notepads—"

"Scanners?"

"Yeah, scanners. Why, you got one?"

"Might."

"That would interest him, sure."

"Like how?"

"For buying. Didn't I say he buys and sells high-tech shit?"

"Where?"

"Down in Fitchville."

Fitchville was the nearest city, if you could call it a city, just off the pike. "What's he pay?" Freedy said.

"He pays good. He's a businessman." Pause. "Like you, Freedy. Think you can get—think you got more extra stuff hanging around?"

"Maybe."

"If the answer's yes, he wants to meet you."

"Twenty bucks for a Panasonic picture-in-picture, the answer's no."

"Not to worry, Freedy. That was just a buddy thing."

Pause. "You've turned into a funny dude, Ronnie."

"Funny?"

"Humorous, Ronnie. Witty."

"Yeah?" Ronnie laughed; one of those little laughs like a giggle, when you're pleased with yourself.

Freedy took an andro from his pocket, popped it dry.

"Freedy? You still there?"

Freedy lowered his voice a little, made it more . . . intimate. Was that the word? Probably: he had a good vocabulary, went with his brainpower. " 'Member that time we went one-on-one, Ronnie?"

"In practice?"

"Not in practice. When we had that little . . . disagreement."

Long pause. "About Cheryl Ann?" Ronnie said at last.

"Was that her name?"

No answer. Ronnie remembered, all right.

Freedy let the silence go on—controlling it, really, which was pretty cool—then said: "Tell your uncle Saul I'm in the book."

"But you're not in the book, Freedy. You've been gone for years."

Freedy hung up.

7

"The noble caste was in the beginning always the barbarian caste: their superiority lay, not in their physical strength, but primarily in their psychical—they were more complete human beings (which, on every level, also means as much as 'more complete beasts'—)." Attack or defend, with reference to the Kennedy family.
—Essay assignment, Philosophy 322

"This is very thoughtful of you, uh . . ."

"Nat," said Nat, handing the gift bottle of pink zinfandel—all wrapped up in red and gold from the wine store, the thickest, shiniest wrapping paper he'd ever seen—to Mr. Zorn.

"Nat what, again?" said Mr. Zorn.

Nat repeated his last name. He and Mr. Zorn shook hands for the second time. Mr. Zorn: whose hand felt small in Nat's; who didn't look particularly distinguished—nothing as impressive as Albert, Mrs. Zorn's personal assistant, or Anton, her personal trainer; who stood shorter than Nat by a few inches, perhaps the same height as Grace and Izzie, but not lean like them, not fair like them; who did have their blue-green eyes, but without the gold flecks that changed the whole effect.

"Nat's the hero du jour," said Grace.

"Yesterday's hero du jour," said Izzie.

"The hero d'hier, then," said Mr. Zorn; a minor witticism,

66

if one at all, and not spoken loudly, but Nat heard laughter from all parts of the room.

Christmas Eve, five o'clock, party in the library. The Zorns' library, on yet another floor, above the bedroom level, wasn't dark-paneled and musty, like the library in an Agatha Christie mystery, but all glass and blond wood, with tall windows and northern views. By now Nat knew that the apartment had 360-degree views of the city, but its size and structure remained unclear to him. The party was not exactly a party, although a waiter was serving drinks and everyone but Nat and the girls was dressed up; it was just a gathering before people—there were about fifteen or twenty in the room, one of whom, a TV network newswoman, Nat recognized— went off for the evening.

Mr. Zorn showed no interest in whatever heroic feat Nat had performed, but peered at the gift bottle, as though attempting to see through the wrapper, and said: "Interested in wine, Nat?"

Wary of a minefield of wine questions, Nat said: "I'm underage."

Mr. Zorn looked up; a quick look, but careful. Then he smiled at him, not warm, not cold, not emotional at all, but an intelligent smile, if that made sense—Nat had never seen one quite like it. "But quick-witted," said Mr. Zorn.

"Very," said Grace.

"Very what?" said Mrs. Zorn, coming up. She wore something black and low-cut that exposed most of her breasts; a huge pear-shaped diamond—had to be a diamond, Nat thought—hung between them. The effort to keep his eyes off the spectacle almost made his head hurt, although no one else seemed to be taking any notice.

"Quick-witted," said Izzie.

"Who are we talking about?" said Mrs. Zorn.

"Nat," said Grace.

Mrs. Zorn looked blank for a moment, then turned to him: "Really?" she said.

Grace and Izzie both frowned in annoyance, their foreheads furrowing identically.

"I guess not, since I don't know what to say to that," Nat said.

Everyone laughed—Mr. Zorn the loudest—except Mrs. Zorn.

Yes, this is fun. Crème de la crème and I'm having fun.

Mr. Zorn raised the gift bottle. "Nat's brought us a little something."

"How thoughtful," said Mrs. Zorn.

"In fact . . . ," said Mr. Zorn, glancing at a nearby door.

"Not now," said Grace.

"Pay no attention to Grace," Mr. Zorn said. "She likes to give me a hard time. That's how I tell them apart."

Grace and Izzie exchanged a glance, beyond Nat's interpretive power. Izzie looked away.

"Not now what?" said Mrs. Zorn. "What is everyone talking about?"

"Too late," said Izzie.

Mr. Zorn had already taken Nat's hand, drawn him away. Nat followed him through the doorway, down a dark corridor, into a vaulted stone room. It had a heavy door, studded, creaking, the kind found in fairy-tale castles. Mr. Zorn closed it. Nat looked around.

"Do you like oxymorons, Nat?" said Mr. Zorn.

"Like a cellar on the seventieth floor?" said Nat.

"Seventy-first."

A wine cellar. Wine in racks, wine in bins, wine in cases on the floor: thousands and thousands of bottles, receding into the shadows. *Something of a hobby with Mr. Zorn.*

"Bordeaux and Burgundy, respectively, along that wall," said Mr. Zorn. "Italian, Spanish, Portuguese—including port and Madeira—at the back, Australian in the corner, and finally domestic. Plus odds and ends, here and there. Someone's coming in from Paris to reorganize the whole shebang. What would you like?"

"What would I like?"

"A little sample. It's to drink. People forget that."

"Burgundy," Nat said; the word was in the air and it was also the team color of Clear Creek High.

"Perfect," said Mr. Zorn. "Especially at Christmas." He set Nat's gift bottle on a dark table as heavy and ancient as the door, and moved down the row of bins. Nat realized he did like oxymorons, liked, too, wine cellars on the seventy-first floor. The thought arose—and he banished it at once, untrue—that he was living for the first time.

Mr. Zorn returned, blowing dust off a bottle. "How about this?" he said, holding it so Nat could read the label.

Romanée-Conti. The name meant nothing to Nat. "Looks good," he said. Then he noticed the date: 1962.

"Crack 'er open," said Mr. Zorn.

"I'm sorry?"

Mr. Zorn handed him a corkscrew. "Do the honors," he said. "We can try some of yours, too."

They both eyed the gift bottle. Suddenly the bright wrapping paper seemed a little too bright to Nat. "What the hell, right?" said Mr. Zorn. "It's Christmas Eve."

Nat glanced at the corkscrew. The first problem was that he'd never used one. The second problem was harder to put into words, but had to do with the contrast between the two labels: the simple black on white of the Romanée-Conti, with no illustration, versus the red, orange, and yellow of Mr. Beaman's wine, Blind River Blush, with its picture of a fish leaping high over a bunch of grapes. The third problem was that Blind River Blush had a screw top.

Nat took the bottle of Romanée-Conti from Mr. Zorn. He noticed a tiny price sticker on the back: $2,500. For a moment his fingers went numb; he could see they were holding the bottle, but had no idea how. The problems all compounded. He actually thought of saying he had to go to the bathroom. But no: he was good at solving problems, wasn't he? He tried to think of some light remark, failed, and went to work.

First, the burgundy-colored foil around the top: he dug his thumbnail under it, stripped it off, exposing the cork. Second, the corkscrew. A strange corkscrew, nothing simple about it. It had at least two moving parts, one the screw itself, which probably wouldn't function until he swung this other, flanged one open. He swung it open, moved the screw to a right angle with the . . . handle, yes, must be the handle, stuck the point of the screw into the cork.

"Tried them all," said Mr. Zorn. "This is the best."

"The wine, you mean?" said Nat, looking up; he felt sweat on his upper lip.

Mr. Zorn laughed. "Some think so," he said. "But I was talking about the corkscrew—these simple Parisian waiters' corkscrews work better than any of the fancy gizmos out there, don't you think?"

A perfect chance to say, *I've never actually used this kind before,* and hand the whole affair over to Mr. Zorn. But Nat let it go by. He could do it. Twisting the screw deep into the cork, he said, "Really goes in there." A light remark, perhaps, but idiotic. He felt his ears reddening, a new sensation. But at the same time, he realized what the flanged part was for—had grasped the underlying mechanics—got it in place, applied pressure, levering pressure. The cork began sliding out. Triumph.

"How's your father, by the way?" said Mr. Zorn.

Nat's arm jerked convulsively, as though he'd lost all control of it. The cork popped free but his arm continued its wild gesture, striking the gift bottle on the table, knocking it over; the bottle rolled, fell, crashed on the stone floor. A muffled crash, the broken glass held inside the thick wrapping paper. Only the wine leaked out, forming a pink pool at Mr. Zorn's feet.

"Looks interesting," he said. "Too bad."

Or some other observation that Nat, staring at Mr. Zorn across the table, barely heard. "My father?" he said.

"Is he still with those Silicon Valley people?"

"I don't have a father."

"You don't?" Mr. Zorn stared back at him. "Weren't you on Grace's floor at Choate?"

"No."

"Not the captain of the soccer team?"

"No. I . . . I think you've got me confused with someone else."

Mr. Zorn's gaze went to the spilled wine, then to the Romanée-Conti and the corkscrew with the impaled cork, still in Nat's hands. He laughed. Nat laid the wine and the corkscrew on the table.

Mr. Zorn picked up the corkscrew. "A happy misunderstanding, then," he said, unscrewing the cork, "since we got to have this nice little visit. Shall we rejoin the others?" He stuck the cork firmly back in the bottle of Romanée-Conti.

The door opened and Grace came in. "Time to go, Nat," she said. "Paolo's here."

"Paolo?"

"Izzie's boyfriend."

"You don't know Paolo?" said Mr. Zorn.

Nat lost his concentration for a few moments and somehow managed to track pink zinfandel on the oriental rug in the library. No one noticed; the colors were similar.

Paolo had a car with a driver and diplomatic plates. He sat in the back between the girls, his arm over Izzie's shoulders; Nat sat in front.

"Paolo's a count," Grace said.

"That's very silly," said Paolo, opening a bottle of champagne. He had a slight accent that somehow made English sound better.

"But true, isn't it?" said Grace.

"Grace," said Izzie.

A difference right there: some character difference, but everything was happening fast, and Nat couldn't put his finger on it.

"Come on, Paolo," said Grace. "Show us some count ID."

"Count ID?" said Paolo, drinking from the bottle and passing it to Izzie. "Have you ever in life heard such a concept, Nate?"

"It's Nat," said Nat.

"Not Nate?" said Paolo. "I am familiar with Nate as a typical American name, but not Nat."

Izzie, glancing at Paolo, drank some champagne and passed the bottle to Grace.

"And kings have scepters," Nat said, "so maybe the concept of count ID isn't so crazy after all."

Grace and Izzie both burst out laughing, spraying little jets of champagne.

"Fuck," said Paolo, even making that word sound almost pretty. He spoke to the driver in Italian; the driver passed him a handkerchief, and Paolo dabbed at his pant leg.

Izzie kissed him on the cheek. In the rearview mirror, Nat saw Grace's eyes narrow. "Sorry," Izzie said.

"It's nothing," Paolo said. He dabbed some more.

Grace extended the bottle over the seat to Nat. Nat wasn't much of a drinker, and had made a promise to his mom never to mix drinking and cars, so the reply *no thanks* formed automatically in his mind. But he hadn't tasted champagne, and, what the hell, it *was* Christmas Eve. He drank. It was good, very, very good. He was alive and he knew it, like never before. The driver kept his eyes on the road.

Paolo took them to parties. There was more champagne, at first very, very good, later simply cold and fizzy, after that just wet.

Parties. A Brazilian party where Nat, wedged next to the conga drums, fell under the illusion that the drumskins were playing the drummer's hands, and not the other way around.

A party in a dance club where they were ushered in past a long line at the door, and where he danced first with Izzie, then with Grace, then with an older woman who had an intense face and cords sticking out on her neck; he shared a frozen rum drink with her and she wriggled her hip against him. He felt immensely strong, strong enough to pick her up and set her on the bar in one easy motion, which he did. She threw back her head and laughed and laughed, the cords in her neck sticking out even more, her stiletto-heeled foot sliding up his leg; Izzie, no, it was Grace, he could tell by her temperature even before he checked the hair, drew him away.

A party in Greenwich Village where he found himself in a bathroom with seven or eight people, where a photograph of the party givers having sex hung over the bathtub, and where a Thai stick, something he'd heard of but never seen, went round and round, with him declining every time until Izzie spoke into his ear: "You're pretty cute, you know that?" No: it was Grace. This time he had to look; their voices were identical, deeper than most girls' and a little ragged at the edges, as though they'd been up all night, or had been singing at the top of their lungs, or were fighting some infection. Grace's tongue tasted smoky.

But how did he know that?

Later, somewhere else, he and Paolo urinated side by side, a bottle of champagne perched on Paolo's urinal. "Ah, Nat," said Paolo, pronouncing the name with great care, almost adding a second syllable: Nat-te. "You know what is everyone asking me tonight, Nat-te?" Paolo said.

"Where your scepter is?"

Paolo regarded him from the corner of his eye. For a moment Nat thought Paolo was going to take a swing at him. But Paolo was in the middle of pissing—they both were—and it would have been messy, and Nat knew from the handkerchief episode that Paolo didn't like messes. "What everyone is asking me, Nat-te, is which one dyes the hair. Because there is one way only to know for sure, if you are following." Paolo winked at him.

Nat had heard a lot about diversity, had answered test questions about it and written his SAT writing sample on the subject, but he hadn't understood how different human be-ings could be, one from the other, until that moment. He thought of Christmas Eve at home: Mom always made an oyster stew, a few friends came over, Patti and her dad the last two years, everyone opened one present, they drank eggnog from little clear-glass cups that appeared only at Christmas, Mom sat at the piano and they sang a few carols. With the time difference, it might still be going on. He turned his wrist to check the time and found his watch was gone.

"I am having a bad feeling you miss the import of the ques-tion," said Paolo, shaking off. "Identical genes, therefore the hair must be identical, therefore one is an artificer. Do I say that right?"

"They're two different people," Nat said. "There are other ways to tell them apart."

"Don't be silly. Is there no biology studies in America? Even their father cannot tell—which is the reason why the hair color in the first place." He zipped up. "So we have a big question, and everyone is asking the person in a position to know. To know beyond a shadow of the doubt. Useless to ask, of course, so don't you bother, Nat-te. I am what used to be called a gentleman."

"What's it called now?" said Nat.

But too late: Paolo was gone. Nat went to the sink. It turned out that counts didn't wash their hands. Maybe he said it aloud. "Counts don't wash their hands." He washed his, laughing to himself. Then he thought he heard someone crying, went still, heard nothing but the running water. In the mirror, he saw that now he did look different, a lot.

Nat was still staring at his image, kind of stunned, when one of the stalls behind him opened and Izzie stepped out. She didn't look at him, either in the mirror or in life, but went out, not speaking.

"Izzie?" Nat hurried after her, but had trouble with the door, somehow locking it for a few seconds, or maybe a minute or two, and when he emerged into a hall swarming with people, she was gone.

"Ever smoked one of these before?" said someone.

"What is it?" said Nat.

" 'What is it?' Who are you, Inspector Gadget?"

Nat didn't remember anything after that.

He awoke in the night with someone breathing against his ear.

"You're pretty cute."

"Izzie?"

"Bzzzz."

"Grace?"

"Boinggg." She slipped her hand inside his shirt; no, he wasn't wearing a shirt.

He sat up; no, tried to. "Where are we?"

"Home is the hunter."

Her hand moved lower. He might not have been wearing pants either. Her hand, so different from Patti's hand; knew exactly what it was doing, for one thing. Nat thought that moment of the conga drummer's hands, a mixed-up thought that went away. He put his hand on hers to stop her.

"How did we get here?"

"Public transportation, like good little citizens. You gave up your seat to a transvestite. Très galant."

Surely she was making that up. "What time is it?"

"Night."

"I think I lost my watch."

"You talk too much." She put her mouth on his, got her hand free, down between his legs.

Nat turned his head away. "I really can't, Grace."

"Different opinion down here."

Nat tried to see her in the dark, couldn't. "It's not that," he said. "We don't know each other."

"I know you."

"I meant we don't know each other well enough."

"If everyone waited for well enough, we'd be extinct."

Nat laughed. "I know, but—"

"But what?"

"I have this—I have a girlfriend."

Grace stopped what she was doing. "At school?"

"Inverness, you mean?"

"What other school do you go to?"

"No," Nat said, "she's not at Inverness."

Grace started up again. "Still on the prairie, then. What's her name?"

"Patti. And there's no prairie."

"Let me guess—she spells it with an *i*. When do we meet her?"

Nat pulled her hand away, sat up, succeeded in sitting up this time, felt dizzy and a little sick. "Yes," he said, "she does spell it with an *i*."

His voice sounded strange to him: harsh and maybe even powerful. Powerful. Was this the immensely strong effect he'd experienced at the dance club, still with him from the champagne? He felt Grace moving away, heard her stand up.

"What convenient morals you have, Grandma," she said.

"Convenient?"

She snorted. "Playing dumb's not you."

"I don't know what you're talking about."

But was he really surprised when she said: "No? What would you be doing right now if it was Izzie in your bed?" He was not.

He said nothing.

Grace said: "Piss on that," and left the room.

Nat lay back down. Was it just that he saw Izzie as the underdog and had always been one of those rooters for underdogs? How could someone like Izzie possibly be called an underdog? Was it instead some crazy competitive thing, that Izzie wasn't available and Grace was? Or simply that he was a little afraid of Grace?

He closed his eyes, thought about returning to Inverness in

the morning, even—but just for a moment—of going home. The steps outlined themselves in his mind: packing, paying Albert what he owed for the gift wine, finding the bus station. He slid down into sleep, and was almost there when it hit him that he'd forgotten all about his hundred foul shots, the first day he'd missed since he'd begun in fifth grade. His eyes opened wide. He remembered the basketball hoop on the deck down below, thought about getting up. Thought about it, but stayed where he was, eyes open.

8

"The degree and kind of a man's sexuality reaches up into the topmost summit of his spirit." In a single paragraph, discuss whether Nietzsche would have said the same for women; if so, why; if not, why not?
—Midterm exam question, Philosophy 322

Christmas morning.

Early morning: Nat was the only one up in the Zorns' apartment; at least, he saw or heard no one else. Showered, shaved, dressed, packed, left $30 on his bedside table for Albert, with a note giving his college address in case the wine had cost more—$2,500!—he waited for the elevator. And while he waited, faced the Renoir.

A pink nude—not really pink, since he could see silver, yellow, violet, red, even blue on her skin, but the effect was pink—a pink nude, one foot resting on the edge of a bathtub, bending to towel herself dry. She was fat, but didn't behave—if the word could be used for a painted figure frozen on canvas—the way fat women did now. *Au contraire,* as Grace or Izzie would probably say, she seemed confident, even liked her body, if that wasn't reading too much into it. The problem, and the reason he didn't like the painting—not liking a Renoir, who did he think he was?—was that he couldn't see anything else inside her but that self-satisfaction. Women he knew, his mom, Patti, Grace, Izzie, might not feel that self-satisfaction—he was almost sure that none of them did feel it, despite the fact that they all had better bodies than Renoir's woman—but there was something important in all of them that she seemed to lack. Was there a word for that something? What was it? An angle? A viewpoint? Or—here came an image—the habit of mind of a chess player forced always to play the black pieces, to go second? Nat didn't know, but he sensed this something in women, wanted to know more about it, didn't see it here. Did that mean that Renoir hadn't known much about women? Nat, shying away from that conclusion, was about to move a little closer to the painting in order to examine the pink lady's eyes and see where he had gone wrong when the elevator opened behind him. He turned.

Mrs. Zorn stepped out. She wore running shoes, black tights, and, despite the cold, a black midriff-baring top. And, despite the cold, she was sweating. A long and serious run: Nat could tell from the line of caked salt running like a blurred thread around her black top. There was a blurriness in her eyes too, but they cleared as soon as she saw him.

"You're up early," she said. "Nat."

"Not as early as you, Mrs. Zorn," he said, his voice sounding a little hoarse in his ears. "Merry Christmas."

She nodded; her gaze rested on his backpack. "Going somewhere?"

"Inverness."

Mrs. Zorn blinked, a long slow blink, much like his mom's. This surprised him. With her flawless skin, high cheekbones, taut muscles—even to the extent of abdominal definition, if not quite a six-pack—and with the grape-sized diamond and the oxymoronic wine cellar and the rest of the life she must lead, Mrs. Zorn didn't seem to have much in common with his mom.

"Weren't you staying for the holidays?"

"That's very nice of you, Mrs. Zorn. But I've got to be getting back."

She looked almost alarmed. "I don't understand."

"No emergency or anything like that," Nat said. "I've got a lot of work to do, that's all."

"Work?"

"Studying and stuff." He thought of the list waiting on his wall: *clean room, laundry, write home, work out, get to know town and surroundings, →on next semester.* Over Mrs. Zorn's shoulder, he could see the Persian cat watching him from the couch in the elevator.

"Schoolwork?" said Mrs. Zorn.

"Yes."

"But it's vacation, and the twins say you're a brilliant student."

"I don't know how they can. First-semester results aren't even in yet."

"The girls are always right about this kind of thing. And you'll miss out on—" She glanced around, like someone seeking help. "How about some breakfast?"

"Thanks, but it's really not necessary."

"I'm fixing myself a little something anyway," said Mrs. Zorn. "It'll be my pleasure."

Mrs. Zorn made an omelette, a beautiful glistening omelette with goat cheese—Nat knew that only from a quick glance at the label—onions, and peppers; the best-looking omelette he'd ever seen. She squeezed a glass of orange juice for him, made her frothy blue drink from a big cube of blue ice she took from the freezer and put in the blender, sat down opposite him in a little alcove jutting into the sky; a sky the color of her drink, the cloud level for the moment a few stories below.

"That's not very fair," said Nat as Mrs. Zorn divided the omelette into two highly unequal portions, taking one tiny end and giving the rest to Nat.

"This is plenty for me," said Mrs. Zorn. "Too much." The alarmed look crossed her face again. "You don't want coffee, do you?"

He did, but thought it best to shake his head.

"One of the deadliest poisons there is," she said.

Nat didn't look up. He cut off a piece of his omelette, tasted it. "My God," he said.

"You like it?" She didn't sound surprised.

"It's great."

"My father taught me how to cook," said Mrs. Zorn. "I hardly ever get a chance, but the staff's off today, of course."

A maid in uniform entered, laid a vase of flowers and some folded newspapers on the table, left. A young maid, Hispanic: she resembled one of the cheerleaders at Clear Creek High.

"The cook's off, anyway," said Mrs. Zorn, who still hadn't touched her food. She sipped her blue drink. "Where are you from, Nat?"

He told her.

"I'm from Denver, myself," she said.

"You are?"

"Do you know the city?"

"Not really."

"My father had a diner in Arvada. He cooked and my mother served."

Nat was amazed. Arvada was where his own mother had spent the first few years of her life, for one thing. "How long have you lived here?" he said.

"New York, you mean, or this place?"

"New York."

"Since I was sixteen."

"Did your parents open another diner?"

"I'm sorry?"

"When you moved here."

"I came by myself. I'd always wanted to be a model, for some reason, and this is where you have to go, here or Paris, and I wasn't ready for Paris back then. Or ever."

"And did it . . . uh, work out?"

"Did what work out?"

"The modeling."

"Yes indeed," said Mrs. Zorn. She stared out the window,

where the cloud level had risen and there was nothing to see but swirling fog. "I'm the third Mrs. Z."

Nat ate more of his omelette, biting down on an onion-filled mouthful that tasted especially delicious.

"You didn't think I was the twins' mother, did you?"

"Oh, no," said Nat. "If anything, I thought you were an older sister." His true thought, but it sounded a little oily out there in the open.

"Aren't you a charmer," said Mrs. Zorn. "I'll let you in on a secret. I work my ass off to stay like this, and it's all fading fast, no matter what I do."

Nat didn't know what to say to that.

"Maybe not such a charmer," said Mrs. Zorn. "You're supposed to say something reassuring, like 'not at all.' "

"You're . . . beautiful," Nat said, and felt his ears reddening again. He'd never said that to a woman, or girl, before; so strange that the first one would be her, so stupid that his voice would crack on the phrase, like he was thirteen or something. "You must know that," he added, making what he hoped was a mature recovery.

Mrs. Zorn smiled. "I know it *officially*. But it's always nice to hear. How's the omelette?"

"Fantastic."

"Enjoy, as the locals like to say," she said. She took another sip of her blue drink; he noticed it was turning her lips and teeth blue. "What do you know about the second Mrs. Z?" she said.

"Nothing."

"No? She's their mother. The girls, I'm talking about. Lives in Paris. A lifestyle you would not believe. What's so funny?"

"Nothing. Sorry."

"She was a model too," Mrs. Zorn continued. "Wanted to be an actress. That became a problem, a marriage buster eventually, because she has a voice like Daffy Duck. With a head cold, but don't tell the girls I said that."

"Was she ever in any movies?"

"He financed one for her in the end." Mrs. Zorn named it, a slasher sequel he'd seen one Friday night at the little two-screen cinema in his town.

"Was she the aerobics instructor?"

"Something like that."

Nat remembered nothing remarkable about her voice.

"But that was it," Mrs. Zorn said. "She overplayed her hand. He didn't like being pressured, not by her, not by those Hollywood people." Outside the sky darkened and lights went on in the kitchen automatically. "He doesn't like being pressured by anybody."

"What does Mr. Zorn do, if you don't mind me asking?"

"It's complicated," said Mrs. Zorn. "Let's just say he takes his cut."

"Of what?"

"You name it." She glanced at Nat's plate, saw it was bare. "What else can I get you?" she said.

"Nothing," he said. "It was great."

"I've enjoyed our little breakfast, too," said Mrs. Zorn, although she still hadn't touched her food. She looked directly at him; she really was beautiful, if a little strange with the blue lips and teeth. "You could do me a favor, Nat."

"I could?"

She reached across the table, touched his hand. If there was a scale of knowingness for a woman's touch, with Grace much higher than Patti, then Mrs. Zorn was at least that much higher than Grace. "By not leaving," she said.

"Not leaving?" Nat drew his hand away. She left hers where it was, a beautifully shaped hand, though it surprised him to see one or two liver spots on the back. "I'm sorry, I—"

"The girls seem to like your company. And now with Izzie so upset. We could all use a change of scene, if you want to know the truth. That's why we're flying down to the islands today. Please don't say no."

"Bora Bora?" said Nat, thinking of Lorenzo.

"Just the Caribbean."

"I can't."

"Why not? You could bring your books, and if you need some more, that's no problem—give Albert a list."

"Thanks, but—"

"If you're really set on Bora Bora, we might—"

"Oh, no. It's not that. It's just—the hotel, the airfare— I can't afford it." Mrs. Zorn started to speak; he held up his hand, not wanting to even hear her charitable offer. "I'd have to pay my own way, Mrs. Zorn, and since I can't—don't you see?"

She laughed. "Let's not make this into a big production," she said. "There is no hotel or airfare. It's not that kind of thing."

"But—"

"And it would be good for Izzie to have friends around right now."

"Why? What's happened?"

"I thought you were there."

"Where?"

The maid entered. "Phone for you, sir," she said, and handed a cordless one to Nat.

"Hello?"

"Nat? Merry Christmas."

"Mom? I was going to call you." And: "How did you get this number?"

"From information. Their name was on the card."

"What card?"

"Don't you know? It's the sweetest thing. They sent flowers, your people. The Zorns. The most beautiful flowers I've ever seen in my life, Nat. Is Mrs. Zorn around, by any chance?"

"She's right here." He handed the phone to Mrs. Zorn. "My mom wants to talk to you."

"Hello," said Mrs. Zorn. She listened. From the expression on her face, Nat could tell that she knew nothing about the flowers; it must have been Albert's doing. And must have happened many times before: Mrs. Zorn didn't even stumble. "Oh, don't be silly," she said. "It's our pleasure. And your son seems like such a wonderful young man."

She handed the phone back to Nat. "Mom?"

"She sounds so nice, Nat. And so . . . grand." Nat, recalling that Mrs. Zorn and his mom were both from Arvada, missed whatever she said next.

"What was that, Mom?"

"I said hang on. Patti's here. She wants to say hi."

"Nat? Merry Christmas."

"Merry Christmas."

"Did you get my package?"

Nat remembered it, sitting unopened on his bed in room seventeen of Plessey Hall. "Yes," he said. She waited for a reaction; he heard her breathing. "I wasn't going to open it till Christmas."

She laughed. "What day do you think it is, you goof?"

"No one's opened anything yet." He hadn't even seen the Zorns' tree, now that he thought about it.

"What's it like there?"

"Nice."

"Your mom says you're staying with some college buddies?"

Nat didn't reply.

"That was nice of them, inviting you."

"Yeah."

"Been to the Empire State Building yet?"

"No," Nat said, glancing out the window; the top of it had been visible before the clouds rose.

"What have you been up to, then?"

"Not much."

Pause. "Nat?"

"Yes?"

"I . . . I wish I could talk to you."

"You can."

"No. I . . . I just . . . miss you so much." There was a muffled sound: she was crying. He caught a word or two—"sorry," "Christmas"—felt Mrs. Zorn's gaze on his face.

"Me too," he said, which didn't even make sense, and therefore couldn't be a lie, even though she might have inferred that he missed her too. But he didn't miss her.

"This is costing money," Patti said, sniffling. "I should go. Love you."

"Have a good Christmas," Nat told her.

"Nat?" His mom.

"Hi."

"Have a wonderful holiday. And do something nice for the Zorns, if you can."

But I should go back to school, Mom. Or maybe home. Couldn't say it, of course, for a number of reasons.

The maid took the phone away.

"Your mother sounds so nice," said Mrs. Zorn.

"She is." He thought he heard that strange, powerful tone in his voice again. Part of it was because she was so much more than that; the rest was the word *nice* itself. Nice, nice, nice: it was starting to grate on him.

"I'm sure of it," said Mrs. Zorn.

Nat saw that she had finally eaten her little bit of omelet, finished the frothy blue drink.

"What were you saying about Izzie?"

"Izzie? Oh, yes. She dumped Paolo. Or vice versa. Or both at the same time. She's not taking it well. It's a vulnerable age." Mrs. Zorn looked down at her empty plate. "Like all the others."

He said yes.

9

> " 'No more exploitation'—that sounds to my ears like
> promising a life in which there will be no organic func-
> tions." Identify the quotation and discuss in relation to
> any one organic function. Five hundred words.

—In-class assignment, Philosophy 322

No airfare, no hotel: not that kind of thing.

It was the kind of thing where you drove to a private air-
field in one of three limousines, sitting beside a friendly-
looking man named Andy Ling who asked friendly questions
about you; where you boarded a private plane with a big
black *Z* painted on the fuselage; where a square-jawed pilot
resembling the hero of *Planet of the Apes*—Nat couldn't remember the actor's name—invited you into the cockpit;
where you sat around a white-clothed table in the tail section
and ate foie gras before you even knew what it was; where
you began to develop a preference for Krug champagne over
the others you'd been trying; where the maid who resembled
a Clear Creek High cheerleader—go Bisons!—plumped up a
soft pillow before placing it behind your head; where you
slept and dreamed one of those soaring dreams you sometimes had, but for the first time within a soaring reality,
soothed like a baby by the hum of jet engines.

To sleep like a baby; to wake over a world of liquid
emerald; to land on a tropic isle; to stand in the open doorway
of the plane, feeling for the first time that air, smelling those

smells; to be aware of all those old boyhood pirate stories stirring in memory, coming to life.

"Welcome to Aubrey's Cay," said Mrs. Zorn; perhaps a little drunk—Nat saw how Anton discreetly helped her down the stairs. "Our little piece of paradise."

"That's not true," Grace said.

Mrs. Zorn, on the black-paved airstrip—it felt soft under Nat's feet—turned quickly, almost lost her balance. "What's not true?" she said. Her eyes were concealed by oversized sunglasses, but he suspected they wore that alarmed look again.

"What you said. It's some kind of lease. We don't actually own it. Do we, Dad?"

Mr. Zorn, talking on a cell phone in the shade of the starboard wing, didn't reply.

"Dad. I asked you a question."

"Your father is busy," said Mrs. Zorn.

"Piss on that," said Grace, and strode toward one of the waiting jeeps.

Nat didn't know what to make of this exchange. Maybe Grace was a little drunk too. All it showed him for sure was that none of this—translucent green sea, white beaches, red-flowering trees by the side of the strip, the air, the smells, not even this tiny orange bird streaking by, which no one seemed to notice—was new to them.

No hotel. None necessary: The Zorns had a big yellow house with red shutters on the east side of the hill that dominated the island. There were two villas on the beach below the house, servants' quarters in a banana grove halfway down the back of the hill, a boathouse big enough for a cigarette boat and a few smaller ones at the head of the little natural harbor on the west side. Not a big island, but beautiful and all theirs, owned or leased.

Nat's room was at the end of a marble corridor in the big house. It opened onto a balcony with a view of Tortola and some other islands; on a chaise longue lay a bathing suit. Nat hadn't brought one. He tried the suit on; the European kind, skimpier than what he would wear, but it fit.

Nat crossed a huge room with a fountain, cool, although all the windows were open to the hot afternoon, looking for anyone who wanted a swim. But no one was around; the house was silent. He walked outside, down stone steps toward the beach. A bright green lizard skittered away from him; he smelled intoxicating smells; passed a tree bearing an apple-like green fruit and a sign on the trunk: *Manchineel—Touche Pas!*; heard a voice drifting down, almost out of range, but clear enough in the still air: "I thought maybe he'd amuse the girls, that's all." Mrs. Zorn, almost certainly; followed by low male rumblings. At that moment it occurred to Nat that the friendly-looking man in the limousine, Andy Ling, hadn't been on the plane.

The path wound past the two villas, both silent, cut through a palm grove—he picked a coconut off the ground, felt its weight, heard the milk sloshing inside—and ended at the beach. Nat walked across the white sand, powdery and hot on the soles of his feet, and into the ocean. This green ocean: pale green by the shoreline, so pale it was almost colorless if you looked straight down; which Nat did, and saw a fish swimming by his feet, a fish similar in size and shape to Lorenzo, but not quite as spectacular, simply deep blue with red lips. At first contact, this water—the Caribbean Sea!—felt the same as his own temperature; then it cooled slightly, just enough to tingle against his skin. All his muscles, his whole body, relaxed at once, a more complete release of tension than he could ever remember, as though his physical self had been waiting a lifetime for this moment, his first immersion in salt water.

Nat wasn't much of a swimmer—Clear Creek High had no pool and the river had become too shallow for swimming—but when the water reached his chest, he slid the rest of the way in and swam a few strokes. Maybe more than a few, because when he stopped and glanced around he was surprised at the distance to the beach. Surprised but not worried: with the increased buoyancy of the salt water, he found he could stay on the surface with almost no effort, and besides, there was that perfect, soothing temperature. He turned his face to the sun, closed his eyes, heard the gentle rippling of the sea around him, the call of a strange bird somewhere above, and nothing else. But that nothing else, that silence, was not like any silence he was used to, but somehow powerful, impending, the background sound, new to him, of the air or sky itself.

Then something grabbed his leg.

Nat kicked out sharply, took a thrashing stroke or two in the wrong direction, out to sea. Whatever was beneath him shot to the surface right before his eyes, a strange and terrifying creature. For a moment Nat couldn't put the pieces together. Then he saw: snorkel, mask, and wet golden-brown hair he'd mistaken for seaweed.

Izzie.

She spat out her snorkel and said, "Boo."

Nat stopped thrashing, tried to tread water in some sort of measured way. Her eyes watched him from behind the mask.

"Did I scare you?"

"No." But his heart was beating fast.

She took off her mask, turned her head, emptied her nostrils into the sea. "That's the dorkiest thing I've ever seen in swimwear," she said.

"It's not mine."

"You stole it from Pee-wee Herman?"

His heartbeat slowed to something a little less crazy. "No need. We're like this."

She laughed. He laughed. He noticed that she didn't appear to be treading water at all, or to be making the least effort to stay afloat, just rose and fell gently with the rhythm of the waves. He also noticed that she wasn't wearing a bathing suit top.

She noticed him noticing. "Maybe you are a bit like him."

He tore his eyes away.

"Aubrey's Cay is topless," she said. "Like St. Bart's."

"What's that?"

"Just another island. But leads the Caribbean in boobs and baguettes. To quote Paolo." Her mood changed; he could see it in her eyes, as though someone had hit the dimmer.

"Nat?"

"Yeah?"

"The thing you said to him the other night—'what's a gentleman called now,' or whatever it was?"

He nodded.

"Thanks."

"Hey," said Nat.

"Grace always said he was a jerk. She was his first choice, by the way."

"She was?"

"She had a boyfriend of her own at the time."

"And now?"

A wave rippled by, a green wave rippling a green reflection in her eyes. "No. He had personal problems."

"Like what?"

"He was sort of married."

"Sort of?"

"You know."

But he didn't. Out there, offshore and separated from everyone else, Nat asked a question he might not have asked on land. "Have you had any married boyfriends?"

"What do you take me for?"

Nat laughed. She raised an eyebrow—her right, the opposite of Grace. Did it have something to do with the way the egg had split?

"What are you thinking about?" she said.

"Eggs."

"Eggs?"

"Eggs and you."

"You're funny," Izzie said.

They fell silent. There was no sound but that of the sea; the sea, which began moving her a little closer to him. Their legs touched under the surface. Since the water was so clear they could have glanced down easily and seen this contact, but neither did: they pretended it was happening somewhere else, out of sight. But it was happening, all right; Nat felt something new going through him, or perhaps something he'd known before, just magnified by the emerald water, the deep blue sky, the scented air.

Izzie backed away. Nat saw for the first time that she had a speargun in one hand, dangling down in the water.

"What's that for?"

"You like seafood?"

"Yes," he said, although his mom almost never served it.

Izzie checked the sun, lower over the island now, and pulled down her mask. "Jukin' time," she said.

"Jukin' time?"

"When the big ones come out, country boy."

She stuck the snorkel in her mouth and swam off at a speed that amazed him, her fins, not quite breaking the surface, churning away. In what seemed like seconds, she had rounded a stony point at the south end of the beach and disappeared.

He thought of Patti. She'd spelled *incident* wrong. He'd made spelling mistakes too. Maybe Izzie couldn't spell it either. He thought of testing her on the word, a disgusting idea he quashed almost as soon as it left the gate. And Patti had nice breasts too, although she'd never dream of swimming topless. All this led nowhere, and was still leading nowhere when something tickled his toes. He didn't panic this time, but peered down through the clear water and saw a little green fish nibbling at him. He swam a few lazy strokes, turned on his back, floated under a purpling sky.

Did he actually fall asleep? It was close: his mind drifted,

drifted, down into one of the seagoing sagas of his child-hood. Pirates, pistols, parrots, pieces of eight. Only a slight chill, the difference between the ocean temperature and his own making itself felt at last, brought him back to full wake-fulness. He treaded water, gazed out to sea.

The sun had sunk behind Aubrey's Cay, graying the water around him, except for the wave tips, still liquid emerald. In the distance, light still shone bright, blazing on the sail of a lone windsurfer. With the wind at his back, he approached very quickly, skimming toward the point that Izzie had rounded, disappearing for a few seconds, then reappearing, much closer, cutting back toward the beach. With a sound from his board like tearing paper, the windsurfer blew by Nat, about ten yards away: a brown-tanned, barrel-chested, skinny-legged man, wearing a bathing suit even skimpier than Nat's and a look of glee on his face. He ran his board right onto the beach, skipped nimbly off, noticed Nat, waved. Nat swam in.

The windsurfer—older than Nat had first thought, with a trim gray beard and gray hair, long, wild, matted with salt water—was lowering the sail.

"I saw you were in residence," he said, nodding up toward the house; a white flag with a black *Z* on it now flew over the roof. "And so dropped in. You're the physical trainer, as I re-call? Angelo, is it?"

"No," Nat said, and introduced himself.

"Not the trainer?"

"A friend."

"Ah. Of the girls." He gave Nat a closer look, or perhaps actually saw him for the first time. "Or of one particularly."

"I'm a friend of the girls."

"As am I," the man said. "A friend of the girls, indeed of the whole lovely family." He held out his hand. "May I pre-sent myself? Leo Uzig."

They shook hands. Leo Uzig's hand was big, out of propor-tion to the rest of him, except for his head. "Where did you drop in from, Mr. Uzig?" Nat said.

"Excellent question. You see that island? No. The one to the north. Not that. To the right. South, then. Got it. Discovered, and please spare me the politically correct boilerplate, by Drake in 1568, thus the name of the simple but pleasant Sir Francis Inn, where I spend my Christmases. Also explaining, to anticipate your question, my long association with the Zorns, the blanks easily filled in. You, I take it, are a student at some Ivy institution."

"Not exactly," said Nat. "I'm at Inverness."

"What luck," said Leo Uzig. "We're fellow inmates, then, you a freshman—you are a freshman?"

"Yes."

"And me chairman of the department of philosophy. If you'll just help me pull my board above the high-tide line, we can be safely inside before the no-see-ums come out."

"No-see-ums?" said Nat. Something bit him on the back of the neck.

Dinner on the terrace: mosquito coils burning on the tile floor, candles burning on the table, more stars than Nat had ever seen shining in a soft black sky, everyone barefoot except the servants. Professor Uzig sat at Mr. Zorn's end of the table, Anton at Mrs. Zorn's, Albert and Izzie on one side, Grace and Nat on the other. They ate the lobsters Izzie had caught, drank something called goombay smash, then Krug, then a Meursault, and more Krug, while a guitarist brought from Virgin Gorda played in the background and the smells of flowers and of the sea took turns drifting by. Could life really be this sweet? Nat had never even imagined it.

"We're taking Phil three twenty-two from Leo next semester," Izzie said across the table to Nat, her nose pink from the sun. "You should too."

"A three hundred course?" Nat said.

"A misnomer," said Professor Uzig, "dating back into the academic mists. Three twenty-two is now for freshmen only, selected freshmen."

"It's full, isn't it?" said Grace.

"Oh, yes," said Professor Uzig, "long full."

"What's it about?" said Nat.

"You haven't heard of the famous course that teaches people to think?" said Mr. Zorn. "Isn't that the one, Leo?"

"You know my thoughts on that subject," said Professor Uzig.

"It's called 'Superman and Man: Nietzsche and Cobain,' " Izzie said. "Isn't that cool?"

"Cool?" said Grace.

The girls stared across the table at each other. Izzie looked down.

"I don't know anything about Nietzsche," Nat said; he didn't know much about Cobain, either.

Professor Uzig turned to him, his hair washed and dried now, but still wild, his teeth and the whites of his eyes the same color as the Meursault. "Of course you do, young man," he said.

"Nat," said Izzie.

A quick smile crossed his face as the professor continued: "That's like saying you don't know anything about Christ or—"

"Walt Disney," said Mr. Zorn.

Everyone laughed, except the professor, and Nat, who wanted to hear what he was going to say.

"Yes, or Walt Disney, I suppose, but that simply demonstrates the power of the trivial in our times," the professor said. "Nietzsche, on the other hand, is not trivial, and, unlike Mr. Disney, is inside all our minds at all times, whether we are aware or not."

"That sounds almost scary," said Mrs. Zorn. "Like that movie, oh, what was it again?"

"*Night of the Living Dead*?" said Anton.

"No."

"*The Little Shop of Horrors*?" said Albert.

"No," said Mrs. Zorn. "Oh, why won't it come to me?"

"Go on, Leo," said Mr. Zorn. Mrs. Zorn's end of the table quieted.

Professor Uzig was sitting back in his chair, arms crossed. "I think I've said enough."

"Please go on, Leo," said Mrs. Zorn.

"Yes," said Grace. "You're just getting to the good part. What's Nietzsche saying inside my head?"

"You already know what he's saying—if you choose to put it that way. None of us would be the way we are without Nietzsche."

Nat saw Anton—flexing his forearm in the candlelight—pause.

"But give us some idea of his philosophy," Izzie said.

"So, you want spoon-feeding," said Professor Uzig. "Since it's Christmas, then, and such a beautiful night, and since the concept of learning to think, by which I mean to think originally, is in the air, and since, as an original thinker, Nietzsche has no superior—" He paused, took a drink, looked at Mr. Zorn. "Here is some idea of his philosophy, then, as it applies to the act of thinking, thinking of the first water. Our supreme insights, he says, should sound like follies, even crimes." He downed the rest of his drink, almost the whole glass, in one gulp. "Even crimes."

"Like Galileo and the Inquisition," Nat said; it just popped out, he had no business speaking at all.

Professor Uzig turned to him, eyebrows, gray and wild, rising. "Exactly."

A bare foot pressed itself against his.

Mr. Zorn laughed. "I love your bullshit, Leo, I really do. World-class. But if you picked that quote—or invented it—to goad me into endowing that Leo Uzig chair of yours, the answer's still no."

"Does he have to be so rude?" Grace said.

"Grace," said Mrs. Zorn.

Grace gave her a furious look. It made Mrs. Zorn's hand

shake. Nat saw the reflected candlelight from her rings making jagged patterns on the far wall.

"Nietzsche didn't mind a little rudeness, did he, Leo?" said Mr. Zorn.

"He was rather correct in his personal dealings, in fact," said Professor Uzig. "Excluding the period of his madness, of course."

"Let's exclude Lizzie Borden's one bad day while we're at it," said Mr. Zorn.

Mr. Zorn was gone by the time Nat got up the next morning; the noise of the takeoff woke him. He went onto his balcony, found the skimpy European bathing suit gone, American-style trunks in its place. He put them on, went down the path to the beach. On the deck of one of the villas lay a pile of snorkeling equipment. He borrowed mask, fins, and snorkel, as well as a large fishnet, and jumped into the sea.

The sea calm, without a ripple, the sun rising directly in front of him, changing the color of everything moment by moment; and the water itself, as he sank into it, still that perfect temperature: it relaxed him to the core. Trailing the net as he'd seen Izzie trail her speargun, he set off toward the point.

Nat saw brightly colored fish, coral heads and fans, a ray, a barracuda, all things the Discovery Channel had prepared him for. It hadn't prepared him for the feeling of this sea, the experience of being in it. He thought of all kinds of metaphors—amniotic, baptismal, blood—none of them quite right.

Nat was around the point, rising and falling with a swell so gradually begun that he was hardly aware of it, watching a tiny purple-and-gold fish nibble at a piece of coral that resembled antlers, and thinking *antlers, St. Nick,* and smiling into his mouthpiece, when he heard a low whine. It grew louder. He raised his head, saw that he'd gone much farther than he'd thought, all the way to the back side of the island,

and, once again, a surprising distance from shore; was there some sort of current? As he oriented himself, he saw the cigarette boat, source of the whining sound, come shooting out of the natural harbor, throwing a frothing bow wave in front, a rooster tail behind. As it came closer, he could make out Grace at the wheel, Professor Uzig in the stern. Their course would take them hundreds of yards to the north, but Grace suddenly changed it and bore straight at him. Nat felt an adrenaline rush, was just about to do something, maybe dive straight down, when the cigarette veered sharply, reared up like a reined-in horse and settled rocking beside him. Grace and Professor Uzig, a book in his hand, gazed down.

"Scare you?" Grace said.

"No."

She laughed. "I'm dropping Leo at the Sir Francis, then going over to Pusser's for supplies. Want to come?"

"Think I'll just stay here."

"Not permanently, I hope," said Professor Uzig.

"Suit yourself," Grace said. "And if you spit in your mask, it won't fog up like that."

"You're supposed to spit in it?"

"Unless you're too dainty."

She gave him a look. Professor Uzig, laughing, didn't see it. The book in his hand had a German title. Grace hit the throttle, circled Nat once—she shouted something at him, might have been "Don't get eaten"—and roared away. Nat caught the name on the stern: *Manchineel.* He spat in his mask, swished it with seawater, kept going, his vision much improved.

Some time later, how long he didn't know, but the sun was high in the sky, warming his back even though he'd begun shivering, Nat swam toward shore. He came to a beach he hadn't noticed before, a small beach beyond the harbor, almost hidden by rocky outcrops at each end. He took off his gear, saw a few strands of seaweed and some shells marking the high-tide line, carried everything above it. That was when he noticed Izzie, previously hidden from his sight on a patch of sand among the rocks. She lay facedown on a towel, reading a book, wearing nothing.

Nat stood there as though cast under a spell, aware of her, aware that his mouth was open. What was the right thing to do? If she'd been wearing something, anything, even just bikini bottoms, he could have spoken. But not like this. Therefore the right thing was to quietly, very quietly, without making the slightest—

Izzie stiffened, jerked her head around, had the towel over herself in a moment.

"Sorry," he said. "I didn't know—"

"That's all right." She sat up. "I thought it was that creep Anton."

"He's a creep?"

Izzie ignored the question, looked past him, saw the snorkel gear, the net. "Catch anything?"

"Didn't try. I was hoping for one like Lorenzo."

"Have to go to the Pacific for that. No clown triggerfish here."

"That's what he is, a clown triggerfish?"

"Yeah. And sit down. You're making me squint in the sun. I'll get wrinkles."

He sat on the sand.

"What are you reading?"

She held it up: *Young Goodman Brown.*

He thought: *We'll be in class together.* "Have you come to the part about him being the chief horror?" he said.

"That's where I am right now. You think it's important?"

"Probably. The ending doesn't make sense otherwise."

She looked at him. "Like it down here?"

"How can you even ask?"

"Is it your first time?"

"Yeah."

"Everyone's like that their first time. After a while you learn the truth about the Caribbean."

"Which is?"

"It's one big slum when the sun doesn't shine."

"I don't believe that."

"Neither do I, actually."

"Is it something Grace says?"

Pause. "Maybe," she said. A shadow passed over them. Nat glanced up, saw a pelican; had to be a pelican, with that fish dangling from its long beak. "Let's go for a swim," Izzie said.

She rose, dropped the towel, ran down the beach, dove in with a whoop. Nat ran down the beach too, dove in too, even gave a whoop, though he wasn't one for whooping. She was already thirty or forty yards out, her stroke effortless, her speed astonishing. Nat splashed after her.

Izzie treaded water over a reddish bottom. "That's my favorite coral head," she said, gazing down.

"How deep is it?"

"Forty feet, on the bottom."

"You use scuba, right?"

"Scuba's for wimps," she said. The next moment she did a duck dive and kicked down; became blurrier, smaller, and stayed that way for what seemed like a long time; then grew bigger and clearer again. She came bursting through the surface, took a deep breath, handed him something.

"What's this?"

"A sand dollar. Keep it for luck."

He tucked it in the pocket of his trunks. "Are you on the swim team?" he said.

"Swim team?"

"At school."

Izzie looked incredulous. "Sis boom bah," she said.

"But you're an incredible swimmer."

"You should see Grace."

They rose and fell with the sea. Again, it seemed to be pushing her toward him. The reply to her last remark had come at once, but he held it in, held it in, while the sea moved them closer and closer, and the sun made gold sparkles all over the surface, just like those gold sparkles in her eyes, and finally it came bursting out, as though he too had come up from a deep dive.

"I want to see *you*," he said.

One more swell and they were touching. This time Izzie didn't back away. Her arms went around him; his circled her; they kissed, warm and salty.

After, lying in the sandy patch between the rocks, they were thirsty. Nat climbed a palm tree, not a tall or particularly straight one, but still a palm tree, plucked a coconut—"no, no, the one to the left"—smashed it open on a rock. They drank its milk. Smashing a coconut! Drinking the milk! Some ran down his chin and she licked it off.

"One thing," she said.

"What's that?"

"It might be a good idea to keep this a secret, at least for now."

"Why?"

"Grace can be funny."

"How?"

"Trust me. Who knows her better?"

"What is it we're keeping secret, exactly?"

"Whatever's going to happen with us."

"Keeping it from Grace means keeping it from everybody, doesn't it?"

"You're so smart."

Smart, sweaty, coated here and there with sand. Did keeping it from everybody include Patti? He had to tell her soon, didn't he? Whether or not he had to morally, he knew that he would tell her the next time they spoke; he couldn't lie to Patti. At the same time, he thought: *Our best ideas should sound like follies.*

He said yes.

* * *

One more vacation note. There was a birthday party for the twins on the thirty-first. Boats overflowed the natural harbor, four or five planes landed, perhaps a hundred party goers came in all, although not Mr. Zorn, en route to Zurich, or possibly Lahore. Nat learned that Grace had been born on the thirty-first, at 11:53 P.M., but Izzie hadn't arrived until 12:13 A.M., on the first. They hadn't been born on the same day, not even in the same year.

10

*Let's have a little fun today. What would Nietzsche have
thought of contemporary American culture?*
—Professor Uzig, opening remarks at a Friday
afternoon seminar, Philosophy 322

Saul Medeiros had an auto body place called Saul's Collision on the outskirts of Fitchville. An auto body place, not a
high-tech store: because of that, Freedy left the HDTV in the
van—that rusted-out VW van of his mother's, with the stupid
flowers painted on the front—and went into the office.

An old son of a bitch with hairs growing on the top of his
nose—no shit—sat behind a greasy desk, and a woman in a
quilted parka stood on the other side.

"Will it be as good as new?" she was saying.

"Oh, sure," the old guy told her, rubbing his chin, unshaven
for three or four days. "Hunnert percent."

"That's a relief," she said, leaning over the desk and
signing some paper; the old guy's eyes followed the movements of the pen. "I know it's crazy, but I'm really attached to
that car."

"Yeah," said the old guy, "it's crazy."

She left. Freedy lounged against the doorpost, cool. The
old guy lit a cigarette, looked him over, dropped the match on
the floor. It came down to who was going to talk first, although Freedy didn't know why. He talked first.

"You Saul?" he said.

"Depends who's asking."

"Says Saul on the sign on the roof."

No answer. The old guy folded his stubby arms over his gut.

"Freedy's asking," said Freedy. "Me."

The old guy nodded. "Ronnie mentioned you. My nephew, up the valley."

"Right."

"What d'ya think of him?"

"Who?"

"Ronnie. My nephew up the valley."

"What I think of him? You know, he's just . . . he's Ronnie, right? We played football."

"How was he?"

"Huh?"

"Ronnie. At football. Any good?"

"You know Ronnie. He's a pussy."

Saul Medeiros smiled; his teeth were the color of nicotine. "And you? Were you any good?"

"I was a fucking leg breaker, Mr. Medeiros."

"Attaboy," said Saul Medeiros. He took a deep drag from his cigarette. "What's the story with this girl Cheryl Ann?"

"Huh?"

"You and Ronnie and this piece of ass, Cheryl Ann."

"That was a long time ago, Mr. Medeiros. How do you even know about it?"

"One of those family legends. All families have them. Maybe it's kind of a legend in your family too."

"It's not."

"No? Don't think I know your family, comes to that. Know a lot of families in the valley, but not yours."

"We're not really from the valley. I am, like. Born here. But my mom came from out of state, back in the sixties."

"And your old man?"

"Fucked off."

"He from here?"

"Don't know where he was from. He was just some hippie, with one of those hippie names."

"Like what?"

"Walrus. They called him Walrus."

"Googoogajoob," said Saul Medeiros.

Freedy, suspecting that Saul Medeiros had lapsed into Portagee, remained silent.

"Lot of hippies came here back then," Saul Medeiros said.

"Must have been a fucked-up time."

"Hell, no. Never got laid so much in my life."

That surprised Freedy. Then came another surprise: a mental picture of this toad with the hair on his nose putting it to his mother. "What was *your* nickname back then?" he asked.

"Some people don't get nicknames," Saul Medeiros said. He stubbed out his cigarette. "That it, then?"

"What?"

"Just getting acquainted, or you got something for me?"

"The second one."

"Thought so. Let's go out back."

Saul Medeiros offered him seventy bucks for the HDTV.

"What's this," said Freedy, "the Comedy Channel?" A good line, real quick, real cool, showing that California polish.

"Seventy bucks," said Saul Medeiros. "Take it or leave it."

Just what Ronnie had told him, probably where Ronnie had got it from. Freedy decided right then he didn't like negotiating with the Medeiroses, didn't like negotiating at all, when it came down to it. For a second or two there, he'd had enough, enough of negotiating, which always meant somebody—like the spics at A-1—cutting a piece out of him. Come to think of it, what was the difference between a spic and a Portagee? Not much, which had to be a brilliant observation, made him feel better and forget all about the speedy little movie that had just flashed through his mind, a movie that ended with Saul Medeiros on the floor. No matter what, bottom line, he himself was no spic or Portagee. He was . . . whatever the hell he was, kind of depended, it suddenly occurred to him, on who his father actually was. What the fuck: he could be any goddamned thing.

"In a coma or just thinking it over?" said Saul Medeiros.

"Another good one, Saul. I like a sense of humor."

Saul checked his watch.

"Know what these things cost new?" Freedy said.

Saul shook his head. "Means nothing. Like with a car. Drive one off the lot, it's worth half. What you pay for that new-car smell."

"I don't think it's half."

"Don't tell me. I'm in the business." He lit another cigarette. "But I'm a soft touch," he continued behind a cloud of smoke, "so I'll tell you what. Think you can get more?"

"More what?"

"Stuff."

"Sure."

"You got some kind of contact?"

"Trade secret, Saul."

"Very smart. Thing is, if you're in a position to get more stuff, then maybe we could build us a working relationship. You follow?"

"Yeah. A working relationship. I can get stuff. Don't you worry about my end."

"Good. Then what I'm going to do, an investment in goodwill like they say on Wall Street, is give you ninety for the goddamn TV."

Freedy smiled. Didn't actually smile on the outside, much too sharp for that, or if he did he wiped it off his face real quick, but, hey—here he was not just negotiating but negotiating the shit out of an operator like Saul Medeiros.

"Appreciate your sentiments, Saul. Sincerely. But you know what sounds better than ninety?"

Saul smiled that nicotine smile. "Some round number, Freedy?"

Freedy smiled back, on the outside this time. He himself had great teeth. "You got it."

Which was how Freedy squeezed a C-note out of Saul Medeiros. He really was an amazing person.

On the way home, meaning on the way back from Fitchville to his mother's place in the flats, all that talk about Cheryl Ann gave Freedy an idea. Cheryl Ann hadn't made the cheerleading squad—lost by two or three votes, as Freedy remembered—and even then had been kind of chubby, and maybe a little annoying with that loud laugh of hers, showing the fleshy thing that hangs down at the back of the mouth and all, but none of that was important about her. What was important about her was that she'd meet him behind the field house after practice sometimes—and that she must still be around. The fact was that Cheryl Ann remained the only girl who'd given him a blow job; meaning by that a complete one and for free. And she'd still be around, for sure: Freedy'd done some growing up by now—hadn't he carved out a place for himself across the country?—and knew that a girl like Cheryl Ann would never go anywhere.

Cheryl Ann didn't live in the flats. Her place was actually on College Hill, on the dark side but still almost halfway up. What was her father? Plumber? Septic guy? Something like that, enough to put them on the Hill. Freedy drove past the Glass Onion, the last of the boarded-up buildings at the bottom, turned onto her street; no need to even think where he was going, not like LA. He parked in front of her house.

Only it was gone. And so were the houses around it, replaced by a huge rounded thing, all glass and smooth red-brown concrete. Freedy drove to the end of the block and checked the street signs. He was in the right spot; everything else was wrong.

Freedy got out of the VW van, walked up to the main entrance, read the bronze plaque: *The Avner K. and Rita M. Budnoy Multicultural Studies Center*. What was this? Some college shit where Cheryl Ann's house used to be? Since when was the college on this side of the Hill? He crossed the snowy lawn to the first normal house and knocked on the door. An old bag answered.

"Lookin' for Cheryl Ann," Freedy said.

"You don't mean Cheryl Ann Crane?"

"Why not?"

The old bag gave him a long look. "Do I know you from somewhere?"

"Nope."

"But you're looking for Cheryl Ann Crane?"

"Yup."

She waved her hand at the new building. "Long gone. The Cranes sold out to the college, as anyone can plainly see."

"Long gone where?"

"Florida. What with the money they got paid they set themselves up in Florida. Why couldn't the college have planned that place just a tich bigger is what I want to know."

"And Cheryl Ann, she went too?"

"She surely did. Climate must of agreed with her. Hadn't been there more than three months but she married a doctor. One of those Cubans, but still, a doctor."

"Cheryl Ann married a doctor?"

"They sent me a picture from the wedding. One of those real dark Cubans, but a doctor."

"With that fat butt, she married a doctor?"

"Some men can't resist a fat butt—don't you know that by now?"

Freedy went home. Not home, but to his mother's. On the way he sniffed up the last of his crystal meth. Tweak. Zing. Snow started falling, or maybe not.

This was all temporary. What he needed to do was put

together one of those nest eggs, and then . . . start a business, say. Since pools were what he knew, why not a pool business? Had to be in a warm climate, not California, too superficial, like everyone said. Warm climate, not California: Florida! And would it hurt to look up Cheryl Ann while he was at it?

The kitchen was a mess: muffin tins everywhere, jars of ingredients with the tops off all over the counters, milk and eggs that should have been put back in the fridge left wherever she'd happened to put them down. He dug a muffin out of a tin, took a bite, threw the rest in the trash. Didn't even taste like food.

Freedy stood over the trash, having smelled a familiar smell. He saw the stubbed-out end of a joint in a discarded tuna can. That meant she was in her bedroom, having one of her naps. Get fucked up, take a nap—part of her life cycle.

Freedy heard the mail falling through the slot, went to get it. Electric bill, phone bill, coupons, something about hunger in Guatemala, and a letter addressed to his mother. He held it up to the light, rubbed it between his thumb and index finger, thought he felt a little crinkling. Made him curious, like Curious Whoever-he-was, some monkey she'd always been reading to him about when she wasn't painting nightmares on his walls. He was curious and she was napping—how the goddamn hippies lost the world.

Freedy had heard about steaming open envelopes but never actually tried. How hard could it be? He plugged in the kettle, always handy for tea—there were dozens of different teas on the shelves, chamomile, lemongrass, raspberry, banana, pick-me-up teas, relax-me teas, teas for thinking, teas for feeling, teas for wiping out cancer. Steam came boiling out of the kettle. Freedy held the envelope over the spout.

Nothing to it. The flap loosened all by itself, and Freedy peeked in the envelope, saw a folded sheet of paper. He unfolded it: no writing on the paper, but C-notes inside. Two of them. Suddenly it was a C-note kind of day: had to be a good omen.

Two C-notes in an envelope and nothing else. Couldn't be her welfare or her disability or whatever the hell it was: the government didn't send cash. Some muffin buyer? With no statement, no name? Some pot thing? But drugs weren't dealt like that. There was an exchange, this for that, at the same time. Still, with her, maybe a pot thing. What else could it be?

Freedy heard her in the hall. Before the kitchen door opened, he had the money resealed and on the counter with the rest of the mail. Moving at the speed of crystal meth.

"Hi, Freedy," she said, yawning and scratching under her tit. "I had the most amazing dream."

Freedy kept his mouth shut; he never wanted to hear another one of her dreams.

"What are you up to?" she said after a little silence.

"Just making tea."

"You are?"

"Want some?"

"Why, sure, Freedy, that's very thoughtful of you." She sat down. "The mango-ginkgo would be nice—that orange box."

Freedy had never made tea before, but how hard could it be? He opened the box, took out a handful of teabags, dropped a few into each cup, poured in the boiling water.

They sat at the table, drinking tea. "My goodness, Freedy," she said after the first sip. "You've got a knack."

"Don't mention it."

She smiled at him. "It's nice having you home, Freedy."

"Yeah."

"Any idea how long you're—any idea what your plans are?"

"Yeah, as a matter of fact. But it's too early to say, if you know what I mean."

"I do, Freedy. I know that one very well." She turned her shadow eyes on him. "We have something in common after all."

The fuck we do. "This, uh, father thing," Freedy said.

"I'm sorry?"

"Walrus."

"Walrus?"

"Wasn't that what he was called? My father, I'm talking about."

"I beg you not to raise your voice, Freedy. You know I can't deal with violence of any kind."

"I'd just like a few facts about him, is all. I'm not a Portagee or something, am I?"

"Please, Freedy, no discrimination."

"But am I?"

"No. You come from bland ethnic stock, just like me."

Freedy missed that one. "What was his real name, for starters?"

"Real name," she said. "I don't even know what that means."

"Like on the goddamn birth certificate."

She leaned closer to him; he could smell the pot smoke trapped in all her hair. "I've told you before, Freedy. It was a one-time thing. Very special, of course, but one-time. He was a stranger, really, passing through. In a mental sense, more than physical. Try not to judge me too harshly. The times were different then, and the person that was me . . ." Her eyes focused on something distant. He heard music coming faintly from her bedroom: Cat Stevens, or some other artist of the first water, whatever that meant.

He finished her sentence for her: "No longer fucking exists."

Later he thought of examining the envelope the money had come in, maybe checking the postmark or whatever that thing was called. By that time the kitchen was cleaned up, sort of, and the envelope gone.

11

I'm aware that this is known as the course that teaches you how to think. Anyone here for that reason should transfer at once. No one can teach you how to think. You must teach yourself.
—Professor Uzig, remarks on the twentieth
  anniversary of teaching Philosophy 322

"**D**id you bring a sample of your writing?" asked Professor Uzig.

Second semester, first day back at Inverness, 8:00 A.M., Professor Uzig's office in Goodrich Hall. Nat, petitioning to enter Philosophy 322, Superman and Man: Nietzsche and Cobain, handed Professor Uzig several essays from the first term, as well as the prize-winning "What I Owe America."

Professor Uzig flipped quickly through the school essays, came to "What I Owe America," paused. His eyes darted back and forth, scanning with a speed and intensity that Nat, sitting across his desk, could feel. Professor Uzig glanced up.

"Do you believe this bilge?" he said.

"Which part, specifically?" Nat said; a composed reply, perhaps, but his face had grown hot at once, a change he hoped his fresh tan concealed.

"Here, for example," said Professor Uzig, turning a page. He seemed so much harsher than the dinner guest at Aubrey's Cay, didn't even look the same. He wore a charcoal gray tweed jacket, white shirt, and navy blue tie, his hair was combed, and his tan, which had been much deeper than Nat's, had almost completely faded. "Where you write, 'The nation is like a monument continuously under construction and the job of the citizen is to make it better.' "

The question: did he believe that? Professor Uzig watched him, the papers steady, absolutely still in his hand, almost an extension of his fingers. It struck Nat that no written material presented any challenge to Professor Uzig, that all texts were instantly transparent to him. "What's the alternative?" Nat said.

"To your metaphor, or to the action of the citizen, the metaphor accepted?"

"The latter," said Nat.

Professor Uzig didn't move, didn't speak, just watched Nat over the papers in his hand. After a while Nat couldn't stand the silence any longer, and said: "I meant what's the better alternative."

Professor Uzig laid the papers on his desk, aligned them neatly, squarely, and sat back in his chair. "You used *continuously* in the proper manner," he said. "And you can write a periodic sentence. Admission is granted."

"Thank you," Nat said.

"The first class is today at one-thirty. You will have read the first part of *Beyond Good and Evil*."

"By Nietzsche?"

Oh, how Nat wished he could have that question back.

As for *continuously*, he'd used it by chance, having no clue that it differed from *continually* until that moment. It was also the first time he'd heard the expression *periodic sentence*.

Back at his desk in room seventeen on the second floor of Plessey Hall, overlooking the quad, Nat had just begun reading the preface to *Beyond Good and Evil*—"Supposing truth to be a woman"—when he heard a knock at the door. Unusual, because almost everybody simply walked in.

"Come in," he said.

A woman in a long fur coat entered. For a moment he didn't recognize her. Then he did: Wags's mom. He rose. "Hi."

"Hello," she said. "Nat, isn't it?"

"Yes."

She glanced around the room, then back at him. "Nose to the grindstone, I see."

"Just trying to keep up. If you're looking for Wags— Richard—he's not in right now. I haven't actually seen him yet."

"You won't. Richard won't be coming back, at least not this semester."

"But . . . but we don't even have the results yet. And he was doing fine. Better than me."

She gave him a look that might have been cold; but why? They didn't know each other at all. She took off her black kid gloves, snagging one for a moment on a ring. "He needs rest."

"Why? What happened?"

"You'd know better than I."

"What does that mean?"

A cold look, beyond doubt. "No one is blaming you, but it might have been nice if you'd drawn our attention, or the college's, to the kind of shape he was in."

"I don't understand."

"Don't you? Richard should have been under a doctor's care. He is now."

"But for what?"

She regarded him in puzzlement, slightly exaggerated puzzlement. "You act like someone not very bright, yet Richard says you are most emphatically the opposite. Are you really saying you had no idea of the mental state he's been in?"

"Everyone's under a lot of stress here."

"I'm sure. But not everyone is driven to a breakdown."

"Wags had a breakdown?" Nat wasn't even sure what the word meant, not in practice.

"Wags, as everyone calls him for some reason, had a breakdown."

"Is he all right?"

"Just dandy."

She stood over Wags's desk, gazing at something he'd scratched into its surface: *Help! We're prisoners of the future!* or something like that, as Nat remembered. Her eyes moistened, but nothing leaked out. When she spoke again, her voice had lost its edge. "He's a little better, in fact, and thanks for asking. They're probably letting him come home next month."

"From where?"

"A very nice place, not far from here." Her hand went to Wags's chem lab notes, stacked neatly on the desk by Nat before vacation; squared the way Professor Uzig had arranged Nat's papers on his own desk not long before.

"Do they allow visitors?" Nat said.

"They do," said Wags's mom. Her eyes moistened again. Nat looked away.

Nat helped her pack Wags's things and carry them down to her car. On the last trip, she came out of Wags's bedroom holding his pillow, and said: "Wasn't there a TV?"

"Oh," said Nat.

"The guest room TV, I think it was."

"Damn it," he said.

"What?"

Nat told her about the theft before Christmas, his call to campus security, and how he had forgotten to file a report the next day.

"You forgot?"

The cold look was back. How to explain about the twins, the shattered aquarium, Lorenzo? "I'm sorry," he said.

She was already on the phone. Someone from campus security appeared five minutes later. Nat recounted waking up, seeing the thief run off, losing him in the basement corridor.

The security officer took notes and said: "Know anything about the TV in the student union?"

"The TV in the student union?" said Nat.

"The high-definition one in the lounge. It disappeared three days ago."

"No," Nat said, "I don't know anything about it." He felt the gaze of Wags's mom. "Why would I?"

The security officer was watching him too. All that scrutiny made Nat feel like he'd done something wrong, not just forgetting to file the report, but really wrong. And he hadn't. He'd never stolen anything in his life, not even a pack of gum. Anger, an uncommon feeling, rose inside him; and he rose with it: a tall kid, and strong. He wanted an answer to that question: *why would I?* No answer came, but in the silence, Nat got past the uniform of the security guard, the implacable expression on his face, even noticed a resemblance to his next-door neighbor back home, the weekend clerk at the hardware store. His anger subsided. "I was away over Christmas," he said. "I got back late last night." He sat down.

The security guard closed his notebook. "A big guy with a ponytail, you say."

"Yes."

The security guard turned to Wags's mom. She was wringing the kid gloves gently in her hands. "We'll do what we can," he said.

"I don't really care," said Wags's mom.

"Beyond Good and Evil—part one," said Professor Uzig. Philosophy 322 met in the small domed room at the top of Goodrich Hall, one floor above the professor's office. Windows all around and lots of wood—mahogany molding, wide-plank pine floor, oval cherrywood table, and sitting at it Professor Uzig, Nat, Grace, Izzie, and four other freshmen, only one of whom, the top student in his English class the previous semester, Nat knew. "Who wants to go first?"

Everyone looked at everyone. No one spoke. Outside, Nat

saw a crow fly by, and beyond it a black plume of smoke rose from somewhere in the lower town, an area he'd not yet set foot in. The flats, they called it, probably where the security officer, and all the hardware clerks, maintenance people, gardeners, secretaries, receptionists lived. He looked back across the table, found Izzie gazing at him. Grace too. They both gave him a little nod, the same nod exactly, and at exactly the same instant. And despite the fact that he had barely had time to get through the reading once, finding it by far the hardest text he'd ever come across, despite his certainty that he didn't understand it well, or possibly at all, a thought came to him, and he uttered it aloud: "Does the very fact that most people think something make it automatically wrong?"

Silence.

The crow, or another one, cawed nearby.

Then the bright girl from English 103 said, "Yeah. What is all that rising-above-the-common-herd stuff about? Sounds kind of elitist to me."

Grace snorted.

Izzie said, "Maybe he is elitist, but there's something almost . . . sweet about him at the same time."

And someone else said: "Sweet? Nietzsche? He was a syphilitic, dangerous bastard."

And they were off.

They talked about the fatalism of the weak-willed, the charm of the refutable idea, and how living things must vent their strength; about the will to power, Wagner, the Nazis and Hitler, and how the true and selfless may be inextricably linked, possibly identical to, the false and appetitive; they talked about the pressure of the herd and the courage of the original thinker; they talked about Friedrich Nietzsche. Professor Uzig hardly spoke, just sat in his captain's chair—none of the other chairs had arms—still and neat in his white shirt, navy tie, charcoal gray tweed jacket, but he dominated completely by the intensity of his concentration. Nat could feel him listening, feel him judging, and was sure the others could too. But what judgments he was coming to remained unknown, with one exception. A bearded student wearing a tiedyed shirt asked when they would be getting to Kurt Cobain, and Professor Uzig replied, "What's the point of developing powerful analytical tools if all you're going to do is waste them on popular culture?"

The bearded student said, "But I thought . . . ," and looked around for help. None came.

Just the same, Nat began to see the connection between Nietzsche and Kurt Cobain, not only Kurt Cobain, but so much of modern life, began to understand what Professor Uzig had been saying down on Aubrey's Cay about Nietzsche's influence. For example, hadn't he read something in part one about how even the laws of physics might be subjective? He was searching for the quotation, leafing quickly through his copy of *Beyond Good and Evil*, when he heard Professor Uzig saying: "Until tomorrow, then."

The chapel bell tolled. Class was over. Ninety minutes, gone like that. The sound of the bell, by now so familiar, seemed strange for a moment.

A foot pressed his under the table. He looked across at Izzie, writing in her date book, her golden-brown hair hanging over the page: dyed hair, he knew that now. His mind, already racing, began racing in another direction.

Grace, sitting beside Izzie, caught his eye. "I'm hungry," she said.

The three of them ate in the lounge at the student union: yogurt for Izzie, chocolate cake for Grace, an apple for Nat, unable to afford much eating off the meal plan. He noticed the empty space where the high-definition TV had been, told them about Wags and the theft of the two TVs.

"Were you scared?"

"A ponytail?"

"He just disappeared?"

Nat took them down to the basement corridor in Plessey

Hall. He showed them the padlocked doors to the storage lockers and the maintenance room, and the only unlocked door, the one to the janitor's closet.

Grace opened it. They regarded the brooms, mops, buckets, cleansers.

"Wags did the same thing the year he was at Choate," Izzie said.

"What same thing?" said Nat.

"The breakdown thing. Drugs."

Grace was inside the closet now, rummaging around. Without looking, Izzie reached out and took Nat's hand.

"Drugs?" he said. "I never saw him with any drugs."

"The damage was done."

Inside the closet, Grace said, "I've had an original thought."

"Don't scare me," Izzie said.

Grace laughed, turned sideways—Izzie letting go of his hand the instant before—raised one foot high like a trained Thai boxer, and kicked the back wall of the closet with a force that startled Nat. The top half of the wall fell out in one solid panel, dropping into darkness on the other side.

They crowded into the closet, peered through the opening. Beyond lay a narrow unlit tunnel, narrow but tall enough to stand in, with one large-diameter pipe and several smaller ones receding into the shadows and finally disappearing into complete blackness.

"This looks like fun," Grace said.

"Uh-oh," said Izzie.

12

"You still have not learned to gamble and show defiance!"—Thus Spake Zarathustra. *Fifteen hundred words on the importance of risk in Nietzsche's philosophy.*
—Essay assignment, Philosophy 322

"This," said Grace as she stepped up and through the open rectangle high in the back of the janitor's closet in the basement of Plessey Hall, stepping up and through as though it were some athletic event in which she specialized, "reminds me—"

"Of Alice," said Izzie.

On the other side, Grace turned, made circling motions with her hands as though blocked by some barrier, a mime beyond the looking glass. She laughed, a little laugh, excited, like a giggle. "Where was that cave?"

"New Mexico."

"The other one—the out-of-bounds one, where the bat flew into your hair."

"Kashmir," said Izzie.

"This is like that, only colder," Grace said. "Nat?"

"Yeah?"

"Close the door behind you."

Nat closed the closet door. Everything went black.

"Where the bat flew into Izzie's hair," Grace said in the darkness. "But I was the one who screamed."

120

"Bats don't bother me at all," Izzie said. "And what makes you think you screamed? You're not the screaming type."

"I'm not?"

Nat reached into his pocket, took out a pack of souvenir matches from Pusser's on Virgin Gorda, lit one. The sudden light captured a surprised look on Izzie's face; and a terrifying one, unless it was some trick of the match light, weak and yellow-edged, on Grace's. A terrifying look, as though she'd been reliving the bat experience, or making faces in the dark, practicing a silent scream. The terrifying look, if it was one, vanished at once, replaced by one of disapproval.

"You're like a Boy Scout," Grace said. "With those matches."

"Or a pothead," Nat replied. There were potheads at Inverness, but not nearly as many as at Clear Creek High.

Izzie laughed. She followed Grace through the opening, just as easily. Nat went last.

The match burned his fingers. He dropped it, lit another. The top of his head brushed the ceiling. "What is this place?" Izzie said.

Hard-packed dirt floor, damp air, a dripping sound, and the three pipes, the fattest one wrapped with asbestos. Nat recognized asbestos: they had some in the basement at home. "I think it's a steam tunnel," he said.

"What's that?"

"For heating the campus."

"That's how they do it?"

Nat laid his hand lightly on the pipe. It felt cold. "Maybe at one time," he said. He noticed a light switch on the wall, flicked it. Nothing happened.

"For heating the campus?" Grace said. "Does that mean there's a whole underground network, connecting every building?"

"Makes sense," Nat said.

"Wow," Grace said, already on her way. He followed with the match, cupped in his hand.

"Does this have anything to do with the TV thing?" Izzie said.

"Who cares?" said Grace, moving on. Nat heard Izzie coming closer from behind, felt her hand on his shoulder, briefly. He lit another match and kept going.

They walked down, down because the floor seemed to be sloping slightly, down the steam tunnel, Nat leading with the matches after the first hundred feet or so, the twins following. "This is so cool," one of them said. One of them: but he couldn't tell which, and it was the kind of thing either might say.

"Who said that?" he asked.

"Me." They answered together, at once, and both laughed. Nat laughed too. What the hell. And it was pretty cool down in the steam tunnel. He tried to figure out their direction— were they under the quad or going the other way?—and could not. Once he thought he heard a guitar playing somewhere overhead, very faint; after that, nothing but the sounds they made themselves, and from time to time, dripping water.

Nat had used up half the pack of matches before they came to a junction, a kind of crossroads, with an intersecting tunnel. He extended the match flame in all three directions: straight ahead and to the left, neither appearing different from what they'd already explored, and to the right. To the right was different: curtained off with spider webs, silvery and furred with dust. That meant—while Nat was thinking about what it meant, his match touched a silver strand, and flame ran up it like a fuse, followed the geometric pattern of the web, burned itself out in the center.

"That's like a whole art project, right there," one of the twins said. But which one: Nat really wanted to know this time. He turned, holding up the match. Their faces glowed in its light; the gold flecks in their eyes sparkled; he learned nothing.

"Maybe we should head back," he said.

"Why?" said Izzie.

"We're running out of matches, for one thing."

"So?" she said. "We can always feel our way back. Why not—"

"Go till the last match," Grace said.

Why not? Nat could think of reasons, but none that wouldn't sound wimpy. They weren't lost or anything like that, hadn't even left campus; and feeling their way back would be easy with the pipes. "Which way?" he said.

"Isn't it obvious?" said Grace. She reached out and swept away the unburned webs. The webs: they meant that no one had gone that way in some time. And the corollary: that there had been traffic in the other passages.

They entered the right-hand passage, Nat leading. Now there were no pipes but the asbestos-wrapped one. There were also spiderwebs brushing their faces, and occasional soft things under their feet. Nat heard water dripping again, louder now, and for a moment thought he felt a warm breeze on his face. He was down to four matches when Izzie said, "I kicked something funny."

They stopped. Nat bent down with his match, saw a magazine on the floor. He picked it up, blew off the dust, rubbed away grime with the heel of his hand: a *Playboy* magazine from May 1963. Grace took it, leafed through. In the match light, smiling nudes from long ago flickered by. "Incredible," she said.

"It is?" said Nat.

"She means the hairdos," Izzie said.

"Not just that," Grace said. "Look how wholesome they are. Like a bunch of virgins with those tits and asses stuck on."

"You think?" said Izzie, taking a step forward for a better view. The next moment, the very moment when the thought *they look pretty good to me* was going through Nat's mind, there was a cracking sound and Izzie dropped through the floor. Nat reached out for her, losing the match, caught her by the sleeve of her jacket; a sleeve made of some slippery material, and he lost that too, and in the pitch blackness, she fell.

No one screamed. The twins weren't the screaming type, and neither was he. Silence; the next sound a thump, down below.

Nat dug the matchbook out of his pocket, almost lost his grip on that too, almost couldn't get a match lit; but he did. Grace was on her hands and knees by then, peering into a hole in the floor: a dirt floor, but beneath an inch or two of dirt lay what was left of a square door or hatch cover. Just the rotted outer frame and the hinges—the rest was splinters and a hole.

"Izzie?" Grace called down into it. "Izzie?"

No response.

Nat knelt beside her, lowered the match into the hole. He saw nothing; or almost nothing. Down there somewhere, how far he couldn't tell, and off to one side, was a globe, a crystal globe that reflected the feeble match light from countless angles.

"What do you think—" he began, and then saw Grace getting a grip on a support beam at the edge of the hole. "No," he said, grabbing her arm. She shook him off in one violent motion, then heaved herself down into the hole, hanging from the beam by her hands. The next moment she swung forward, like a gymnast on the high bar, but unlike a gymnast, went hurtling into the dark. Her body overprinted the crystal globe, then came a shattering sound, but light and almost musical, and Nat thought: *chandelier*. Grace, trailing a comet's tail of match-lit crystals, fell from sight.

Nat heard a thump, much like the first, followed by the tinkle of crystals raining down, and then:

"Ow."

Followed by: "Iz? Are you all right?"

"I was until you landed on my ankle."

"Then why didn't you say anything?"

"Spiderwebs in my mouth."

The match went out.

"Nat?"

"Yeah?"

"We can't see you."

He lit another match. Two left in the pack.

"That's better. Doesn't he look like the Cheshire Cat?"

Nat leaned through the hole as far as could, held out the match at arm's length, saw what must have been their faces, two pale ovals tilted up in the dark. "No one's hurt?"

"We're fine."

"It's kind of soft."

"Like a bed."

"What's down there?"

"Hard to tell."

"But it's promising."

"Oh, yes."

Silence.

"Wait right there," Nat said. "I'll be back."

"Where are you going?"

"For help."

"Who said anything about help?"

"How are you going to get out?" Nat said.

He heard a soft crash, followed by tinkling glass, then silence.

"Could this be—?" one of them said.

"Not a—?"

"Mais oui."

"Like a sign."

He heard them laughing together. "What's going on?" he called.

"Nat? Come on down."

"What?"

"We've got a candle."

"From above."

"A big fat one."

"So?"

"What do you mean—so?"

"I mean what about getting back up?" Nat said.

Pause. Nat heard them talking, but too low to distinguish the words. "Just toss the matches down, if you're going to be like that," one of them said. Had to be Grace. She must have realized it was a chandelier before she jumped, must have thought she could hang on to it and somehow lower herself down. But still: she'd leaped into darkness, an unknown darkness. He'd seen it.

"Grace?" he said.

"Yeah?"

The match went out. One left. "How will you find them in the dark?" Nat said.

"No clue," said Grace. "Wasn't my idea."

"If everyone just shuts up," Izzie said, "we'll hear them land."

A dumb idea. Nat heard a giggle: Grace's giggle, surely. Then came silence, a deep silence down there under the campus. He thought of the land above, the way he'd seen it on the drive out of town in the Rolls, ancient and austere. An uncomfortable thought from down where he was, beneath it, although he didn't know why. They weren't lost, or anything like that.

"Trust me," Izzie said; had to be Izzie.

"Was that you, Izzie?"

"Who else?"

Only one left. A dumb idea. Nat dropped the matchbook through the hole, just let it go. He felt the friction strip as it slid off his fingertips.

13

"Thus speaks the red judge, 'Why did this criminal murder? He wanted to rob.' But I say unto you: his soul wanted blood, not robbery; he thirsted after the bliss of the knife." Identify the quotation; then, if you must watch a movie this weekend, rent the robbery-gone-wrong video of your choice.

—Friday afternoon seminar assignment,
  Philosophy 322

"Freedy?"

He grunted.

"If you're going to be staying for a while, and of course you're always welcome, as I'm sure you know—we're a family, after all, it only takes two, and—"

"Just spit it out."

"I wondered whether you were considering getting some kind of job. For contributing to the communal pot, to coin a phrase."

Freedy stared at her across the kitchen table—he was only trying to drink his coffee in peace, for Christ sake, but there she was, head twisted a little, having trouble with the clasp on a huge hoop earring—he stared at her and said nothing. No comment. No comment, at first because he thought he'd heard her asking him to pay for her dope, then when he understood, because it didn't deserve comment. She was his

127

so-called mother. And look at her. Didn't she owe him, owe him big-time? And why was it so fucking cold in the house?

Click. The clasp snapped into place. Couldn't she see how ridiculous she looked, like some gypsy wanna-be? He checked out his own reflection in the little mirror framed with seashells hanging over the sink. No gypsy there: a fuckin' animal, but with a brain, as the ponytail showed.

She was saying something: ". . . when you used to help out in the maintenance department, up at the college?"

Was she still on the job kick? "I remember a lot of things."

A good line. She waited for him to say more, sitting absolutely still. She was good at sitting absolutely still. He remembered a lot of things, but nothing at that moment. Outside the window, an icicle broke off and dropped with a faint thud in the snow.

"That wasn't so bad, was it?" she said. "The maintenance."

He thought of answering, *No comment. No comment* was what people with brains said. But she was pissing him off. "Are you telling me to look for a job?"

"Not telling, Freedy. Nothing like that. And just something temporary. As temporary as you like."

As temporary as he liked. Was there some meaning in that, some hidden meaning? Freedy was mulling over that when he was hit, from out of nowhere, by an amazing idea, the kind of idea that proved his braininess. It tied things together so nicely, at the same time backing her right against the wall. He showed her that smile of his—a ten-thousand-dollar smile, according to a friend of Estrella's who worked for a dentist, and said: "Then I'll need my birth certificate, won't I?"

"Birth certificate? Why?"

"Job application, what else?" Complete bullshit, of course—all they ever asked for was your license and social, but did she know that? Not a chance: never held down a real job in her life. So now he had her. No surprise there. They weren't on the same field, not when it came to brainpower. His brainpower came from elsewhere.

She did have one little surprise for him. Freedy had expected the birth certificate would be lost, or unavailable, or not around for some reason or other, but after a minute or two in her bedroom, she came back with it. "Here you go, Freedy."

He scanned it. Freedy hated official forms. They never made any sense. Like this one, with all these boxes and lines and different size print, even print in different whatever they were called, like Old English or something. *Standard Certificate of Live Birth:* what the hell was that? Like they had certificates of dead births? Didn't have them for abortions, which he knew for a fact because of Estrella's. He'd had to drive her. Hours in the waiting room, hours on the freeway going back—flipped-over truck blocking the lanes, he could still see the blood on the pavement—but no certificate.

Freedy's eyes roamed the stupid form, picked out his own name, and farther down hers, Starry Knight, and down below that was what he was after, must have taken five minutes to find it: *FATHER. Full name: Unknown.*

Huh? Freedy didn't say *huh*—if he did it was real quiet—but that was what he thought. He'd set such a nice trap for her, because Walrus's real name should have been there, right? Maybe not real name, but the legal one, the way Starry Knight was her legal name. And it wasn't. The space was blank. Meaning? He looked up at her. She was watching him.

"Don't lose it, Freedy. It's the only proof of your existence."

"Is that supposed to be funny?"

"Yes, Freedy." Her hand came up a little off the table, as though for defense. "You know the way bureaucrats think."

"That makes it funny?" But he didn't know what she was talking about.

They stared at each other across the kitchen table.

A job with maintenance: out of the question. Down in the tunnels with his flashlight, although he almost didn't need it, knowing his way around so well, Freedy got angry just thinking about the idea. What did she want him to do: go backward in life? That wasn't the way to financial success. Freedy knew the way to financial success; he and Estrella had watched hundreds of infomercials and she'd figured out what they all had in common: make a plan and stick to it. There was one other part, Freedy recalled as he came to the junction of D36 and Z13—aboveground everything had a fancy name, but down in the tunnels it was just A this and B that, the letters standing for tunnels and the numbers for buildings—one other part to the formula, what was it? Oh, yeah: have an idea. First have an idea, then make a plan, then stick to it. He already had his idea, a big one—own a pool company in Florida. And a plan—raise the money for it by ripping off high-tech shit at the college and unloading it on Saul Medeiros. Sticking to the plan meant doing it a lot.

Freedy took the turn into Z. Building 13—Lanark, was that the name?—was a girls' dorm on the quad, or maybe coed; they were almost all coed now. He hated those words: *coed, quad.* He hated the whole college scene, the backpacks, the notices stuck up all over the place, the sitting in the grass and talking. And the football team: biggest hoax of all. His high-school coach had once taken them all to a game. They—the fucking high-school team—could have beaten the shit out of Inverness. And he himself could have wrecked anyone they had out there. A joke. Didn't mean some of the college girls weren't all right; some were. But what he'd never been able to figure out back then was how any of them could be interested in those college boys. Now that he'd been around a bit, he could see how growing up isolated in their rich little suburbs meant the girls never had a chance to meet a real man, let alone a fuckin' animal. Back then, he'd never made a move on any of them. He'd been just a kid—a big kid, but not as big as now, and no ponytail—and besides, there'd been Cheryl Ann. Those blow jobs. Married a doctor. The only two thoughts he had about her. He tried to fit them together and could not. Wasn't she a townie just like him?

Night: no maintenance guys in the tunnels at night. Freedy followed Z tunnel under the campus. He hadn't liked working maintenance but he liked it down in the tunnels. On slow days the workers would sometimes curl up in corners here and there and sleep, but not him; he'd always roamed around till quitting time.

Freedy liked the sounds too. There were sounds down in the tunnels, but not his. He moved silently. Just another one of his skills. He moved silently, heard switches click, the skittering of tiny animals, and sometimes voices from up top, carried weirdly down by the pipes. Like now, at the junction of N, he heard someone laughing. That was kind of weird too, because the sound was louder than the human sounds he remembered, too loud to have been carried by the pipes. He glanced down N, saw it all screened off with cobwebs, remembered it had always been like that, at least as far back as the time he was a summer worker. N led to the old field house, torn down long ago, and beyond that to building 41, now heated with gas. The college was always doing something new, building, tearing down, switching the distro systems, buying up Cheryl Ann's old house. What gave them the right? Freedy stood there at the junction of Z and N for a minute or so, listening for that laugh again—a woman's laugh—but it didn't come.

Freedy moved on. Z did a funny little thing just before building 13. It came to a sort of drop-off, like one of those manholes, except uncovered. No railing or anything, just a sudden black hole in the floor. The tunnel continued straight down for thirty feet or so, maybe more, and you had to pivot and climb down a steel ladder bolted to the walls. The maintenance guys—old drunks, most of them—liked to scare the high-school boys with their stupid stories. Freedy didn't remember this particular story—something about a broken neck—but he remembered the drop-off and had his beam on it in plenty of time. He climbed down the ladder, crossed a brick floor, shut off his light, put his ear to the door and listened in the perfect darkness.

Silence; not complete, with that low humming of machine noise, but no human sounds. He opened the door a crack, saw little zones of machine glow in the shadows. All systems go. Freedy stepped into the utilities room in the subbasement of building 13, silent as, as some animal known for silence—tiger? wolf?—but much, much smarter.

He shone his light around, spotted a fridge in one corner, a small fridge where the maintenance guys would keep their lunches and snacks. Freedy opened it. Each shelf bore a different name tag; he remembered the way they kept their food to themselves. Workies. Freedy helped himself to a ham sandwich intended for someone named Griff. A thick sandwich, the kind wifey might pack for hubbie, but mustard instead of mayo; what kind of wifey was that, Griff? He took a bite or two and dropped the rest in the trash on his way out.

Not out right away of course, but after a careful wolf- or tiger-like peek both ways, and into the subbasement hall under building 13. Widely spaced low-voltage bulbs in the ceiling cast a dim light. No switches. This was new: had to be a security thing. Freedy didn't worry. No one around, no reason for anybody but maintenance to be down here—and what difference would it make if anyone did see him? They'd take him for a student, or somebody's date. It was safe, at least going in. Going out, with the goods—that was a little different. But all of it, the in part and the out part: fun. Yes. At that moment, Freedy understood why people got into sky-diving or climbing Mt. Everest. On Everest, though, you wouldn't have to put up with any of the college shit, like this flyer taped by the stairway: *Curious? Come to the weekly Lesbian, Gay and Bisexual Club Dance. Music! Food! Prizes!* He tore the sheet off the wall, crumpled it up—the sound of the crumpling so clear in contrast to the silent way he'd been moving, clear like the sound system he'd once checked out at some Hollywood guy's place when no one was home—and went upstairs, into building 13. Lanark, or whatever they called it, a residence, and all the residences had a basement lounge. Freedy checked it out.

TV—but not HDTV; VCR—dying technology, DVD was what the market wanted; microwave—who gave a shit about microwaves? What he had a hankering for, maybe because of the recollection of that killer sound system, was one of those compact stereos, the new kind that hung on a wall, and a laptop or two for dessert. For dessert! That was funny, unlike so-called jokes about bureaucrats. Idea, plan, stick, stick, stick. Freedy left the lounge and went up to the dorm rooms, where the real goodies were.

Stone stairs, each step worn with a depression marking the tread of feet over a hundred years or more; the kind of thing that should have been repaired but was instead considered a point of pride. College shit—they had no idea what the country was all about. Freedy, maybe because of the Everest thing, maybe because he got a little zoned out planting his feet in those depressions, went all the way to the top floor, the third, and entered the hall. Three rooms on each side, all with closed doors but the two at the end; blue light leaked out of one, yellow light, very faint, from the other. Freedy, tiger, wolf, but much, much smarter—there was a word for that kind of animal, started with *p*, it would come to him—treaded silently down the hall. He peeked into the yellow-lit room.

Good choice. Freedy saw something nice, real nice. The room itself, the living room, sitting room, whatever the hell they called it, wasn't lit at all; the yellow light came through the partly open bedroom door at the back. And through that opening, Freedy saw a woman, a college girl. A fat college girl, maybe, or if not fat, still far from perfect; and she wore glasses. But that wasn't the point: the point was she wore jeans and nothing else. Even more—she was doing something interesting. The college girl, kind of fat, glasses, was standing sideways, from Freedy's viewpoint, and facing a mirror. Freedy couldn't see a mirror from his angle, but he knew it had to be there, possessed as he was of a brain capable of mental leaps. This girl, not too fat, really, had one of her tits cupped in both hands, was shifting it around a little, gazing at the mirror Freedy couldn't see; a few moments later, she went through the same routine with the other tit, like she was checking to see if they were identical. Did girls do that? Learned something new every day. An up-close-and-personal moment: it was like they knew each other already, no bullshit, no expense. Add to that the fact of her not being perfect, meant she was probably lonely for a man. In her wildest dreams would she ever think she'd have a chance with a man like him, diesel, buff, a man like him a matter of a few feet away? If he cleared his throat right now, for example: wow. One other thing, an image, a memory. Wasn't the mind funny, the way it worked? This image Freedy recalled from a porn video, maybe seen on that trip to Mexico, or else the time he'd rented one to watch with Estrella, but she'd been grossed out, letting him down bad. This video memory: a girl with glasses—

Action central. The girl turned abruptly toward the door, toward him. Started to turn would be more accurate, because Freedy, so quick, was out of sight in the hall almost before the movement began.

But why? Shouldn't he have stayed where he was, let her see him? He could have delivered some line, like: *They both look pretty good to me.* How cool was that? Then: *Come in, big boy.* The college girl saying that, not the video girl. His reflexes had gotten the better of him. He was about to make up for it, to step back into the room and hit her with that line, when the door closed. Then the lock clicked. And some kind of fucking bolt slid into place. Not hard, not frantic, she hadn't spotted him, simply noticed the open door. Shut out, just like that, by seconds, or tenths of a second. Bad luck, nothing more.

But Freedy was getting tired of bad luck. Now he was in

a bad mood. Idea, plan, stick, stick, stick. They made it seem so easy.

Freedy took a deep breath, a trick he'd learned from Estrella, or maybe from the other waitress, the one who worked days, and got a grip. Stick, stick, stick. Meant doing it again and again. Meant sucking it up, being a man. He knew how to do all that, had learned in high-school football. A fucking leg breaker, a Thanksgiving crackerjack. Freedy dug down deep, stuck his head into the blue-lit room.

No one there. He walked right in, on a mission now, in search of stuff and plenty of it.

The blue light came from a computer, a laptop, sitting on a desk. Dessert, but he was in a bad mood, and the joke had lost its appeal. The laptop's light illuminated another laptop—a second helping, to put it in dessert terms, but he didn't see the humor in that either—this one closed, on the adjoining desk; a sound system, but not the kind that hung on a wall; a cell phone and a regular phone; and something else, reflecting blue light in the corner. He went closer, saw that this something else was a fish tank. In the fish tank hovered a single fish, bigger than a goldfish and not gold. Some other colors— Freedy didn't really notice. What he noticed were its eyes, blue from the reflection, focused on him like it was watching. Freedy wished he had something sharp to stick right through them, but not because he was unkind to animals—he'd owned a dog, a pit bull, for a few months after his arrival in LA, and fed it practically every day. He was in a bad mood, period. Could happen to anyone.

Cheer up, he told himself. The laptops, the cell phone: a decent night's work. Freedy walked over to the open laptop, read what was on the screen:

To: Phil. 322

From: Prof. L. Uzig

Re: Due to the late arrival of the Kaufman edition of Zarathustra, the assignment due

And other college bullshit that he would have stopped

reading even if he hadn't heard a sound. A voice; distant, female. He ripped the plug out of the machine, snapped it shut, glanced out into the hall. Saw nothing, but heard footsteps, faint then less faint, on the stone stairs at the far end. He banged through the exit at his end—*Emergency Only, Alarm Will Sound,* but it didn't, the college kids disabling everything they could—and zoomed down, two, three, even four stairs at a time.

Easy for him. His body handled it; his mind was elsewhere, working on something important. If he had a problem with women, and that was debatable, it had always been getting past the first step or two in meeting a certain type. Only get past that hurdle, begin from a position already inside their lives, as he had been on the point of doing with the college girl in the yellow-lit room, then they'd see him for what he really was, a stud on the road to big success. After that, well, who wouldn't jump at the chance to hook up with the CEO of a major pool corporation in Florida, maybe the entire Southeast one day? Freedy reminded himself to keep financial control out of greedy little hands, to draw up one of those agreements—prenups, there'd been an infomercial on that too—if he ever got married. Damn: he thought of everything.

Freedy's bad mood lifted just like that. Out into the night, laptop under his arm. He felt good again.

14

> *"Clever people are not credited with their follies: what a deprivation of human rights!"* Give one example, citing the U.S. president of your choice.
> —Homework assignment, Philosophy 322

"You caught it?" Nat said.

"Not cleanly," said Izzie.

Not cleanly, but she'd caught the matchbook in the dark, with the last match inside, and now a candle burned, down in the hole. Not a hole, Nat could now see, but a room, a bedroom, and as far as he could tell in the dimness, a bedroom of the kind he'd encountered only in stories set in English country houses. Grace and Izzie were sitting on a bed, a redcanopied bed like Scrooge's except that the canopy had been torn off by Izzie's fall. Nat could make out something of the intricately carved bedposts, and beyond that, dark-paneled walls and the glint of gilt-framed paintings hanging on them.

"What is this place?" he said.

"Like in that expression," said Grace.

"Sanctum sanctorum," said Izzie.

"Yeah," said Grace. "Sanctum sanctorum. You joining us, Nat?"

Nat paused. There was still the problem of getting back up, of course, candle or not, a problem no one else seemed to recognize. And other problems: he had the feeling there were other problems, but couldn't think what they were.

"Just jump," Grace said.

"It's safe," said Izzie.

They got off the bed, Grace holding the candle, their faces tilted up at him. He hesitated. The jump itself was no big deal, not with a bed to land on. Then what was stopping him?

"What's it going to be?" Grace said, and Izzie started smiling as though she knew what was coming. "Man or Superman?"

He jumped.

A long fall, surprisingly long, maybe a bigger deal than he'd thought; a long fall, with those faces tilted up at him and the candlelight catching the gold flecks in their eyes; long enough for an odd image to pop up in his mind: Lorenzo falling out of his aquarium.

A surprisingly long fall, feetfirst until the thought of Lorenzo broke his concentration, and he dipped out of the perpendicular, landing on the bed, but on his back and hard. He bounced right off, out of control, and caromed into Grace, pinning her to the floor.

"Well, well," she said.

Izzie picked up the candle, dropped by Grace, peered down at them. "Everyone all right?"

Nat got off quickly. "I'm fine."

Grace rose more slowly. "He's heavier than he looks."

Izzie nodded, an expression that could have meant anything on her face. Grace took the candle, held it up, gazed at what remained of the chandelier: thousands of cut-glass crystal teardrops still shimmering from the impact, and twenty or thirty fat candles like the one Grace held, set in glass holders.

"No electricity?" she said. She turned to the lamp on the bedside table, an oil lamp, Nat saw, with a chimney and a wick. He examined it, found the reservoir dry. Underneath lay a book, coated with dust; everything in the room was thick with it. Grace picked up the book, blew off the dust; she and Izzie blew it off simultaneously. A leather-bound book.

With Nat and Izzie looking over her shoulder, Grace leafed through. A French book, probably a novel because of all the dialogue, but he could pick out only a few words—*fesses*, *jolie*, and one he didn't know, *couilles*—before a picture flashed by.

"Whoa," said Grace, paging back to it.

The picture: a black-and-white drawing, pornographic, of a woman wearing nothing but one black stocking, in the lap of a mustached man sitting on a piano stool and wearing nothing at all, both of them gazing out at the reader in a matter-of-fact way. A second woman, fully dressed, leaned against the keyboard, gazing down at them.

Silence.

Then Grace said: "This is better."

"To say nothing of the dress," said Izzie.

"Better than what?" said Nat.

"Playboy," said Izzie. And to Grace: "What's the pub date?"

Grace turned to the front of the book: *Mon Jardin*, published by Editions Bleues in 1919. She leafed through again, finding a few more illustrations, all featuring the mustached man with different women. "Remind you of anyone?" she said.

"Not funny," said Izzie.

And Nat knew they were talking about Paolo. He also wondered whether on their little journey under Inverness they would keep unearthing porn. He was about to ask if anyone knew the year the college had gone coed when Izzie said, "What's that?"

"What's what?"

"Shh."

They listened, heard nothing.

"I thought I heard something."

But there was nothing to hear except the candle flame sizzling in a pool of wax. "I didn't hear anything," Grace said. "And I've got better hearing."

"Is that even possible?" Nat said.

"She does," said Izzie.

"How do you know?"

"We know," Grace said, closing *Mon Jardin* and putting it on the table. She moved toward the nearest wall, ran her hand over the paneling. The light shone on an ornate picture frame. They examined the painting, a nude bathing in a stream. Even in the poor light, Nat could see it wasn't very good; compared to the Renoir, not worth looking at. There were other paintings, much the same.

They came to a leather-padded door studded with brass. Grace opened it. On the other side, a much bigger room, full of shadows.

"It's like that club," Izzie said.

"Except more lively," said Grace. Izzie laughed.

"What club?" said Nat.

"Some old-farts club in New York we had to go to once. Just like this, the furniture, the rugs, the paintings, everything. Except for dust."

"And the spiderwebs."

Nat walked into one at that moment; it clung to his eyelashes. He wiped it away, and as he did noticed Greek writing high on one wall—he knew some of the letters from math—painted in gold.

"Were there fraternities here?"

"Something like that," said Grace. "Didn't Leo mention it?"

"They kicked them out," Izzie said. She was opening a glass cabinet full of bottles. "During Prohibition."

Grace held the candle near the bottles, dust-free in the cabinet: scotch, bourbon, gin, rum, cognac, Armagnac, many still sealed. "This looks good," she said, taking out a heavy, square bottle: Bas Armagnac, Domaine Boingnères, 1913. She chipped off the wax seal, found a tarnished silver corkscrew on the top shelf, drew the cork. The scent reached Nat a moment later and grew and grew: a heady smell, fiery, sweet, strange; as though France, which he'd never seen, and a long-ago time, when he'd never lived, could be kept in a bottle.

Grace tilted it to her lips, drank. "Ah," she said, and passed it to Izzie. Then to Nat. He took a sip and decided not to romanticize too much. It was just booze, after all, the very best quality, but just booze. Then the aftertaste hit him and he changed his mind again: yes, France and a long-ago time, in a bottle. He took another drink.

"He likes it," Izzie said. Nat saw she was watching him closely.

"What else does he like?" said Grace.

The girls looked at each other in silence, their expressions beyond his power of interpretation. But an awkward moment, certainly. Was this the time to bring everything into the open? But what was everything? He and Izzie hadn't been together alone for more than a few minutes since that one time on the beach at Aubrey's Cay. More guests had arrived the next day, and Nat had had to share his room with a banker from Singapore. And Grace had always been around. But the biggest impediment was this need for secrecy. It was almost as though that in pretending nothing was happening between them, they were making it reality. Maybe nothing *was* happening: there was lots of hooking up at Inverness, or at least some, that neither party intended to repeat, if not before it happened, then after. Were he and Izzie like that? And what about Patti? Nat realized he had to do some clear thinking, but down here in this strange place, that wasn't easy. He found himself taking another drink.

"Hey," said Grace, "my turn."

The bottle went round again.

"What's this?" Izzie said.

"A record player," Nat said. He'd seen one of these before, probably at a lawn sale. Opening the top, he found a record on the turntable. *Victor*, read the label: *Caro Nome (Rigoletto— G. Verdi), sung by Amelita Galli-Curci.*

"Turn it on," Grace said.

Nat wound a crank at the back, moved a switch beside the turntable. The record began to spin. He lowered the needle onto it.

A little musical intro, almost lost in the fuzziness and scratchiness of the recording, and then came a voice, high, light, penetrating, strange, that made Nat forget about the recording quality. If anything, it made it better. The room, the drink, the music: all from a long-ago time. He'd heard of Verdi, was pretty sure that *Rigoletto* was an opera, but otherwise knew nothing, had no idea what the song was about, couldn't understand a word. Still, he stood motionless until it was over.

"Play it again," Izzie said.

"Isn't there anything else?" said Grace.

Nat checked a compartment at the base of the player, found a bill from a record store in Albany for $4.45, dated October 6, 1919, and more records, a few by Caruso, the others by singers he'd never heard of. They played them all, Nat operating the machine while Grace and Izzie sat in high-backed purple chairs they dusted off and drew up. The candle burned down, the bottle went around and around until it was empty.

"Time travel happens," Izzie said.

"Whenever we want," said Grace, "if we keep this our little secret."

"But what's it all about?" Nat said. "No one's been here in eighty years."

"How do you know that?"

"The booze would be gone. The question is, who left it like this, and why?"

"Maybe there was an earthquake or something," Izzie said.

"In New England?" Grace said.

"Possible, isn't it, Nat?"

"Who cares?" said Grace before he could answer; a good thing because he didn't know. "The point is we've made an amazing discovery."

Nat found himself nodding in agreement. He didn't know

exactly what the discovery was, or its implications, but he knew she was right.

"Let's try another bottle," Grace said.

They tried another bottle, found a few more candles, lit them, put "Caro Nome" back on the turntable, explored. There were no other rooms, and just one other door, directly under the Greek writing. They opened it, saw a stone staircase, followed it up ten steps—Nat counted them for some reason—came to another leather-padded door with brass studs. "This is so much fun," Grace said, turning the knob, "like one of those interactive-theater evenings, only for smart people."

The leather-padded brass-studded door opened onto a brick wall.

Izzie did something then that made an indelible impression in Nat's memory. She gave the wall a push with the fingers of one hand, just a little push, as though it were a prop that would topple at the slightest touch. The bricks were real; it didn't.

There, at the top of the stone stairs, the bottle went around again. Grande Champagne Cognac, Berry Bros. & Rudd, 1908. Nat, trying to remember what furniture he'd seen, building a mental tower that would allow them to climb out of the hole in the bedroom ceiling, realized he was a little drunk.

Grace said: "I could get on your shoulders and Izzie could get on mine."

"That's not as easy at it sounds," Nat said.

"Let's try it," said Izzie.

Nat smiled. There was something about her that made him smile, smile right at her in a way he didn't think he'd ever smiled at anyone else. But she didn't smile back, didn't even meet his eye for more than an instant before looking at Grace. Grace was looking at him.

Nat stopped smiling, was about to mention the furniture idea, when he felt a current of warm air flowing past his face. He glanced around, noticed a square metal grate high up in the wall opposite the bricked-in doorway. A big grate, but the wood around it was old and rotted. He got a grip on the bars and tugged. The grate came free in his hands.

Grace laughed, that excited little laugh of hers, full of pleasure. Nat took a candle, stood on his tiptoes, peered into the square hole. He felt the warm air—it fluttered the candle flame—and saw down a tin-lined duct, perhaps just big enough for him to squeeze into. Standing the candle on the floor of the duct as deep in as he could reach, he pulled himself up and inside. Just big enough. He felt one of them giving him a little push from behind, heard them talking:

"Did something like this happen in those *Alien* flicks?"

"It was James Bond."

But there was nothing frightening about this, and it didn't require courage. Nat had already spotted a little pool of light not much farther ahead. He wriggled toward it with the candle in front of him.

The light came from above. Nat reached it, squirmed over onto his back, looked up through another grate. High above he saw a dark wooden ceiling, laid out in squares and decorated with carved scrollwork and bunches of grapes. It seemed familiar. Nat was trying to place it when he heard voices. He blew out the candle.

Silence. Then footsteps approached, two sets of footsteps, Nat thought, on a hardwood floor. A foot came into view above him, and another, shod in Birkenstocks with heavy socks underneath; the Birkenstock feet walked over the grate and out of sight. Then came two more feet, these in tassel loafers. A woman said, "I only want to do the right thing." She stepped forward, a wiry woman with long hair, gray and frizzy.

The tassel loafers stopped, planted right on the grate. Paper rustled. The woman said, "Oops," and something fluttered down, came to rest on the grate: a hundred-dollar bill. The tassel loafers shifted slightly, and the man wearing them stooped to retrieve it. His face, his furious face, came within two feet of Nat's: Professor Uzig. He picked up the bill, thrust it at the woman. The footsteps, both sets, moved off. A heavy door opened and closed. Nat waited for a minute or two, heard nothing more, then pushed up the grate and raised himself into the ground-floor lounge of Goodrich Hall. Through the tall windows he saw the night sky, full of stars. The clock on the wall said 3:30. That wouldn't have been his guess.

15

Anyone interested in extra credit will receive a one-third grade step-up for any citation from life undermining the following Nietzschean precept: "The will to overcome an emotion is ultimately only the will of another emotion or of several others."
—Standing offer, Philosophy 322

Nat slept through a dream in which he stood at the foul line, shooting one and one, with no time on the clock and his team down by a single point. He had actually lived such a moment in his senior high-school year against their big rival, Western Tech. But in the dream, he wore the red and white of Western Tech, instead of Clear Creek High's burgundy and gold. He stood at the foul line bouncing the ball, bouncing and bouncing it, but never taking the shot. An uneasy dream made more so by the hardwood floor that looked like any other court but made cracking and splitting sounds with every bounce; still he remained inside it, sleeping through the ringing phone in the outer room—dimly aware of it, sleeping on. Sleeping on through biology class, the first class he'd missed, unaware of missing it, although as class time came and went the anxiety of his dream might have increased. Then someone's lips touched his, and he woke up.

Izzie.

"Morning, sleepyhead," she said.

"What time is it?" He tried to sit up; she rolled on top of him; was already in his bed.

Izzie gazed down on him. "Going somewhere?"

"Biol—" Nat started to say, but from the intensity of the light coming through the window, he knew it was too late.

"Biology—the science of living things, correct?" Izzie said; raising an eyebrow the way she did, her right eyebrow, questioning, mocking.

"Correct."

"Then you've got nothing to worry about."

"Why is that?"

"This counts for extra credit."

"A-plus," said Izzie, after.

After sex, but still under its spell. They lay in Nat's narrow bed, the room quiet except for their breathing. Nat noticed that the period of their breaths seemed similar. He held his until her next inhalation, and inhaled at the same time. After that, they breathed in unison, a coincidence, of course, and maybe a bit sappy, but there it was.

"What's that word," Izzie said, the vibrations from her voice buzzing against his ear, "when bad beginnings have a good result?"

"Serendipity."

"Then what happened to Wags was serendipitous for us."

"Because he's not around?"

"What else?"

Nat couldn't agree; on the other hand, his scruples were dwarfed by the power of that *us*. It seemed to toll in the room, like a steeple bell at the beginning of a story.

"Or am I being too pushy?" Izzie said, sensing but misinterpreting his resistance. "Maybe you don't want me to come here."

"I do."

"Then give me a kiss."

He did.

From beyond came all the normal sounds of Inverness: voices raised across the quad, maniacal laughter in the hall, music from everywhere, someone's barking dog. "Grace thinks this is like living in the projects," Izzie said after some time.

"Do you?"

She thought. "I don't know. Maybe not. Grace doesn't really think so either. She's got a big personality, that's all."

"It must be interesting," he said.

"What?"

"Living two lives at once."

She looked at him, didn't speak. He leaned forward—he was on top now—his gaze on her whole face, then her eyes, then only one of them, then on those gold flecks in the iris, as though a really close examination of them would reveal everything about her. Her eyelid closed just as his lips touched her. The softest thing. He stayed right there. Had time ever slowed down like this for him before? He got the feeling that he and Izzie had entered a powerful circle of some kind, impermeable. Was this what all that poetry he'd had to study was about, all those novels? Maybe not, because something permeated the circle right away, at least his part of it: the image of Mrs. Smith's and Miss Brown's happy faces on the Fourth of July, an unwelcome image that let in unwelcome thoughts: the effort it had taken to get him here, the missed biology class. And Patti.

"What's wrong?" Izzie said.

"Nothing."

She opened her eyes—he felt the eyelid's tiny struggle against his lips—and turned her head so she could see him. "You're thinking about something."

"No."

"Is it Grace?"

"Of course not. Why would I be thinking about Grace?"

Izzie didn't speak.

And Patti. Now messy memories from the Thanksgiving party threatened to spill out in his mind, but the most important, more important than how drunk Patti had got, or the way she'd vomited in bed that night, all over both of them, was the way he'd seen everyone back home, his old friends, changed. He was the changed one, of course. The cliché at the heart of so many coming-of-age stories, but that didn't make them false. He would call Patti today. He'd changed. It was normal. Out of the corner of his eye, he was suddenly aware of her picture on the upside-down crate at his bedside. Something writhed inside him.

"Then what are you thinking about?" Izzie said.

"Nothing."

"That's not true. I can tell."

He was wondering whether to drag her through the whole thing, or to simply answer *you*, which was true—his mind was full of her—if not factually correct at that exact moment, and also might sound a little buttery, when he heard someone entering the outer room. Izzie went still.

"Nat," called a voice. Grace. He saw fear, real fear in Izzie's eyes.

"Just a sec," he said, hurrying out of bed, pulling on sweatpants. He stepped into the outer room, closing the door, he hoped casually, behind him.

Grace looked up from reading something on his desk as he came in, her gaze going to his bare chest first, then to his face. "Morning, sleepyhead," she said. "And hungover, too."

"A bit."

"Moi aussi," she said, although she didn't look it. "But isn't it great?"

"What we found?"

"And the way we found it," Grace said. "Defines *serendipitous*." She glanced around as though someone might hear. "You haven't mentioned it to anybody?"

"No." He noticed she was wearing overalls, with a hammer, screwdriver, pliers sticking out of the pockets.

"I've already been down there today," she said. "It really is like Alice—through the looking glass *and* down the rabbit hole."

"What have you been doing?"

"Fixing up."

"How?"

"You'll see." She pulled a book from her back pocket. "And look at this—plot summaries of all the major operas, so we'll know what we're listening to. For example . . ." She flipped through the pages. "Rigoletto: Gilda—she's the one who sings that song, 'Caro Nome,' means 'dear name,' she sings it to her lover, but it isn't even his real name . . . and then it looks like there's some kind of kidnapping—her own father, that's Rigoletto, helps without knowing it."

"Helps who?"

"The kidnappers."

"Why?"

"Doesn't say," Grace said, running her eyes over the page. "She dies at the end, by mistake."

"What kind of mistake?"

Grace checked the text again. "It's convoluted. And not very believable. But the music makes all that irrelevant, I guess."

"Last night it did," Nat said.

"Exactly," said Grace, closing the book. Her eyes went to his chest again, then back to his face. "I guess it's my fault," she said.

"What is?"

"That we got off to maybe a bad start."

"What do you mean?" he said, wishing she'd talk a little more quietly.

"You and me. That night in New York. At my da—at my father's. Too much to drink and smoke, et cetera. And I was probably a little too forceful. For you, I mean. For other men, though . . ."

Her voice trailed off. Nat thought of Paolo, and the married man Izzie had told him about. He felt a little sorry for Grace. "Forget it," he said.

"You mean that?" The way she asked that little question, the words, the intonation: pure Izzie; he revisited the most obvious fact about them, one he'd been leaving behind, the fact of how alike they were.

"Yes," he said. "I mean it."

"A clean slate, then?"

"Sure." Who could say no to that?

Grace smiled a bright smile. "See you in class," she said, and left the room; very light on her feet, almost skipping. He went over to the desk to see what she'd been looking at and found Patti's letter.

Nat went into the bedroom. No Izzie. He opened the closet and, as though it were a children's game, there she was, hiding behind his Clear Creek letter jacket, worn once at Inverness and never again.

"Has she gone?" said Izzie.

"Yes. What's this all about?"

"I told you—I just don't want her to know right now."

"Know what?"

"That anything's happening between us."

"Why not?"

"Just give me time."

"But why not?"

Izzie watched him over the letter jacket. "I never did better than Grace in anything, not a single race, a single essay, a single exam, not ever."

"So what?"

"Until the SATs. I scored twenty points higher on the verbal."

"Do we have to talk about the SATs?"

Izzie smiled. "I never met anyone like you."

"That's because you haven't led a sheltered life."

She laughed. "You see? Every time you open your mouth

you prove it." Her eyes went to the Clear Creek jacket. "Can I wear this?"

"You want to wear that?"

"It's not something Wags left behind, is it?"

"No. It's my old high-school jacket."

"Then I want to wear it. Just for a while," she added when he was silent.

"Okay."

Izzie put it on. She wasn't wearing anything else. "Now close the door."

"We're in the closet."

"That's right."

Nat closed the door. In the darkness she leaned against him.

"But you've had boyfriends before," he said.

Izzie knew what he meant. "Only ones she'd rejected or didn't want in the first place, like Paolo," she said.

"What makes you think she's interested in me?"

"I know it."

"How?"

"I just do."

"But—"

But she grabbed the back of his head, pulled him close, kissed his mouth, deeper and deeper. He had sex in his closet with Nat, Clear Creek Basketball, number 8. He'd never had sex three times in a row before—except for Patti hadn't had sex at all before Izzie—but for some reason this time was the best of all.

After Izzie left, Nat reread Patti's letter. He held it up to the light, tried again to see what she'd crossed out, with no success until he thought of turning the page over. Then, reading backward, he was able to make out a bit more: what he'd thought might be *kissed*, *pissed*, or *missed* was definitely *missed*; and the next word was *my*. The rest remained obliterated. His gaze went to the PS: *my present should be there by now.*

He'd forgotten all about Patti's present; last seen on his bed before Christmas. Nat searched the bedroom, found it under the bed. A small package with reindeer wrapping and a card with a reindeer, candy canes dangling from its antlers, on the front: *Merry Christmas to the very best person I know. Love, Patti.* He sat slowly on the bed, the present in the palm of his hand.

The phone rang in the outer room. He let it. Slowly, more slowly than he'd ever unwrapped a present, he unwrapped Patti's, taking great care not to rip the paper, also not like him. Inside was a little cardboard box, and on it the words *Assad and Son.* Assad and Son was the jewelry store on the main street in his town. Nat opened the box, pulled aside some tissue paper, and exposed a small gold number 8 on a gold chain.

Eight, the number he'd worn at Clear Creek. And a gold chain. He'd never worn a gold chain or had any desire to. Nat closed the box without touching the pendant or the chain.

He went to the phone, called Patti at her mom's. With the time difference, she might not have left for her classes at Arapaho State. *I wish I didn't have to say this on the phone, Patti, but:* his mind rehearsed as it rang at the other end. The answering machine took his call. He listened to Patti's mom's taped message—she said "God bless" at the end—and at the sound of the beep, hung up.

You'll meet all kinds of girls, prettier than me. Prettier and smarter. And richer. And richer: she'd said that too. He had a funny thought: *what else does she know about my future?*

In the small domed room at the top of Goodrich Hall, the smart girl from English 103 was saying, "There's a lot here we're going to have to filter out, isn't there?"

"Such as?" said Professor Uzig, his face so composed and

dignified it was hard for Nat to imagine it any other way, certainly not furious. But the memory, not twelve hours old, was strong, reinforced by a quick glance on his way up at the hot-air grate in the ground-floor lounge.

"Like on page one-oh-one," said the girl from English 103. " 'In revenge and in love woman is more barbarous than man.' And he's got sexist opinions like that all over the place."

"Is it possible to mount a defense in this particular case?" asked Professor Uzig. An odd thing had happened: although the professor's voice remained unchanged, calm, cultured, confident, he'd gone pale. Did he dislike being challenged? Nat had already seen some of the others challenge him, seen how he turned them back with ease. Then what was it?

"You're asking us to defend that statement?" Grace said.

"For the sake of argument, Grace, as a lawyer would."

"That's what's wrong with—" She broke off at that moment: Izzie had just entered, a few minutes late, and she was wearing Nat's letter jacket. Grace's eyes were on her as she sat down; everyone's were. Nat had two sudden revelations; the first, what a juvenile garment a high-school letter jacket was, certainly his, burgundy with gold sleeves, the big gold *C*, *Nat* in burgundy on one sleeve, 8 on the other; the second, he now understood the meaning of a word that had always been doubly foreign to him: *chic*.

Izzie, aware of everyone watching, said, "Sorry I'm late." She might have been addressing Professor Uzig, but she was looking at Grace.

"Carry on, Grace," said the professor.

Grace faced him, opened her mouth, but nothing came out. Nat, sitting beside her, realized she'd forgotten what she'd been saying. "Lawyers," he said, softly, so only Grace could hear.

"Lawyers," said Grace, her tone more passionate than it had been before, almost angry. "That's what's wrong with lawyers."

Professor Uzig, his color back to normal, said, "As your

punishment for tardiness, Isobel, it's up to you to defend Nietzsche's one hundred and thirty-ninth maxim from *Beyond Good and Evil*. Page one-oh-one."

Izzie riffed through her copy, read the sentence, looked up. "Women are more barbaric than men?"

"Barbarous," said Professor Uzig. "The words are not synonyms, *barbarous* invariably implying moral condemnation, as *barbaric* does not. Barbarous, then, and in only these two areas, love and revenge."

"Barbarous love?" said Izzie. "Isn't that an oxymoron?"

"Is it?" said Professor Uzig.

"And what about domestic violence?" said a girl who'd never spoken before; she had an up-from-under way of holding her head that reminded Nat a little of his mother.

"What indeed?" said the professor.

"Well, it's indefensible, isn't it?"

"Anyone else?" said Professor Uzig.

Silence. Nat expected Grace might speak, but she was doodling on her pad, a flower with something dripping from it. Professor Uzig's gaze found him. He had yet another thought about that jacket: wasn't it the descendant of knightly finery, what a princess-rescuing fairy-tale character might wear? He never wanted to see the goddamn thing again.

"Nat?" said the professor.

"Yes?"

"Have you done the reading?"

"I have."

"And your response to this question?"

"A question of my own," Nat said. To his surprise he said that aloud, the kind of remark that until very recently, maybe until that moment, would have remained inside. Then he asked the question: "Did Nietzsche believe it?"

"Referring to this passage that seems to shock everyone so much?"

"Yes."

"Go on."

"That's it. How do we know he believed it?"

"And if he didn't believe it?"

"Maybe he was just trying to be provocative."

"In order to provoke what?"

"I don't know."

"Guess."

"Thought. To provoke thought."

"What kind of thought?"

"Fresh," Nat said. "And maybe that's the connection to Kurt Cobain," he added, the words popping out on their own, "the provocative part."

"Oh, dear," said the professor, "and you were doing so well."

The bearded student who liked Kurt Cobain leaned forward and said, "Wait a minute. He's on to something."

"Something that you can discuss outside class," said Professor Uzig. "We will begin to separate Nietzsche the provocateur from Nietzsche the philosopher, now that Nat has shown the way."

"But what about the whole *Incesticide* CD?" said the bearded student. "The one with 'Hairspray Queen' and 'Mexican Seafood.' It fits perfectly."

Grace had been working. She'd repaired the hatch cover, or trapdoor, in the tunnel, replacing the hinges and adding a pull ring and a rope ladder that unfurled all the way from the frame to the floor below. She'd swept, dusted, cleaned; and that night, by the glow of dozens of candles—in wall sconces, candelabras, and the great chandelier—they saw how magnificent the two rooms really were. They lounged on plush furniture with elaborately carved legs, while the paneled walls gleamed all around, but through pockets of candlelight and shadow, more like an artist's rendering of Victorian splendor than the real thing, and while Amelita Galli-Curci sang "Caro Nome," her voice, perhaps because of the recording quality, like some rediscovered instrument from a dead culture.

"We need a name for this place," Grace said.

"How about the frat?" Nat said.

They both gave him a look.

"The club?" said Izzie, still wearing the letter jacket.

"Yuck," said Grace.

"The Rigoletto Room?" said Nat.

"That's the dumbest thing you've ever said."

"Then what?"

"Something underground, like . . ."

"The burrow?" said Izzie.

"I've got it," Grace said.

"What?"

"The cave."

"Oh, I like that," said Izzie. "Didn't Plato have a cave? This can be Nietzsche's."

"I wouldn't push it that far," said Grace. "Just 'the cave' will do. Nat?"

"The cave," he said, raising his glass. He gazed through it and saw into the long-ago, or thought he did, and while he was doing that Grace opened another bottle. She poured more cognac in their glasses, heavy crystal glasses she'd found in one of the cupboards, poured cognac from 1899, its color the same as the atmosphere in the room. "Here's to the cave," she said, tilting back her head, exposing her perfect throat, draining the glass. Her face reddened at once, and when she spoke her voice was thicker and deeper. "And to Nat's letter jacket, if that's what the thing is called."

Nat sat up straight. Silence, except for Galli-Curci singing her song to the wrong lover, or whatever it was, the details of *Rigoletto*, never clear in Nat's mind, now less so.

"It's sort of funny, isn't it?" said Izzie, her voice going the other way from Grace's, thinner and higher; anyone could have told them apart at that moment.

"What is?" said Grace.

"This silly jacket," Izzie said. "As a fashion statement, I mean. That's why I borrowed it."

Enough, Nat thought, and was about to bring everything into the open when he thought he heard a muffled sneeze, not far away. "Shh," he said. "Did you hear that?"

"What?" they both asked.

They all listened, heard nothing but water dripping, very faint.

Grace turned to him. "You a little wired or something?"

"No."

"Spooked, down here in the cave?"

"Not at all. I like it."

"Me too. The best thing about this dump." She got up from the divan she'd been lying on, filled everyone's glass again. "A fashion statement," she said, pausing before Izzie. "What a weird concept." She continued to pour, candlelight-colored liquid rising to the top of Izzie's glass and spilling over.

"Grace!"

"Oops. You forgot to say when." Grace paused—Izzie's eyes glued to her—plucked at the fabric of the jacket, rubbed it between finger and thumb. "Nice," she said.

"Want to try it on?" said Izzie, very quiet.

"That's up to Nat, isn't it?"

"Of course not," Nat said.

"I wouldn't want to violate any high-school code."

"What are you talking about?" said Izzie; every note false in Nat's ear. "It's just a jacket." She shrugged it off.

Grace put on Nat's high-school letter jacket, saying, "At least we know it's going to fit."

And it did. At that moment Nat realized that Patti had never worn it. Wearing your boyfriend's jacket had been uncool at Clear Creek High, at least while he was there.

"How do I look?" Grace said.

16

*"Once you had wild dogs in your cellar, but in the end
they turned into birds and lovely singers." What does
Zarathustra teach about "suffering the passions"?*
—Midterm exam question, Philosophy 322

"**T**hought you had a laptop," said Ronnie Medeiros,
rummaging through the stuff in the back of the goddamn
hippie van as they drove down to Fitchville. "My uncle has a
thing for laptops."

"You thought wrong," Freedy said. There was a laptop, of
course. Freedy had decided to keep it for himself. He'd never
owned a computer before, knew nothing about them, but the
CEO of a pool company would need to be completely whatever the word was with computers. So he was going to learn
in his spare time. How hard could it be?

"Still," said Ronnie, climbing into the front, "not a bad
haul. My uncle says you're doin' good."

It was starting to snow again, little dark pellets more like
buckshot than flakes. Freedy turned on the wipers, turned up
the heat. "Why's it so fucking cold?" he said.

"Maybe you're low on coolant," said Ronnie. "Or else the
coil's fucked."

Freedy glanced sideways at Ronnie, all toasty warm in
his plaid hat, wool mittens, and padded jacket out to here.
Looked like a complete asshole. He hadn't been talking about
the goddamn car. "Why's it so fucking cold *in general*?"

159

"You mean because there's s'posta be global warming?"

Freedy wanted to hit him; not brutally, just hard enough to straighten things out, clear the air. "How can you stand it?"

"Hey, it's home."

"The flats," said Freedy. "You call that home?"

"Could do worse."

"How the fuck would you know? You never been anywhere."

"That's not true. I was down to see my cousin in Fall River just last spring."

"Fall River," said Freedy. "You heard of Bel Air, Santa Monica, Rancho . . ." Rancho what? He couldn't remember. Like: was the whole thing, his whole California life, his real life, fading away? That scared him. This pool thing—pool business, concern, corporation—was going to happen. No matter what. Have an idea, make a plan, and then . . . for a moment, he couldn't remember the third part.

"Jesus," said Ronnie, throwing his hands up over his face, "you almost hit that guy."

"Fuck you, Ronnie. I'm in total control." He must have said it loud, because everything was quiet after. And in the quiet, having a chance to think for once, he remembered the third part from the infomercials: stick to the plan. Idea, plan, stick, stick, stick.

"Everything's cool," he said.

"Okeydoke."

"Say, Ronnie."

"Yeah?"

"Got any access to crystal meth?"

"You into that?"

"Wouldn't say *into*. It's just, you know, an enhancer."

"I tried it. Couldn't sleep for two nights."

"That's what's fun."

"Not for me. I need my sleep. Can't perform otherwise."

Perform? What the hell was he talking about? He wasn't

some high-powered something—Jew word—he was Ronnie Medeiros, Portagee loser. "You got access, yes or no?"

"It's around."

"I know it's *around*, Ronnie. This is the U.S. of A. What I'm sayin' is can you get me some?"

"Sure, for a price."

"You fuckin' people."

"What's that mean? Who fuckin' people?"

"What I said."

They drove the rest of the way in silence, Freedy shivering because of the coolant or the coil or whatever the fuck it was, and still wearing California clothes, and Ronnie toasty warm hunched inside his padded jacket out to here, looking like an asshole. Imagine Ronnie in California. The thought made Freedy laugh out loud, a good long laugh. He could feel Ronnie thinking, *What's so funny?* but he didn't explain. Does the wolf explain, or the tiger?

"Thought there was a laptop," said Saul Medeiros. It was cold in his office back of the collision place; cold in the office, cold in the car, cold everywhere, like all the heat was on the fritz.

"No laptop."

"You sure?"

"Fuck I'm sure," said Freedy. "Think I got it hidden in that goddamn toaster?" A good line, California cool, especially if he'd said it quieter.

" 'Kay," said Saul, wiping his nose on the sleeve of his greasy jacket, that nose with the hair growing right on top. "If there's no laptops, there's no laptops. But you know why I like laptops?"

" 'Cause they make you think of pussy," said Ronnie, smoking in the corner. They both turned to him. "That's what they make me think of," Ronnie said. "Every time I see a laptop I think of one of those lawyers, like on TV in a miniskirt."

"Ronnie?" said Saul.

"Yep."

"How about takin' the dog for a walk?"

"What dog?"

"The junkyard dog, for fuck sake. What other dog is there?"

After Ronnie left, Saul opened a drawer in his desk, took out two nips of V.O. and a jelly donut with sprinkles. He pushed one of the nips across the desk, tore the donut in half, leaving a black thumbprint on powdered sugar, said, "Help yourself."

"Not hungry," said Freedy, unscrewing the tiny bottle.

Saul shrugged, ate the donut, speaking between mouthfuls, or actually during them. "What I like about laptops is the way they fly out of here."

"Yeah?" said Freedy, downing his drink.

"Fly. You're doin' pretty good, but you start bringin' in laptops you'll be doin' better. 'Pendin' on the model, I pay up to three C's for a laptop." He raised the V.O. to his lips—lips with sugar powder in the corners—paused. "One thing."

"What's that?"

"You bein' discreet?"

"Sure."

"Discreet means you never mention my name."

"Why would I?"

"Otherwise I get anxiety. That's no good for anybody. Me because of my hypertension. You because . . ." The ugly little bastard stared at him with his ugly little eyes, one of them bloodshot. Then he polished off his drink and said, "Let's do business."

They did business. For Saul that meant shaking his head a lot, saying, "This I can't move for shit," "No one wants these anymore," "There's a new model out now," "It's missing that thingamajig at the back"; for Freedy it meant getting ripped off.

"You're doin' good," said Saul, paying him off.

"Then how come this is all I get?"

Saul did that head-shaking thing again. A tiny green drop quivered at the end of his nose. "Has nothin' to do with me," Saul said. "Market forces goin' on here. Globalization market forces."

A hundred and seventy-five dollars. Driving back by himself up the highway, Freedy knew he just had to work harder. He was willing. This was the U.S. of A., and he was a native son. Men just like him had built the whole goddamn country, so there was no problem with work. He wasn't some lazy name-the-ethnic-group. He popped an andro dry, ready to work at the drop of a hat.

But what about fun? There had to be fun too, or what was the point? Female fun, especially. The image of the video girl in glasses, and what had happened to those glasses, jumped up in his mind. He toyed with the idea of paying for it. He'd never paid for it in his life: with his body, it would have been like—something, one of those complicated comparisons. But where, as he rolled into Inverness, shivering now from the cold, would he even find a hooker in this town? In LA . . . but that was another story.

He had an idea. It came to him, just like that. Proved how amazing he was: he figured out, with help from no one, where hookers might hang out in Inverness. The bus station. Pure inspiration, the kind of inspiration that makes all the losers say, "Why didn't I think of that?"

Freedy cruised by the bus station. It was empty. What a town. Not just no hookers. No nobody. He had to really assert control over his hands to stop them from squeezing into fists. While that little struggle was going on, a bus pulled in at the back of the building. Freedy parked in front of the station door, waiting to see who would get out.

One person got out, one measly person. But a woman. Freedy watched her through the glass wall of the station, coming across the floor with a suitcase. Probably not a hooker, not with the suitcase, but how would you tell a hooker in this fucking cold? This woman, a young one, was wearing jeans, hiking boots, a long, hooded sweatshirt. Probably not a hooker. She disappeared into the rest room.

Freedy waited. Why not? The day was shot. And what did that matter? He worked at night. Plus, those jeans—as far up as he could see—had looked pretty good on her.

She came out of the rest room. Surprise: maybe she was a hooker after all, because the hiking boots and jeans were gone, replaced by shoes, not high-heeled but not flat either, and a clingy blue skirt or dress, one of those cocktail things. She still wore the sweatshirt, but even a hooker had to stay warm. Freedy rolled down the window as she came outside.

A good-looking girl, and if a hooker, one of the innocent-on-the-surface types. She turned this way and that, new in town, no doubt about it, and then spotted him. He showed her that smile. And she came; slow, hesitating, shy, but she came.

"Excuse me," she said, standing on the sidewalk, not putting down the suitcase.

"Hey," said Freedy, not the smoothest line, maybe, but he made it extra smooth with his voice.

"I'm looking for Inverness College," she said.

"The college?" *What the fuck do you want up there?* But he didn't say that, didn't even let it show on his face, kept smiling, even bigger.

"Yes," she said, taking a piece of paper from her jacket pocket. All crumpled up, and she had trouble uncrumpling it, like she was nervous or something. Probably aware all of a sudden of the vibe between them, of how big and buff he was: that would explain it. "Plessey Hall is the name of the building," she said, reading what was on the paper.

"I just know the numbers," he said.

"I'm sorry?"

The numbers. Not what he'd meant to say at all. Plessey— which one was that? Forty-six? Eighteen? "Tell you what," he said, "since you're a stranger and this is a real friendly town, how about you just hop in and I'll run you right up there."

"Well . . ."

"Lickety-split, you know? And you'll be out of this fu—this wicked cold."

"That's very . . ." Her gaze shifted past him toward the passenger seat. Lying on the seat was a skin magazine that Ronnie had brought along, which was really unfortunate. She backed up two steps. "Very nice of you, but . . . I just remembered I was supposed to call. When I got in. If they're already on the way, you see . . ." And she retreated a few more steps, said, "Thanks so much anyway," turned, and went inside the station. On the back of her sweatshirt it said *Arapaho State College.*

Really unfortunate. He could have taken her somewhere, not home because of his goddamned mother, but somewhere—like down in the tunnels!—and then. And then. Lickety-split, down in the tunnels. Instead; instead he picked up the skin mag and flung it out the window. He was going to have to do something about Ronnie Medeiros.

Freedy had calmed down a little by the time he went to work that night. For one thing, Ronnie called to say he had some crystal meth, and he'd gone over to Ronnie's and scored it for a cheap price, then pumped some iron. For another, he'd done some thinking. CEOs, like Bill Gates, say—oh yes, he'd done his homework, think Bill Gates's name didn't come up on infomercials?—CEOs like Bill Gates, who started companies in their garage, did they hang around bus stations, sniffing for cunt? No—first came the money, and then cunt came sniffing for you. That was what Bill Gates and the rest of them had found out. Idea, plan, stick, stick, stick. Clipping a flashlight to his belt, Freedy raised a grate in the parking lot behind the football field and entered tunnel F.

He felt good right away, optimistic, psyched. He was

investing in his future. Besides, he just liked being in the tunnels, especially appreciated the current of warm air stirring in this one. Down F he went, down because F was the deepest tunnel, passing under the football field and the rink, intersecting Z, then crossing right under another tunnel—N, as he recalled—somewhere beneath building 68, the one with the dome, going on all the way to building 17, the science building, had some Jewish name. But that wasn't the point. The point was: science building. Why? Because science meant computers, and computers meant laptops! Inspiration had struck again. Freedy had a vision of himself in his headquarters office down in Florida in the not very distant future, and voices out in the hall whispering, *The guy's fucking brilliant.*

It was really going to happen. He was going to do it, and do it by stripping the college bare. His stake sat waiting up above, the stake to get him started in the pool business. It was—what was the word? A perfect word existed, he could feel it coming, coming, coming—*justice!* The word was *justice.* The college would get him started: justice. What were colleges for, anyway? Cobwebs brushed by his face; he hardly noticed, just sneezed a good big one and kept going.

How much did he need to get started in Florida? Thousands, right? Saul paid three C's per laptop. That meant ten laptops was three grand, right there. And what was ten laptops? Cake. There had to be thousands of laptops on College Hill. Say he only got a hundred, for Christ sake. He giggled aloud as he worked out the math. Three zero zero times one zero zero—so many zeros!—that made—

Freedy stopped dead. Someone was singing, real clear and real close by. A woman, no doubt about it, with a high voice. Sometimes sounds drifted down pipes from above, but never this clear—like it was coming from the other side of the goddamn wall—and never down in F, F being so deep. But she was singing, singing in some foreign language, and what was more, there were instruments playing too. What the fuck?

Instruments too, and way down here. That scared him, like something was happening to his mind. Where was he? Freedy flicked on the flash—hadn't even been using it, hadn't felt the need—and shone it around. It was just F—steam pipe, cable pipe, phone-line pipe—dipping down a little ahead and bending left, where it passed under N. Just F: but his heart was beating, too fast, too light, not the heavy boom boom it usually did. How much of Ronnie's meth had he tweaked? Couldn't recall. He took a few deep breaths, felt better.

But the woman was still singing, still close by. He put his ear to the tunnel wall. Fucked if she really wasn't singing just on the other side.

What did he have on him? Pliers, couple of screwdrivers, pocketknife. He opened the knife, took it to the drywall, cut out a fist-sized hole. The singing grew even louder, even clearer. And what was that? A woman's laugh? He stuck his hand in, felt not cement or brick, what the tunnels were usually lined with, but nothing. Taking the knife, he cut a neat door in the drywall, stepped through.

He shone the flash. He was in a little square room with a dirt floor, nothing in it but a stool, a heavy old wooden stool—he'd seen a few like it over in storage—placed by the opposite wall. If you sat on it, he saw, you'd have access to a hinged flap in the wall. Freedy blew the dust off the stool, sat down. He opened the flap.

A tiny round hole: he put his eye to it. A spyhole! Amazing. He snapped off the flash.

What Freedy saw he couldn't take in, not all at once. Candles burning, dozens of them, in a room—no, more than one room, there was at least another through a door at the back—a room straight out of a palace or castle. Music came from somewhere, horrible old scratchy music, not live. But there were live people in the room, live people from the present day, a guy and two girls.

Two girls. One sat on a couch near the guy, the other was

standing in front of them. She, the blond one, said, "How do I look?"

She looked fucking incredible. So did the other one, the brown-haired one. Also fucking incredible. The girl at the bus station was pretty, but these two. *Fox* wasn't the word. Freedy shifted his peering eye from one to the other, trying to decide which was better-looking, unable to make up his mind. Then the guy said something Freedy missed, and the two girls laughed. That kind of pissed Freedy off. He took a look at the guy—some kid, college kid, that he could break in two. Bust through the wall, break the college kid in two, take the girls back into that other room, where he could see some sort of weird bed, and fuck their brains out. Get them to do a few things together, and then—*whoa, Freedy. Getting ahead of yourself, boy.* He reached for his stash, took one little sniff, just to stay grounded.

When he peeked back through the hole in the wall, things had changed. They were all up, finishing their drinks, drinks a little lighter in color than Saul's V.O., and blowing out the candles. The room went dark candle by candle. They went through the doorway to the other room, started blowing out candles there too. Freedy thought he could make out a rope ladder hanging down from above. One of the girls climbed it, then the other, finally the college kid, carrying a candle with him. They all went up the ladder easily, the college kid easiest of all, like he was an athlete or something, but that didn't fool Freedy. He could snap him in half. Like Thanksgiving. Crack.

The college kid disappeared from view, and everything went dark. Completely black. That didn't bother Freedy. What bothered him was the fact that the music was still playing, the woman with the strange, high voice singing on and on.

When Freedy got back home that night, his mood was mixed. The bad part was he hadn't gotten into the science building. He'd found it all right, building 17 at the end of F, but from the other side of the door leading to the utilities room had come voices, maintenance guys working on some electrical problem. So no laptops, just a fax machine and a cordless phone with speed dial he'd grabbed from the lounge in 51. The good part, though, the very good part, was the strange place he'd found where F passed under N somewhere beneath building 68; and those girls. He'd worked in maintenance with guys who were lifers, sorry assholes, and no one had ever said anything about rooms, fancy rooms, under 68. But it existed, and those girls knew about it. That was so promising. Freedy didn't know how exactly, or at all, just knew that it was.

He went in the house real quiet, what with the phone and the fax, past her bedroom, toward his bedroom at the end of the hall. The door was open and blue light leaked out. Freedy looked in, saw his mother, in that Arab getup, standing before the open laptop. He walked in behind her, but real quiet, stuck the phone and the fax under the bed before he spoke.

"Little Boy is home," he said, reading the poem title right off the wall.

She jumped, actually got airborne, which was pretty cool, jerked around, said, "Oh my God," holding on to her tits. "Why do you scare me like that?"

"I said hi. You just didn't hear me, what with concentrating so hard on my laptop."

Her gaze went to it. He moved closer to see what was on the screen, saw what had been there before:

> To: Phil. 322
> From: Prof. L. Uzig

and all that.

Then her gaze was on him, that dark, stoned gaze, right into his eyes, like she was trying to see inside. "What's going on, Freedy?"

"It's for business purposes," Freedy said. "I got it off Ronnie Medeiros for a song."

"I didn't know Ronnie took Phil three twenty-two," she said.

"What's that got to do with anything?" Freedy said.

17

The consequences of our actions take us by the scruff of the neck, altogether indifferent to the fact that we have "improved" in the meantime.
—Professor Uzig's citation from Nietzsche in banning makeup work from Philosophy 322

After midnight, aboveground. Grace and Izzie left Plessey Hall to cross the quad, Nat continuing upstairs to his room, seventeen on the second floor. He stopped at the landing, looked out the window. Snow was falling, dark flakes blowing through cubes of light outside the dorm windows, through ovals of light under the Victorian lampposts on the quad. Grace and Izzie were about halfway across, both wearing ski hats with tassels, their gaits, their carriages identical, impossible to tell apart. One swept a handful of snow off Emerson's bronze leg, flung it at the other. Then they were both running across the quad, chasing each other like little girls, and disappearing in the shadows; Nat thought he could hear their laughter, very faint. At that moment, with the laughter and all, he knew that everything was going to be okay.

It wasn't that he was drunk—oh, maybe just a little from the cognac, much more from the fact of it being one hundred years old, and from the whole magical experience down there—but the realization that "everything" didn't amount to much, so why wouldn't it be okay? What was wrong? He made a short mental list. First came Izzie's insistence on keeping their relationship secret from Grace. He would have to persuade her to change her mind. Her fear of Grace's reaction was exaggerated, probably due to years and years of Grace's dominance, now coming to an end. He reminded himself to learn the ending of the SAT story.

Second, there was Patti. She had to be told—no, he corrected himself—he had to tell her, and as soon as possible. First thing in the morning, even if it meant waking her: he would call Patti, tell her the truth. There was someone else.

Third, he had to catch up in biology. He hadn't come all this way to miss classes. That was for tomorrow as well. In twenty-four hours he would be caught up.

There. He felt better, as he should have with only three problems in his whole life, the last one trivial; all solvable and solvable soon. Meanwhile, although he hadn't really known what to expect at Inverness, any half-formed expectations had already been exceeded. He loved the place. Loved it, and knew he could do well. Not only that, but there were other kids from his town who could do well here too. He would make sure Mrs. Smith knew that when he went home for the summer. Mrs. Smith, and how she had brandished the Fourth of July special edition of the *County Register* at the sky: he understood her now.

Nat came to his door. A note was tucked under the brass 17. He opened it. A note written on economics department stationery, from his first-semester professor:

Nat—Your final exam grade last semester is being changed from a B minus to an A plus, a change that will be reflected in your course grade as well. I've reexamined your answer to the last question. I was looking for an analysis of capital and current account theory as it related to the hypothetical and since you didn't give me that, I gave you zero. On reflection, and having conferred with several colleagues, I believe that your application of monetarist methodology is

*fresh, cogent, and quite defensible. Have you given much
thought yet to your choice of major?*

Nat loved Inverness. Had he ever been happier in his life?
He was so lucky. He owed them—Mrs. Smith, Miss Brown,
his mom; and all the others back home.

Nat opened the door. It was dark in the outer room, the only
light coming from his screen saver, but not dark enough to
hide the person sleeping under a blanket on Wags's couch,
still not picked up by the movers. Was it Wags himself, released or escaped? Nat found himself smiling at the prospect.
But going closer, he saw it was a woman, her face turned
away, her hair longer than Wags's and curlier. He bent over. It
was Patti.

Patti. Nat froze right there, and *froze* was the word, with
that icy tingling in his fingertips. What's she doing here? Answers came, none convincing: some vacation he didn't know
about, a school trip, an internship in an eastern city. To find
out, all he had to do was wake her. He didn't want to. He
wanted to let her sleep, there under Wags's afternoon nap
blanket. To simply let her sleep, because nothing had gone
wrong yet; to let her sleep before he told her the news. He noticed a small but bright red zit in that curved indentation on
the side of the nose where zits liked to form.

"Patti?" he said quietly.

She didn't wake up, didn't stir.

"Patti?" A little louder, but only a little, not wanting to
scare her, and no more effective. She was probably tired from
her trip; had she taken the bus? The bus all the way from
Denver? Nat remembered his last trip, a flight in a private jet
with a black *Z* on the tail. He touched her shoulder.

Patti's eyes opened. For an instant she didn't know where
she was. Then she saw it was him, and the look in her eyes
changed completely. She smiled, a smile that could only be
called sweet, as sweet, in fact, as he'd ever seen.

"Nat," she said.

"Hi."

She sat up. "Your hair's longer. It looks nice." Her hand moved, no more than an inch or so, as if she'd thought of touching his hair and reconsidered.

"I called you a couple times," she said, "once from Chicago and once from . . . somewhere else. I can't even remember, isn't that weird? Especially since I was trying to take it all in."

Like him, him until a little while ago, she'd never really been anywhere. Nat remembered the phone ringing while he'd been in the bedroom with Izzie. He had to tell Patti and tell her now. It would be too cruel to allow her another one of those sweet smiles. He forgot whatever it was he'd rehearsed, just opened his mouth and hoped something not too terrible would come out.

But Patti spoke first. "Oh, Nat," she said, her voice suddenly unsteady. "I'm pregnant."

Thoughts poured into Nat's mind, first—whatever it said about him, good or bad—first came the knowledge of what Patti must have crossed out in her note: *I missed my period.* Then came more: it could only have been at Patti's house, before Julie's party, before the drinking. But they'd used a condom. That raised the possibility of some other guy. Man. Of some other man. Out of the question: he knew Patti, and she wouldn't be here if it wasn't him. It had to be true. Patti was pregnant and he was the . . . father. He squirmed from that idea, that word. But he knew there would be no getting away from it, he wouldn't let himself get away from it, because he'd had a father, too; he'd had a father, briefly, a father who'd ignored his responsibility, who'd walked away.

"Nat?"

"Yes."

"Aren't you going to say something?"

He nodded. "How are you feeling?"

"Horrible."

What was the name for it? It came to him. "From the morning sickness?" he said.

She smiled at him again, almost as sweetly as before. "Not that," she said. "I feel great. My body feels great. Inside is where I'm so messed up." Patti started crying, first just a silent tear or two, then, maybe catching some expression in his eyes, many more, and far from silent. "And now I'm messing you up too. The best thing that ever happened to me." Or something like that. Nat couldn't really tell because of the sobbing. He sat down on Wags's couch and held her, awkwardly, sitting on the edge.

She leaned against him, leaned with all her weight, holding nothing back. "Oh, Nat," she said.

He hugged her. If he'd been at all drunk before, physically or psychologically, he wasn't now.

Her lips moved against his chest. "I can feel you thinking," she said. Her voice vibrated through his skin. "What are you thinking?"

"I don't know," he said. But he did: he was remembering what had happened when they got to Julie's party. Julie's family had money, at least what he'd used to think of as having money. Julie's father, brother of Mr. Beaman, Nat's mother's boss, was a pharmacist. They could afford to keep two or three horses in a barn behind their house. The loft had been turned into a guest bedroom. He and Patti had ended up there, in the bed where the vomiting incident happened. But before that, they'd been asleep. He'd awakened with Patti on top of him. She'd rolled off a moment or two later, saying she didn't feel well. Had he been inside her? Had it happened then? He didn't know. It was all vague, half remembered, half aware in the first place, the horses stirring uneasily beneath them the only sure thing.

"Are you mad at me?" Patti said.

"No."

"Something, then."

"No."

"You're thinking."

"I'm not."

But she was right. Thoughts like: *Are you sure you're pregnant? How do you know?* Those remained unspoken: Patti wouldn't have been here if she wasn't sure. And: *abortion.* He didn't even know where Patti stood on abortion. He assumed she was for it—he assumed he was for it—but they'd never discussed abortion, not the right and wrong of it. And then there was Patti's uncle in Denver, a big red-faced Broncos fan who'd taken them to a game, bought them beer and hot dogs, screamed like a maniac at the ref; Patti's uncle, the priest.

"Nat?"

"Yes."

"What are we going—what should I do?"

He looked down at her: curly hair, pale face, blue-lit from the computer screen, against his chest, his shirt dampening with her tears. Her gaze shifted up to his, like a baby watching its mother. That was the image that came to mind, and he hated it.

"Do you love me," she said, "just a little bit?"

He was silent.

"You don't have to answer," she said. "I'm sorry, sorry for everything."

"You have nothing to be sorry about," he said.

She clung to him. "You're such a good person."

"That's not true."

"Yes, it is."

He didn't love her. There had been times last summer when he'd thought maybe he did; now, because of the contrast with what he felt for Izzie, he knew for certain he never had. He also knew she was wrong: he had to answer the question. "I don't love you, Patti," he said. He said it as plainly as he could, deliberately closing the door to interpretation, but at the same time he held her tight, as tightly as he ever had. Completely crazy, but he couldn't help it.

Patti sobbed. Half a sob, really, cut off sharply through an effort of will he could feel in the muscles lining her spine. After that, they were silent for what seemed like a long time. Blue-lit snow piled up on the window ledge; his shirt got damper. Then it got no damper, and later less and less, almost dry again.

The chapel bell tolled. Patti yawned, the kind of big yawn impossible to stifle.

"You're tired," he said.

"A little." So quiet, both their voices, but very clear.

"Then sleep," he said. "It can wait till tomorrow."

"You're sure?"

"We'll think better in the morning."

"All right."

He made her sleep in his bed. She lay on her back, under the covers, curly hair spread on the pillow. "You can come in, if you want."

"That wouldn't be a good idea."

"Why not?" Patti said. "What could happen now?"

She laughed. That was Patti. He laughed too. At that moment, and just for that moment, he came close to something like love: more craziness.

Patti took his hand. "Nat?"

"Yes."

"What's gone wrong?" She wasn't crying anymore; her face was puffy but somehow peaceful too.

"How do you mean?"

"People used to get married at our age. Settle down, have . . . kids, and everything was all right."

"Not in my family," he said.

She let go.

Nat took his sleeping bag into Wags's room, lay down on Wags's bed. Wags hadn't showered enough, especially toward the end, Nat realized now, but he'd compensated with spray-on deodorant, some brand that smelled like evergreens and coconut. Nat closed his eyes; the evergreen-and-coconut smell, rising off the mattress every time he moved, grew stronger and stronger,

You want me to flunk out, don't you?

Right. And then all this will be mine.

Nat rose, went to the couch in the outer room, tried to sleep where Patti had been sleeping.

At dawn he stopped trying, got up, shaved, showered, put on fresh clothes, tried to look fresh. Patti was still asleep, her face still peaceful, her breathing almost unnoticeable. He left a note on the bedside crate, laying a granola bar on top of it: *Gone to class. Back by noon. N.*

Nat went to the bio lab, made up the work he'd missed. Problem three, from the old set of problems, taken care of; the precious premed option preserved. Problems one and two were now buried under the new ones.

English 104. Izzie wasn't there. The professor, handing back the *Young Goodman Brown* essays, said, "I'm a little disappointed with these. Only two of you—" She glanced around the table. "—one of whom is absent, identified the pathos at its core."

"Which is?" someone asked.

"Page ninety-five," said the professor, opening her book: "Referring to Goodman Brown: 'But he himself was the chief horror of the scene.' " Nat stuffed the paper in his backpack without checking the grade and hurried back to Plessey, taking shortcuts through the snow.

Izzie was at his desk in the outer room, playing solitaire on the computer. She turned as Nat came in. He went into the bedroom. The note and granola bar were where he'd left them, but Patti was gone, the bed neatly made.

Izzie was watching him through the doorway. "They went out," she said.

"They?"

"Grace and . . . Patti."

"Where did they go?"

"For food. She hasn't eaten in two days."

Nat glanced back at the bedside crate; perhaps it was just the empty wrapper of the granola bar that he'd seen. But no. And also on the crate, the little box from Assad and Son. Was that where he'd left it? He didn't think so, and he'd certainly not left it open, as it was now, the gold number 8 and chain nestled in the tissue paper: never worn, as would be clear to anyone who looked inside. He thought of putting the chain on now; his fingers almost touched it.

"Do you want me to leave?" Izzie said.

He would have if Izzie had said anything like *She seems so nice.* But Izzie didn't. "No," Nat said.

They waited in the outer room, Izzie at the desk, Nat on the couch. "You went to English?" she said.

"Yes."

"Did she give the papers back?"

Nat nodded.

"What did you get?"

"I don't know." He handed her the paper. She flipped to the back. "A," she said. "I guess you were right about that chief horror line."

"You used it too?"

"Of course."

"Why of course?"

"Don't you remember? We discussed it on the beach."

"But I might have been wrong."

Izzie shook her head. "I trust you."

"You do?"

"Completely. I didn't even know what the word meant until you came along."

"You haven't known me very long."

"So? Just look at you."

"What do you mean?"

"That chipped tooth, for starters."

"That's why you trust me?"

"And a million other things."

"What's number two?"

Izzie thought. She flushed, very slightly. "I'm not telling."

They looked at each other, Izzie at the desk, Nat on the couch, but within touching distance in the cramped dormitory room. Nat could feel some force pulling them together, knew that at almost any signal from him, a word or gesture, they could be in the bedroom the next minute. He said no word, made no gesture. They both looked away.

Snow started falling again. It changed to rain. "I hate that," Izzie said. And back to snow.

Nat checked his watch. "I'm going to look for them."

"I'm coming."

They searched the student union, the freshman dining hall, the snack bars, the Rat. They tried Grace and Izzie's room, the Lanark lounge, the gym. Then they went off campus to the nearby coffee shops and delis where students gathered. It got colder and colder. They stopped at the bottom of the Hill, in front of a boarded-up building with a faded sign: *The Glass Onion*.

"Where else?" Nat said.

"The cave?" said Izzie.

"Why would she take her down there?"

"Who knows?" Izzie said. "But I'll look."

Izzie went down to the basement of Plessey to enter the tunnels through the janitor's closet. Nat returned to his room. He checked his voice mail, his E-mail: nothing. Grace walked in, alone.

"Where's Patti?"

Grace glanced at her watch. "Still at the airport."

"Airport?"

"I took her there."

"What airport?"

"She asked me to. She wanted to go home."

"What airport?"

There was something strange in his tone, strange and new. Grace heard it too. "Albany," she said, backing up a step. "It's the closest one with connections to Denver."

Nat was on his feet. The airport was thirty miles away. He flung open his closet, snatched all the money remaining in his shoe— $32—all the money he had until his next paycheck from the Alumni Office job.

"It's what she wants," Grace said as he left the room. And: "Departure's in twenty minutes. You'll never make it." Down the stairs, out the main gate, into a taxi. It was only after he was on his way that he realized Grace was still wearing his Clear Creek letter jacket.

At the airport, Nat checked the first screen he saw. No mention of Denver, but a flight to Chicago, delayed by weather, was now boarding, boarding, boarding at gate eleven. He ran toward the gate area, stopping sharply at security. He'd forgotten about security.

"I need to see someone at gate eleven."

"Gotta have a gate pass."

"Where do I get it?"

"Back at ticketing."

"But there's no time."

Shrug.

He raced back to ticketing, got a gate pass, went through security.

"Place your pocket change in the tray and try again."

He went through again, this time successfully, and ran as fast as he could to gate eleven. Patti, now wearing jeans instead of her blue dress, was handing her boarding pass to the attendant at the ramp.

"Patti." Too loud: the handful of people still in line all turned to him.

Patti stepped out of the line, not very steadily. "You shouldn't have come."

"Of course I came."

"How?"

"Doesn't matter. In a taxi."

"It's so expensive. Or did she—did Grace pay for you too?"

"Of course not."

Patti flinched. He saw how pale she was.

"What is it, Patti?"

"I'm going home, that's all."

The last passenger started down the ramp. The attendant waited by the door.

Nat lowered his voice. "But we haven't talked about anything yet."

"There's nothing to talk about."

"What do you mean? We have to make some decisions."

"There's nothing to decide."

"What are you saying?"

"I'm not pregnant anymore."

Nat's first thought was that she'd lost the baby, had a miscarriage caused by stress, travel, not eating. Then came the second thought.

"The people were very nice," Patti said. "Didn't even ask for money, but Grace made a donation."

"Grace?"

"She's very nice too. I'll pay her back for the ticket when I can. That's how we left it."

"Oh, God. Don't go, Patti."

"I'm going." She looked right into his eyes, spoke without bitterness, with hardly any inflection at all. "I'm just not exactly clear on which one is the one," she said, "Grace or Izzie? You don't have to answer."

"Izzie."

Patti nodded. "Good choice."

"Closing the flight, honey," said the gate attendant.

Patti turned and walked down the ramp.

18

A married philosopher belongs to comedy.
—Friedrich Nietzsche, *On the Genealogy of Morals*
   (not on the syllabus for Philosophy 322)

Nat worked.

He worked on his bio experiment, the effects of trichloroethane and trichloroethylene on *Palemontes vulgaris*; he worked on his "Faith and Hypocrisy in *The Scarlet Letter*" essay for English 104; he worked on the Apollonian/Dionysian paper for Philosophy 322; he worked overtime in the Alumni Office; he worked out at the gym. He didn't socialize, didn't see anyone, let all his calls, not many, go through voice mail, answered all except the one from Izzie and the one from Grace. There was none from Patti.

Nat worked, without enjoyment, involvement, or even interest. But only for a while: after two days, he began to feel more like himself, at first guilty about it, then less so, finally working the way he always worked, time forgotten. He couldn't help it.

One of the phone calls he returned was from Professor Uzig, inviting Nat to the traditional Philosophy 322 dinner at his house, Saturday at seven.

"Thanks, but—" said Nat.

"It's a requirement, actually," said Professor Uzig. "And you might even win the prize."

"The prize?"

"In the cake. There's always a prize in the cake."

"Is this alcoholic?" said the quiet girl who'd tried to connect Nietzsche and domestic violence.

"Kir?" said the hired waiter, passing out drinks in the great room of Professor Uzig's house. "Yes, ma'am."

She put her glass back on his tray.

Professor Uzig had a big brick house on College Hill, surprisingly big, surprisingly luxurious, inside and out. A fire blazed on a stone hearth brought from Provence, a portrait of the professor by a famous painter Nat thought he'd heard of hung on the wall, and there were other similar details, pointed out by the host. Professor Uzig was wearing one of those silk things—ascot? foulard?—around his neck, the first time Nat had seen one off the movie screen. Now, having witnessed the scene between the waiter and the girl, the professor, his back to the fire and his students around him, was telling a story about a recent faculty party where some new TA had thought that *in loco parentis* meant "like a crazy parent."

Everyone laughed, some more confidently than others. The whole class was there, all dressed up except the Kurt Cobain fan, probably making a statement, and Nat, who hadn't known. The two of them, in their jeans, stood together next to the shrimp. "What's this kir shit?" said the Kurt Cobain fan.

"Wine and something else."

"Think it would be all right to ask for a beer?"

"What's the worst that could happen?"

"I get an F and lose my scholarship."

Nat laughed.

"You on scholarship too?" asked the Kurt Cobain fan.

"Yeah."

"Went to a public high school?"

"Yeah."

"Been to Europe?"

"No."

"I'm Ferg."

"Nat."

"I know," said Ferg. "Want to see something?"

"Sure."

He led Nat out of the great room, into the library. Books from floor to ceiling, a table covered with papers, periodicals, correspondence, and on a pedestal a bust of Nietzsche, his walrus mustache resembling, in bronze, the armament of an unusual animal. Ferg took a book off a shelf, leafed through, handed it to Nat.

An Inverness course catalog, twenty-five years old, opened to the philosophy section. Philosophy 322, Professor Uzig. Nothing had changed but the name of the course: Superman and Man: Friedrich Nietzsche and Bob Dylan.

"Can you believe it?" said Ferg.

"Pretty funny," said Nat.

"Funny? You call bait-and-switch funny? He's been perpetrating a consumer fraud for twenty-five years. I'm seriously thinking of filing a formal complaint to the academic dean."

"Ask for the beer instead," Nat said.

Ferg glared at him. "I won't stop there," he said, and left the room.

Nat saw more catalogs on a higher shelf, wondered whether there were any from a really long time ago, say, 1919. He was reaching up when he felt someone in the room behind him, knew it was Izzie even before he turned.

"I brought you this," she said; a glass of beer. Izzie wore black pants, black turtleneck, black headband. *Walks in beauty like the night:* that was the phrase that popped into his mind. It now made perfect sense.

"I don't want anything, thanks." He hadn't touched alcohol since Patti left, didn't want to.

She nodded, as though he'd confirmed some impression. "You're mad."

"No."

Nat saw that the beer was trembling in its glass. Izzie put it down. "You blame me for . . . Patti."

"Why would I do that?"

"I didn't even know she existed."

"Grace didn't tell you?"

"You told Grace about Patti?"

More than that, and worse, if his memory of that drunken and stoned night in New York was accurate: he'd used Patti as a shield. "I did," Nat said. "The thing is—"

Izzie held up her hand. "You don't have to explain anything," she said.

"There's nothing to explain. It was over. I just didn't do it right." Couldn't have done it worse.

"And us?" Izzie said. "Are we over too?"

A door, not to the great room, but another one, opened and Grace came in, carrying a framed photograph. "Hey, Izzie," she said, then saw Nat. "Oh. Nat."

"Hi."

"Still speaking to us?"

"Why wouldn't I be?"

"You're not returning calls."

He was silent.

"Maybe you misinterpreted what went on," Grace said.

"Which was?"

Grace paused. Her gaze went to Izzie, back to Nat. "Didn't Patti explain at the airport?"

That raised several questions in Nat's mind. He voiced the simplest. "How do you know I saw her at the airport?"

"She called me the next morning."

"She did?"

Grace nodded. "Didn't have to. No thanks were necessary. But she's so . . . sweet. Worried about the money and everything."

Let me guess—she spells it with an i. "I'm paying," Nat said. Why hadn't he thought of that earlier?

"Don't be silly," Grace said.

"I'm not being silly."

"No need to get angry. The amount's inconsequential."

"That's not the point. I'm paying."

Grace laughed.

"What's funny? I can pay." But not right away—it would probably have to be in installments drawn from coming Alumni Office checks; should he also start looking for a second job, down in the town? How he wished he could just whip out his wallet and hand over whatever the amount was on the spot.

"It's not that," Grace said. "Don't be so touchy."

"Then what's funny?"

"I just don't want this to degenerate into farce, that's all."

"What are you talking about?"

"Farce. The maid under the bed, someone else in the closet, British accents, you getting stuck with the bill."

"I don't understand."

"Do I have to spell it out?"

Izzie shook her head at Grace, almost imperceptibly, but Nat caught it from the corner of his eye.

"What the hell's going on?"

"Nothing," Grace said. "Look what I found." She set the photograph down on the table. Nat took it in at a glance: Professor Uzig when he was young, not much older than they were. Took in that, and the resemblance to the bust of Nietzsche—not the features, Uzig's being much sharper— but the similar thinking poses, and the fact that the professor when young had worn a mustache much like Nietzsche's. He stood in front of that place at the bottom of the hill, the Glass Onion, its sign unfaded.

Nat waved his hand in the air, waving away distraction. He clipped the edge of the frame by accident, knocking the photograph over. "Spell it out, whatever it is."

"No, Grace," said Izzie.

"Why not?" said Grace. "He'll feel better in the end."

"Say it," said Nat.

Grace said it: "You may not be—you may not have been—the father."

Nat felt sick, didn't want to hear another word.

"Something about too much to drink, homecoming weekend at Pismo State or whatever it is, a football player. She wasn't really too clear. But the kind of thing that goes on here every weekend. A moment of weakness, in this case followed by another—coming here. Her words, not mine. Call her if you don't believe me."

"You think I'd do that?"

"I apologize," Grace said, laying her hand briefly on his. Her fingers were icy; it was cold in Professor Uzig's library, snow blowing by the leaded windows. Nat sat down, resisted the impulse to put his hands over his face.

"What did that accomplish?" Izzie said.

Grace turned to her, eyes narrowing. Before she could reply, Professor Uzig stuck his head in the room and said, "Dinner, young people."

"Ah, dessert," said Professor Uzig when the cake appeared. "The course America likes best."

"Where are you from, anyway?" said Ferg; he'd built a little palisade of empty beer bottles around his place setting. Everyone else, except for the domestic-violence girl and Nat, was drinking wine.

"Brooklyn," said Professor Uzig. "Your native soil as well, if I recall."

Ferg's mouth opened but no words came.

A startling revelation: Nat had expected some answer like Prague, Munich, Trieste. Startling and with a lesson that applied to him, cut through his misery about Patti, not making it go away, but showing why it must: he was in the right place, doing the right thing. And therefore while he might return to his hometown, would for sure, he would never live there again. As for Patti, who wasn't in this place: as for Patti—but he hadn't completed that thought before Izzie, sitting across the table, caught his eye. She smiled, a hesitant smile, as though asking if he was okay; at least, that was his interpretation. He smiled back and started pouring himself a glass of wine. Why not, after all? Then he remembered: *He'll feel better in the end.* Feeling better so soon? He stopped pouring, the glass half full.

"With the question of origins out of the way," said Professor Uzig, rubbing his hands together—white hands, long and hairless, the fingernails gleaming as though coated with some colorless polish—"who wants to play the future game?"

No one said they didn't. Professor Uzig passed out three-by-five file cards. "Simply write in a sentence or less what you imagine you'll be doing in twenty years."

Everyone wrote. Professor Uzig collected the cards, read them silently to himself, his face expressionless. "First card," he said: "Inner-city doctor."

That was easy—the domestic-violence girl.

"Record producer."

Ferg.

"Dead."

"Not funny, Grace," said Izzie.

"A writer."

A writer. Everyone guessed the smart girl from English 103, promoted by the English department beyond Nat and Izzie's 104 to some sophomore-level course.

"I confess," said the smart girl.

The funny thing, known only to Nat, was that *writer* had been his thought too, but, not wanting to jinx it, he'd written *teacher* instead.

"Teacher," said Professor Uzig, looking around the table. His expression changed abruptly; he went still. Everyone followed his gaze. A woman had appeared between the open French doors to the dining room, an old woman with a ring of white hair. She wore a quilted white housecoat, a white tissue sticking out of one sleeve, and white slippers.

"I thought the department meeting was next week, Leo," she said; an old person's voice, all the bottom sounds missing.

The note cards slipped from Professor's Uzig's hand. "Correct," he said. "This is Phil three twenty-two."

"Phil three twenty-two?" she said. "That's still going on?" She scanned the faces around the table. "What a bushy-tailed bunch, Leo. I'd forgotten how bushy-tailed these bunches can be. What's the craze this year? Aboriginal rights? Prescription drugs? Ritual baths?"

Ferg laughed; a loud laugh, choked off almost at once.

The old woman advanced into the room. "What are we drinking?" she said.

"I understood you weren't feeling too well," said Professor Uzig.

"You understood right, Leo, as always. I feel like Marie Antoinette after the guillotine, like Cleopatra after the asp, like . . ." She couldn't think what else. One of her eyes was tearing; she dabbed at it with the tissue, had trouble sticking it back in her sleeve.

A nurse entered, straightening her cap. "I'm so sorry," she said. "I went to relieve my—I went to the rest room, and the next thing I knew Mrs. Uzig had . . ." She took the old woman's elbow.

"Like Anne Boleyn after the . . . after . . ."

"Then why not go back to bed?" said Professor Uzig, his voice much gentler than Nat had ever heard it. He hadn't imagined certain things about Professor Uzig, that he could have been born in Brooklyn, that he'd be caring for an aged mother.

"Come, dear," said the nurse.

"Come, dear," mimicked the old woman. "Why should I, when all the fun's down here?" She picked up Nat's glass. "How's the wine?"

"I haven't actually tried it yet," said Nat.

"Proving youth is wasted on the young. Are you familiar with that expression?"

"I've heard it," Nat said.

"A careful reply." She took a sip. "Can't taste a thing, of course. But I'm sure it's good—I taught him everything he knows about wine, paying for it in the bargain."

The nurse tugged a little harder at her elbow.

"You don't mind sharing your wine, do you, young man?"

"No," said Nat.

"What's your name?"

Nat told her.

"Enchantée," she said, extending her hand as though she expected him to kiss it. "I am Helen Uzig." Nat shook her hand: skin like paper, green veins almost on the surface, pulsing light and fast against his fingers. "Enchantée," she repeated, "accent aigu on the second *e*."

"Please, dear," said the nurse, pulling now.

"Keep your panties on," said Helen Uzig. She looked right at Professor Uzig and repeated the remark. The nurse pulled again, a little harder, and this time the old woman gave way, half walking, half in tow, toward the doorway. "Good night, my bushy-tailed friends," she said, as the nurse got her out of the room. "And never forget that Nietzsche is something one must grow out of," she added from down the hall.

There was a silence. Ferg, on his sixth or seventh beer, broke it. "Your mother's pretty cool."

"My mother is dead," said Professor Uzig.

"Huh?" said Ferg.

But Nat got it.

The prize in the cake was a well-preserved piece of eight, found by Professor Uzig himself off Jost van Dyke, pierced to make it wearable as a pendant. It turned up in Grace's portion.

*　　*　　*

Once, in Boulder after a high-school student government conference, Nat had found himself in a pickup basketball game that included a few CU players. It was the only basketball he'd ever played where everything had happened too fast. Now, leaving Professor Uzig's house, snow falling but the moon somehow shining at the same time, an effect—black snow streaks over the disk of the moon—that he'd never seen before, he had that feeling again. He needed to slow things down, to go back to his room, to do nothing. The three of them went down to the cave instead. They were college freshmen. It was Saturday night.

19

Does the superman make you uneasy?
—Professor Uzig in class, Philosophy 322

Saturday night. Freedy's favorite night of the week, by far. What else was there, if you thought about it? Sunday, Monday, Tuesday nights all sucked, everyone knew that. Wednesday was a little better, Thursday better yet—he'd even been known to cut loose on a Thursday night, like one time down in Tijuana after those fires or earthquakes canceled the Friday schedule. Friday night was famous coast to coast, of course; but at jobs he'd held, A-1 Pool Design, Engineering, and Maintenance, and others not worth remembering, Saturday was a working day—not a normal working day, because no one expected normal work when everyone was a little wasted, although he would expect it, by God, when he got set up down in Florida, whose money was it, anyway?— but still, a working day, taking some of the fun out of Friday night. That left Saturday night, just one goddamn night to be totally . . . totally whatever. Freedy came alive on Saturday night. He was in the habit.

Totally whatever. That put it perfectly. Saturday morning Freedy lifted over at Ronnie's, feeling real strong, stronger than he had for a long time, since California, in fact. Then he and Ronnie had a few beers, watched an infomercial about real estate or maybe getting into retail, Freedy wasn't sure.

Didn't matter: they were always the same, as he told Ronnie. Idea, plan, stick.

"Fuckin' A," said Ronnie. "I never thought of that."

"Works for everything," Freedy said.

"What do you mean, everything?"

"Give you a for instance, Ronnie. What do you want to do tonight?"

"Huh?"

"Just answer. I'll show you how it works."

"What I want to do tonight?" said Ronnie. "Get laid, I guess."

"Okay. That's the idea part. Now for the plan. How are you going to make it real?"

Ronnie thought. "Head over to Fitchville?"

"Fitchville? What the fuck are you talking about?"

"Thing is," said Ronnie, "there's sort of a girl."

"You've got some piece in Fitchville?"

"Nothing what you'd call serious."

What the hell was going on? Ronnie had a girlfriend? How did that compute? "What's the story?"

"No story. She's pretty nice."

"Pretty nice?"

"Yeah."

"How did you meet her?"

"I still do a little reffin'."

"Reffin'?"

"You know. Reffin' basketball. Pays twenty-five bucks a game. I got my certificate way back."

"So?"

"So she plays on the team. Point guard."

"Fuck are you talking about? What team?"

"Fitchville South."

Fitchville South? "You're fucking some high-school girl?"

"I wouldn't say fucking, exactly," said Ronnie. "She's not ready yet."

"She's not ready yet?"

"She's just a sophomore," said Ronnie. "But I get hand jobs."

Fuckin' pathetic. But that night—sitting in a bar near the state line, a stripper bar, but because of the snow only one stripper had shown up and she was on a break—Freedy's mind gravitated to the subject of hand jobs. Nothing wrong with hand jobs—American as apple pie. Once Estrella had given him a hand job in the Burger King drive-through in West Covina. Home of the Whopper. He kind of missed Estrella. But what good would that do? She'd fucked it all up with that brother scam or whatever it was. He ordered another beer, and a shot of V.O.; he was starting to like V.O.

He liked hand jobs, too: but a sophomore? Some pimple-faced kid with baby fat? Not cool. The cool thing would be a hand job from some classy girl, the drop-dead fuck-you kind. Not Estrella: take away all her good points and what was left? Just another wetback among millions. Did he know any classy girls of the drop-dead fuck-you kind? No. Had he even actually seen one in real life? The surprising answer to that question came as he was knocking back the last of the V.O. He'd seen two!

Two. Double your pleasure, double your fun. Two, as drop-dead fuck-you as they came. As drop-dead fuck-you as those TV miniskirt lawyers of Ronnie's, except these two were real, real flesh and blood, down there in that underground palace where F tunnel hooked beneath building 68. The underground palace—what was that all about? Some mystery, some college shit from the past, buried down there. Who cared? What mattered was that those two classy girls had discovered it too. Probably thought of it as their little secret. An amazing, what was the word? *Insight.* That was it. An amazing insight. They thought of it as their little secret. But he knew! Amazing. And he was amazing too, because just like that he'd figured out where ideas—the first step on the infomercial road to success—came from. Get an idea, they said, step one, they said, but they never told you where ideas came from. And now he knew. He'd figured it out, all by himself. Was he some unit in the common herd? Oh, no. He was an original, like, thinker. One day he'd be making infomercials of his own. He knew that with absolute certainty. Why? Because he'd figured out where ideas came from. They came—

"I said c'n I get you another?"

Freedy looked up, up into the face of some waitress, not a classy, drop-dead fuck-you face, more like the opposite. Just the basics—face, tits, cunt. "Saturday night, why not?" he said. So cool.

"Phew," said waitress, "thought you were on one of those toxic-shock trips there for a sec. Bud and a shot of V.O.?"

"Make it a Bud Light." Had to keep his head clear.

She went away. Ass. He'd left out ass. Face, tits, cunt, ass. Easy to make a joke of it by saying *forget about the face part*. That would be crude. There were crude guys around, but not him. He sipped Bud Light like a gentleman, tried the V.O., went back to the beer, back and forth, but like a gentleman, taking his time, cool and moderate. Had to keep his head clear. Why? Because things were happening, were going to happen. He didn't know what things, but the . . . elements, yes, the elements were in place. Take Einstein. Had Einstein known what those theories of his were leading to? 'Course not—he just knew things were going to happen. Ka-boom.

But—as Freedy went to the can to piss away several beers and V.O.'s—one thing Einstein must have known about, just like him, was where ideas came from. He went into a cubicle, snorted the tiniest possible snort of meth. Ideas: they came— this was incredible!—from the crashing together, the collision, of two . . . two things. Two . . . forces! Yes. Such as: those two drop-dead fuck-you girls thought the underground palace was their little secret. That was force one. But he knew. That was the second force. Ka-boom. And out of that ka-boom—Freedy stepped from the cubicle, saw himself in the mirror, more diesel than ever, smile whiter than ever, like

Superman with bigger muscles and a ponytail—out of that ka-boom came an idea, new and fresh: he would go back down to the palace, down where F tunnel hooked under building 68. When? Why not now? It was Saturday night.

He popped an andro, and as he did saw another cubicle open behind him. A guy came out zipping up, a guy in a state trooper's uniform. A fuckin' statie, wearing the Smokey hat. *You wear it in the crapper?* Freedy came close to saying that aloud, probably would have if it hadn't been for the way the statie was eyeing him in the mirror. What the fuck was that all about? Then he remembered the meth. What cubicle had he been tweaking in? Couldn't have been the one next to the statie, could it? Hard to tell. Freedy turned on the tap, washed his hands. The statie broke off eye contact—his image stopped staring at Freedy's was what really happened, as nice a bit of meth thinking as you could ask for, but the main point was that Freedy could stare anybody down, what with those eyes of his that resembled some British actor's— and went out. "Ever heard of hygiene?" Freedy said; but not loud. He wasn't afraid of some statie with bad personal habits, wasn't afraid of any cop, for that matter, but this was no time for distractions. Idea, plan, stick, stick, stick.

Before he even got to his spyhole, Freedy knew they were there. That creepy music, coming down tunnel F: he didn't like any music, but this kind was the worst. Wasn't even in English, like the singer was rubbing your nose in it.

Freedy removed his drywall door, went into the little room, put his eye to the spyhole. Ka-boom: drop-dead, fuck-you, better than he'd remembered, one, the darker-haired, dressed all in black, the other, the blonde, in red. And that guy. Freedy had forgotten all about him, the college kid he could break in half.

They were lounging on couches, purple couches with gold fringe, drinking some golden liquid from sparkling glasses and talking, the whole room golden too, from the candlelight.

The funny thing was that the blond one, hanging something silver around her neck, was saying exactly what she'd said the first time he'd seen her: "How do I look?"

Some weird time warp, like they'd been waiting for him to come back. But what a ridiculous fuckin' question. How could she even ask? Drop-dead fuck-you is how she looked. The drop-dead fuck-you ones had to know they were drop-dead fuck-you, didn't they? Otherwise nothing made sense. Freedy toyed with the idea of saying it, not loud, just cool and matter-of-fact, speaking right through the spyhole. *Drop-dead fuck-you is how you look, babe.* Then their heads would whip up, real quick, to where the sound came from, and he'd come crashing through the wall. Ka-boom. Toyed with the idea, but remained silent. He was good at silence when he wanted to be; right now, he couldn't even hear his own breathing.

"Like a pirate," said the darker-haired one. "Do you think Leo actually found it, or just bought it somewhere?"

"Who knows anything about Leo anymore?" said the blonde.

The darker-haired one thought that over. The college kid, so breakable in two, watched her do it like something special was happening. "Do you think Dad knew all this?" she said.

"Knew all what?" said the blond one.

"Brooklyn," said the darker-haired one. "Mrs. Uzig."

Mrs. Uzig? Leo? Bells rang. Maybe something special *was* happening.

"It would be just like him, wouldn't it?" said the blond one. "To keep the good stuff to himself."

"I wasn't suggesting that," said the darker-haired one.

The blonde shook her head. "Daddy's little girl."

Daddy's little girl. What the fuck was this all about? Suddenly it hit him, another one of his amazing insights: they were sisters! And this other one, the college kid, was their brother! Three rich kids, fooling around down in the tunnels.

It all made sense. Lucky for the college kid, that brother angle—might save him from being broken in two.

"What do you mean, daddy's little girl?" said the darker-haired one.

"You find that obscure?" said the blonde.

Totally obscure, but Freedy didn't care: their bodies! Meanwhile they were exchanging some sort of look. The darker-haired one broke it first, just like the statie with him. Hey! Was this a fight? And were they a little drunk? Probably not—they weren't behaving like fighters and drunks he knew: no snarling, for one thing; no punching, for another.

The music stopped. It got very quiet. Freedy pressed his forehead to the wall, his eye almost in the room. He could hear the candles burning. "More music?" said the college kid, getting up.

For fuck sake.

"How about the Caruso?" said the blonde.

" 'Caro Nome,' " said the darker-haired one, real decisive for some reason.

" 'Caro Nome,' " said the blond one. "Aren't you getting sick of it?" The darker-haired one didn't answer. The blond one turned to the college kid. "Aren't *you* getting sick of it, Nat?"

"Not yet," said the college kid, Nat.

From his angle, Freedy had a good look at the blonde's face when he said that. She was pissed. He had no idea why, but she was. The others didn't see it: the one called Nat was winding up some old-fashioned record player—maybe an antique, maybe worth a bundle—and the darker-haired one, the little sister, was watching him.

More music. A female voice, the same hideous song that had been playing the first night. The big sister didn't like it either; Freedy could see that. She got up right away and said: "I'm going to call him."

"Who?" said the little sister.

"Daddy," said the big sister, said it funny, like it was in quotes.

"Why?"

"See what he knows about Leo."

"It's the middle of the night."

"Not in Manila."

"How do you know he's in Manila?"

Her voice took on an edge: "Or Singapore, Shanghai, what difference does it make? They'll track him down." She was walking toward the unlit room, the bedroom. "See you later," she said.

"You're leaving?"

"Bonsoir."

Or some foreign shit; this was like another goddamn country.

Freedy's angle was perfect for seeing what happened after that. The little sister and the Nat guy exchanged a look, like they didn't know what the hell was going on. *Join the club,* thought Freedy. Meanwhile, big sister was climbing up the rope ladder in the bedroom. There was just enough spillover light from the candles in the big room to gleam on her blond head. Up and out of sight she went. Freedy heard something close like a lid.

The little sister and the Nat guy made eye contact again, different this time. The little sister got up and walked over toward the record player where the Nat guy was standing. Why did he keep calling her the little sister? She was just as tall as the big sister, with a body just as good in every way. In fact—another one of his insights was coming, he could feel it—they were identical, except for the hair. Except for the hair, they could have been twins.

And the Nat guy was not their brother, oh no, not unless something sicko was going on. Freedy knew that from the way she put her arms around him, the way they kissed, swaying to the music but not dreamy, much hotter than dreamy. Freedy was just settling into what might get pretty interesting when he saw something that actually scared him, scared *him*, Freedy; made his heart jump inside his chest. It wasn't that first gleam, barely flickering in the unlit bedroom that did it; he didn't make the connection. It was when that blond head materialized in the darkness, and big sister, her body hidden in shadow, took in the scene by the record player. Her face.

Actually scared him.

"I love this song, don't you?" little sister was saying.

"Yes," said the Nat guy.

"Do you understand the words?"

The Nat guy shook his head. "Is this before the kidnapping or after?"

"Just before," said the little sister.

Freedy looked beyond them, to the bedroom. Big sister was gone.

20

"That which is done out of love always takes place beyond good and evil." Why? (Or why not?)
—Optional midterm exam question, Philosophy 322

"I love that," Izzie said.

"What?"

"Your chipped tooth." She ran the tip of her tongue over it again.

"It's a flaw."

"That's why." They stood beside the wind-up record player, down in the cave, their arms around each other, music of long ago all around them; the words incomprehensible to Nat, the emotions not. "How did you do it?" Izzie asked.

"Do what?"

"Chip your tooth."

"I was born with it. My mom has the same thing, same tooth."

"Your mom—" Izzie began, and stopped herself.

"What about her?"

"Oops," Izzie said.

Nat backed up a little, still holding Izzie, but at arm's length. "What about her?"

"I hope to meet her one day."

"That's not what you were going to say."

Izzie sighed. "She sounds nice, that's all."

But he'd never really discussed his mother with Izzie.
"Who says?"

"You can be relentless."

"Sorry."

"I'm used to it. Patti told us about her. There—happy
now?"

"Yup." He was; the sound of her name stabbed him, but he
was happy at the same time.

Izzie laughed, moved closer to him. The music played, the
candles burned. Happy, and on his way to exhilaration. He
spun her, just a half a little spin, to the music.

At that moment, something caught Nat's eye on the far, and
distant, wall. He looked over Izzie's head, saw only the biggest
of all the oil paintings, hanging halfway up. Fauns, sheep, a
centaur spying from behind a rock, three nudes bathing by
a waterfall.

"Is she relentless too?"

"My mom? No."

"What does she do?

"I thought I told you."

"Must have been Grace. Happens all the time."

"She works in a law office."

"Your mother's a lawyer?"

"Receptionist."

"How big a practice?"

A question that would never have occurred to him. "In
what way?"

"How many lawyers?"

"Just one."

Izzie's eyebrow rose, that right eyebrow that took care of
nonverbal communication.

"It's a small town," Nat said.

"What's he like?" said Izzie. "Or she."

"My mom's boss?" Mr. Beaman: *Whatever you've got,
Evie. Paper cups will do.* "He's all right, I guess." She never
complained. "Why do you ask?"

"It's about you," Izzie said. "And we have something in common."

"We do?"

"I lived in a small town once myself. In Connecticut. Not Grace. Just me. We were very little and it was just for a year. This was after the divorce. Grace stayed with our mother in the city, my father and I moved to the country. I went to first grade at an ordinary public school."

"And survived?"

"Very funny. I loved it. Especially snow days. They were the best. Did they have snow days where you were?"

"Some." But not many; Nat's town prided itself on keeping the schools open no matter what, and anyone with a pickup and a plow was on the road with the first falling flakes, fighting for a chunk of the public-works budget.

"There's nothing like a snow day," Izzie said. "Not Christmas, or any other holiday or vacation. You wake up and ka-boom."

"Ka-boom?"

"Everything's changed."

"What do you mean?" Nat said. He himself had earned extra money on snow days, shoveling driveways.

"It's a different planet," Izzie said. "This feeling—I couldn't put it into words back then—of freedom. Real freedom, like I was no longer in the grip of all these forces."

"What forces?"

"The forces, Nat. The responsibilities, the duties, the relationships."

"Life as we know it."

"Exactly. Snow days are different. Like after the world ends but you survived."

"And you get the same feeling down here."

"Close. How did you know?"

Later they were in the bedroom, on the canopied bed, the candles all out, the silence complete.

And not long after that: "The things you do," Izzie said.

Anything. They seemed to be able to do anything together, without need of consultation, without fear of a misstep. He moved slightly so she could put her head on his chest if she wanted; she did.

"Think it's still snowing?" Nat said.

"Got to be," said Izzie. "That's why I picked this place—it was snowing when I interviewed."

Picked this place. Nat thought of Mrs. Smith and Miss Brown, all it had taken to get him here. "And Grace? Is that why she picked it too?"

"She didn't really care."

"Didn't care?"

"Where she went. College isn't really that big a deal, is it? If I liked it, that was good enough for her."

Silence.

"And when you went with your father and Grace stayed with your mother?" Nat said. "How was that decided?"

"What a funny question."

"Why?"

"Because it's one of my earliest memories, maybe the first. It was supposed to be the other way, me with my mother, Grace with my father. Then there was this goodbye scene in Grand Central Station. Suitcases, porters, the old nanny and the new one, probably the Albert of the time, the four of us. The four of us of the time. And Grace—do you know Grand Central?"

"No."

"There's a mezzanine with a restaurant above the main concourse, or at least there was then. This was before the renovation, when it was still full of homeless people. We were having hot chocolate while someone got the tickets for Connecticut. Grace's chocolate spilled—I can't remember how, but I can still see the chocolate flowing across the table and dripping onto her lap. She just watched it, didn't even flinch. Then she looked up and said she wanted to go with Mommy."

Silence. And yes, like a snow day, everything muffled, the world disconnected.

"But it was all arranged. That's what they said, my mother, my father, one of the nannies, someone. No one took her seriously. The next thing, she'd climbed on top of the railing, over the concourse, and spread her arms. I can see that too, much stronger than the spilled chocolate, even. On tiptoes on the railing, like Acapulco. It was in my dreams for years."

Silence.

"What was that?" Izzie said.

"What?"

"That noise."

"I didn't hear anything."

They listened, heard nothing but snow day silence, insulated from sound by the earth around them.

"Then what happened?" Nat said.

"This homeless guy, going from table to table with a paper cup, grabbed her and sat her back down in her chair, like it was part of his routine, kind of roughly. Couldn't have happened now, of course, the way it's all cleaned up. Then the tickets came. I went to Connecticut and Grace went back to the apartment with our mother. This was on Fifth Avenue, not where we are now. And that was that. The next year, our mother met someone new and moved to Paris, and my father ended up with both of us, back in the city."

Silence.

"But I never understood what she was basing her preference on," Izzie said.

"How do you mean?"

"We hardly spent any time with either of them. I don't know why it made such a difference."

Nat didn't either, but he could see that chocolate dripping into Grace's little lap as though he'd been there. In the darkness, he felt Izzie's eyes on him.

"What's *your* earliest memory?" she said.

"The same kind of thing."

Izzie took it for a joke, and laughed.

They climbed the rope ladder, started back through the tunnels, Nat leading the way with a flashlight. "A teacher?" said Izzie; he felt her breath on the back of his ear. "Is that really what you want to be?"

He replied with a question of his own. "What did you put?" The rest of the cards had been forgotten after Mrs. Uzig's appearance.

"Guess."

"Spearing fish," Nat said.

Pause. "I wish I had," Izzie said. "I'm starting to think you know me better than I do."

He had a troubling thought. "You didn't put what Grace did?"

"Oh, no."

"Then what?"

"Now I'm not telling."

"Even if I guess?"

Somewhere during this dialogue they'd stopped, faced each other, embraced; the flashlight beam pointing here and there without guidance.

Izzie started to reply, then made a little sound, a quick inhale. "Look," she said, and pointed to the quivering circle of light on the tunnel ceiling.

A bat hung upside down from a plastic pipe, its eyes wide open, liquid, intelligent.

"Our cave," said Izzie. "Our bat."

The thing hung motionless.

They climbed into the janitor's closet in the basement of Plessey, out into the hall, upstairs to the main floor. Late night, snow coming down hard.

"Snow day tomorrow," Izzie said, "for sure."

She led him out the door and onto the quad, the snow in her

hair, on her eyelashes. "Kiss me," she said. "Kiss me right now."

He did. Everything was all right, would be all right; whatever problems there were lost their power, like normal forces on a snow day, just as Izzie had said. He loved her, no doubt about it, and would have said so; but she was already gone, running across the quad toward Lanark, snow falling behind her like curtains.

In the morning snow still fell, but not as hard. Nat put on his boots, warm and waterproof, sixteenth-birthday present from his mom, now a little tight, and walked over to the student union cafeteria. Breakfast smells woke him up. He piled food on his tray—scrambled eggs, bacon, cornflakes, English muffin, banana, milk, juice, coffee. The cashier took his meal card, swiped it through the machine, swiped it again, once more. "Card's blocked," she said.

"Blocked?"

"Got a block on it."

"Why?"

"Have to ask the financial office."

"But it's Sunday."

"Comes to four twenty-five."

But Nat didn't have $4.25 on him, had no money at all, and the shoe in his closet was empty. He'd used up all his money getting to the airport and back, would have no more until his next check from the Alumni Office, due the next day.

"Can I owe you?"

"Owe me?"

"I'll pay tomorrow."

"The machine don't allow that."

All at once he was very hungry. "I could leave a note, and my student ID."

"Won't work." She put a hand on his tray.

Nat abandoned it, walked away. As he went out the door he glanced back, saw the cashier chewing on a piece of his bacon. That put him in a good mood, a mood that lasted all the way home through the snow. He even took off his gloves, made a snowball, and threw it at Emerson, hitting his oxidized copper head from fifty feet.

He sat at his desk, opened *Beyond Good and Evil* to where he'd left off, part two, "The Free Spirit," section 30. His mind felt sharp, much sharper than usual, so sharp he noticed the change. *Our supreme insights,* he read, *must—and should!— sound like follies, in certain cases like crimes*—Nat's gaze left the page as he remembered Professor Uzig referring to this same passage on Aubrey's Cay, and, as it left the page, happened on the blinking phone light, indicating a message in voice mail.

He checked, found one.

His mom. "Nat? Please call as soon as you—when you can. Okay? It's me. Mom."

Eight twenty-five, 6:25 at home. Too early to call. But something was wrong; he could hear that much. Then it hit him: *Patti. Something's gone wrong with Patti.* She would never do anything to hurt herself, never—say it right— commit suicide, not Patti; but then he recalled a girl at Clear Creek a few years ahead of him who had committed suicide, and how everyone in the halls had said they couldn't believe it, not someone like her.

He phoned home.

His mom answered in the middle of the first ring; probably the phone on her bedside table, but there was no sleep in her voice. "Nat?" she said. "Nat."

"Hi, Mom. I didn't wake you, did I?"

"Oh, no, I've been up all—no, you didn't wake me."

"What's wrong, Mom? Is it Patti?"

There was a pause. He knew she was doing that long slow blink. "Patti? I haven't heard from Patti."

"Then what?"

"Oh, Nat."

"What, Mom?"

"I've let you down."

"That couldn't happen, Mom."

She started crying. "I'm so sorry."

Nat just waited. He didn't have a clue.

She got herself under control. "I lost my job."

That made no sense. She'd worked for Mr. Beaman for fifteen years. "Did Mr. Beaman retire?" Stupid question: Mr. Beaman was much too young to retire.

"He . . . he let me go."

Mr. Beaman fired his mom?

"I was getting stale. That's what he said. He hired someone much fresher. Barely older than you, Nat."

"I'm sorry, Mom."

"I begged him."

"Mom."

"The day after Christmas. That's when he . . . he did it. I've been looking for work ever since, but there's nothing. And meanwhile the bank found out—why wouldn't they, he does all their closings—and they called in the home equity loan."

Nat found himself doing something he'd never done in his life: the long slow blink. When his eyes opened, he saw that it had stopped snowing.

"This was Monday, the day before I was going to mail the check for the second semester."

Card's blocked.

"How can they do that?"

"The bank? Change in financial status—it's all in the fine print, all legal." She started crying again. He'd hardly ever heard her cry, not since he was a kid, couldn't stand it. "I've let you down so bad."

"No you haven't, Mom. Stop saying that."

"You don't understand. I can't keep you there, Nattie. You have to come home."

21

"A living thing desires above all to vent its strength."
Identify the quotation; what does it imply about the creation of moral values?
—Essay assignment, Philosophy 322

A problem, maybe not like any other; still, a problem, and he was good at solving problems, wasn't he?

He was hungry. There was only the granola bar untouched by Patti, still lying on the bedside crate. He didn't want it; a granola bar, yes, even three or four, with a tall glass of cold milk to wash them down, but not this particular granola bar.

Nat dressed in warm clothes, went for a walk. A long walk—temperature cold and dropping, the sky brilliant now, its blue almost glaring—through pockets of the campus he hadn't yet seen. After some time, he wandered down the north, sunless side of College Hill, across some railroad tracks, and into what they called the flats. A dismal place, he saw, bringing to mind the town he'd come from, although his town couldn't be called dismal, could it? He thought about the yellow legal pad in the kitchen at home, on which he and his mom had done the figures; he thought about the figures themselves, still clear in his memory. He thought about the home equity loan. He shifted numbers around in his head, began to feel the cold.

His mind kept returning to that home equity loan. He was forgetting something, but what? He walked back up to the campus, trod every path, the wind picking up now from the west, lifting some of the new snow, blowing it around; trod every path and fought the impulse to commit it all to memory. He walked until the western sky turned orange and the tree branches went black, but didn't solve the home equity loan problem.

The answer didn't come until he was back on the quad, almost at the main Plessey door. The problem wasn't with the home equity loan itself, he finally realized, but the original mortgage on the house. How would they make the payments now? Specifically, how would they make the payments without him going back and finding a job? That meant that even coming up with money to pay the bills at Inverness wouldn't be good enough. Thinking had only made the problem worse.

Back in his room, he took off his boots, warm boots but a little tight, which was why his feet were blue. He rested them on the radiator, gazed out the window as shadows fell over the campus, the golden dome on Goodrich Hall holding the last of the light. Later the moon rose. He ate the granola bar.

Nat was at the financial office the next morning, 8:00 A.M. He told the story of his mom's job and the home equity loan.

"I'm so sorry," the woman said.

Nat could tell she meant it. "That's all right," he said.

"I feel so bad," she went on, "whenever something like this happens. The good news is that as a student in good standing, you're welcome back at any time, any time, that is, after the resolution of these financial difficulties."

And the bad news?

"I wish there was something we could do," she said.

What about making up the difference, he thought, *just till the end of the semester? I'll work two jobs this summer, maybe three, and . . .* But he didn't say any of that, was already on his feet. They'd been generous with him; wouldn't they do it if they could? He couldn't make himself ask for more; and pointless, too, when the answer had already been given.

Nat picked up his check in the Alumni Office, cashed it at the Student Union, filled a tray: bacon and eggs, French toast, cornflakes, juice, milk, coffee; paid cash. He sat at a table by the window. Someone had left the campus newspaper, the *Insider*, behind. He started reading automatically: he'd eaten many meals alone growing up, liked to read at the same time. The lead story was about a survey of the current activities of last year's graduates. They were impressive.

Crème de la crème.

Nat stopped reading. He heard talk all around him, student talk rising from other tables. There was only one other solitary eater, a middle-aged man in heavy olive-green work clothes, warming himself over a bowl of something steaming. Nat's appetite vanished. He left the rest of his food untouched despite all his mom had taught him about waste, despite how hungry he thought he'd been.

Monday: bio, English, econ. He cut them all. Hadn't paid for them was the fact of the matter.

Nat knocked on the door of Professor Uzig's office in Goodrich Hall.

"Yes?"

He opened the door.

"Ah, Nat." Blue blazer, blue fountain pen; white shirt, white paper. "How nice to see you. Do we have an appointment?"

"No."

"Then?"

"Something's come up."

"You intend to drop the course."

"Drop the course?"

"Your friend—Ferg, is it?—has preceded you."

"He dropped the course?"

"Within the hour, but still, well before the deadline, and therefore no harm done."

"I'm not dropping the course," Nat said. "Not intentionally."
Professor Uzig looked interested.

"I love the course." He'd meant to say *like*. "Nietzsche . . ."

"Yes?"

"I'd barely heard of Nietzsche before I came here. Do you realize that?" That just came bursting out. And more: "Izzie's right. He was a sweet man." What was this? He was suddenly close to tears; hadn't cried since he was a little boy.

Professor Uzig watched him. Nat could sense the power of his mind. He made his face a mask, watched him back.

"Sweet," said the professor. "A remarkable observation. Izzie's a remarkable young woman."

Professor Uzig paused. Nat said nothing.

"Grace is remarkable too," Professor Uzig went on. "Both remarkable, as one might expect, each in her own way, as one might not." The professor smiled, as though just happening upon something witty. Nat didn't: it was the plain truth.

"A sweet man—perhaps true, to some extent," said Professor Uzig. "But of no use to him in the end. Sweetness is a self-defeating characteristic in combination with genius of that order."

Nat understood perfectly: *Because ambition should be made of sterner stuff.* He kept that to himself.

"But you're not here to bat around peripheral ideas. You came to deliver your unintentional rationale for dropping the course."

Nat told him. Professor Uzig had a way of listening that Nat had felt before, as though some powerful device, like a radio telescope, was at work. He'd felt it at Aubrey's Cay, in the classroom under the dome, in Professor Uzig's dining room on College Hill. He didn't feel it now.

"That's the story, then?" said Professor Uzig.

Did he no longer look interested? Was he disappointed, as though the account lacked drama, originality, or something else he valued? A weird idea, even paranoid, Nat decided: his imagination was out of control.

"That's the story."

"Very considerate of you to tell me in person," said Professor Uzig.

Nat didn't quite get that, wondered where it was leading. When it led nowhere, he said: "I thought you might have some ideas."

"Ideas? Of what sort?"

"Some way I could stay."

"This seems to be a purely financial matter."

He paused as though expecting a reply, so Nat said, "Yes."

"Those I avoid," said Professor Uzig.

There was nothing wrong with Nat's imagination.

He went back to his room in Plessey Hall. Almost immediately he thought of a modification for his bio experiment, a new test run conducted at a higher temperature that might—

Forget it.

Nat began packing his stuff, first actually folding the odd thing, but soon packing only in his head, staring out the window. Snow lay deep on the quad. Some students were building a huge mound, or ramp, as he realized after a while, a ramp leading up to a tall window over one of the entry pediments of Lanark. He heard laughter and shouting; condensation clouds rose from their mouths; the sunshine was dazzling.

The tall window over the pediment opened and someone emerged; flew out, really, surfing down the ramp on a cafeteria tray. A girl: her hands outspread, body poised, balanced— actually in some control of the tray. It was Izzie. She hit the soft snow at the end of the ramp, went airborne, dove like a surfer bailing out. A male student, two male students hurried to help her, but she was up on her own, laughing and covered with snow, before they reached her.

Nat turned away.

He was good at solving problems. What about calling Mrs.

Smith? What about calling Mr. Beaman? What about calling his mom again, to be sure he'd heard right? Could he put her through that? No.

That left winning the lottery. He didn't have a ticket, had never bought one.

"I don't get it," Grace said.

They were down in the cave, the three of them, that night.

"It's pretty simple," Nat said.

"You have to go home?" Izzie said. "I don't understand that part at all."

"Tomorrow?" said Grace.

"Or the next day. I still have to change my ticket." His return ticket, to have been used at the end of the semester.

"Home equity loan?" Izzie said. "What is that, exactly?"

Nat explained again.

"But what's it got to do with Inverness?" Grace said. "It should be none of their business."

He went over that too.

"And I thought you were on scholarship anyway," Izzie said.

"Partial. This is about the rest of it."

"The rest of what?" Izzie said.

"Tuition. Fees. Room and board."

"Partial?" said Grace. "Can't they make it complete?"

Nat shook his head. "But I can come back under the old terms whenever we get this straightened out."

"Like next week?" Izzie said.

"It's a technicality, then," Grace said.

Nat smiled. "Next year at the earliest."

"Next year?" said Izzie.

"You're leaving Inverness," Grace said, "just like that?"

"You talk like I'm doing something whimsical."

"Aren't you?" Grace said. "This is silly. How much money are we talking about?"

Izzie nodded, as though a shrewd point had been raised. "Good question," she said. "How much?"

"Over seven thousand dollars."

They turned to him, each doing that raised-eyebrow thing, Grace the left, Izzie the right.

"This is about seven thousand dollars?" Grace said.

"Closer to eight."

Grace and Izzie laughed.

"What's funny?"

"You," they said together.

"I don't get it," Nat said.

"He doesn't get it," said Grace. "What's in the account, Izzie?"

"What account?"

"Our bank account, here at school."

"Do we have one? I've just been using the ATM in Baxter."

"There must be a bank account," Grace said. "What does it say on the checkbook?"

"Checkbook?" said Izzie.

Nat held up his hand. "It doesn't matter. I couldn't take anything from you."

"You couldn't?" Grace said, her glance going quickly to Izzie.

"No."

"You don't really want to be here," Izzie said. "Is that it?"

Didn't she know better than that? And how it would be without her? "That's not it."

"Then what?"

"What I said. I couldn't take money." They looked blank. His gaze went to the big oil painting: at that moment Grace and Izzie were almost as unreal to him as the nudes, the fauns, the centaur behind the tree.

"You wouldn't be taking it," Grace said.

"We'd be giving it," said Izzie.

"That's what can't happen."

Silence. They stared at him.

Izzie cocked her ear. "What was that?"

"What?" said Nat.

"That sound."

"I didn't hear anything," Grace said.

They listened, heard nothing.

"I have an idea," Grace said. "What if it was in the form of a loan?"

"A loan!" said Izzie. "You could pay it back later, down the road, whenever."

"No."

"Why not?"

"It's no different."

"Sure it is," said Izzie. "Completely different. This would be like the home equity thing."

"A Nat equity loan," said Grace.

That was why. "No," Nat said. "And there are other complications." He told them about the mortgage payments that had to be made, the utility bills, the food, the car expenses, all of it out of his mom's pay, now cut off.

They made identical flapping motions with their hands, as though shooing flies.

"This is—" Izzie began.

"—ridiculous," said Grace.

"What about talking to Leo?" Izzie said.

"Forget it," said Grace.

"Why do you say that?" Nat asked.

"I talked to my—our father," Grace said. "He knows all about Helen Uzig, Brooklyn, the whole thing. He checked Leo out when discussions about this faculty chair endowment started getting serious. Leo grew up in Brooklyn, family owned a dry-cleaning business—or was it a candy store?—went to City College of New York, Ph.D. Columbia, got a job at Inverness, where Helen, not Uzig at the time, was head of the phil department. Head of the phil department, and had some money, too. Made him shave off that ludicrous walrus mustache. It's her house, of course."

"Does this mean that Ferg guy's right?" said Izzie. "He's some kind of fake?"

"Fake?" Nat said. "He's a brilliant teacher. Anyone can see that. Besides, he's famous, in philosophical circles. I've looked him up."

"Then go see him," Grace said.

"I did."

"And?"

Nat didn't answer.

"See?" said Grace.

"See what? It has nothing to do with his qualities as a teacher."

"Nietzsche would disagree," Grace said.

Nat was thinking about that when Izzie said: "So what's he going to do?"

Nat wasn't sure who she meant.

"About the endowment?" Grace said. "Take his time deciding. Quote."

Izzie nodded, as though that made sense to her. Nat doubted that either of them really knew what a home mortgage was, but they had no trouble understanding whatever manipulations were going on between Mr. Zorn and Professor Uzig, or Mr. Zorn and the phil department, or Mr. Zorn and Inverness, or whatever it was. Maybe it was a simple matter of Mr. Zorn delaying his decision until after the girls had graduated. Nat discounted that: a small-town, been-nowhere kind of notion; he remembered the gas station owner back home with a son in the Clear Creek football program, and the coach's free fill-ups.

They were both watching him.

"You're not trying to find a way," Grace said.

"I am." Nat's voice rose, taking him, taking them all, by surprise.

"You can't just go," Izzie said. "You're here. You're right here."

"This kind of thing happens. I'm not the first."

"So what?" said Grace. She rose. "Let's have a drink. We'll think better."

She poured from the oldest bottle yet, Domaine des Forges, 1893; Izzie wound up the record player, put on "Caro Nome." Nat didn't think any better, but probably because he hadn't eaten, the drink's effect was immediate.

"We're lucky," Izzie said.

"Because we have money?" said Grace. "They say that causes problems of its own."

"But they're problems of freedom," Izzie said. "Other people don't even get to those."

They both turned to him, awaiting confirmation from the land of other people. He suspected it wasn't that simple, but before he could organize his thoughts, Grace said:

"She's right. Home equity, mortgages, all that step-by-step bullshit—by the time most people get past it, life is over. Piss on that. Working for decades just to get—just hoping to get—where Izzie and I are right now."

"That makes me feel better," Nat said.

Izzie laughed, then Grace. "Here's to the problems of freedom," Grace said.

They drank. Izzie restarted "Caro Nome." "Unless," she said, turning from the record player, "Nat gets lucky too."

"In what way?" said Grace.

"I don't know. Writes a best-seller or something."

Nat was astonished: he'd never mentioned wanting to write to anyone.

Grace and Izzie looked at each other. Nat had the crazy idea that for a moment their brains had hooked up, doubling normal human power.

"That's the point, isn't it?" said Grace.

"This isn't about seven thousand dollars," said Izzie.

"Or scholarships, home equity, watching our pennies," said Grace. "It's about getting all that out of the way."

"In one stroke," said Izzie.

"I thought of Powerball," Nat said.

They glanced at him, said nothing. Grace got up, walked over to Izzie by the record player, refilled her glass, came to Nat on the couch, refilled his, started to refill her own—and dropped the bottle. A heavy, cut-glass bottle that just slipped from her hand, smashed at her feet.

She didn't seem to notice. "I'm having a thought," she said.

"Uh-oh," said Izzie.

"Shut up," said Grace. "It's—it's so good. And it's all right here, even the sound track."

Izzie's eyes widened; maybe she saw it coming. Nat didn't.

"What are you talking about?" he said.

"We'll kidnap Izzie."

"For God's sake."

"Or me, then. It doesn't matter. We'll kidnap me for ransom."

"How much?" said Izzie.

"I don't know," Grace said. "Tuition, room and board, home equity, mortgage, miscellaneous—how about a million dollars?"

"Sure that's enough?" said Izzie.

"In terms of the expenses?" Grace said. "Or do you mean—"

"—what a real kidnapper would ask. It has to look realistic, doesn't it?"

"You're way ahead of me, Izzie."

Izzie looked pleased.

"This is a joke, right?" Nat said.

"A joke?" said Grace. "Is that still a negative word in your lexicon? Shouldn't our supreme insights—"

"—sound like follies," Izzie said. She giggled, a little

giggle just like Grace's, but that Nat heard now for the first time from her.

"Like follies," said Grace, "or even crimes."

She opened the leaded-glass cabinet doors, took out another bottle. "Hey," she said. "Rouge." She showed it to Nat.

Romanée-Conti, 1917.

"Is it a good one?" Izzie said.

"Who knows?" said Grace, looking around for the corkscrew, not spotting it immediately.

"Wait," Nat said, because he knew. Mr. Zorn's 1962 bottle of the same wine was worth $2,500. And therefore—

"Not to worry," said Grace, striking the neck of the bottle sharply against the edge of a table. It snapped off; she found new glasses, poured.

And therefore that might have been tuition, room, and board right there. Was there more, even one bottle? Nat checked the cabinet, found none.

They drank. "My God," said Grace.

"Like having a drink with the czar or something," said Izzie.

The things she sometimes said: perfect, at least to his ear.

Grace raised her glass. "To crimes and follies."

"You're serious," said Nat.

"Why not?" said Grace.

"Why not? Because it's wrong."

"Is it?" said Izzie; that surprised him a little; perhaps things would have been different had it been Grace, but it was Izzie. Or if he had eaten more than a granola bar in the past two days, or hadn't been drinking nectar on an empty stomach, or hadn't been drinking at all since he'd never been much of a drinker, or this or that. "First of all, it's not much money," Izzie said, "nothing at all to him. He wouldn't even notice."

"It would do him good," Grace said.

Izzie glanced at her. "What do you mean?"

"Nothing. Forget it."

After a pause, Izzie continued. "Take that horse farm—how much do you think that's costing?"

"And we don't even ride anymore," said Grace.

"Second, there's no victim, no real crime, no one gets hurt or even scared."

"I just hide down here for a day or two," said Grace, "there's some sort of ransom demand, Izzie goes to pick up the money, I reappear, ka-boom. Nothing's real."

"And third," said Izzie, "it's just."

"Just?"

"Like land reform in Latin America," said Grace.

"Exactly," said Izzie. "What fortune didn't start with a little hanky-panky?"

"Hanky-panky?" said Grace, and started to laugh; then Izzie started too, and finally Nat. It seemed like the funniest combination of syllables ever uttered. They laughed till they cried.

Then they sat quietly for a few moments. Izzie looked at Nat, right into his eyes. "Fourth, you can stay." Nat met her gaze, the candlelight catching those gold flecks in her irises, kept meeting it until he felt Grace watching.

"The best part, of course," said Grace. "And all those worries—home equity, mortgage, your mother's job—"

"Finis," said Izzie.

"So," said Grace, "how about it?"

Nat was silent. It wasn't the money itself, but the freedom, just as Izzie had said. To be free of that yellow legal pad and future legal pads with their columns of figures adding up to worry, constriction, settling for second-best, or less. What was that cliché? Play the cards you're dealt. He'd been dealt a new hand. He'd entered this world of Grace and Izzie where some words—*money*, for one—had a different meaning. *Money* perhaps the most different of all: a world where a cash machine was no more than a box where you pushed buttons and out came money, as demanded.

"Or maybe this place is a bit too much," Grace said to Izzie. "Maybe he's not that ambitious."

Izzie turned to him.

That word: and the stern stuff that went with it. To be sweet and brilliant, a self-defeating combination. And if not sweet and brilliant, at least reasonably kind and fairly smart. He had a horrible vision of dying promise, promise dying, dying down the years, its first stage the long flight home. Come east but hadn't cut it, for one reason or another. The candles, dozens of them, burned, the old wine glowed in the fine glasses, Galli-Curci sang her song from *Rigoletto*, romantic and alien at once: their sound track. If he went home? It would be the end of him and Izzie, he didn't fool himself about that. And other changes: change would follow like falling dominoes. Maybe his mom would never find another job; things like that happened every day. Then he'd be working full-time. Living at home. Night school. And then? What could he shoot for, what would he end up as, best-case scenario? A small-time lawyer like Mr. Beaman? A nauseating prospect. He suddenly knew one thing for sure: he wanted the big time. Perhaps the desire had been in him from the very beginning, but distrusted, denied, disowned, buried. He wanted it, more than Mrs. Smith, Miss Brown, the whole town put together. He remembered then a quotation from Nietzsche, one he'd highlighted a few days before, meaning to raise it with Professor Uzig: *The great epochs of our life are the occasions when we gain the courage to rebaptize our evil qualities as our best qualities*. Ambition wasn't necessarily an evil quality; still, he had no need for the professor's explanation now.

"I'll think about it," he said.

"Think about it?" said Izzie, disappointed, even shocked, as though he'd just revealed some unsuspected and damning flaw. Again: if only that had been Grace's line.

"What do you want me to say?"

Izzie said: "Say yes."

He said yes.

They drank. The brief exposure to air had turned the Romanée-Conti 1917 into something thin, tasteless, not wine at all.

22

"God is refuted but the devil is not"—*inevitable conclusion of Nietzschean philosophy?*
—Topic for class discussion, Philosophy 322

*W*hat the fuck? Freedy almost said it out loud. Bad idea, of course, with him at the spyhole and big sister, little sister, and the college kid on the other side, like in a dollhouse. Freedy knew about dollhouses because there'd been one in his room, his room with the wall paintings and the "Little Boy" poem, when he was very young. Some theory of his mother's about boys' toys and girls' toys, making boys into girls, world peace, more of her crazy shit. He'd smashed it to bits, of course, but only when he'd gotten a little older. Before that, he'd kind of played with it, reaching in, moving the tiny people around, maybe undressing that straw-haired one in the red-and-white checked skirt, and the boy one in the blue overalls, and then ... His memory got hazy. But the point was he knew about dollhouses, knew about looking down on the world like a giant, hey!—like God. It was pretty cool.

Like God. Amazing.

Pretty cool, to stare through the spyhole, watch a whole kind of movie happening. Hey!—God the movie nut. Amazing. But there was a downside, he knew that already: not an easy job, what with all the information, coming so fast, so confusing, even for someone with his kind of brainpower.

He felt a moment's passing respect for God: who'd want to do this forever?

Confusing things, like some situation involving the college kid, impossible to understand. Home equity loans, tuition, rooms, boards, seven grand, a lost checkbook. Didn't add up.

Unless that seven grand was lying around somewhere. Now that would be nice. Freedy was thinking how nice it would be—seven grand, three hundred per laptop, how many laptops was that?—when the college kid looked up, looked him right in the fucking eye. Or almost; his gaze slid up the wall a foot or two, fixed on something Freedy couldn't see.

But a close call.

And then right away, another: he had to sneeze. What was going on? Did he have allergies all of a sudden, like those women whose pools he'd cleaned in California? He put his finger under his nose the way you were supposed to. That worked, or almost worked: the sneeze that came was tiny, made no sound at all.

Except little sister got a funny look on her face. Smash. Ka-boom. He could be through that wall in a second.

But the moment passed. Freedy's muscles relaxed, just hung on his bones, heavy and still. Felt good.

Felt good, but that didn't help him deal with the confusing things. Confusing things, like big sister and little sister were swatting flies or something, and then: *Leo. Leo Uzig.* This name kept popping up. Professor. On his laptop. Taught a course his mother thought Ronnie was taking. Ronnie? How could that be? Had a wife. Helen Uzig. A wife with money. Wife made him . . . made him what? What was that? Shave . . . shave off that—some word he didn't catch and then two words he did—*walrus mustache.*

Something walrus mustache. The something word sounded a bit like *ridiculous*, but wasn't. He tried to recall it exactly, gave up.

But *walrus mustache*: he'd caught that.

Walrus.

Plus it turned out Leo Uzig was famous. And his wife had money.

Confusing: but Freedy was an amazing person. Why? Because, despite all the confusion, with all this information whipping by, the moment he heard that Leo Uzig's wife had money, what was the first thing he thought of? Yes. Money. Specifically, the envelope he'd steamed open, so wisely, it turned out, with the two C's inside.

It was all coming together. Everything had a meaning. He'd heard that. He'd also heard that nothing meant anything. So what? None of that mattered. What mattered was his future. Pool company. Florida. Stick, stick, stick. And as for getting his hands on big sister and little sister, showing them what a man was, a real man, a buff, diesel, andro-popping, meth-tweaking fuckin' animal like him? That would be nice.

Meanwhile, he was missing stuff. Action central, Freedy, action central. Action central, like the room with all the monitors, where you could watch everything coming together.

Someone else's name came up, a name even stranger than Uzig; sounded Chinese maybe, Ni Chi. One of them, Uzig or Ni Chi, was a fake, but before Freedy could sort that out, the dolls in the dollhouse were drinking and talking about money again.

Fine with him, except that the music started up, with that horrible singing.

Turned out that big sister and little sister had money, possibly from hitting the Powerball number. Seven grand meant nothing to them, chicken feed. Why would it, you hit the Powerball number? Maybe this was a celebration. That would explain the wild look on big sister's face—she was something, drop-dead fuck-you and wild. Was she a little drunk too? Or a lot. She dropped the bottle; it shattered on that thick purple rug with the blue flowers, but none of them seemed to notice.

And then. Whoa. Kidnapping? A million dollars? They were afraid of kidnappers, because of the Powerball score?

No, no no. They . . . they weren't afraid of kidnappers—they were planning a kidnapping of their own! To get their hands on the Powerball money? And kidnapping who, exactly? That had to be important.

What was this? They were planning to kidnap one of themselves? Which one? Little sister? Big sister? Before he could get a handle on that, they shifted to the home equity thing again. Out came another bottle. More breaking glass. Were they all stoked on drugs or something? What drugs? Freedy wanted to know.

Something was going down. Big sister and little sister were hot. They were *physical*. Couldn't keep still. Freedy could see that. The college kid, he was the still one. Dragging his feet about something or other. A wimp, of course, and so breakable in two. First Freedy would let him have a good one, right in the gut. Then—

A million dollars wasn't much money?

No victim? No crime?

Big sister? They were going to kidnap big sister? Maybe yes, maybe no. A strange kind of kidnapping. Big sister was . . . going to hide out right here, down in the dollhouse? Did he get that right?

And then what? Little sister picks up the money?

Ka-boom? Big sister said *ka-boom*, the exact same word that had been on his mind at the exact same moment. Had to be an omen, an omen of the very best kind.

Then: they were laughing their heads off. Why? *A little hanky-panky*. They were going to get naked and fuck each other's brains out, after all, as he'd secretly hoped, all of them this time, and, for Christ sake, let it be right there in the big room, instead of sneaking off to the bedroom the way little sister and the college kid had last time, where Freedy couldn't see, not even hear very well.

Freedy waited for the hanky-panky to begin. They took their sweet time. A little bit of talk, mostly silence and waiting. Waiting for what? Waiting for the college kid to stop dragging his feet. That was it. Freedy got it now: as soon as the college kid said yes to whatever they wanted him to say yes to, the sisters would come across.

Say it, you asshole. To get those two to come across who wouldn't say whatever it took? *Yes* was easy.

The college kid said it. Finally. And guess what? They didn't come across. Women. Did the college kid know how to handle that, did he get pissed, slap them around? No. Instead they all had another drink, like the best of friends, then started blowing out the candles, climbing that rope ladder, clearing out. Next minute, they were gone, leaving nothing but the blackness, the smell of melting wax, the horrible singing. Nothing had happened, nothing at all. Was it just some sort of game, more college shit? What the fuck?

Maybe because of all these questions, all this confusion, Freedy got a little lost on his way out of the tunnels. He thought he was in F, headed for the subbasement of building 87, at the edge of the backside of the campus and therefore closest to home. Problem was, it took way too long. He finally flicked on his light to see where he was. Good thing: he was in Z, two steps—two goddamn steps—before the drop-off near building 13. He shone the light over the edge, illuminating the steel ladder bolted to the wall and the brick floor thirty feet below, at least, where some workie had broken his neck long ago.

Don't think he was scared or anything like that. First, his instincts—he was a fuckin' animal—had protected him, always would. Second, even if he fell, so what? Think he wouldn't land on his feet, bounce right up? 'Course he would. He shut the light off immediately, just to show the kind of . . . started with *p*—*predator*! Yes! The kind of predator he was, like the wolf or the tiger.

Freedy climbed out of a ventilation hood behind the hockey rink. The snow had stopped falling but lay all over the place, on every roof and tree branch, and piled high on the ground. He hated snow. He hated the cold. A cold wind was blowing from the west, right in his face as he left the campus, started down the Hill. The west, where California was: explain why California was warm while the wind that came from it was cold. There was a lot of shit they didn't know.

A million. A cool million. Freedy understood the expression now. A million made you cool, inside and out, simple as that. He pictured his corporate HQ, a blue tower, blue being the color of water, eight or nine stories high, with a gym on the roof, overlooking the ocean. And the name: he needed a name. Freedy's Fine Pool Business. Freedy's First-Rate Pools and Maintenance. What was that expression she used? First water. Freedy's First Water Corporation. Nah. Then it hit him. *Aqua*—or was it *agua*?—meant water, didn't it? The Aqua Group. The classiness of that *Group* part! Or maybe the Agua Group. Which sounded better? He tried them out loud, several times, as he passed the Glass Onion, crossed the tracks, entered the flats, turned onto the old street. Someone was having septic problems, often happened down by the river; he could smell their shit through all that snow.

Freedy went into the kitchen. A fuckin' mess. Every dish dirty, hardened yellow batter caked to this and that, fridge door hanging open. Why should he close it? Had a pig for a mother. He sniffed once or twice: a pot-smoking pig. And the ants were out, ants in winter, which was pretty unusual.

He switched on the lights in his bedroom, tried to ignore the wall paintings—unicorns, toadstools, dopehead elves, the lion man, the poem with that planet spinning, out of fucking control. He was so busy ignoring things that at first he didn't notice that the laptop, which he'd left on the bed, was gone.

That laptop was worth three hundred bucks. More important, much more important now, he wanted to have another look at what was on the screen. So where was it? Not there. Crash. Or there. Splatter. So where the fuck was it? Was it possible that someone had ripped him off? Ripped *him* off? A good way to die. Oh, to get his hands on whoever it was: a killing desire swelled rapidly inside him, like he would burst, and what was this? He had: blood was seeping out of his hand. Or maybe it was just a cut, by-product of the laptop search. Still, a mystical moment: everything did have meaning.

He went into the hall. Next door was the bathroom, next door to that her bedroom. He knocked. No answer. No light shone under the door, but he could hear music, tinny and faint, the way it sounded leaking from headphones, and he could smell pot, stronger than in the kitchen. He opened the door.

Lights out. A good thing: darkness hid the paintings on *her* walls, paintings he hadn't seen in years, and never wanted to again. One of them was the picture of his birth, based on that photo she had. A circle of women, all naked, although it couldn't have been that way in real life, all naked like witches with their unshaved legs and armpits, and in the middle her with her legs spread, and one of the witches holding him up, bawling and red.

His eyes adjusted to the weak light penetrating the shade from the streetlamp. She lay in bed, eyes closed, singing along to the music in the headphones, singing that came and went, more like muttering, but he identified it: "Winterlude," fucking Bob Dylan song he hated. Every winter, from the first flake till the last melting patch in the trees, "Winterlude." He thought of ripping the headphone jack out of the machine, was seriously considering it, when he noticed the green light flashing under her bed. He bent down—so close he could smell her breath, but there was no chance of her hearing him, not with Bob Dylan in her ears—and retrieved the laptop.

Freedy took the laptop to his room, opened it, pressed the on button. Words popped up on the screen, but nothing about Leo Uzig:

snow falls like velvet down

More of her poetry shit. Were all poets ignorant? Down, for example: everyone knew it was made from goose or duck

feathers, not velvet. He hit various keys, combinations of
keys, trying to make the poetry go away, trying to find out
what the computer knew about Leo Uzig. For example, he
typed *Leo Uzig*, spelling both names several ways since he
couldn't remember exactly what he'd glimpsed on the screen
that first time, then hitting control; or hitting control first and
then the names. But he couldn't even make the poetry disap-
pear. He closed the thing, not hard, but hard enough to send a
message.

Why should he be a computer expert? Soon, very soon,
he'd be hiring them. On the other hand, he needed one now.
What about Ronnie? It was possible.

Freedy walked over to Ronnie's, less than a mile away, its
yard backing onto the river. The river showed through the
gaps between the low shadows of the unlit houses, frozen
whiteness under a black sky. Late, probably very late, but
Freedy wasn't the least bit tired; full of energy, in fact. The
whole town sacked out except for him: showed how much
stronger he was, stronger than the whole town. They'd all
faded, collapsed, passed out, while he still patrolled the
streets.

Ronnie's place was dark like the others. Not much of a
place, but because of the slope down to the river it had that
basement, with sliders around the back, unlike most of the
places in the flats, the land being so goddamn wet. That was
where Freedy went, around to the back: Ronnie wasn't the
type who'd remember to lock the sliders.

But he had. That Ronnie. The thing with sliders, though,
Freedy thought, as he got his hand on the frame and bent his
knees a little, the thing with sliders was—

Pop. Scrape. In he went. That Ronnie. Would he even remember Ronnie in a year or two? He tried to imagine himself
sitting in his blue HQ, Agua Group, and remembering
Ronnie, a Portagee with that hairy thing growing under his
lower lip. No way.

Freedy avoided the bench press, a low shadow in the darkness, heard drip-dripping close by, went upstairs to the kitchen. The house was quiet, the only sound the fridge humming away. Hey! He was hungry. Freedy opened the fridge, found a tub of KFC, polished off a drumstick and a wing—bones and all when it came to the wing, just a small one.

Fueled up, he walked down the hall to Ronnie's bedroom, laptop in hand. Door closed: he opened it, real silent, first turning the knob all the way. In the darkness, he could make out Ronnie's head, a dark circle on the less dark rectangle of the pillow. The surprise was the second dark circle on the pillow next to Ronnie's.

Freedy, gliding softly over to the side of the bed with that second sleeper, remembered the cigar smoker in the Santa Monica bar—*nothing surprises me anymore*—remembered that was supposed to be his attitude too. But still, he was only human. Careful, gentle, he got hold of a corner of the bedcovers, pulled them back, real slow.

A girl. Asleep on her side, facing Ronnie, and: her hand wrapped around his limp dick. A girl with a big butt, light enough to see that, a big butt that reminded him of Cheryl Ann. In a flash he figured it out. This was the sophomore from Fitchville South, the one who hadn't been ready to go beyond hand jobs. She looked ready now. But to make sure, Freedy flicked on the bedside light.

Oh, yes, good and ready, and in the second or so before their eyes opened, Freedy saw how like Cheryl Ann she was, not just the fat butt, but other things too, especially her age. She was about the same age Cheryl Ann had been back in high school, back when Ronnie had made his little play for her, and he and Ronnie'd had their little rat-tat-tat.

Because of those memories, Freedy's mood was already changing a bit as their eyes opened, becoming less playful. Ronnie gets the girl: what sense did that make?

Moment they saw him, they both jerked wide awake, made

startled noises, Ronnie's higher-pitched than the girl's. Very next thing, the girl let go of Ronnie, yanking her hand back off Ronnie's dick like it was on fire, which it most certainly was not. This was fun.

"Well, well," said Freedy. "Nothing surprises me anymore." He laid his hand on that fat butt. Why not? He was a regular guy. Should he get rid of Ronnie for ten minutes or so? Was that what Bill Gates would do? Not when he was on a mission, and Freedy was.

There was a funny sound in the air, electric and silent at the same time. It ended when he took his hand off the girl. At least she'd gotten to feel what a real man felt like, if only for a moment. "Done your homework?" he said to her, which was pretty good. No one laughed, but so what? Not everyone appreciated wit, which was why the entertainment industry always ended up appealing to the lowest common whatever it was. "See you in the kitchen, Ronnie," he said, "if you've got a sec."

Freedy went to the kitchen, switched on the light, opened the laptop on the table. Gray screen with nothing on it. Ronnie appeared a minute or so later, shirt on backward.

"This is kind of unexpected, Freedy."

"My bad."

Their eyes met. Ronnie licked his lips. "She's older than she looks."

"Do I care?" said Freedy. "It's your constitutional right. But this isn't just a social visit." He hit the on button. "I could use some tech support."

No answer. Normally, you say something normal like that and the other guy says something back. Freedy looked up from the screen—nothing had happened yet; wasn't there supposed to be a warm-up routine?—and caught an expression he didn't like on Ronnie's face.

"Something on your mind, Ronnie?"

"Thought there was no laptop," Ronnie said.

He'd forgotten all about that. Made him look stupid, stupid in Ronnie's eyes. Pissed him off. This whole computer business pissed him off. All he wanted was to find out what it knew about Leo Uzig: how hard could that be? He glanced down at the screen to see how it was getting along with the warm-up, saw a message:

Total system failure. Computer will shut off in ten seconds. All files will be

The screen went black. The green light stopped flashing.

That swelling-up thing, like he was going to burst? He felt it again.

"You want it, Ronnie?"

Ronnie was fingering that hairy thing. "Depends on the terms," he said.

Ronnie, even Ronnie the pervert, was trying to cut a piece out of him. "These terms," said Freedy, and flung it across the table. An awkward object for throwing, but Ronnie, so slow, managed not to get out of the way, managed not even to block it, managed to get hit in the head. He lay on the floor.

That was when Freedy remembered something important. "Meant to ask you Ronnie—ever take Phil three twenty-two?"

No answer.

That Ronnie.

Freedy found a phone book, looked through the *Y*'s and then the *U*'s. *Uzig*. Not one of the spellings he'd tried on the laptop, but there it was, a single listing. More than one way to skin a cat. Not that he'd ever actually skinned a cat. Had skinned a squirrel once, one he'd snared in the woods back of—

But no time for that now. A single listing, the address up on the Hill, high on the Hill, over on the sunny side.

Dawn was just breaking as Freedy arrived. All that meant was the sky switching from black to dark gray. Still, there was enough light for Freedy to see what a big, solid house it was—nice brickwork, a tall black door with shiny brass fittings, expensive-looking extras all over the place. For a moment he felt a little funny, realized that the swelled-up feeling, like he was going to burst, hadn't quite gone away. He went around to the back.

23

"Youth as such is something that falsifies and deceives."
Identify the quotation and discuss in five hundred
words. No personal references, please.
—In-class essay assignment, Philosophy 322

Nat woke suddenly in the night. He checked the time, saw that he'd been asleep for less than three hours, rolled over, closed his eyes. Sleep had always come easily to Nat and, if interrupted, returned just as easily. But now he couldn't get back. Couldn't get back, although he was tired, and the night was still; even more than that, he could almost feel snow blanketing the roofs and windowsills and pediments and cornices, sticking to the friezes and architraves and pilasters and capitals—and all those other architectural features of Inverness for which he now knew the names—surely a sleep-inducing image; but sleep wouldn't come. Did it have to do with the Romanée-Conti 1917? There was a strange taste in his mouth, strange and unpleasant. Was this the taste of Romanée-Conti, too long bottled up? Nat got out of bed to brush his teeth.

Brushing his teeth meant going through the outer room and into the hall bathroom. He opened the bedroom door, and in the darkness of the outer room saw someone crouching by his desk.

Nat flicked on the overhead light. Not someone, not crouching, but a snowman, normal size for a snowman, a robust snowman with green buttonlike things for a smile. Right away, he felt a chill.

He touched the snowman, making sure the snow was real. It was. A snowman in his room, with a red ballpoint for a nose, a baseball cap on backward for a hat, those green buttonlike things for a smile. First he thought: snow days, Izzie's snow days, keep on snowing, snow days from now until forever. What sense did that make? Something wrong there. Too much to drink, too little sleep, too mixed up. Therefore, second thought: a prank, a college prank. No frats at Inverness. So who would do this? And why? A lot of work in the middle of the night, just for a prank. On the other hand, there had been frats, or something like them, long ago, and he could easily imagine Grace and Izzie putting in that kind of work, Grace especially. Or Izzie especially, given her snow days; snow days, when the forces relented and indoor snowmen became possible. So he was right back to thought one.

Nat stood in his room, gazing at the snowman. Inverness was silent, a rare thing. No banging of the pipes behind Plessey's walls, no scraps of talk from above, below, beside, no music drifting by from somewhere, no one quietly typing away, not even traffic sounds from beyond the campus. Nothing was happening, nothing but the snowman silently melting, leaving a growing puddle on Nat's floor. He plucked one of those green buttonlike things from the snowman's smile, read the single tiny word stamped on it: *Pfizer*.

Nat turned to the other bedroom, Wags's old bedroom. The door was closed. Wasn't it always open these days? He opened it now.

Wags lay on the bare mattress, reading by flashlight.

"Nattie boy," he said, sitting up, holding out his hand. "A sight for sore eyes, whatever that might mean."

Nat shook his hand; hot and moist.

"Keeping busy?" Wags said.

"Yeah."

"Still in there pitching?"

"I guess."

"Grinding away?"

Nat was silent. Wags wore a trench coat with a price tag hanging from the sleeve; underneath he had on flannel pajamas and mismatched boots, one an expensive-looking hiking boot—Nat spotted the Timberland logo—the other, paint-spattered rubber.

"I'm teaching myself Japanese," Wags said. He showed Nat what he was reading: a comic book. Two Japanese men were about to torture a Japanese woman. The only word on the page was *Eeeeee*! "I may get a job in the Ginza district," Wags said, "or possibly come back here and finish up."

Nat looked around for luggage, books, any of Wags's possessions, saw nothing but a hospital bracelet on the floor. He remembered Wags's mom: *Are you really saying you had no idea of the mental state he's been in?*

"Wags?"

"Present and accounted for."

"You all right?"

"Never better, Nattie boy. Better never, if you want the obverse, reverse, perverse. Free verse." Wags laughed, a little hee-hee-hee that petered out. "Sometimes when my mind gets going . . . ," he began. There was a long pause. "They tested my IQ," he said at last. "Off the charts. What's yours?"

"I don't know."

"You forgot?" Wags laughed his new hee-hee laugh again. "That would say it all, wouldn't it? An answering nonanswer of the truest sort."

Nat laughed too.

"Did you know I spotted a mistake in a PSAT math section my year?" Wags said.

"No."

"That must have been your year too, it occurs to me. In retrospect. There's also introspect, disrespect, and plain old R-E-S-P-E-C-T, find out what it means to me. Remember that question with the hexagon and the isosceles triangle?"

"You remember the question?"

"Nothing wrong with my memory, Nattie boy. Nattie boy-o."

"Do you remember why you built the snowman?"

Pause, even longer this time. "Right there," said Wags, "that's why I don't like you."

Nat picked up the hospital bracelet. The name of the place was on it, and a phone number.

Wags watched him. "You're pissed about Sidney," he said.

"Sidney?"

"Sidney Greenstreet. The snowman, if that's how you want to think of him. He was supposed to be a sumo wrestler, but he ended up like Sidney Greenstreet."

"Who's he?"

"Who's Sidney Greenstreet? Is that what you're asking? Who's Sidney Greenstreet? I despair. I give up. I just give up, completely and utterly." Tears welled up in Wags's eyes, spilled over onto his cheeks, kept coming.

Nat glanced down at the hospital bracelet in his hand.

"I'm on leave," Wags said; there were still tears but his voice sounded normal, a combination Nat had never witnessed before. "Paid leave, or maybe administrative leave. Semiauthorized. It's the medication, Nat—they have all these studies, but they're clueless about what it feels like inside your head."

"They let you carry your own pills around?"

Wags gave him a long look. "Still in there pitching," he said again, but without animosity this time. "No, they don't let you carry your own pills around. Not officially. But I'll make a deal with you. I'll defenestrate Sidney."

It took Nat a moment or two to figure that one out. "And then?" he said.

"And then we'll be even."

Wags got up. They went into the outer room, Wags moving stiffly, as though he'd just returned from football practice. They gazed at the snowman. Footsteps sounded in the hall.

"Gestapo," Wags whispered. His fingers dug into Nat's arm.

The door opened. Grace came in, then Izzie. Wags let go.

"We couldn't sleep—we were so—" They saw Wags, broke off.

"Sight for sore eyes," Wags said. "To the second power."

"Back already?" Grace said.

"And raring to go. Remember all the defenestrating we used to do at Choate?"

"What are you talking about?"

"Or maybe it was the next year, when I was . . . wherever I was. Doesn't matter. The point is we're going to defenestrate old Sidney." He extended his hand toward the snowman, as though presenting a friend.

"Sidney?" said Grace.

Wags's eyes narrowed. For a moment he looked almost dangerous. "Greenstreet," he said.

"Looks more like Burl Ives to me," said Izzie.

"Burl Ives? You know about Burl Ives?" Wags's eyes went to Izzie, to the snowman, back to Izzie. "You may be right," he said.

Grace walked over to the snowman, removed one of its green teeth, examined it. "I'm glad you're here," she said, sticking it back on the snowman, but in the middle of its forehead.

Wags bit his lip. "You are?"

"I want to pick your brain."

Wags went to the snowman, replaced the green tooth where it belonged. He turned to Grace. "Pick away."

"Still into movies?" she said.

"More than ever. They've got HBO, Showtime, Cinemax, plus a decent video library. Why do you ask?"

"I'm writing an essay."

"On movies?" said Wags. "What course is that?"

"Independent study," Grace said. "It's on plot construction."

Wags nodded.

"In kidnapping movies specifically," Grace said.

"Right," said Wags. "You've got to focus."

"Seen any?" said Grace.

"Name one I haven't."

"Any ransom demand scenes that come to mind?"

"Ransom demand scenes? Like how they go about it?"

"That kind of thing."

"Excellent subject." Wags rubbed his hands together. "Can I read it when you're done?"

"Why not?"

"This is so much fun," Wags said. "What college should be all about." He paused. "We're just dealing with ransom-type kidnappings, now, not the sicko or political kinds? Or kidnapping by accident or kidnapping to make a nice little family group?"

"Ransom," said Grace.

"*Ruthless People,* of course. Pretty recent. Judge Reinhold demands five hundred thousand dollars, unmarked and sequentially numbered one-hundred-dollar bills. On the phone. No notifying the cops, of course, that's pretty standard. There's *High and Low*, also on the phone." Wags smacked his forehead, much too hard. "And my God," he said. "Kurosawa. Japanese. Patterns, patterns, patterns." He turned to Izzie. "I may be taking a job in the Ginza district."

"Lucky you," Grace said. "What's *High and Low*?"

"Haven't seen *High and Low*? Where they kidnap the chauffeur's kid by mistake?" A tiny spray of spittle flew from Wags's mouth when he sounded the *s* in *mistake*. "Thirty million yen, as I recall—going to have to find out what that is in dollars—same nonsequential thing, same specifying the denomination. Speaking of chauffeurs, there's *After Dark My Sweet*. Patterns and more patterns. Bruce Dern sends a ransom note. But the kid's got diabetes and Jason Patric's escaped from an . . . asylum." He fell silent, looked down.

"What does it say in the ransom note?" Grace asked.

No answer. Wags kept looking down, hanging his head,

bent like one of those old people who can't straighten. His eyes got silvery. Nat waved Grace and Izzie away. They backed out of the room, Izzie first, then Grace.

"Maybe you should lie down," Nat said.

Wags looked up, didn't seem to notice that the girls had gone, maybe because his eyes were overflowing again. "Don't you want to hear about *Night of the Following Day*?"

"Later." But Nat didn't want to hear it at all. At that moment, looking at Wags in his misery, Nat knew that the kidnapping thing was out. He didn't understand the connection, but he knew. "First you're going to lie down," he said.

Wags stared at him. "Good idea," he said at last. "Your very best." Wags started moving in that stiff way, but not toward his old bedroom. Instead, he went to the snowman, gouged all the pills out of his face in one swipe, threw the window open wide, flung them out. The cold wind blew his hair straight back, as though he were going very fast. Then he had his head out in the night and one foot up on the sill.

Nat grabbed him, pulled him back into the room. Who would have imagined that a skinny kid like Wags would be so strong?

"Jason Patric dies at the end, you asshole," Wags said, wriggling free. Nat went to grab him again. Wags threw a punch. No one had ever thrown a punch at Nat before. He saw it coming, had time to block it or duck, or at least turn his head and not get hit flush on the nose. But no one had thrown a punch at him before, and this one did hit him flush on the nose. His eyes stung, he saw stars and, stepping back to recover, slipped in the snowman's puddle and went down.

Wags stood over him in fury. "You're just like all the others," Wags said, "only worse." Then Wags's foot swung into view and Nat started to roll; *the foot with the rubber boot, not the Timberland, thank God*—Nat's last thought for a while.

* * *

When he opened his eyes, dawn was breaking on a dark day, hardly lighter than night, and his room was cold. The window was open. His head hurt.

He got up, went to the window, looked out. No sign of Wags, no sign that he'd jumped and been carried off or jumped and walked away. Nothing down there but the baseball cap. Nat turned back to the room. The snowman was gone, the floor where he'd stood almost dry. He closed the window.

What next? His head hurt; he felt slow and stupid. Next would be the hospital bracelet, the phone number, a call. Where had he last seen it? Couldn't remember. He searched the outer room, searched Wags's old bedroom, didn't find the bracelet. Wouldn't need the bracelet if he could remember the name of the place. But he couldn't. Or he could call Wags's mom and get the name of the place from her. Rather than that, he went down on his hands and knees to try again. The door opened.

Grace; no, Izzie, he saw, as she came in from the dark hall and the light hit her hair. Izzie. She looked as though she'd just had eight hours' sleep followed by one of those runner's-high workouts; her hair still wet and gleaming from the shower. He rose.

"Nat! What happened to you?"

"Me?"

"Your nose."

He resisted the urge to touch it. "I'm fine."

She glanced around. "Wags cleared out?"

"Yes."

"Good." She closed the door, lowered her voice. "It's done."

"What's done?"

"The plan, of course. Sure you're okay?"

But the plan was out. "Done?" he said. "Done in what way?"

"Don't worry. Everything went smoothly. Grace called, as

me, and said she'd been—" She lowered her voice still more.
"—you know, kidnapped. We toyed with the idea of asking
for yen, the kind of interesting twist that makes things au-
thentic, but then we—"

"Called who?"

"Our father. You're acting funny, Nat, like you're hearing
this for the first time. Sure you're—"

"She called as you?"

"Why not? No one can tell us apart on the phone. 'This is
Izzie, something terrible's happened, I'm so scared,' blah blah
blah, million dollars, sequential, nondenominational, whatever it was, blah blah." Izzie laughed; she had that untamed
look of Grace's in her eye.

"We have to stop this."

"What are you talking about?"

"We just do."

"Nat. I told you. It's done. Grace is hiding down in the cave
and the money's on its way."

"The money's on its way?"

"It's nothing to him—didn't we mention that? He's
sending someone. Someone gives it to me, I give it to no one,
Grace reappears. We get back to normal life. Voilà."

He shook his head. That hurt, and had no other effect.

"You and Wags had a little disagreement, didn't you?" She
came closer, brushed her lips against the tip of his nose,
barely touching it. "Give me a kiss."

He kissed her. They'd kissed maybe dozens of times by
now, but never like this.

24

"The fantasist denies reality to himself, the liar does so only to others." Illustrate with examples from history or literature.
—From the final-exam study guide, Philosophy 322

All those years, growing up in this town—Inverness, the name itself snotty and hateful—all those years and he'd never once been inside a house on the Hill. Been in their yards, as he was in the backyard of Leo Uzig's house now, the summers he worked for one landscaper or another, but never inside. They had nice yards up on the Hill, and this was a nice one, surprisingly big, with different kinds of trees and a high stone wall. A snow-covered terrace led up to double back doors, heavy and black with brass fittings, like the door at the front. No cheap sliders, no bulkhead with stairs down to the basement, nothing easy. Funny thing, though, about people who lived on the Hill, especially those who'd lived there since the time when no one locked their doors—some still didn't lock them. Freedy tried the polished brass handle. Locked.

He stepped back, almost knocking over the bird feeder, checked the house, hoping for balconies, windows cracked open an inch or two, maybe a—

One of the double doors opened. An old woman came out with a bag of birdseed in her hand, saw Freedy, stopped. She was all in white—a long white housecoat, white slippers— except for her hat, red with earflaps sticking out to the side.

She looked like somebody's old gran. He himself had no old gran, his mother's mother, whoever that might have been, belonging to some earlier life. Not to mention the other side, where—

The other side. Freedy had maybe the most amazing thought of his whole life, a kind of jump or leap, like you turn the key in the ignition and then you're there, without doing the actual drive. This, this old thing with the watery eyes and the Kleenex sticking out of her goddamn sleeve, could be his gran! They stared at each other. Freedy knew he should say something, but what? No idea. Had he run into a situation he didn't know how to handle? That would be a first.

He got lucky—a nice change. The old lady spoke first. "Can I help you, young man?" she said.

"I, uh, represent the Aqua Group," Freedy said; meant to say *Agua*, too late.

"We're happy with what we have now."

"With what you have now?"

"Poland Spring, I believe. Or possibly Mount Monadnock."

What the fuck was she— Then he got it. "This is swimming pools," Freedy said. "I was just checking out your space for possible swimming pool installation."

"Were you?" she said, making a big thing out of that *were*, like she was pleasantly surprised.

"Yes, ma'am."

"But it's the middle of winter."

"The early bird," Freedy said.

The old lady smiled. "How right you are." She gazed beyond him, scanning the trees in the backyard, the smile slowly fading, but not completely. "Perhaps you can help me," she said, indicating the birdseed. "Before we get to the actual spiel."

Freedy took the bag from her, spread seed in the feeder.

"Richie," she called, in a yoo-hoo kind of voice, although she didn't say *yoo-hoo*. "Richie."

"Richie?" said Freedy, glancing around, seeing no one.

"My cardinal," said the old lady. "Short for Richelieu, of course, but I don't have to tell you that."

"None of my business anyway," said Freedy.

The old lady laughed. "I love a sense of humor. Swimming pools, you say?"

"The best."

"But now? In the middle of winter?"

"The early bird," Freedy said again, since it had worked so well the first time.

The old lady nodded. The sky had brightened slightly and he got a good look at her face. Did he resemble her, at all? "Those folk sayings," she began; but a crow swooped down at the feeder and she threw up her hands in horror. "Oh, no."

Freedy took a swat at it. He was quick, yes, and a fuckin' leg breaker, yes, but not bird-quick, so some luck must have been involved. Good luck—a nice change. Supposing, on top of all his other qualities, he was starting to get lucky too? Shudder to think, whatever that meant.

Some luck must have been involved. Why? Because he caught that crow a pretty good one, not on the button, but close enough. It went down and stayed down, a black feather or two drifting in the air.

"My goodness," said the old lady, gazing down at the crow, then up at Freedy. "What a competent fellow!"

Freedy tried to think of some aw-shucks folk saying that fit; he knew there must be some, even felt one on the tip of his tongue, but it didn't come.

"And modest as well," she said. Yes, even things he didn't do were paying off. This was the start of a lucky day, had to be. He should buy a lottery ticket, maybe go on *Jeopardy*.

Something caught her eye, something red. "Good morning, Richie." The cardinal settled on the rim of the feeder. "Isn't he the most elegant little man you've ever seen?" the old lady said, lowering her voice.

Quicker than a crow, Freedy wondered, or slower? Not the time to experiment. "Yes, ma'am," he said.

She turned to him. "I'm glad you agree. Now get on with it."

"Get on with what?"

"Why, swimming pools. I was a champion swimmer."

"You were?"

"At Camp Glenwhinnie. Many, many ribbons, red and blue. Do you know Camp Glenwhinnie, Mr. . . . ?"

"Just call me Freedy."

"Freedy. What an interesting name. I don't believe I've met a Freedy before. Camp Glenwhinnie, on Lake—is it a diminutive?"

"Huh?"

"Freedy. Is it short for anything?"

"Friedrich, I guess."

"Friedrich? Is that true?"

"Sure." How dense could she be? "Like the *Freed* part's in both of them," he explained patiently, reminding himself that she was old.

"I meant is that really your name—Friedrich?"

"Want to see my birth certificate?" he said. Amazing. He actually had the goddamn thing in his pocket, almost pulled it out.

Her laughter, abrupt and unexpected, stopped him. "Aren't you the funny bunny," she said. "How about coffee?"

"Sounds good," said Freedy.

"Excuse the mess," she said, leading him inside. "It's everybody's day off."

Freedy sat at the kitchen table, in a little nook with a good view of the feeder. There was no mess that he could see. Why would there be in a house on the Hill? It was all very nice. He stretched out his legs, trying to get comfortable. And he did, right away; comfortable, up on the Hill.

"Richie," called the old lady, although the bird couldn't possibly hear her, "eat up, there's a good boy." The fat red fuck stood on the rim of the feeder, doing nothing.

She gave Freedy coffee, poached eggs on toast, bacon—a gran breakfast. They talked about swimming at Camp Whatever-it-was on some lake whose name he didn't catch, up in Vermont or maybe New Hampshire.

"What kind of pools do you install?" she said.

"All kinds."

"Like what, for example?"

"There's the Malibu. One of our biggest sellers. If that's a little too pricey, we've got the Miami. The Mediterranean's pretty popular too."

"This is so exciting—and they all start with *M*. More bacon?"

"Yeah."

"Why didn't I think of this before?"

"Don't ask me."

"I'll have to check with Leo."

"Leo?"

"Not because of the purse strings—don't think that for a minute. But he's sensitive to noise."

"Leo?"

The old lady nodded toward a framed photograph on the wall. Freedy went over for a look. He saw a guy with wild gray hair, wearing a tuxedo and standing at a podium; behind him sat some famous person whose name escaped Freedy. He peered at the man in the tuxedo. Laid his eyes on him but felt no chill, nothing. Did he resemble this man, at all?

"That was last year, in Vienna," said the old lady.

"Your son, right?"

No answer.

He turned to her. She was glaring at him.

"What's up?" Freedy said.

"I hate when people say that," she said. "Have always hated, hate now, will hate. Leo is my husband."

Freedy tried to remember what he'd heard in the dollhouse, all so complicated. "You're not my gran, then," he said; said without thinking, the words just popping out.

"Your gran?" said the old lady.

The way she said it pissed Freedy off, all that Hill-and-flats shit, just in her tone of voice. He'd been so nice, so polite, even making sure to eat with his mouth closed. And now this. He whipped out his birth certificate, slapped it on the table in front of her, stabbed his finger at the space marked *FATHER*. *Full name: Unknown.*

The old lady—old lady, but Leo Uzig's wife, and therefore the other woman, the one who'd broken up the family he'd never had—gazed at the sheet of paper with her watery eyes. "Is this the contract?" she said.

"Contract?" The voice—male—came from the kitchen door. Freedy turned quickly, saw Leo Uzig. Not a picture on the wall, but the man. Leo Uzig wore a crimson robe and under it a white shirt and knotted tie, but his feet were bare. His feet: he had the kind of second toes that were longer than the first. Freedy's were the same way. Now he did feel a chill.

"The swimming-pool contract, Leo," said the old lady. "We have to make a decision. Malibu, Miami, Mediterranean. All beginning with *M*, as I'm sure you noticed. You most of all."

"What swimming pool contract?" Uzig said.

"This gentleman is from the pool company," said the old lady. "Freedy, my husband, Professor Leo Uzig. Leo, Freedy, last name to come."

"How's it goin'?" said Freedy, slipping the birth certificate in his pocket.

Uzig didn't look at him. "Have you signed anything, Helen?"

"And if I have?"

They stared at each other until Freedy said, "Hey. Nothing's signed. This is just the whatchamacallit. Checking out the dimensions. We're strictly aboveboard. You know, integrity."

Now they were both looking at him.

"Thank you, Freedy," said the old lady, "but I don't require your help."

"Huh?"

She glanced at Uzig, back to Freedy. "May I present my husband? Professor Dr. Leo Uzig, Freedy. Short for Friedrich."

She was introducing them again? What the fuck was he supposed to say? Freedy was wondering about that when he noticed that the expression on Uzig's face, still turned toward him, had changed. Hard to describe how: kind of like Uzig had suddenly realized he'd eaten something bad; Freedy recalled his own very first night in Tijuana, an all-you-can-eat bar called Gringo's. Leo Uzig looked the same kind of sick. Why wouldn't he, being married to a crazy old bag and her with the money? Freedy'd figured that one out in two seconds. She had the money, she wanted a pool, and he didn't. He was way ahead of them. *If I don't watch out, I'm going to make my first sale, and I haven't even got a fucking backhoe.* That was really funny. Freedy caught himself smiling broadly, smiling in the direction of Leo Uzig. No harm in that: no harm in showing him those white teeth, big and perfect.

Uzig smiled back, the kind of smile where teeth don't show. "Perhaps it's not such a bad idea," he said.

"What isn't?" said Freedy.

"A swimming pool—isn't that the subject at hand?"

Subject at hand? What was he talking about? Freedy, who'd never talked to a college professor before, expected them to make more sense than that. "Malibu, Miami, and Mediterranean," he said, because he had to say something and that sounded pretty good. "You've got choices."

Now Uzig's teeth showed, not bad teeth, but not as good as his. Probably smiling because he liked those names. Who wouldn't? They were fucking brilliant, and created—yes, created, like those Budweiser lizards—created by him out of the goddamn blue. Maybe he didn't even need a backhoe. Freedy realized he could have been a college professor himself, probably should have been. His rightful—what was the word? *Birthright.* He stopped smiling.

"Why don't we go out and survey the site?" Uzig said.

"Hey," said Freedy. "Sure."

"Me too," said the old lady.

"It's much too cold," Uzig told her. He pressed a button on the wall phone. A nurse entered moments later. What about her day off? Freedy almost said something.

"Bath time," said the nurse.

"I'm clean," said the old lady.

The nurse led her away.

Uzig put on boots. They went onto the deck. Richie pecked up one last seed and flew away.

They stood on the deck, almost side by side, gazing at the snow-covered yard. Uzig wasn't as tall as Freedy, but Freedy could sense he was built sort of solid. Nothing like Freedy, of course, but Uzig was older, and probably hadn't lifted much, maybe didn't know about andro.

"I don't believe there are many swimming pools in Inverness," Uzig said.

"Just another one of the fu—of the dumb things about this town."

Silence. Silence when the next question should have been where he was from, or how long he'd lived in town, or something like that. Freedy tried to figure out why it hadn't been asked, gave up, answered it anyway.

"You've heard of the flats?"

"Of course."

"That's where I grew up." Did his voice sound a little angry? He softened it and said, "The pool business I learned in California."

"Naturally."

What was natural about it? He could have done other things in California, sold cars or tried Rollerblading. Something impressive occurred to him. "The demand curve for pools," he said. "Up and up."

"I'm not surprised," said Uzig.

Demand curve. How sharp was that? Freedy thought of a

selling point, remembered someone saying it, really, but it
was a good one just the same. "Kids love 'em."

"I don't have kids," said Uzig.

Silence. They looked at each other. Freedy got a very weird
feeling: like he was seeing into his own eyes. Reverb, reverb,
reverb. That was the feeling. His own eyes resembled the
eyes of some British actor, according to his mother. He tried
to remember British actor names, came up with only one,
the James Bond guy. Were his eyes like the James Bond
guy's? Were Uzig's? Freedy didn't know. Still, it couldn't be
bad. The James Bond guy was a big star.

"No kids," said Freedy. "That's a shame." Just toying now.
Toying, which proved he was as smart as, maybe smarter
than, a college professor. Came by it honestly. That was
a good one. "But you know what would be even more of
a shame?" he said. "Even more of a shame than having
no kids?"

Uzig watched him. His face was still, hard to read. Hard
to read if that reverb thing hadn't been going on. But it was,
so Freedy knew him through and through. It was sweet,
knowing everything about the other guy when he knew
nothing about you; especially when it was a father-son deal.
How about that for a mindblower?

"What would be even more of a shame?" Uzig said at last.

"Not to have a pool in a space like this." *Space* was the
word you used—Freedy'd watched an architect use it over
and over on a woman in Palos Verdes. "A crying shame.
That's what it would be."

"What do you propose?"

Freedy liked that. It made him want to clap Uzig on the
back and say, *I get the feeling this is the start of something
good.* It made him want to, so he did; even the clap-on-the-
back part, maybe a little harder than he'd meant, but still well
within the boundary of two guys hanging out, father-and-son
style. "I propose to build you a pool you'll never forget,"
Freedy said. He held out his hand. After a second or two,

Uzig extended his. They shook. The old man didn't have much of a grip, and Freedy did his best to back off on the squeezing part. "How about I throw some specs together and get back to you?" he said.

"As you wish," said Uzig.

Which Freedy took for yes. He tried to think of something else to say, some way to extend the conversation. Or maybe Uzig would say something. But he didn't, so Freedy finally said, "Get back to you then. Real soon." Plenty of opportunity for conversation in the future. He walked home, down College Hill, across the tracks, into the flats, jazzed all the way.

She was on the kitchen phone when he went in, up early for her. Saw him, said something quick and low into the phone, hung up.

"Freedy," she said.

"The one and only."

"I'm . . . glad you're home. We should have a little talk."

Fine with him. He had lots to tell her. Should he hit her with the whole thing at once, or—

But she spoke first. "I—we've had some good news, Freedy."

"Yeah?"

"The fact is . . ." She bit her lip. "Maybe artists shouldn't even have children at all."

Stoned again. Out of her goddamn mind. He would have pushed past her, gone into his room, except for that good-news part. He waited instead.

"Do you know that song, Freedy, 'Last Thing on My Mind'?" She started singing, in a little-girl voice that irritated him even more than normal singing: " 'Could have loved you better, didn't mean to be unkind, you know that was the last . . .' " Her voice trailed off.

Pathetic. He could see Leo Uzig as his father, especially after the reverb thing. What didn't add up was her as the mother.

"But now maybe I can make it up to you," she said. "The fact is, I've come into a little money."

"How much?"

"Some. I know you don't like it here."

"Who said that?"

"You, Freedy. What with the cold and the lack of opportunity. Maybe I could help . . . set you up. In a warmer place, if you had some idea."

"What kind of idea?"

"About what you'd like to do."

Yes, a lucky day. What was it all about? Choice. He heard that all the time. Bill Gates, all the others, they had choices, they chose from different possibilities. Malibu, Miami, Mediterranean: choice. "I've got some ideas," Freedy said. "How much are we talking about?"

"Some," she said again.

"Can't start a pool—" Whoa, don't give anything away. "*Some* won't cut it in the business world."

"What . . . what would be a likely amount?"

"Depends what's available."

Her eyes went to the phone. What was she going to do, call the bank? Had to be a dope deal, although he couldn't imagine her making a big score.

"How would ten thousand do?"

Meaning there had to be four or five times that. Freedy was impressed. "Be a start," he said.

She nodded, like it wasn't out of the question, like it could happen.

"There'll be some travel expenses too," Freedy said.

"To where?"

"Florida." Said it out loud. It was real, a real choice. "Let's call it another two."

"Two?"

"G's."

She nodded again. Should have said three, four, even five. "When can I have it?"

She glanced at the phone again, opened her mouth to reply. Freedy heard a car door close.

He went to the window. A state police cruiser was parked on the street, a statie coming up the walk, but slow because she hadn't shoveled. Freedy's first thought: *there goes the dope deal.* Then he got a good look at the statie's face: the same statie who'd eyed him in the men's room of the stripper bar. He backed away from the window.

Didn't make sense. Ronnie had filed a complaint? What was wrong with him? Did he want to get seriously hurt? That wasn't Ronnie. But if not Ronnie, what?

No time to figure it out now. He turned to her; her mouth was still open. "I've gone back to California," Freedy said.

"Not Florida?"

"That's just what to tell him, for fuck sake. Address unknown."

"Tell who, Freedy?"

There was a knock on the door. Freedy could move. He moved: down the hall to his bedroom, out the window, into the backyard, through some trees, angling toward the river; heading for Ronnie's. Nothing to it; but he was pissed. This was supposed to be a lucky day.

But as for getting away clean, that was never in doubt. Freedy had only one bad moment, when a helicopter suddenly appeared. What was this? LA? It swept low over the river, passed above him at treetop level, close enough for him to see it had no police markings; no markings at all, except a big black *Z.*

25

*"You must become who you are." Identify the quotation
and relate to the concept of the Superman.*
—Final exam question 1, Philosophy 322

That Ronnie.

Just when things were getting promising, just when Freedy's
hard work was starting to pay off, who fucks it all up but
Ronnie? Calling the cops? Calling the cops because he was
too clumsy to avoid bumping his head on a laptop? This
wasn't like the hairy thing under Ronnie's lower lip, or the
girl from Fitchville South, both a bit funny in a pathetic way.
There was nothing funny about this. Calling the cops about a
private matter crossed the line—everyone in the flats knew
that, and no one would blame Freedy, whatever he did.
Ronnie was a disgrace.

The slider to Ronnie's basement was open a foot or so, off
the track, askew. Ronnie had probably gone back to bed, was
probably still asleep, maybe even with the girl. Was it a
school day? Freedy realized he didn't know what day it was.
Cool, in a way. Did the wolf keep track of the goddamn days,
or the tiger?

Freedy went in, saw the weights lying around, saw someone's cut-off sweatshirt—his Planet Hollywood sweatshirt,
found by some pool in the Valley, how the hell did that get
here?—on the bench press, heard water dripping. He went
upstairs to the kitchen.

All quiet, the fridge still humming away, the tub of KFC on the table. Freedy couldn't remember taking it out of the fridge, but maybe he had. He helped himself to another drumstick, then noticed the laptop, still lying open and unblinking on the floor. Drumstick in hand, he went down the hall to Ronnie's bedroom. Door closed. He opened it, went in.

Ronnie was back in bed all right, and alone. Eyes closed, maybe sleeping. Oh yeah—and his head was all wrapped in bandages. Freedy moved to the side of the bed. "Ronnie?" he said, swallowed what he was chewing, and said it again, more clearly, "Ronnie?"

No response, like he was in a . . . coma, or something. Impossible. Not even Ronnie. Freedy was thinking about giving him a little pat, a little poke, a little shake, when he heard footsteps in the hall; very light footsteps, but would anyone be surprised to learn that Freedy's hearing was second to none? That was why he was already turned toward the door, readying some high-school joke for the Cheryl Ann substitute, when the footstepper walked in.

But not the girl: Saul Medeiros, Uncle Saul, gnawing on a drumstick, just like him. Saul paused, paused in midchew, and said something, possibly not clear because the drumstick got in the way. It sounded like, "Boys."

Boys will be boys. Must be what he means, thought Freedy, and he started to relax. The laptop incident—no more than a boys-will-be-boys thing to Uncle Saul. Saul knew what Ronnie was all about; he remembered how Saul had smiled his nicotine-colored smile when Freedy said Ronnie was a pussy. Besides, he and Saul had developed a good working relationship. Not that they'd reached the mentor stage yet, but—

Two guys appeared behind Uncle Saul.

"Look who's here, boys," said Saul.

The two boys were big boys, one about Freedy's size, the other a lot bigger. Both wore black satin jackets with *Saul's Collision* in gold letters and crossed bowling pins on the front, plus gold crests reading *Runners-Up '99*. Freedy wanted one.

"This here's Freedy, boys," said Saul Medeiros. "Numbnut I was tellin' you about. Don't unnerstan' the . . . what'm I tryna say? The importance of business ethics."

The boys didn't look happy to hear it.

"How can you say that, Saul?" said Freedy.

"Mr. Medeiros," said Saul.

"How can you say that?" said Freedy, compromising by dropping the *Saul*; at the same time glancing at the window, hoping to gauge the distance to the ground. Surprisingly far from upstairs at Ronnie's: that would be the fucking slope to the river, why Ronnie had that basement with the weights, why they were friends.

"How can I say what?"

"Ethics. When you're the one that called the cops."

Saul and his two boys all wrinkled their foreheads. "What the fuck are you talking about?" said Saul.

"The statie over at my place right now is what I'm talking about."

"Nothin' to do with me," said Saul. "Never called a cop in my life, never will, except for setting up a payment or some other legitimate business purpose." The boys nodded their heads. "So don't question my ethics. You're the one broke the laptop agreement."

"The laptop agreement?"

"You forgot?" said Saul. "Forgot we talked about laptops, you and me? Then all of a sudden—no laptops. Okay. I'm reasonable. If there's no laptops, there's no laptops. Supply don't meet demand. Happens all the time—why you got scalpers. But if it turns out there is laptops all along, is laptops but I'm gettin' some bullshit story there isn't laptops, then what's a reasonable, ethical businessman s'posta do?"

"There were no laptops," Freedy said.

"What's that—some hallucination on the kitchen floor?"

The boys got a kick out of that one.

"There's just the one," Freedy said, "and it wasn't for sale."

"How come is that?"

"I was keeping it."

"Getting into programming?" said Saul.

The boys liked that too.

"I needed it for research," Freedy said.

"Research?"

"Nothing you'd be interested in. It's a family matter."

Pause. "Family."

"Right."

"Family," said Saul, "is very funny coming from you."

The boys nodded.

"What's that mean?" said Freedy.

"Means we now come to the main event, laptops being like the undercard."

"Lost me," said Freedy.

"Don't you worry—I'll find you," Saul said. "Refresh your memory—didn't we talk about family, you and me? Or are you tellin' me you forgot that too? Not surprisin', your ma being a hippie cocksucker down at the old Onion. I done some checkin', unnerstan' why you might want to forget the importance of family. Forget family legends. Forget Cheryl Ann."

Family legends? Cheryl Ann? And that wasn't very nice about his mother. Was this some kind of Portagee shit? These people were stuck in the past, going nowhere, total losers. It pissed Freedy off to be in the same conversation with them. This was America, after all. "Is this some kind of Portagee shit?" he said.

The drumstick fell from Saul's hand. "I hear you right?"

Freedy put his drumstick tidily in the ashtray by Ronnie's bed. "I mean Christ almighty, Saul, Mr. Medeiros, whatever. Is that what this is all about? Portagee shit? Were you getting a piece of Cheryl Ann too? Or—" It suddenly hit him. "—or is it the new one, the schoolgirl from Fitchville South?"

Okay, maybe he wanted that last one back. But how did

that work? How did you get things back? Besides, it was another one of his amazing insights. He could believe it, Saul and the sophomore, easy. So he said it. You had to be who you are, had to be who you are and make it work for you—right from the infomercials. Nothing wrong there. But jeez, that girl from Fitchville South: how could she do it with an old prick like that, hair on his nose? Freedy found himself smiling at the thought, shaking his head, maybe not the best time for that either.

Ronnie made a little noise in his sleep, coma, whatever it was, a relaxed sound, almost happy.

"Boys," said Saul, not loud, almost a question.

"Now, Mr. Medeiros?" said the smaller one, Freedy's size, or maybe a bit bigger, Freedy realized.

Saul stepped aside.

The boys came into Ronnie's bedroom, reaching inside their satin jackets. They pulled out tire irons. 'Course, you had a wrecking yard, you had tire irons.

Freedy felt jacked right away, like he was full of andro, stoked on meth. Was he? He'd have to think about that later. Right now he had to deal with the boys. Just because you were big, just because you were strong, just because you dug beating the shit out of somebody, just because you weren't afraid, none of that made you a fuckin' leg breaker. What made you a fuckin' leg breaker came from inside, and the boys didn't have it.

Ronnie's bedroom wasn't big. It could scarcely contain Freedy, the boys, Ronnie and his bed. But that was neither here nor there, whatever that might mean. What was here and there was the smaller of the two boys, the one just a bit bigger than Freedy, moving in on him first. No surprise there: you expected the smaller guy to be quicker. He was quick, had that tire iron swinging sideways at Freedy's head—smart, much harder to block than a high-low—had the tire iron swinging at him quick. But not crow-quick, and even crow-quick might not have been quick enough. Freedy ducked:

takes some nerve to just duck, but it works. Didn't even duck a lot, only the two or three inches necessary. The tire iron actually clipped his ponytail, for a moment floating free of gravity before his ducking head pulled it down.

The smaller big boy spun halfway around from the force of the missed blow. Freedy kicked him good and hard behind the knee; weak spot on most everybody. Freedy heard a cracking sound—that Thanksgiving sound, he felt like a kid again—and the smaller big boy went down.

Bit of a surprise at that point. The bigger big boy turned out to be just as quick as the smaller one, maybe quicker. He actually connected with the tire iron, actually made Freedy feel pain, shoulder temporarily out of service, maybe the arm too. Someone shouted: might have been Freedy. Then the big boy was on him, like a house. Three hundred pounds or more, saliva slobbering down, some growling: disgusting. Three hundred pounds on top, Freedy on the bottom, one arm not in tip-top shape. Oh, yeah: and the tire iron raised up high, cocked back, now coming down at his head. But what was this? Freedy felt something funny under his hand—left hand, but that was the only one working at the moment—almost as though some angel had put it there. His fingers closed around it—the goddamn KFC chicken bone, dropped by Saul, pig that he was, and gnawed on a bit. One end could almost be called sharp. That was the end that Freedy jabbed up with, up and up with his kind of quick, right up the nose of the bigger big boy, way, way up. The bigger big boy stopped whatever he was doing at that moment, whatever he was doing consciously. The tire iron left his hand, flew across the room, crashed into something; the bigger big boy fell on Freedy, lay there still.

The boys didn't have it, not what it takes inside.

Problem was, while Freedy struggled to get out from under all that weight, he forgot about the one other guy in the room besides him who did have it inside, who was a fuckin' leg breaker, as he should have kept in mind the whole time. Just because a guy is old and scrawny and has that sickening hair growing on the top of his nose doesn't mean he hasn't got it.

Saul Medeiros kicked him real hard in the balls. The look on his face when he did it was the genuine fuckin' leg-breaker look. All the air left Freedy's lungs, and there was no hope of getting more anytime soon. Uncle Saul reared back to give him another one. He wore filthy, oil-stained shit-kickers, what you'd expect down at the wreckers.

But at that moment, when things didn't look so good, Ronnie came through for him. He sat up, squinting, and said, "Can somebody close the goddamn shade?"

Saul glanced at him, an expression on his face that might have amused Freedy at some other time. A glance that lasted for a second or less, but enough time for Freedy to dig down deep, start a sideways turn, lash out with his top leg. Not a hard lashing out, not hard for Freedy, but Saul was old and scrawny. He fell without any resistance Freedy could feel.

Saul started scrambling to get up. Freedy, still needing that breath, a little sore here and there, started getting up too, but slow, like Superman exposed to whatever that stuff was, k-something. Slow for Freedy and scrambling for Saul turned out to be about the same. Saul had a sharp, shiny hooked thing in his hand, something from the yard Freedy didn't even know the name of. Didn't matter. That nose with the hair growing on top? Freedy flattened it with one punch, a left hand by necessity, flattened it flush into the rest of Saul's mean little face.

That left Saul and the bigger big boy motionless on Ronnie's floor, the smaller big boy crawling on his belly toward the door making moaning sounds, Ronnie sitting up in bed, his room a mess.

"Hold it right there," Freedy said to the smaller big boy.

"Don't," he said, and kept moving.

Freedy went over to him, bent down.

"Don't," said the smaller big boy.

"What are you going to do about it?" said Freedy, and he

tore that black satin jacket with the gold letters and the gold crest right off the smaller big boy's back.

Freedy walked over to the bedside, putting on the jacket, not easily because of his right arm. He looked down at Ronnie. Ronnie squinted up at him.

"Freedy?"

"Yeah?"

"Mind getting me a glass of water?"

"Guess not."

Freedy stepped over the smaller big boy and went down the hall.

"And maybe a couple aspirin," Ronnie called after him. "In the drawer by the sink."

Freedy came back with water and two aspirin in his hand. Ronnie took the aspirin off his open palm, gulped them down.

"Ronnie?"

"Yeah?"

"Call it even, right?"

Ronnie nodded, winced, stopped nodding.

Down in Ronnie's basement, on his way out, Freedy had a moment of . . . not weakness, more like he was tired for a second, what with missing a night's sleep and all. He sat down on the bench, the padded bench they used for presses, and swallowed an andro. What was this? Three left? As for the meth, he had enough for about that many hits in the Baggie in his pocket, the main supply stowed under his bed in the "Little Boy" room. The question: was this the time to go back and get it? Saul had said he hadn't called the cops and Freedy believed him. You could say what you liked about Saul Medeiros, but he was true to his word. That meant it was some pot deal of his mother's, nothing to do with him. So it was safe to go back and get it, right?

Or wrong. Freedy couldn't make up his mind, which was

weird. Just fatigue, probably, and his right arm dangling like that. Good time for a tweak, in fact. What was he thinking of?

Freedy used up a little of his meth, had an idea immediately. Why not call and find out? Ronnie's cordless lay right there on the stereo. Freedy dialed the number.

"Hello?" said his mother.

"Hi," said Freedy.

She lowered her voice. "What happened in California?"

She'd mixed it all up. "Happened? I told you to say I'd gone back there, that's all."

She spoke faster. "I did. But they're saying they've got a war—"

In the background a man said, "Who is that?"

The line went dead.

Something happened in California? Not that he was aware of. She'd mixed it all up: no surprise there, her head full of smoke, year after year. Still, probably not a pot thing in this case, so it wasn't safe to go home yet. When would it be? What about the money she'd promised, the ten grand, plus travel expenses? She ruined everything. He pounded the bench, in his frustration forgetting and using his right hand. Made the shoulder, the arm feel a little better, actually.

What now? He needed to sleep, to rest, to sort things out. Where? Only one place he could think of.

Freedy popped up the vent hood behind the hockey rink. He heard sirens down in the flats. Not unusual. He glanced around; no one in sight, nothing to see but his own footprints, leading right to him across the snowy playing fields. What could he do about that? Nothing.

But maybe he wouldn't have to. As he watched, the sky, already dark for even a cloudy day, darkened more, and the first flakes started falling. The wind picked up. Snow and wind would take care of the footprints for him, like nature was on his side. Luck, on this lucky day, was still with him. One or two more breaks and he'd be golden.

26

*"All my writings are fish-hooks . . . If nothing got caught
I am not to blame. There were no fish."* With reference to
Nietzsche's critics, describe three major arguments of
the fish that didn't bite.
—Final exam question 2, Philosophy 322

The aquarium was missing. They were sitting in the twins'
room on the third floor of Lanark, Nat at one of the desks,
Izzie on Grace's bed. Outside, the sky, a morning sky but
dark, darkened more, and a few flakes began falling, almost
invisible in the weak light.

"Where's Lorenzo?" Nat said.

"We took him down to the cave. She—Grace wanted company in case it was a long wait."

They fell silent, waited. After a while Izzie picked up a
mirror, made a few adjustments to her hair. "I wish you
wouldn't be like this," she said.

"Like what?" Nat said.

"Brooding, or whatever it is. What's the point? It's done."

"Maybe not."

"Maybe not? The only way to undo it is to make us look
like idiots."

Nat said nothing. There was an unfamiliar sharpness in her
tone; he put it down to tension.

"You know what your problem is?" she said.

Tension, for sure. He'd never heard her on edge like this,

268

not close. She wasn't herself. Perhaps the girls had made a mistake: maybe Izzie should have waited in the cave while Grace handled things up here.

"What's my problem?" Nat said.

"Fear of success," Izzie told him. "Which I always took for psychobabble. Now I'm thinking it exists after all."

He felt that one, so close to *ambition should be made of sterner stuff*. It didn't matter now. Someone with the money was on the way. Someone gave the money to Izzie. Izzie gave the money to no one. Grace emerged. A little hanky-panky, then back to normal life. It sounded simple, like a beginning case study in economics.

She came over to the chair, stood behind him. "Let's not fight," she said, and rubbed the back of his neck. "Mmm," she said. Her hands were cold.

There was a knock at the door. Nat's eyes met Izzie's. Was her heart suddenly beating faster too? Probably not, from the casual way she said, "Come in."

The door opened: a UPS man in his brown uniform.

"Izzie Zorn?" he said, reading the name from the package in his hand.

"I'll take it," said Izzie, and laid the package on the other desk. The UPS man went away.

"Aren't you going to open it?" Nat said.

Izzie opened the UPS package, unwrapped bubble wrapping, pulled out what was inside: a laptop. She looked puzzled for a moment, then laid it aside.

"New computer?" Nat said.

"The old one disappeared."

"Disappeared?"

"Stolen, I guess."

"When was this?"

"Not too long ago."

"You never mentioned it."

She shrugged.

"Did you report it?"

"Report what?"

"The theft."

"To whom?"

"Campus security."

"What good would that do?"

"Maybe none," Nat said. "But there was Wags's TV, the TV from the lounge, now this."

"Probably Wags doing it himself," Izzie said.

That had never occurred to Nat. "Why would he?"

"Why would he build a snowman in your room?"

Nat realized he still had a headache, very faint. "I don't think Wags—"

Another knock on the door.

"Was I supposed to sign?" Izzie said; and, as casually as before: "Come in."

The door was opened again, but not by UPS. Two men in suits came in, very nice suits—even Nat knew that. The first man, the smiling one—not Albert, not Anton—was Andy, who'd sat beside him in the limousine to the airport; behind him, not smiling, was Mr. Zorn.

Someone coming with the money: why hadn't he expected Mr. Zorn? Nat had no idea what to say or do; and felt transparent.

Not Izzie. She leaped up, ran to her father, threw her arms around him, started crying. Actually shaking, wracked with sobs: Nat was amazed, would never have thought her capable of this. It was almost as though she were really afraid for Grace. Mr. Zorn watched him over her shoulder.

The smiling man extended his hand. "Hi, Nat. Andy Ling. Met you over Christmas. More pleasant circumstances."

They shook hands. "Maybe I'd better go, Mr. Ling."

"Not necessary," said Andy. He turned to Mr. Zorn, patting Izzie's back, his eyes still on Nat. "Is it, Mr. Zorn?"

"We'd appreciate your staying," said Mr. Zorn.

Nat nodded.

"Good man," said Andy. He opened a closet, peered inside, beckoned Nat over. Was Nat supposed to notice something? He noticed shoes; had never seen so many outside a shoe store. Andy Ling lowered his voice. "Why don't we give them a moment or two?" Andy led Nat into Grace and Izzie's bathroom, shared, because of their corner room, with no one.

Andy closed the door. He glanced in the toilet, drew aside the shower curtain. "Scared, Nat?" he said.

"Yes," Nat said. It was true.

Andy opened the medicine cabinet, closed it, ran his eyes over the bottles on the shelf above the sink: nail polish remover, body lotion, shampoo, conditioner, Clairol. "Scared of what, exactly?" said Andy.

"This . . . this situation."

Andy turned to him, still smiling. He had one of the friendliest faces Nat had ever seen: asymmetrical, lumpy, cheerful. Nat tried to remember his job description. Albert was Mrs. Zorn's personal assistant, Anton was her personal trainer, and Andy? He didn't recall anyone ever telling him.

"I don't blame you," Andy said. "Being scared." He dumped the wastebasket on the floor, poked through the mess, poked through it with his gloved hands; not till that moment did Nat notice he'd kept his winter gloves on the whole time.

The mess: tangled strings of dental floss, balled-up tissues, Q-tips, an empty bottle of Clairol, another bottle, also empty, that Nat recognized: Bidoit Paradis, Grande Champagne, 1880. Andy picked it up, sniffed at the opening, set it on the sink. "Don't blame you one bit. Something happen to your nose?"

"Just a bump."

Andy opened the bathroom door and reentered the bedroom. Nat checked himself in the mirror—the nose wasn't bad, but there were other problems, hard to define—and followed.

Izzie, no longer crying, sat on Grace's bed, hugging her knees. Mr. Zorn stood by her, gazing out the window.

"Imagine spending four years here," said Mr. Zorn.

"Doesn't get any better," said Andy.

"You agree, Nat?" said Mr. Zorn.

Nat couldn't manage a reply of any kind.

Mr. Zorn looked past him. "Anything?"

"Nope," said Andy.

"What's going on?" said Izzie.

"You're asking the right question," said Mr. Zorn.

Andy got down on his hands and knees, checked under the beds. Nat had a premonition of what was coming. *Stop,* he thought. *Enough.* He almost said it.

"What are you doing?" Izzie said. "And where's the briefcase?"

"Briefcase?" said Mr. Zorn.

"Or whatever you brought the money in."

Mr. Zorn sat down beside her. "Why don't you tell us the whole story?"

"But I already did," said Izzie.

In fact, Nat realized, it was Grace who had told the story, told them on the phone as though she were Izzie. How well did she herself remember it? *Sequential, nondenominational, whatever it was, blah blah.* How well had she listened in the first place?

"Please tell it again," Andy said, soft and gentle.

Izzie shrugged. She told the story, second hearing for Mr. Zorn and Andy, first for Nat. She didn't try to sell it at all, didn't even look at anyone as she spoke, just sat there on Grace's bed, still hugging her knees, spoke as though it was all unfolding again in her head. She told how Grace had risen in the night, complaining of an upset stomach; how Grace had gone down to the Coke machine in the Lanark basement; how she, Izzie, had fallen back asleep and been awakened by the kidnapper's phone call. A male voice. Perhaps a slight Japanese accent. He'd put Grace on the line for a moment, to prove he had her. "I'm all right," Grace had said. Grace had been Grace, poised and cool. But Izzie could tell she was just being brave; they'd have to take her word, the word of a twin, for that. Then the man came back on with the demand: one million dollars in nonsequential low-denomination bills. He would get in touch again to arrange the delivery. Click.

"Click," Izzie said again, now looking up at her father. She'd done beautifully. Nat's premonition had probably been false; certainly false, he would have thought, except for one thing: there was no briefcase.

Silence in Grace and Izzie's room.

Andy sighed. He rose, slowly, as though his legs were tired, and went to the phone on Grace's desk. "The call came on this phone?" he said.

"Yes."

"About what time, Iz?"

"Exactly?"

"As close as you can'll be all right."

"I didn't check. Around five-thirty this morning."

"Give or take how much?"

"Ten minutes either way."

"Could it be more?"

"I guess."

"How much more?"

"I don't know. Five minutes, ten, fifteen.   was pretty upsetting."

"I understand," Andy said. "So give or take a half hour, either side?"

"I guess."

"Maybe a little more?"

"Maybe."

"But not, say, ten hours."

"Ten hours? What are you talking about?"

Andy turned to Nat. "And where were you at that time, Nat? When the call came."

"In my room."

"Which is?"

"In Plessey. Across the quad."

Andy went to the window. "Mind pointing it out?"

Nat pointed to Plessey Hall.

Andy shook his head. "All so picturesque," he said. "I can't get over it. The call didn't come on your phone, by any chance?"

He was still gazing out the window; Nat wasn't sure for a second if the question was directed at him.

"Mine?"

"Yours," said Andy.

"No, sir."

Andy turned to Mr. Zorn. "That it, Mr. Zorn?"

"Other than asking Izzie if there's anything she'd like to change, yes, that's it."

"Change?" said Izzie. "About what?"

"Your story," said Mr. Zorn.

"I'm not getting this," Izzie said.

"No?" said Mr. Zorn. "For one thing, there haven't been any calls, in or out, on this phone since . . . when, Andy?"

"Seven thirty-three P.M. yesterday. Incoming from room nine in this same dorm. Something about the arrival of a pizza, according to the student who made the call. The next one, the only other one, was Izzie's call home this morning."

"Second," said Mr. Zorn, "Andy made a phone call of his own on our way up here."

"Spoke to Nat's mom, out in Colorado," Andy said. "A very nice woman. She explained all about her unfortunate new circumstances, and their implications. I felt bad."

"Third," said Mr. Zorn, "I know your sister."

"What is that supposed to mean?" Izzie shifted down the bed, away from him.

"I know people, Izzie."

"What are you saying?"

"I'm saying I know all I need to know. I did a billion-dollar deal last year—meaning I made a billion-dollar decision—on less information, less essential information, than this. So if you'll just tell me where Grace is, we'll get back to work."

"Have you all gone crazy?" Izzie said. Nat knew they hadn't. It was over, just like that, the whole plan blown apart effortlessly, as though they'd posted it on the Web by mistake. Nat tried to catch Izzie's eye, get her to stop. Izzie didn't look at him.

"She probably has a suite at the Inverness Inn," said Mr. Zorn.

"Want me to check?" Andy said.

"It really doesn't matter. She'll turn up."

Izzie rose, stood over her father, getting it at last. "You're not paying?"

"Why pay ransom when there's no kidnapping?" said Mr. Zorn. "Make any sense to you, Nat?"

"No, sir." He hated letting Izzie down, but that was the answer. He also hated the way Mr. Zorn was watching him, without anger, without hostility, without scorn, but still punishing. He'd been a guest in this man's house.

"I take that as a confirmation," said Mr. Zorn.

"Yes," said Nat.

"Thank you," said Mr. Zorn. He rose too. Now they were all on their feet; the room seemed small. "It's beautiful here, Andy, as you say. The thing to remember, though, is it's just a big playpen. Won't do to get too caught up with people like Leo. It might interest you to know, Nat, that I never hire people from this kind of place. I harvest from the top five percent of the state schools every year." He checked his watch. "Anything else, Andy?"

"I don't think so, Mr. Zorn."

Mr. Zorn faced Izzie. "I'm not blaming you, angel. I know what's going on."

Izzie was white. "You're abandoning her? She's not worth one little million out of that last billion?"

"Izzie, the game's over."

"What if . . . what if it was . . . me, instead of Grace?"

"You're not making sense, Izzie."

Izzie laughed, a strange laugh of real amusement. "You don't know anything."

Mr. Zorn gave her a careful look. "Maybe you should have gone to separate schools," he said. "To escape her influence."

"Influence?" said Izzie. "You think I don't know whose bidding *you're* doing?"

"Who would that be?"

"Your present wife, of course."

"You couldn't be more wrong. She wanted me to hand the money over, on the assumption it was going to Nat." Mr. Zorn turned to him. "She liked you. But it doesn't work that way, Nat—might as well learn now." He paused, looked Nat in the eye. Nat met his gaze; it took just about all the willpower he had. "I can relieve your mind on two things," Mr. Zorn said. "First, we didn't tell your mother what was happening, and have no intention of doing so. Second, there will be no legal consequences—as long as you do what I'm sure you knew was the right thing from the beginning."

"Which is to go on home," said Andy. "Plus no hard feelings, right, Mr. Zorn? You said to remind you."

"Of course not," said Mr. Zorn. "No hard feelings, no recriminations, no threats. I never threaten people."

The nature of the threat—his mother and the law—was clear.

"They're at the age for adolescent pranks," Andy said.

"Good point," said Mr. Zorn. "Imagine if they'd been funneling— is that what they call it, Andy?"

" 'Fraid so."

"Funneling quarts of vodka or something." Mr. Zorn shivered.

"Every parent's nightmare," said Andy.

"So we dodged one this time. Let's think of it that way. Have Grace get in touch when she cools down."

*　　*　　*

Nat and Izzie stood by the window, watching Mr. Zorn and Andy Ling walk across the quad. Andy said something that made Mr. Zorn laugh; a big breath cloud rose above him.

"We ended up looking like idiots anyway," Nat said. He felt worse than an idiot, embarrassed and ashamed; but deep inside he agreed: *We dodged one this time.*

"Speak for yourself," said Izzie.

He looked at her in surprise.

"Sorry," she said; came to him, wrapped her arms around him, shivered, just as her father had done. Mr. Zorn and Andy disappeared from view. "There is a positive side," Izzie said after a moment or two. Was she, too, aware that they had dodged one this time? Izzie surprised him again. "It's not often," she said, "you get the chance to find out what someone really thinks about you."

"He likes you," Nat said. "He loves you."

"You don't understand."

"It couldn't have been clearer," Nat said. "If he's got problems, they're with Grace."

Izzie's grip on him tightened. Outside snow was falling harder.

"We'd better go tell her," Nat said.

"What's the rush?" Izzie said, her mouth close to his ear; the sound sent one of those odd nerve reactions down his neck and spine. He knew what Izzie was thinking: Grace would say they'd blown it.

But they had to tell her, tell her about the failure of their little scheme; and while they were at it, there was more: "We should tell her about you and me."

"Both at the same time?" Izzie said. "How much can the poor girl take?"

Nat turned her sideways a little so he could see her face. "You're acting funny," he said.

"Am I?"

He looked into her eyes, saw the gold flecks, took in Izzie's whole golden effect. "Maybe there's no point telling her about us," he said, "now that I'm going home."

Did the idea upset Izzie? Nat couldn't tell. Before, she'd said, *You can't just go*. Now she said, "Let's worry about that later." She kissed him; then kissed him deeper. At first, he felt nothing. Then he realized this might be the last time—Albany-Chicago-Denver, there was a flight that very afternoon at three—and felt a great deal, much more than he was prepared for.

"Now?" he said.

"Why not?"

Izzie drew him toward the bed; the closest bed, which happened to be Grace's. He steered her the other way, toward her own bed.

"What's the difference?" she said.

They lay on Izzie's bed. The last time, he thought: and maybe because of that knowledge, nothing went quite right. It was clumsy, awkward, quick—clumsier, more awkward, quicker, than any of the other times, even the first, on Aubrey's Cay. He was surprised once more, then, when Izzie cried out at the end, loudly, passionately, instead of making the low moan she sometimes made, or no sound at all.

Izzie came out of the bathroom. "I've been thinking—it might be better if I tell her myself," she said. "Why don't you wait here?"

"No," Nat said. Grace almost certainly would blame them—Izzie especially—and he wanted to shield her. "I'm coming."

"I'd rather do it myself."

That was Izzie. He smiled at her. "I'm coming."

She opened her mouth as though to argue, closed it, came over. "Why not? It can't get any crazier." She kissed him, running her tongue over his chipped tooth. "What's that?"

"My chipped tooth."

"You can always get it fixed."

* * *

Taking a flashlight, they crossed the quad, went down to the Plessey basement, shifted the panel at the back of the janitor's closet, entered the tunnel. They walked, deep under the campus, Nat leading, their feet silent on the hard-packed dirt floor. All familiar now: the downward slope, the dampening air, the dripping sound from somewhere nearby. At the junction, they turned into the right-hand passage, no longer hung with spiderwebs because of their coming and going. The dripping sound grew louder. Suddenly Izzie screamed and dug her fingers into his shoulder, hard enough to hurt.

"What's that?" she said.

In the flashlight's beam, a bat hung from the valve on the steam pipe. "Just the bat," Nat said.

"Kill it."

"Don't be silly. What's wrong with you, Izzie?" But he knew: she was afraid of her sister. It made her jumpy. "Why don't you go back? I'll tell her myself."

"Piss on that," said Izzie.

They walked on, past the bat, hanging motionless. Izzie released her grip on his shoulder.

Nat raised the trapdoor, saw it was dark down in the cave, at least in the bedroom part. Grace was probably asleep. He climbed down the rope ladder, Izzie following, shone the light on the bed. Grace wasn't in it, but something lay on the pillow. Nat went closer. Because of its color—that of putty—Nat didn't recognize it until he was within touching distance. He didn't touch. Lorenzo: Lorenzo lying on the pillow, dead in the open air, all his gaudy beauty faded away.

"Grace?" he called. "Grace?" And hurried, running at the end, into the big room. No candles burning in the big room either. Nat stabbed his light here and there. "Grace? Grace?" The room was a shambles—furniture overturned and broken, paintings knocked off the walls, cabinets smashed, shattered glass everywhere—and Grace was gone.

27

*According to Nietzsche, "Man and woman never cease
to misunderstand each other" because (a) women have
less need to vent their strength, (b) the religious nature
is less developed in men, (c) their emotions run at different tempos and thus are never in sync.*
—Multiple-choice question one, final exam,
  Philosophy 322

Izzie lit a candle. Huge shadows appeared on the walls.
"Where is she?"

She picked up a chair, one of those dainty gilt chairs, a leg
now broken off, tossed it aside. Then something else, bang, and
something else, crash, as she moved through the two rooms,
faster and faster, the huge shadows in wild motion on the walls.
"Where is she?" Then, much louder: "Where are you? Where
are you?" No response; Nat thought he heard a distant dripping
sound. She turned to him. "What's going on?"

He didn't know. Where was Grace? His first thought was
the studded door in the big room, bricked-in on the other side.
He opened it, shone his light around, then up at the grate that
led to Goodrich Hall. She wasn't there. She wasn't under the
bed, under the couches, behind what was left of the old wind-
up record player. He knelt over fragments of a record: "Caro
Nome," the label still intact.

Izzie cried out. He hurried to her. "What is it?"

"Nothing." She pulled a shard of glass from her finger. A fat drop of blood rose to the surface, quivered.

Nat shone his light on the smashed aquarium at her feet, on the chunk of coral Lorenzo had liked to hide behind, on the seaweed almost invisible on the pattern of the rug. He raised the beam up to Izzie's face. She was sucking on her finger.

Izzie shielded her eyes; he aimed the light away. "Where are you?" she called, so loud and sudden it startled him. "Where are you?"

A painting fell from the wall, startling them both. Nat went to it: the nude bathers with the centaur spying from the bushes. He passed his light over the wall, saw a small hole where the hook must have been.

"Something bad is happening," Izzie said.

Nat wasn't so sure. "Suppose she was out in the hall."

"What hall?"

"Your hall, in Lanark. When your father was in the room. What if she came up to tell us something and heard what he was saying about her?"

"What are you getting at?"

"Wouldn't it make her angry?" Nat said. "It made you angry."

Izzie watched him, saying nothing.

"Maybe she was angry enough to come back here and . . . do this." Do this, down at the subterranean level, in the time he and Izzie had spent in bed, above.

"You don't know her," Izzie said. The candle she held lit her face from below, casting cheekbone shadows over her eyes, at the same time lightening her hair. "You talk about her like she's some kind of monster."

"Not a monster. But she can be funny. You're the one who told me that."

"Did I?"

"On the beach."

"How loyal of me," Izzie said.

He overcame the urge to shine the light on her face again, to get a better look at her. "What's wrong with you, Izzie?"

"How can you ask a question like that? Something bad is happening. And you don't care. You think she's off by herself, in a sulk."

"What other explanation is there?"

She gazed at him. "You're starting to remind me of my father."

An uncommon feeling stirred inside him, that same anger he'd felt when the campus security officer had implied he knew something about the theft of the HDTV from the student union.

"But here's an explanation if you need one," Izzie said. "Wags."

"Wags? Wags doesn't even know about this place."

"Maybe he found out."

"How?"

"Maybe she did come up, as you said, but went to your room. What if he was there?"

"Why would he be?"

"Why not? Where else can he go? What if he was there, popping those green pills, kidnapping plots buzzing in his brain?"

"So?"

"So he made her bring him here."

"Wags couldn't make Grace do anything."

"Or tricked her, then."

"He couldn't trick her either."

Izzie's face softened. "You think pretty highly of her."

"It's not so much that," Nat said. The soft look faded. "More that Wags is—" He started to say *harmless*, stopped himself. Wags wasn't harmless. Plus: leaving Lorenzo on the pillow. That was Wags; he'd probably seen something like it in a movie. "We'd better check my room," Nat said. He shone his light around the wreckage one more time. There were movies like that, too.

They started up the rope ladder, Izzie first. As he reached for the ladder, Nat stepped on something slippery. He shone his light on it, picked it up: a black satin jacket.

"Wags's?" said Izzie, coming back down.

Nat had never seen it before.

"The kind of thing that would amuse him," Izzie said. A black satin jacket, two snaps ripped from the material, with *Saul's Collision* in gold and crossed bowling pins on the front, and a gold crest, *Runners-Up '99.* "Especially that runners-up part," Izzie said.

"Sure it's not Grace's?" Nat said.

"You think she'd wear something like this?"

"It's not impossible."

"Trust me," Izzie said.

Nat's room. And there was Wags, sitting at Nat's computer, fingers on the keyboard, face almost touching the screen.

"With you in a sec," he said, not turning toward the door. "Just checking out the Fatty Arbuckle Web site."

Nat glanced in the bedrooms. No sign of Grace.

Izzie jabbed off the monitor.

"Hey," said Wags as the screen went dark. "I was downloading." His eyes went to Nat; actually to a spot in midair a few inches off target. "Hope you're not pissed about our little . . . debate last night, or the night before, Nattie, my friend. No harm done. And I brought you some chocolates, as a bribe."

A box of chocolates lay on Wags's old desk. They'd been gift-wrapped, but now the wrapping was ripped off, the box open, and three or four of the chocolates gone.

"Fact is, roomie, I'm moving back in. I can't afford to neglect my education for another second. So if you'll excuse me . . ." He reached for the monitor button.

Izzie grabbed his wrist. "Where is she?"

"That hurts a bit," Wags said. "Ouch. I mean it."

"Where is she?"

"Where's who?"

With her free hand, the back of her free hand, Izzie smacked Wags across the face; harder than a smack, from the way his head jerked to the side, stunning him. Nat was stunned too.

"Where is Grace?" she said.

Wags gazed up at her, wide-eyed. "Is that like metaphysical or something?"

She raised her hand again; he winced in anticipation, like a dog Nat remembered in his neighborhood.

"Izzie," he said. She froze, slowly lowered her hand. Her other hand still gripped Wags's wrist.

Nat went to them, put his hand on Izzie's. Her hand, so cold, relaxed. He uncoiled it from Wags's wrist, looked down at Wags. "Do you know where she is?" he said.

"I don't understand the question," Wags said, his eyes still locked on Izzie. They filled with tears, like the eyes of a child badgered by the teacher.

"Did you take her down in the tunnels?" Nat said.

"The tunnels?"

"The tunnels under the campus."

"There are tunnels under the campus?"

"You didn't know?"

"Real, physical tunnels?"

"Yes."

"You've been in them?"

"Yes."

"And you never told me?" Wags smiled, a smile Nat didn't like at all, with only one side of his mouth turning up and the eyes not participating. "Why am I surprised?"

"No time for therapy," Izzie said. Wags's smile, what there was of it, vanished. "Does this belong to you?" She held up the black satin bowling jacket.

"No."

She shoved the jacket at him. "Put it on."

Wags rose, unsteady, as though his legs were weak, put

on the jacket. "Is this like Cinderella?" he said. It was much too big.

Izzie reached behind the collar, turned it out. "XXXL," she said.

"He's got nothing to do with it," Nat said.

"With what?" said Wags.

They didn't answer.

"These tunnels—are they scary?" Wags said. "I'd like to see them, at your earliest convenience. Also, I'm growing partial to the jacket."

"You can't have it," Nat said.

"Can I borrow it?"

"No."

Wags took off the jacket, handed it to him obediently.

"What do you want to do?" Nat said.

"Resume my education, I already told you. Beginning with Fatty Arbuckle."

"I meant do you want me to call your parents or do you want to go back to the hospital?"

"Give me a hard one," Wags said.

They sent him to the hospital in a taxi.

"Now what?" said Izzie, back in Nat's room.

"I don't know," Nat said. But what could it be? Either Grace had heard her father's analysis and had some sort of violent psychological reaction or . . . what? He couldn't think of anything else. "She must have overheard."

"What makes you so sure?"

"It's part of a pattern."

"Pattern?"

"Grand Central Station," Nat said, "all over again."

"Grand Central Station?"

"When your family was splitting up and Grace stood on the railing."

A look he hadn't seen before, at least on her, appeared on

Izzie's face. He wouldn't have thought her capable of a look like that if he hadn't seen what she'd done to Wags.

"You know everything about us, don't you?" she said.

"You didn't have to tell me."

"I shouldn't have."

They sat in silence. The wind was blowing harder now, driving snowflakes against the glass; they made a soft drumming sound.

"We just sit here, then," Izzie said, "waiting for her to reappear. Is that the plan?"

Nat had no other; but this one had a flaw. First he just sensed it, an uneasy feeling, then he identified it, then it grew bigger in his mind: the bowling jacket, size XXXL. He picked it up and did what he probably should have done in the first place. He searched the pockets. There were two. Nothing in the left-hand one. Something in the right; something his fingers identified before he even pulled it out: a switchblade knife. There were always a few kids at Clear Creek High who carried them. He pressed the button. The blade, longer than the ones he'd seen, snapped out. Nat knew then that she was right and he was wrong. Something bad was happening.

Izzie held out her hand.

He gave it to her.

"Like this?" she said.

Like that.

She folded the knife, stuck it in her pocket.

"Let's go," he said. She was already moving.

They went down to the cave. Everything, the whole mess, was exactly the way they'd left it, except for the painting of the nude bathers and the centaur, the painting that had fallen. Now it was propped against the wall, facing the wrong way. On the back, in big black letters: *A milion sounds nice. Right here soon say by dark. Call the cops and she die$.*

Identify and explain: "There is so much goodness in cunning."
  —Single-paragraph essay question one, final exam,
    Philosophy 322

Was luck still with him? Bottom line: yes. The expression *bottom line* pleased him; the kind of expression he was going to need in the future. A golden future. He'd asked for a break—who deserved one more?—and maybe he'd gotten one, maybe the breaks would finally start breaking his way. The kid from the flats, on his way to the big time. For one thing, he had the girl.

Drop-dead fuck-you, and he had her! Had one of them: they were twins, of course, not just sisters, he knew that now, had figured it out, maybe a little late; twins, so one couldn't be bigger than the other, none of that big-sister-little-sister shit. And the one he had probably wasn't as good-looking as the other one right now, not after their little—not fight, he didn't want to say fight, more like a dustup. But any—he didn't want to say damage, more like nicks and scratches—any of that was probably temporary, and even if not, she was still drop-dead fuck-you, the best-looking girl ever in his life, bar none. Wouldn't trade her for a million bucks.

Just joking.

"Babe," he said. They had funny names, these twins,

names he had never really grasped, couldn't relate to. He just called this one babe. "Babe?"

She wasn't answering.

Freedy could live with that. They both, he and she, needed a little breather, were both a little banged up. His right arm was still funny, not dangling useless anymore, but not right. That was one of the reasons his initial encounter with the girl hadn't gone smooth as planned. He hadn't been 100 percent, but take nothing away from her. A girl, and she'd given him a bit of trouble, more than Saul and his big boys. Amazing. Was it possible that at one point he'd even been lying on the floor while she climbed that rope ladder, almost to the top, almost free and clear? And those scratches on his face, and one eye half shut, not as bad as hers, but still. She was amazing.

She was amazing and he liked that. "Babe?" he said.

Not answering. He liked that too. He was getting more mature. A man, a diesel, buff, ripped fuckin' animal such as himself needed a woman to match. That was the revelation that had hit him while he lay beside her in the spyhole room between F tunnel and the dollhouse, both of them just breathing for a while. He liked her. And would he answer in her place? Hell no.

Having a woman of your own power, making the right match—it went back to Adam and Eve. Had he ever had a woman like that, an equal, in his life? Not close. Nothing against Estrella, he'd learned a lot from her, especially practical things, like how to make dreams come true, but she wasn't close.

"Going to need some information from you," he said.

Not answering. No sound in the spyhole room but the drip-dripping, nothing to see but total blackness.

Needed information, to make this dream come true. He'd already made—didn't want to say a mistake—not the best moves once or twice, no fault of his own. Like forgetting to write a ransom note at first—maybe not the best move. Had to give people guidance, right? Had to provide leadership.

Meant he'd had to leave the spyhole room, go all the way back, down F, into N, over to the trapdoor, down inside again, retracing the whole route he'd dragged her, just to write that note like he should have in the first place. He needed a—what did they call it?—detail person. He hadn't dragged her all the way back with him, of course, hadn't had to since she'd still been, not unconscious, more like sleeping, or whatever.

"Need that information," he said.

Not answering.

And maybe there'd been one or two other—glitches, that was it—glitches, too, but how could they be blamed on him? Want to grab a million bucks as it flies by? Have to act fast. He'd acted fast, pounced on her as soon as he knew what was happening, soon as the other sister had left. Hadn't expected that much resistance, who would have? That, and forgetting the note, two glitches. What if no one came down again and saw the note, or came when it was too late? Too late? A funny thought: how could it be too late?

Wasn't like him to fret this way. He felt in his pocket: one andro left, two hits of meth. Sampled the meth, felt a little better. And not to fret, because the next moment, or not long after, Freedy heard people moving again on the far side of the wall. That meant they'd be seeing the ransom note. It also meant she could maybe hear them too, maybe cause a little trouble. He lit a candle—all he had, one little candle, her flashlight all busted during the dustup—looked over at her, lying nearby on the dirt floor. Oh yeah, slipped his mind: her face, the mouth part anyway, was taped up with electrician's tape from the utilities room in the subbasement under building 31.

Mouth taped up, probably the reason she'd hadn't been answering him, because she wasn't sleeping anymore. Her eyes were open; eye, actually, the one that would open. Open and on him, but she was listening, he could feel it. He put his finger to his lips, letting her know it wasn't a good time for talk, and rose—slowly, even painfully—to look through the spyhole.

Freedy saw a flashlight beam pointing at the back of the painting with his note. On track. He heard a voice, the other sister: "I suppose you're going to say that's her own writing."

"No," said someone else; the college kid. The college kid started shining his light here and there, right into Freedy's eyes for a second. Freedy shrank back, blew out the candle. And the moment he did, the girl, the sister that was his, made a thumping sound. How? He'd thought of everything, had her arms and legs taped tight to the utility pipe. So she had to be doing it with her head. She was banging the floor with her head to get their attention. Freedy was on her with all his weight just as she did it again, a muffled thump on the dirt floor. Could they have heard? He listened; no sound came from the other side of the wall.

Freedy lay on her with all his weight. She was amazing: imagine doing that, with the way her head must be feeling after that sleep, or whatever. He lay on her, subduing her, kind of. Could have forced himself on her right there, felt like it in a way. But was that how he wanted it? No. A man like him didn't need to force himself on a woman; all he had to do was give her a taste of what he was about, and she'd be forcing herself on him. Was it unreasonable to think that given time to forget all the unpleasantness, this drop-dead fuck-you American dream girl would see what a good match they were? He'd been joking when he'd had that thought about not trading her for a million dollars, but why did he have to make a choice at all? Wasn't—yes!—wasn't the hero supposed to get the money and the girl at the end?

Freedy rolled off her, got up, felt along the wall till he found his spyhole, peered through. The room was silent and dark. They were gone. That meant he had work to do.

"Need a little help here," he said. A detail person: what he'd always been missing. "We have to plan this out."

He relit the candle, gazed down at her. She was awake,

the one eye that could open, open. It was pure gold in the candlelight, which was kind of cool, pure gold, fixed on him like that.

"We got some thinking to do," he said. "You know how it works, right? Start with an idea, make a plan, stick to it." He liked talking to her, liked the way his voice sounded talking to her, quiet, casual, close, like they were soul mates. Potential soul mates: he didn't want to be unrealistic at this stage. "The idea we already know," he said. "A million dollars. Now we just have to figure out the plan and stick to it."

They watched each other, watched each other by candlelight. Women had a thing for candlelight. Candlelight, flowers, candy: what the hell was that all about? A man likes that kind of shit and he's gay. So did women want their men to be gay? Made no sense.

"You like candlelight?" he said. "Flowers? Candy?"

No answer, what with the tape job. The gold eye just watched him, blinking now and then.

The idea: a million bucks, a cool million. The plan: the money would appear in that room on the other side of the wall, less than ten feet away, by dark. He'd take it, leave the girl, be in Florida the next day. Sounded good, better than good. The life he had ahead of him—he went cold, actually went cold thinking about it.

Were there any holes in the plan, any weak spots? He lay back on the dirt floor, tried to think of some. Couldn't come up with any and was ready to stop, to just enjoy that feeling of success around the corner, when one cropped up. What if they did call the cops? Then came another: what if they didn't call the cops, but brought fake money, too well made for him to tell? And a third: what if he wasn't ready to give her up? And there were others. He could sort of see them, shapeless dark things slouching in his mind.

"A situation like this"—Freedy didn't want to use the word *kidnapping*—"turns out to be complicated. Hell if I know why—there's only two parts to it. You and the money. So how come everything's so . . ." He couldn't think of the word. The gold eye watched him. Whatever the word was, she knew it.

Freedy sat up. His shoulder gave him a twinge. Maybe that made his voice harsher than he'd intended when he spoke to her. "I'm going to take the tape off your mouth, babe. But any glitches and it's right back on, good and tight. Comprendo?"

Comprendo: could he have picked a better moment to slip in a foreign word?

No response. The gold eye watched him. She was something else. Made for him. He pinched a corner of the tape between thumb and index finger and ripped it off. She didn't make a sound. Made for him in heaven.

Her lips parted. Some blood, not a lot. She took a deep breath. He could hear it, like a warm breeze. He seriously considered leaning over and giving her a kiss.

She spoke; real quiet. She didn't have a strong voice like her sister, shouting through the walls. "I need a doctor," she said.

"Me too," said Freedy.

The gold eye watched him.

"Won't be long," Freedy said. "First I need that million."

"Let me go," she said, and paused for breath. "Let me go and I'll make sure you get it."

"Think I'm stupid or something?"

"No."

"The fact is I own my own business."

She was silent.

"Built from scratch. You wouldn't understand. College girl. College girl up on College Hill, everything handed to you on a silver spoon, if you see where I'm coming from."

No answer. Now maybe it wasn't quite so cool, this silence of hers. He leaned over, went and did it: kissed her on the lips, real light, but sending a message. She didn't move a muscle.

"No more bullshit, that's all. Promise?"

Pause. A real long one.

"Say yes or the tape's back on."

Another pause, but not as long. Then: "Yes." He could barely hear it.

Her lips were warm. That feeling lingered on his own lips. He knew for a fact: life, his own life, was going to be sweet.

"Familiar with the flats?" he said.

"No."

"Why would you be, right?"

"I need a doctor."

"Why would you be? That's the whole point. Even though the flats is this whole town, except the goddamn college. Say hello to the kid from the flats."

She didn't. The gold eye closed. He closed his own eyes, went over the plan. What if they did call the cops? He'd hear them coming, of course, hear them in the tunnels, but what good would that do? He'd be trapped. Have to kill her then— that's what it said in the note. Then what?

He opened his eyes. "Time for a little . . . ," he began. What was the word? The gold eye opened, watched him. A little what? He knew the word, had heard it a thousand times on the infomercials. Something about thunder, lightning: "Brainstorming!"

Maybe he'd said it a bit loud. He lowered his voice, back to that intimate level he liked to use with her. "Time for a little brainstorming," he said. "You understand what I mean by that term? It's an entrepreneurial kind of thing."

"Yes."

"This friend of mine, she and me used to do a lot of brainstorming. Back when I was just starting out."

Freedy got the feeling she was going to say something. He waited, heard the dripping sounds. She spoke: "What happened to her?"

"Happened to her? Nothing happened to her. She's out in California, leading the good life. Why would anything happen to her?"

"No reason."

He heard that warm breeze breath again, slow and long.

"Been to California?" he said.

"Yes."

"Whereabouts?"

"Heavenly Valley."

"What the hell's that?"

No answer.

"Been all over the fucking state, from Tijuana to LA. Never heard of it."

"It's a ski place."

"A ski place?"

No answer.

"A ski place, I said."

"Yes."

"That's what you do in California? You ski?"

"I did."

"The college kid go with you?"

No answer.

"I asked you a question. The college kid, you know who I'm talking about, who the two of you are so hot for—what's his name, again?"

No answer.

"That was another question."

Nothing, zip. Couldn't allow that. But what to do? All he could think of was kissing those lips of hers again. Weird: what kind of reprimand was that? No explaining some things. But it was what he wanted to do, and he started to do it, rolling over, lowering his face to hers.

"Nat," she said.

He paused. "Huh?"

"His name is Nat."

The answer to his question, but not what he wanted to think about right now. "Don't tell me. He owns a condo out there."

"No."

"But he's got money to burn. I know the type. Never worked a day in his life."

That got her angry. Was it possible? "He works right now."

Another long slow breath. "And in the summer he works in a mill."

"What kind of mill?"

No answer.

"His old man probably owns it."

"His old man's not around."

Freedy felt another twinge, more than a twinge, but he'd call it a twinge, in his shoulder. He rolled over, lay on his back. They lay there, breathing together. Shadows made jittery motions on the ceiling. Water dripped. Sleeping would be a bad idea.

Blackness.

"You awake?"

Candle out.

"Babe?"

He had a horrible thought—she'd escaped somehow—and as he had the thought his good arm lashed out. Struck something sort of soft. She screamed, like in agony. He jumped a mile.

"Hey," he said. "That wasn't even a hit."

She was already quiet. Then she took one of those breaths. "I need a doctor," she said.

"Me too."

They lay there. Freedy tested his bad arm. Hey! Felt better, a lot better. What a little sleep would do, especially when you were a fuckin' animal. "Me too," he said, "but you don't hear me complaining."

He relit what was left of the candle, had a look at her. Nothing wrong that he could see, beside the obvious, that eye, one or two other things. "That was a nice little siesta." *Comprendo, siesta*—he was on a roll. "Now we're feeling refreshed, how about we get back to brainstorming?"

No answer, just that warm breezing breath.

"You know that word, *siesta*?" he said.

Zip.

"It's a spic—Spanish—word for, like, sacking out." He thought: a cool million, the girl, siestas in the Florida sun, maybe by the rooftop pool of Agua Group HQ. "You like pools?" he said.

No answer.

"Swimming pools."

Zip.

"I asked you a question."

No reply. Maybe she was going to say something, but before she could, Freedy heard a little scratching sound. It came, it went, a rat probably, or something like that, not important. But it got him thinking.

"We got to think," he said.

Silence.

"Say 'About what, Freedy?' "

"For God's sake," she said.

He liked that. Breaking in a horse: he'd seen it in the movies. "We got to think about our plan. There's . . ." He wasn't sure exactly how to put it, about those problems slouching in his mind.

Time passed while he thought. At last, she said: "What is the plan?"

"Like I said, there's you, there's the million."

Another long breath. "Do they know?"

"Now they do. They saw the note."

"What does it say?"

"The exact words? Can't give you the exact words. Something about the money, where to leave it and such."

"Where?"

"In the room down there."

"When?"

"Tonight."

"What time is it now?"

"Don't have a watch."

"I do."

He rolled over, held the candle near her wrist. Her watch was all smashed up.

"No you don't," he said.

The gold eye watched him. "And if the money doesn't come?"

"Like, worst-case scenario? That's what we say in business." He waited for her to speak. When she didn't, he said: "No need to talk about that. It'll come. The cops is what I'm—not worried—more like, you know."

"What makes you think they'll be involved?"

"Hey. Exactly right. I wrote it in plain English, what would happen."

"Which was?"

"That'd be a deal breaker."

The gold eye watched him.

He watched her back, let her get a good look at him. "Ever seen a man like me?" he said.

The eye closed. "No."

Freedy smiled, his first smile in a long time. There was pressure, oh yes, but he could handle it. Pressure was part of the big time, one thing they didn't mention on the infomercials. "Babe?" he said.

No answer.

Breaking a horse, but a valuable one, and a horse he liked. He reached over, put a hand on her tit. The gold eye opened. She tried to move away, but couldn't, of course.

"The plan needs work," she said, real quiet.

He stopped what he was doing. "Yeah?" he said. "Like what?"

She—that eye of hers—watched him.

"I asked you a question."

"Why should I help with the plan?"

"I'm asking the questions here."

Silence. He had an idea. "You know why you should help?" he said.

She watched him.

"Because we're in this together," Freedy said.

She laughed. Cut off real quick, with a gasp like she was in pain or something, but still: an actual laugh.

"What's funny?" he said.

"Nothing."

"You laughed."

No answer.

"Come on," Freedy said. "I've got a sense of humor."

"I know you do."

He liked that. He looked at her, so close. Soul mates. Only potential right now, but the potential was there. Couldn't he just see it: the two of them walking out of his HQ, his beautiful blue HQ down in Florida, at the end of a working day, climbing into the coolest car in the world, peeling off to somewhere. "What time do you think it is?" he said, real relaxed, real intimate, like man and wife.

"No idea."

She had a great voice. Had he noticed that before? She was worth a million bucks. Should he say that? Why not, since she knew he had a sense of humor, had just finished saying so? The hero gets the money and the girl, and everyone else stands around like assholes. That was what he found himself saying, instead of the joke: "You know the way the hero gets the money and the girl and everyone stands around like assholes?" he said.

The gold eye closed, opened, watched him. "The plan needs work," she said.

"You already said that."

"The money and the . . . hostage can't be in the same place."

"Huh?"

"They can't be in the same physical place."

"How come?"

"You can't figure it out?"

He couldn't believe he'd heard that. "What did you say?"

"Nothing."

Nothing? He was back on top of her, not as quick as usual, but still quick enough that she hadn't finished saying *nothing*. She made that gasping noise again, this time ending with a high-pitched little note. He felt her breath, warm on his face.

"Think I'm a loser?" he said.

"No."

"Then don't talk down your fucking nose."

"I need . . ." She didn't finish it.

He felt her tits under him, saw those lips, undamaged so far, inches away. They were perfect. His own lips parted. This would be a good time.

"You don't have any control unless the money's in a separate place," she said.

He paused. "I don't?"

"If you're with the hostage," she said, "that makes you a hostage too."

Had he ever heard anything as smart in his life?

"Especially in a place like here," she added, nailing it down.

"How do you know all this?" he said.

She watched him, watched with the gold eye. The other eye, the closed one, had some kind of liquid seeping out.

He rolled off her, sat up. She took one of those long slow breaths, making that gentle breeze sound.

"But I already wrote where to bring the money," Freedy said, seeing a problem right away.

"You'll have to change it."

"How?"

"By calling them."

"Who?"

"My sister. Nat. I'll give you the numbers."

Freedy didn't like it. "What if no one answers?"

The gold eye watched him. He got the feeling the next thing she said was going to piss him off. But it didn't. "Leave a message," she said.

"Saying what?"

"Where to leave the money."

"Where's that?"

"This is your territory, isn't it?"

Freedy thought. His mother's: no. Ronnie's: no. The high-school parking lot: no. "What kind of place?" he said.

"The woods."

"With all this snow?"

"A vacant lot, then. An empty building."

"I don't know anywhere like . . ." But he did.

She watched him. "You've thought of something."

"Maybe."

"Where?"

"Tell you later. Just give me the numbers."

She did. Pen, yes, paper, no; he wrote them on his hand.

"Now," he said, "what about you?"

"You have to leave me here. Especially if it's still daytime."

"Do you think it is?"

"Yes."

"I'll have to keep you taped up to the pipe."

"I know."

"And gag you again."

She was silent.

And what else? There was something else, something important. "There's something else," he said, hoping she'd tell him what it was.

She watched him.

"Oh yeah," he said. "What if someone comes down while I'm gone?"

"I'll be tied up and gagged."

"But—" This was the point: "What about the head-banging thing?"

"Why would I do it?" The gold eye closed, opened. "They didn't hear."

"Still," Freedy said.

Still. Which was why he had to do something. He checked

out the way she was, the tape job, the pipe. Going to need some adjustments.

"Babe?" he said.

No answer.

"Have to untape your hand for a sec." He tore at the tape, unwound it. Her arm, one arm, came free. She sort of groaned. The rest of her, legs and the other arm, remained taped tight to the utility pipe. "Have to lean your head a little this way," he said. He was looking at the pipe, reaching in his pocket for a roll of tape, not really watching, not really noticing that her arm, her free arm, was feeling around under her. "Let's have that arm," he said.

The arm came up, came up with something glinting in it, came up quick, even by his time scale. A sharp thing, goddamn piece of glass from that fucking aquarium, stabbed him right in the neck. Not in the neck, exactly, because he was even quicker, but in his shoulder, the one just starting to feel better, deep. Had she known it was under her, that piece of glass, even brought it somehow, waiting for a chance? That hurt most of all. Why? Because of the money and the girl thing, the hero's reward, now gone and wrecked.

He let her have it. Let her have it but good, as they said, and Freedy knew why: because of how good you felt, doing it.

Freedy taped her arm, now limp, back up to the pipe, taped her head to it too, to prevent that head-banging shit. He popped the last andro, tweaked the last of the meth, stopped the bleeding; his bleeding. New plan. Action central.

29

Which of the following was not written by Nietzsche? (a)
It is our future that lays down the law of our today. (b)
The sick are the greatest danger to the healthy. (c)
Money is the root of nothing.
—Multiple-choice question two, final exam,
   Philosophy 322

The ransom note.

It defied Nat's understanding, like a superficially simple
poem packed with allusions he didn't even know were there.
He was sure of only one thing: it wasn't Grace's writing. Nat
still believed Grace might have wrecked the two rooms in
their cave; could even imagine Lorenzo dying in the fray; but
could not accept that she'd written that note on the back of the
centaur painting. *A milion sounds nice. Right here soon say*
by dark. Call the cops and she die$. Not her. Could she have
disguised her written self to persuade her father and Andy
Ling that a kidnapping had really taken place? Maybe, Nat
thought, but not like this. The longer he stared at the note, the
stranger it got—didn't even read like a ransom note, left out
all those points Wags had made; and the middle sentence almost didn't make sense. Something else about the note bothered him even more, something he couldn't identify.

So when Izzie said, "I suppose you're going to say that's
her own writing," he said, "No."

On the way out, Izzie went by Lorenzo's body without a glance.

Grace and Izzie's room. Even with what he'd just seen, Nat still wouldn't have been surprised to see Grace there. She wasn't. Izzie snatched up the phone.

"Calling your father?" Nat said.

"Who else?"

"To say what?"

"To say what? That my sister's been kidnapped."

"We already told him that."

"So? Now it's true."

"But—"

"But what?"

"He didn't believe it."

"The room, the note—that changes everything."

"Will he think so?"

"What are you talking about?"

Odd, to have to explain her own father to her. "We need more facts," he said.

"What kind of facts?"

"I don't know. We have to think. Who could have done this?"

"Kidnappers, for God's sake. Do you expect them to identify themselves?"

"Have there been any other attempts?"

"Other attempts?"

"In the past—threats against your family."

"From whom?"

"Workers with a grievance, business rivals—you'd know better than me."

Izzie, punching out the numbers, gave him a quick look. "All you're doing is complicating this. It's simple. We need that money and we need it now."

She reached someone, spoke a word or two into the phone, hung up. It rang within the minute.

"Dad?" She pressed the speaker button.

"Yes?" said Mr. Zorn. Nat heard traffic noises—he was back in the city—and impatience in his tone.

Izzie told him about their place in the tunnels and what had happened to it, told him about the ransom note, told him they needed the money and needed it now, told him that this time it was real.

Silence, followed by a muffled conversation; Nat thought he heard Andy Ling's voice. Mr. Zorn came back on the line.

"What did the note say?"

"The exact words?"

"Yes."

"I don't remember the exact words, but—"

"I do," Nat said.

"Ah," said Mr. Zorn. "Nat. Let's hear them."

Nat quoted the ransom demand verbatim.

Pause. "Would you repeat that, please?"

Nat repeated it.

Another pause. Then Mr. Zorn laughed. In the background, Andy said, "A million sounds nice," and started laughing too, a low, pleasant laugh of real amusement, different from Mr. Zorn's, Nat couldn't help realizing even at that moment: Mr. Zorn's laugh had an edge, almost like a weapon.

"Is something funny?" Izzie said.

"Kids," said Mr. Zorn: "It's enough now."

Click.

Izzie paled, then went red. He'd never seen her face like that; she was almost a different person. For a moment, he thought she was going to throw the phone across the room. Grace probably would have. The color faded slowly from her face. She turned to him and said, "Doesn't anyone understand what's happening here? She's going to die. I can feel it."

"What about trying Professor Uzig now?" Nat said.

"Stop calling him that," Izzie said. "He's just Leo. What about him?"

"Maybe he can persuade your father."

"He didn't come through for you."

"This is different."

They brought Professor Uzig down to the cave. He shone the flashlight they'd given him here and there; not lingering, Nat noticed, on the wreckage, Lorenzo, or even the ransom note; but more on the undamaged parts: the gilded molding, the velvet chairs and couches, the fine old rugs. "My God," he said. "This couldn't be better." Izzie shone her light at him. He shielded his eyes. "Did you say there were candles?" he said.

Nat and Izzie lit some. Professor Uzig gazed at the high ceiling, with its coffered woodwork, carved with leaves, flowers, grapes, horns of plenty. "Metaphorically, historically, culturally—it's perfect, perfect in so many ways."

"What do you mean?"

"You must know, if you've been coming here. What shall I call it? A time capsule, and planted with the same sort of deliberation. Can you read that?" He pointed to the Greek writing on the wall. "From the *Republic*," he said, reading it in Greek and then translating: "Let early education be a sort of amusement."

Didn't Plato have a cave? This can be Nietzsche's. Izzie had said that, when they were naming this place.

"There were social clubs at Inverness in the nineteenth century," Professor Uzig was saying. "Not fraternities— more in the Oxford-Cambridge style. They had a powerful influence, almost independent of the college. The board of trustees outlawed them after World War One, bought up their houses, Goodrich Hall being one. There must be a direct route into Goodrich, sealed off."

"There is," Nat said.

Professor Uzig nodded. "Sealed off by the club members, of course, in order to preserve this secret space. A kind of defiance, do you see, an underground resistance forever in opposition to whatever modernizing forces they despised.

Metaphorically, historically, culturally perfect, as I said." He eyed them. "And motivationally," he added.

"Motivationally?" said Izzie.

Nat felt it coming.

"There couldn't be a more seductive setting for dreaming up little schemes like yours," said Professor Uzig. "A place like this can almost be said to dream them up by itself. And the consequent destruction in light of the failure of the scheme makes perfect sense."

"Mr. Zorn called you?" Nat said.

"I was hanging up when you knocked on my door."

"You're saying you don't believe us?" Izzie said. "What about the goddamn note?" She took him by the front of his tweed jacket—seized him, really—and yanked him toward it. Professor Uzig, barrel-chested, fit for his age, didn't like being yanked, resisted, but not successfully.

"Yes," he said, smoothing his jacket when Izzie had released him, "I heard about this note." He looked it over. All texts, as Nat recalled, were transparent to him. "Don't you realize you're starting to embarrass yourselves?"

"What's wrong with everybody?" Izzie said. "We didn't write it."

"Your father doesn't doubt that. He knows it was Grace."

Izzie turned on him. "When I say we, Grace is included."

Professor Uzig took a step back. "Who else could have written it, then?"

"I thought you were the one who knew how to think. Some real kidnapper, of course."

Professor Uzig's voice rose, but only slightly. "This is not the note of a real kidnapper. And what real kidnapper would know about this place? For that matter, have you told anyone else about it?"

"No," Nat said. "But . . ." An idea was starting to form in his mind.

"But what?" said Professor Uzig.

"There's a thief on campus."

"There are always thieves on campus, almost invariably your fellow students."

"But this one knows about the tunnels," Izzie said.

"Why do you say that?" said Professor Uzig.

Nat told Professor Uzig about the theft of Wags's TV, how he'd followed the thief until he'd disappeared in the Plessey basement.

"That doesn't mean he knows about the tunnels."

"There was nowhere else he could have gone."

Professor Uzig didn't looked convinced. "Could you identify this person?"

"I only saw him from behind," Nat said. "Big, with a ponytail."

A strange expression crossed Professor's Uzig's face. Nat's mom would have said he looked a little green; as though he'd eaten something bad or was seasick. "It won't work," he said.

"What won't work?" Izzie said.

"Whatever you kids are up to," said Professor Uzig. He turned to Nat. "Time for you to go home. Worse things have happened."

"Worse things are happening now," Nat said. *A milion sounds nice.* Whatever was bothering him was in that sentence. *A milion sounds nice.* And it wasn't the spelling. He walked along the walls of the room, tapping here and there, listening for hollow sounds, although not sure why. They sounded hollow everywhere.

"You're not going to talk to him?" Izzie said.

Professor Uzig shook his head. "You've given me nothing to talk about."

"Nicely put," said Izzie, "as usual. But would you be saying that if he wasn't dangling this endowed chair in front of your nose?"

There was no persuading Professor Uzig after that. He didn't say another word. They went upstairs in silence.

*　　*　　*

"What about calling the police?" Nat said to Izzie when they were alone; not because he thought it was a good idea, more because it seemed the kind of thing people said at a time like this.

"Brilliant," Izzie said. "If we forget about what the note says, and about what will happen when the police call my father and ask when the money's coming."

"Izzie," he said; not because she was wrong, but because of how she'd spoken to him. She was acting so strange.

"What?"

She was acting so strange, but he'd already said that.

Izzie took a deep breath. He could almost feel her getting hold of herself, slowing down.

"Sorry," she said. She gave him a kiss, soft and quick, on the cheek. "Better?"

That left the bowling jacket. *Saul's Collision.* Nat knew a bit about bowling—his mom had been in the Tuesday league for years, always fixing chicken pot pie that night, so he could warm it for himself when he got home from basketball—and had noticed lanes at the bottom of College Hill, not far from the tracks. All-Star Bowling, or something like that. He looked them up in the phone book, called the number.

"Does a team from Saul's Collision bowl there?" he said.

"Sure does."

"Because one of them lost his jacket. I'd like to return it."

"We're open till ten."

"I meant personally."

"Personally?"

"I'm looking to join a team."

"You could do better than Saul's, you're any kind of bowler at all."

"But I like their jacket."

"I hear you. Tell you what. Where you calling from?"

"Here—in Inverness."

"There's only one team member lives in town. That would be Ronnie Medeiros, over on River Street. He's in the book."

The wind was blowing off the river, driving the snowfall in waves that seemed to bound through the air. Tracks, back and forth between Ronnie Medeiros's house and the street, were disappearing fast. Nat ignored the buzzer dangling loose on its wires, knocked on the door. No answer. He knocked again, louder. They listened, heard the wind, the snow hissing through bare trees, a plow grinding along some nearby street. Izzie turned the knob. The door opened.

They went into a living room that had space for a big TV and not much else. On the TV sat a framed photograph of a referee posing with a girls' basketball team.

"Hello?" Nat said.

No answer.

They went into a hall, opened a door. A bedroom: in no way like their cave rooms under the campus except that it too was a shambles. Only the bed was undamaged. The basketball referee was sleeping in it. Nat knocked on the doorjamb.

The sleeper's eyes opened.

"Ronnie Medeiros?" Nat said.

"Who'dja expect in my bed, for Christ sake?" His eyes went to Izzie, back to Nat. "You the guys Saul sent?" he said.

They didn't answer.

He got impatient. "To help me clean up. My fuckin'—my freakin' head is killing me."

"What happened here?" Nat said.

"Saul didn't tell you?"

"No."

"Just a little party, you could call it. Got out of hand. He promised me that if I kept my—that he'd send someone to clean it up."

"You're talking about Saul of Saul's Collision?" Nat said.

"Huh?"

Nat held up the bowling jacket.

"Where'd you get that?" He sat up with a groan. "Lemme see." Nat handed him the jacket. He ran his hands over it, as though it bore a message in Braille, then squinted up at Nat. "You cops?" He lowered his head gently to the pillow. "Fuckin' A. That was quick. I told him there's no way to keep something like this a . . ." He paused, his eyes again shifting to Izzie and back. "You don't look like cops," he said. "Least not cops from around here." His gaze went to Izzie. "Unless you're FBI," he said. "There's girl FBI agents on TV and they always look like you." His eyes narrowed. "I get it now—that fuckin' Freedy."

"Freedy?" Nat said.

"Sure. Crossing state lines."

"Who's Freedy?" Nat said.

"Think I'm stupid? Not sayin' another word till I speak to my lawyer. That's my right, and no one ever accused Ronnie Medeiros of not sticking up for his rights."

"We're not from the FBI," Nat said, "not police at all."

"Expect me to believe that?"

"Whose jacket is this?" Nat said.

Ronnie clamped his mouth shut, sucked both lips into his mouth like a child, raising the little growth of hair under his lower lip into prominence. Izzie made a disgusted sound and left the room.

"Is it yours?" Nat said.

Ronnie, mouth still clamped shut, shook his head.

"How do you spell *million*?" Nat said.

Ronnie looked interested. His mouth relaxed. "Million?" he said.

"Spell it."

"M-i-l-l-i-o-n."

"Are you sure?"

" 'Course I'm sure. I graduated high school. And *billion*'s the same, just with a *b*."

Izzie came back. She had a laptop in her hands. "The laptop," she said.

"How do you know?"

"It's not working, but . . ." Izzie flipped open the protective flap at the back. Nat read the label inside: *Property of Zorn Telecommunications*.

She stood over Ronnie, about to do almost anything. "Where did you get this?"

"Don't," he said.

"Don't what?"

"I already been clobbered with that thing once."

"By who?" Nat said.

Ronnie looked at him, at Izzie, at the laptop. He licked his lips. "I'm ready to make a deal," he said.

"Let's hear it," Nat said; he felt Izzie's glance.

"First I want immunity. Not the bullshit kind, the other one."

"You got it," Nat said.

"Guaranteed?"

"Guaranteed."

Ronnie nodded. "The thing you gotta understand, I didn't have nothin' to do with any stealing. All I did was tell Freedy about my uncle Saul. Whatever happened after that was all them."

"What happened after that?"

"The stuff Freedy . . . acquired, must have got bought by Uncle Saul."

"So Uncle Saul is a fence and Freedy's a thief."

"If you want to put it that way."

"Describe Freedy."

"Describe him?"

"What he looks like."

"He's a fuckin' animal." Ronnie Medeiros glanced around the room. "Big, like. Buff. Works out like you wouldn't believe. Has this scary smile." He shrugged. "That's about it."

"You left out the ponytail," Nat said.

Ronnie gazed at him. "For a minute there I thought maybe you looked a bit too young to be FBI. Just goes to show."

"Where is he?"

"Who?"

"Freedy."

"Haven't got a clue."

"Where does he live?"

"That I can tell you," said Ronnie.

30

The true Nietzschean teacher values his own worth only in relation to his students. True or false?
—True/false section, final exam, Philosophy 322

Freshmen couldn't have cars. Following Ronnie Medeiros's directions, Nat and Izzie walked the mile to the house where Freedy lived. A plow passed them, spraying sand out the sides, sand covered almost at once by blowing snow; the streetlights came on, triggered by the growing darkness, although it was still long before night. Nat thought of a poem, not a poem he had read, but for the first time a poem he might write. Why now? Almost shameful, when all his resources should have been devoted to getting Grace back, to undoing what they'd done, but there it was, a poem about clocks, all the clocks in life, everything a clock, measuring time in different ways: the stars moving across the sky, the spinning earth, the tilting earth, light and dark, snakes shedding their skin, Izzie's heart beating beside him, his own heart.

Izzie took his arm. "I'm changing my mind about you," she said.

"In what way?"

"A good way. You were great back there, with that sleazeball. I never knew you were so strong inside." He felt her gaze. "We're a good match, don't you think?" she said.

Nat, who'd thought she already liked him, didn't understand

in what way she'd changed her mind. He looked at her in confusion. She misinterpreted the expression on his face.

"Is everything going to be all right?" she said.

"We'll find her."

"That's not what I asked."

Nat didn't understand that either, but there was no time to go into it. They were at the house where Freedy lived. A woman answered their knock.

Nat recognized her at once: the woman he'd seen through the grate in the lobby of Goodrich Hall, taking a hundred-dollar bill from Professor Uzig. She wasn't wearing her Birkenstocks now: her feet were bare and she had on a striped Moroccan robe. There were a few drops of what looked like blood, not quite dried, on the front, although she didn't seem to be bleeding. Her eyes were open much too wide.

"We're looking for Freedy," Nat said.

"He's not here."

Over her shoulder, Nat could see the kitchen. Another wrecked room: even the fridge was tipped over, spilling food over the floor, and smashed pottery lay everywhere. A ceramic shard that might have been a cup handle was lodged in her frizzy graying hair. Nat thought: *Grace is here.* He even felt her presence, the kind of paranormal thing that wasn't him at all. He pushed his way past the woman, inside.

"Grace?" he called. "Grace?"

He went through the kitchen, jerked open a closet door, then into a hall, another bedroom, wrecked, and another one, also wrecked. This last bedroom had strange wall paintings of mushrooms, elves, rainbows; a deformed lion held up a poem on a scroll, an inept, unpleasant poem called "Little Boy."

"Grace? Grace?"

Not under the beds, not in the closets, not behind the upside-down chairs and couches; but still he felt her presence. He strode back into the kitchen.

"You're Freedy's mother," he said to the woman.

"Yes."

"Where is Grace?"

"Grace?"

Maybe there was no reaction because Freedy's mother hadn't heard the name. "Her twin," he said, indicating Izzie, "but with lighter hair. Where is she?"

Freedy's mother looked at Izzie. Nat saw no sign of recognition, and knew in that moment that Grace wasn't there, that this woman had never seen her. He knew that, but the paranormal feeling lingered.

"I don't know what you're talking about," Freedy's mother said.

"He may have given you some other name for her," Izzie said.

"Who?" said Freedy's mother. "I'm not getting any of this."

Izzie grabbed her robe, right at the throat. "Where is she, you stupid cow?"

Nat reached out to pull Izzie's hand away, but before he could, Freedy's mother started crying, a horrible cawing cry with tears and snot, her face all cubist. Izzie let go, backed away. Freedy's mother's legs folded under her; she sat on the floor, hard. "Are you going to rape me too?" she said.

"Someone raped you?" Nat said.

She covered her face with her hands, red hands with cracked knuckles and bitten nails.

"Did this just happen?" Nat said.

Freedy's mother nodded, face still hidden.

"Who did it?"

She made another cawing sound. "They came looking for Freedy." And another. "Just like you."

"Who did?"

"I'm so afraid."

"Of what?"

"That Freedy's done something terrible."

Izzie stood over her. "To my sister?"

Freedy's mother shook her head. "I don't know anything about anyone's sister."

"Then what terrible thing did he do?" Nat said.

She lowered her hands. "What if he hurt one of them, very badly?"

"One of who?"

"S-S—"

"Who?"

"S-Saul M-M-Medeiros's people."

"That's who came here?"

She nodded.

"And they raped you?"

She shook her head.

"What's going on?" Izzie said. "Does this have anything to do with us?"

"One of them raped you, is that it?" Nat said.

She nodded. "S-Saul Medeiros raped me. His—his nose was all squashed up. He bled all over my face." She cried out again, and covered it, covered where Saul Medeiros had bled, with her hands. Her bare feet were turned inward and the toes curled under, like twins, Nat thought, in the fetal position. His mind paused right there, on the verge of something. Was it the answer to whatever was bothering him about the first line of the ransom note, or something else? Whatever it was didn't come.

A photograph lay on the floor, a framed picture, the glass cracked, of a kid in a muddy football uniform, posing unsmilingly after a game, helmet in hand. He picked it up. "Freedy?" he said.

Freedy's mother peered through her fingers, nodded.

"The ponytail came later?"

"Yes." She reached out for the picture. Nat handed it to her. She gazed at it, composed herself a little. "I used to love this town."

Silence. It went on until Nat said, "But?"

She shook her head. Nat went to the sink, full of smashed

things, found an unbroken glass with the stub of a joint in it. He washed the glass, poured water, brought it to Freedy's mom, helped her to her feet. She took the glass in both hands—still it shook—and drank a mouthful. Not drank, exactly; but filled her mouth, went to the sink, and spat it all out, with force. Then she swallowed the rest of the water. Izzie glanced at her watch.

"Thank you," said Freedy's mother. She must have felt the cup handle in her hair at that moment. She plucked it out, regarded it uncomprehendingly.

"You used to love the town," Nat prompted her.

"A long time ago," she said. "Back when the Glass Onion was still open."

"The boarded-up place at the bottom of the Hill?"

"Everyone met there—townies, college kids, even some professors. It was a very positive space. Positive things happened to me there. I thought they were positive."

"Like what?"

"Personal growth experiences."

"This is getting us nowhere," Izzie said. "What about Freedy?"

"He should never have come back from California," Freedy's mother said.

"Why not?"

"Why not? Look what's happening. But I suppose there was no choice. Something bad happened out there, too."

"What?" Nat said.

"I don't know what. No one actually died. And the truth is it's not the whole reason he came back. I see that now."

"What's the rest of it?"

"Do we have time for this?" Izzie said.

Freedy's mother looked at Izzie. "I'm still not sure who you people are, or what you want."

"We told you already," Izzie said, her voice rising. "My—"

Nat cut her off. "If your son is a kidnapper—"

"He couldn't be."

"You're wrong," Nat said. "Shouldn't you help us stop it now, before anyone else gets hurt? Before the police are involved?"

"I guess so," said Freedy's mother; her eyes, still open much too wide, looked confused. "But I've never heard of any kidnapping."

"Just tell us where he is," said Izzie.

"I don't know."

"You're lying," Izzie said. "You'll end up in jail with him."

"Could that happen?" Freedy's mother's voice had gone soft and high-pitched, like a little girl's. "I'm a good person. Freedy's basically a good person, too. He went out to California to make something of himself."

"And did he?"

"I think so."

"In what way?"

"He's ambitious now."

"What does he do?"

She thought. "Did he tell me the details?"

"We're getting nowhere," Izzie said.

"What did he do when he was here?"

"Went to the high school. Played on the football team. I didn't watch—too violent."

"What else did he do?"

"Hung out, I guess. Like a teenager."

"Did he have a job?"

"Oh, yes." She brightened. "He was always very hard-working. He worked for the college every summer."

"Doing what?"

"In the maintenance department."

Nat glanced at Izzie. She was quiet now, watching him.

"And the other reason he came home, the reason you see now?" Nat said.

"That would be a private thing," said Freedy's mother. "More of a personal quest."

"Look around you," Nat said. Freedy's mother obeyed. "This has gone beyond a private thing."

She nodded. He took her glass, refilled it, handed it back. "He got interested in his father," she said; water trembled in the glass. "Why did I think that wouldn't happen?"

"Who's his father?" Nat said.

"That's just the point," said Freedy's mother. "It was only a one-night . . . experience. I shouldn't say only, because it had its own validity. But it was part of another world that had nothing to do with Freedy. That explanation used to satisfy him."

"But not anymore."

"No."

"Did you tell him?"

"No. But he might have found out anyway, I don't know how."

"Who is he?" Nat said.

"I can't tell you," said Freedy's mother. "It's a private—" She stopped herself. "I'm sworn to secrecy."

"Or is it that you're being paid?" Nat said.

She stared at him. "Who are you, again?"

"Who's paying her?" said Izzie.

"The father," Nat said, watching Freedy's mother. "Someone she met a long time ago, down at the Glass Onion."

Freedy's mother didn't deny it; her lips parted slightly, gripped by the narrative, as though hearing her life turned into a story by someone who knew how.

"So he's hiding her at his father's," said Izzie. "Is that what you think?"

"Yes," said Nat.

"Then we have to know who he is, and that's that," said Izzie. Freedy's mother backed up against the counter. "Who's the father?"

She looked up at Izzie, started crying again. Was there something false in her crying now? Nat thought it was possible.

"It doesn't matter," he said.

"What do you mean?" said Izzie.

"We already know."

They left Freedy's mother like that, crying in her blood-spotted Moroccan robe. There was no time to do anything about her; and not much desire, either.

The nurse answered the Uzigs' door. "The professor's not in," she told them.

"Where is he?"

"You'll have to speak to Mrs. Uzig about that. Right now she's sleeping."

"We have to talk to her," Nat said.

"I'm sorry," the nurse said, closing the door; but they were already inside.

Helen Uzig wasn't sleeping; she was sitting at the kitchen table with a cup of tea, watching the snow fall. She smiled at them.

"Bright-eyed and bushy-tailed," she said. "Welcome."

"Where's Leo?" said Izzie.

"You missed him, I'm afraid. He was called to a sudden conference. Some Nietzschean emergency—perhaps they've discovered a long-lost retraction of the whole thing."

"Where is the conference?" Nat said.

Helen noticed the nurse. "Stop hovering." The nurse left the room. "Milan, I believe. Leo is probably on the connecting flight out of Albany at this moment, unless the airport is closed."

"Did he go alone?"

"Alone? What is the implication of that, floozy-wise?"

"Was he with a big, ponytailed man?"

"Do you mean Freedy?"

"Yes."

"How interesting you should know him. No, he wasn't with Freedy. Why would he be?"

"Is Freedy here now?"

"Here?"

"In the house."

"Of course not. I don't expect him till spring."

"Why?"

"He can't very well do his excavating in frozen ground, can he?"

"Excavating?" Nat, in his winter clothes, felt cold.

"For the new pool. Malibu, Mediterranean, and the other one escapes me. An enterprising man—just think of that crow—although I wouldn't describe him as bushy-tailed." She lowered her voice. "And between you and me, I wouldn't be surprised if he had a serious drug problem."

"Why do you say that?"

"His perceptions get a bit wobbly. At one point he thought I was his grandmother. Although it could have been because I fixed him a slap-up breakfast, just like the nicest granny in the world. You young people aren't hungry too, by any chance?"

"We have to search your house," Nat said.

"How exciting," said Helen. "But you won't find Leo."

"We're looking for Freedy," Nat said.

"You won't find him either."

"What about Grace?"

"Grace?"

"My sister," said Izzie.

"Ah," said Helen, turning to her, "the beautiful twins. How Leo does go on and on. Which beautiful twin are you?"

"Izzie," said Izzie.

"So many z's in my life. Well, Izzie, your beautiful twin isn't here either, except in the sense that you are."

"I don't follow you," Izzie said.

"What's so hard? Being identical, of course, you're always in both places. But no one's here today, not even the birds."

Nat and Izzie searched the house. No sign of Grace, no sign of Freedy, no sign of Leo, except three plastic wrappers on his bed, the kind dry cleaners use for shirts.

They tried the garage last. It contained gardening supplies and an old Mercedes convertible under a drop cloth. The keys were in the ignition.

"We may need this," Izzie said, getting behind the wheel. Nat opened the garage door. She drove out. Nat closed the door, hopped in the rolling car. Helen Uzig watched them from a front window.

They couldn't figure out how to put the top up. Snow had been falling when Grace and Izzie drove Nat to New York for Christmas in the Rolls-Royce and the top had been down then, too. But it hadn't been snowing hard like this, and the feeling he'd had then, of being inside a protective bubble, was gone.

There were two banks on campus. They identified the one where Grace and Izzie had their account, entered just before closing, withdrew all the money in cash—$13,362. More money than Nat had ever had in his hands, ever seen, but still almost useless. They went back to Grace and Izzie's room to find some clever way of making it look like a million; their only idea. The message light was blinking. Izzie hit the button.

An intake of breath; Nat knew who it had to be before the voice spoke. "Little change of . . . can't think of it, starts with *v*. Call it a change of plan. What with the snow and all. Know the Glass Onion? Bring the package to the back door. Six o'clock. Sharp. Any questions?"

"Thank God," Izzie said.

"What do you mean?" said Nat. It was 4:45.

"Because this will change everything, of course." She was already calling her father to play him the message. Nat watched her face, said nothing.

An operator at some Zorn number said he would call back. Izzie tried again, every fifteen minutes, every ten, every five, using expressions like *life and death*. She tried her stepmother, Andy Ling, Albert, even Anton. She reached none of them. No one called back. The bone structure of her face grew more and more apparent.

At 5:50, Nat got to his feet. His heart started racing, lightly at first, then harder and harder but just as fast. Izzie raised her eyebrow, her left eyebrow. "Is it going to be all right?" she said. Or something like that; Nat was aware of little more than his heartbeat. She took his hand as they went out the door. Hers felt like ice.

31

Identify: "When you gaze long into an abyss the abyss also gazes into you."
—Two-point bonus question, final exam,
   Philosophy 322

Freedy felt pretty good. He kind of liked the way things were going down. Sure, the arm wasn't tip-top, his right arm, almost like another person, ready to go to war for him at the drop of a hat. And he was all out of andro, all out of crystal meth. But funny: he didn't even need them anymore. Had he ever felt stronger? No, not even close. He could knock down brick walls, lift cars right off the ground, smash things to smithereens, whatever smithereens were. Had to be momentum. Momentum was on his side at last. Everything was easy now. Take just walking down College Hill in the darkness, right in the middle of the deserted street, snow swirling around him and he didn't even feel it. Didn't feel the cold. Momentum: all he had to do was let it take him.

Soon, very soon, he would be a millionaire. A millionaire! Was that the most beautiful word in the language or what? A millionaire, and out of this goddamn town forever. Tomorrow—a matter of hours—he would be in Florida. The beach. The biggest cigar in the world. One of those drinks with an umbrella. Cool shades, the very best, like Revos, not ripped off somebody's towel, but store-bought, legitimate. He pictured it all, saw it as clear as life, or clearer. A picture in his mind tonight; tomorrow: reality. He was an entrepreneur, a risk-taker, one of the daring few, who, as they said on all the infomercials, made things happen. The kid from the flats makes good. At that moment, reaching the bottom of College Hill and trudging through knee-deep snow in the alley that led to the back of the Glass Onion, Freedy felt not just pretty good, but better than he'd ever felt in his life.

Only one problem. Not a problem, really, just something he hadn't made up his mind about. The girl. Would he ever find another girl like that, a girl so right for him? She was something: a girl who'd given him more trouble than Saul and his big boys. Remembering what had happened to Saul's nose, he smiled to himself in the darkness. He'd taken Saul down a peg or two, but good. I got you last—a game he'd played at recess as a kid. Freedy always won, had now won again. Florida tomorrow. He'd finished with Saul Medeiros forever, would never even think of him again, had got him last.

Much more fun to think about the girl. An amazing girl. She'd actually helped him—*if you're with the hostage, that makes you a hostage too*. She'd even suggested this place, in a way; a vacant lot, she'd said, or an empty building. The Glass Onion was perfect. Freedy saw just how perfect when he moved behind it.

The alley made an L-shaped turn back of the Glass Onion and ended there. On one side was the loading dock of the old hardware store, also boarded up; at the end of the alley, a Dumpster; before him, the service entrance of the Glass Onion, the door padlocked, the bulkhead buried in snow. He was happy about the snow, another sign of the momentum on his side. Supposing they *had* been stupid enough to call the cops, didn't it stand to reason that the cops would already have checked this place out? But they hadn't: he could see, dark as it was, that there were no footprints except his in the snow. He crouched under the loading dock, giving himself a good view back up the alley, all the way to the street. The alley was dark, but the entrance glowed orange from a street-light; the blowing snow came and went as black streaks. Freedy pulled an old pallet from the shadows under the loading dock, upended it in front of him, waited.

Out on the street the storm was making noise, but it was quiet in the closed-in space behind the Glass Onion. The Glass Onion had been boarded up for almost as long as Freedy could remember. He had to say almost because the truth was he'd been inside once. Must have been very young, but he had a clear memory of a guitar-playing singer with a long beard up on a stage, a yellow drink with a straw, a dish of noodles or some shit in a sauce the same color—ginger, was that the word?—as the singer's beard. The beard and the noodles and that yellow drink had got all mixed up in his mind and he'd ended up puking on his mother's lap. She'd been wearing one of those striped Arab robes. The stripes, the noodles, the beard, the puke—all the same ginger color. She'd never taken him to the Glass Onion again, so it worked out fine.

Something was bothering him about the girl. Oh, yeah. Even though she was amazing, he was a little pissed off with her. For one thing, there'd been that business with the broken glass. He admired it in a way, but she could have actually hurt him. Worse than that, though, was this tendency she had to maybe not respect him enough, maybe talk down her nose a little. Had she even laughed at him at one point? Of course, with the way things had been left between them, she might be reconsidering her attitude by now. She would come around. Human beings were animals, after all, not in a bad way, that was simply scientific fact. So what he'd thought before—breaking a horse—was right. If he decided to take her along with him, take her into this golden future—and the decision was his, not hers—she'd end up—what was the word? *Infatuated.* Like a broken horse. She'd end up infatuated with him. Could he picture her with her hands all over him, staring up at him with big horse eyes, going down on him by request? Yes, he could. He could have both: the money and the girl. But the decision would be his.

And first, the money. What time had he said? Six. Six sharp. Freedy was wondering what time it was now, the plan kind of depending on it, when he heard, very faint in the storm, the bell tolling up at the chapel on College Hill. That bell was part of his life, one of the bad parts, but this—the last time he'd have to listen to it!—was different. This time it was working for him. He counted: six bells.

Six o'clock. Sharp. But what if they didn't come? That would mean they thought he was bluffing. Freedy knew what had to be done in a case like that, no matter how perfect for him this girl was, no matter how infatuated she could become with his body and his mind. In a case like that, when you said if something doesn't happen then something else is goddamn well going to, in a case like that, you had to follow through. Every infomercial said that; it was, like, one of their Ten Commandments.

He'd been getting ahead of himself. There, down at the end of the alley, in that orange light with the black snow swirling around, someone stepped into view. Someone fairly tall, although not as tall as Freedy, but who did look a bit like a certain type of football player, the quarterback type specifically. Freedy had always hated quarterbacks. The wonderful Thanksgiving leg-breaking hit? That had been on a quarterback.

Whoever it was came closer, and just as he reached the point in the alley where the orange light ended and the shadows took over, he glanced back for some reason. And, in glancing back, revealed his profile. The college kid. Nat. He had a backpack—those college kids all went around with backpacks, like life was a camping trip—but he had it in his hand, not on his back. The college kid: born on top of the Hill. But then Freedy remembered: *He works in a mill. His old man's not around.* That made him even angrier.

Now the college kid was entering the quiet, closed-in space. How to handle this, exactly? The first idea that came to Freedy's mind was to take him out, take the money, take off. Break him in two, just like he'd wanted to do since the first time he'd seen him. Then—goddamn it, yes—then go back and get the girl. Why not? He couldn't think of one good reason. The first idea, the best, the only. He had momentum, he had the power, he had the element of surprise. Like the wolf or the tiger, he got ready to spring.

The college kid was looking around. Looking at the back of the Glass Onion, the Dumpster. What was this? He'd noticed the footprints, was following them with his eyes, like he was tracing Freedy's movements or something. Freedy didn't like that at all. The college kid's gaze came up, directly on the pallet propped up under the overhang of the old hardware loading dock.

The college kid, Nat, spoke. "Where is she?" he said. Didn't raise his voice; sounded almost steady, in fact, like he wasn't afraid or some bullshit. "I've brought the money."

Freedy pushed the pallet over, came out from under the overhang in a crouch, a little awkward, rose to his full height, making up for it. Yes: taller than the college kid, and much, much stronger. A fuckin' animal of another species. "Let's have it," he said.

It was Freedy. Nat made no move to hand the backpack over. Freedy, without question. Nat recognized him from the football picture; there wasn't much light, but enough for that. Freedy looked older, of course, but the expression on his face was the same. Enough light, too, to make out the scratches over his eye and on his chin: not good signs. Nat's heart still pounded, but slower now. "First I have to see her," he said.

Freedy was silent. They stood there—if both had held out their arms at full length, their hands would not quite have met—stood there behind the Glass Onion, the snow drifting in corkscrew patterns down through the partly sheltered space between the rooftops. A smile appeared on Freedy's face; he had big white teeth, like a movie star.

"It's not that kind of kidnapping," he said.

"Yes, it is," Nat said. "There's no other kind." He was aware of a strange assurance suddenly in his tone, as if some older self had stepped inside him when he most needed it.

Freedy's smile faded. "What's that supposed to mean?" he said.

"It's a trade. I bring the money. You bring her." Nat looked beyond Freedy, tried to shape another person from the shadows under the loading dock, could not.

"Don't blame me," Freedy said.

A remark that Nat didn't understand, but he asked for no explanation, just waited. He felt a certain rhythm coming from Freedy, sensed that it was important to break it, and that silence, waiting, might do that. In the silence, he watched Freedy's face, saw nothing of Professor Uzig, except around the mouth. Their mouths were similar—almost identical, in fact, if you allowed for the difference in age.

"What're you staring at?" said Freedy.

"I'm waiting."

"What for?"

"For you to say where she is."

"I already told you—don't blame me. It was her idea."

Her? Was Freedy talking about his mother? Was she somehow involved, was that why they were meeting here, behind the Glass Onion? Had he misunderstood everything?

Freedy was smiling again. "Not so sharp, huh, for a college kid. She, me, and the money in the same place means I'm a hostage too. Get it now? *I* got it right away."

Nat didn't get it. He realized that Freedy was talking about Grace, not his mother, but what did that mean? If Grace was giving Freedy ideas, were they in some sort of collaboration? Was it still a fake kidnapping? Would she take it that far? No:

the scratches on his face, the phrase *hostage too*, the note—she'd never have worded it, or let him word it, like that—all told him no. It was real. Therefore the fact that Grace was giving Freedy ideas probably meant she'd been trying to trick him in some way, and almost certainly meant she was still alive.

"Is she in there?" Nat said, nodding toward the Glass Onion.

"I'm getting bored with this," Freedy said. "Hand it over."

"And then what?" Nat said.

"Hey," said Freedy, "I'm not a prophet."

"That's clear," Nat said.

Could those eyes of Freedy's be said to harden, to become even harder than they were? They did. "You better explain that," Freedy said.

"If you could see at all into the future," Nat said, "you wouldn't be doing this."

"Are you, like, threatening me?" Freedy said.

"I'm stating a fact." Freedy seemed a little closer to him, although Nat wasn't aware of any movement; if they held out their arms now, their hands would be in contact.

"Shows how much you know," Freedy said. "By tomorrow I'll be down in Flor—I'll be in fucking clover."

"Only if there's been an exchange," Nat said. "You don't get the money until we get her."

Freedy was even closer now; Nat sensed his physical strength—like a magnetic field, except repellent. "This is starting to feel like negotiating," Freedy said. "I don't like negotiating."

"Then you shouldn't have done this," Nat said. "It's not too late to undo it."

"Shake hands," Freedy said, "and go out for beers?"

"Just walking away with no more damage will be good enough."

"Nope," said Freedy. "Doesn't work that way, got to take

risks if you're going anywhere in this life. Got to put it on the line. Everybody knows that, except you rich boys."

"You can drop that one," Nat said. "I grew up with no more money than you, maybe less."

"What the hell do you know about how I grew up?"

"And you're putting another person, an innocent person, on the line, not yourself." Nat was getting angry now—bad strategy, bad timing, bad self-control—but there it was.

"What're you getting at?" Freedy said.

"If you think you're some sort of daring risk-taker, you're full of shit," Nat said. "That's what I'm getting at."

Had he heard right? Freedy couldn't believe it, couldn't believe this college kid would say something like that to him, but he had to trust his hearing; his hearing, like all his senses was very sharp, the best. No one could talk to him like that without being punished. He'd handed out punishment for a lot less. But was this the time? Not quite. Instead, he thought of something amazing to do, something cool and amazing, while everything bottled up in him had a chance to get bottled up more. He reached across the space between them, not much of a space now, reached real slow, and laid his finger on the lips of the college kid. Shushing him, like. Was it the coolest thing he'd ever done? And at the most important moment in his life? What did that say about him?

The college kid got this pissed-off look in his eyes, more than pissed off, angry you could call it, and batted—yes, batted—Freedy's arm away. With some force, even, a surprising amount. Thing was, since Freedy'd been intent only on shushing, he'd used his right arm, the one that wasn't working so well on account of that tire iron business. Also, the one that would hurt if someone batted it. And now someone had.

"You know what I'm going to do to you for that?" Freedy said.

"You're going to take me to where she is," the college kid

said. "I'm going to give you the money. After that, you can try whatever you want."

The answer confused Freedy. Truth was, he couldn't recall a moment of confusion like this, ever. Made him look away for a second, almost like he needed a break from staring the college kid down. Good thing, though—momentum was still on his side—because in that moment of looking away, he saw someone else in the alley.

"What the fuck?" said Freedy.

The college kid turned to see what he was talking about.

"Get back," he called to whoever it was.

Making that turn, of course, the college kid took his eyes off Freedy. Mistake. Beginner's mistake, taking your eyes off old Freedy, especially at a moment like this, when things were a bit confusing, maybe even getting out of hand, and when there was so much bottled up inside him, due to all the composure he'd been keeping. Freedy let him have it. A left hand, yes, not like his right, not like another whole person, but still, he put everything into it, legs—those legs of his!— hips, back, chest, all those reps, all those sets, all those curls, dips, presses, raises, all those years in the gym, all those sup- plements, all that andro, he put that kind of everything into it, and hit the college kid a good one, bang on the side of the face, a crusher. Orgasm? Orgasm had nothing on the feeling that spurted through him at that moment.

College kid went down, no surprise there, and Freedy grabbed the backpack. Bit of a surprise there; he didn't grab it clean. The college kid kind of held on to it, kind of fought him for control of the thing, didn't let go—never let go, in fact—until Freedy booted him one in the gut, making his grip soften enough for Freedy to snatch the backpack away.

Turned out a million was easy to carry. Freedy slung it over his good shoulder, gave the college kid another boot, aiming for the head, but maybe not connecting square, what with all the snow on the ground. No time to do any better, with who- ever it was in the alley, and the alley the only way out.

Freedy ran into the alley, a funny, heavy run in the deepening snow. Out on the street the storm was howling now, but between him and it stood this other person, at the edge of the orange light. Freedy switched the backpack to his other shoulder even though it smarted at bit, freeing his left arm.

This other person stepped right into the middle of the alley, blocking his way.

"Stop," she said.

Turned out to be a she, and with a familiar voice. Then Freedy got a good look at her—snowflakes in her light brown hair—and it gave him a shock. She'd somehow gotten free! Undone all that tape, climbed out of the tunnels, come after him. Was it possible? No, not with her face like that. Not a mark on it, both eyes open, no sign of all they'd been through. Somehow, this had to be the other one.

"Stop right there," she said, in a real commanding voice, like he was a dog.

He was no dog. Two more steps and he let her in on the secret of that left, caught her a nice one, marking her, making them more like twins again. But: something hurt. In his left forearm, something hurt awful, awful enough to make him cry out. He looked at that forearm, held it up in the orange light, that mighty mighty forearm: and what was this? A knife, a goddamn switchblade, angled deep into it, deep in the heart of the muscle. Freedy boiled over. He hit her again with his left, the knife still in it, but didn't connect the way he'd wanted, only staggering her. She was moving away, running now, down the alley, calling, "Nat, Nat."

Freedy looked at that knife in his arm and felt like puking. Funny, to be puking again at the Glass Onion. He didn't let himself. *Get a grip,* he thought, or maybe said aloud. Getting a grip meant figuring out what to do. First, the knife. He got his right hand on it—right hand not at its best either, they were maddening him, maddening him like a bull—sucked in some air, yanked out the switchblade knife. That hurt too— even though there wasn't much blood—hurt enough to make him cry out again, although he kept it inside. Or maybe not. Meth: oh, how he wanted it, and lots of other drugs. He dropped the knife in the snow and stepped out into the street.

At least he had the money. At least? What was he thinking? That was the whole point. No pain, no gain: how true. A millionaire! A millionaire at last! And right away, his life started changing, because parked by the curb, just a few feet away and motor running, was a Mercedes convertible. An old one, but immaculate, and very cool. Not only that, but the top was down, like it was all ready for Florida. Did he need an invitation? He did not. Freedy slipped behind the wheel. No CD player, but he could always add one later. Which way to Miami?

The girl? What about her? The girl maybe wasn't so perfect after all. That part was confusing too. These girls, coming at him with jagged glass, with switchblades, could he ever really trust one of them? Could he ever really be sure she was broken like a horse? He made a decision, an executive decision: forget her. There were girls in Florida, girls who'd be hopping into this new car of his every time he stopped to take a piss, for Christ's sake. No, he would start his golden future alone, like a man.

Miami: what a word, a perfect match for *millionaire.* Which way to Miami? He knew: south. South meant the turnpike; the turnpike meant Route 7, Route 7 meant driving his cool new car down the Hill and taking a right on Main. Freedy was doing that, had switched on the headlights and released the clutch, was actually rolling, when he realized he'd forgotten something important, maybe even basic. He hadn't checked the money. He pulled to a stop beneath the nearest streetlight and picked up the backpack. What if they'd cheated him? Was it possible? He tore it open: no, it wasn't possible, because there, inside the backpack, was money, beautiful, beautiful money. Hundred-dollar bills, in thick wads held together with rubber bands, wads and wads and

wads of them. He pawed through. This wasn't orgasm time,
but a pretty good feeling just the same. He was rich! It was
that easy. Real life begins.

But hey, what was this? Another little wad down in there, a
little deeper, held together by a rubber band like the others,
but didn't feel like the others. In fact, it felt like—he held it up
in the orange light—it was: just a stack of goddamn note
cards. And here was another. And another, and another, and
another. He was hurling them around now, out of the convertible, into the snow, maybe hurling around some of the
money too. A million dollars? Wasn't anything like that here,
not even close. He wasn't a millionaire. He wasn't rich.

They were maddening him, maddening him like a bull,
inciting violence. Wasn't that a crime? He wheeled the car
around, tires spinning crazily in the snow, skidded to a stop
outside the Glass Onion, jumped out, slamming the door shut
hard, but nothing like the way he was going to slam them
around. Slam. The streetlights went out.

The whole town went dark. Everything disappeared: the
street, the buildings, the ground, the sky. Even the blowing
snow was now invisible, but Freedy could feel it stinging his
face, maddening him more. He entered the alley, felt his way
along to the space behind the Glass Onion.

Couldn't see a goddamn thing, no people, no footprints,
only darker shadows and lighter shadows. He slogged his
way through the snow, bumped into what had to be the overhang of the loading dock. A good hiding place, as he knew
well. He lashed out with his boot a few times, hit nothing.

"I want the money," he said, not hysterically, just making
an announcement. He found the Dumpster, one of the darker
shadows, kicked out at any small dark shadows he saw
around it, connected with nothing human.

He made another announcement: "I'm going to murder
you." Then he had a disturbing thought. What if they'd
slipped by him, were already out of the alley? What about the

car? Freedy hurried back to the street, slipping once and falling in deep snow. So cold. He hated the cold.

The car was still there, filling up with snow. He got in, turned it on, fiddled with switches. This and that happened, but the top didn't go up. He sat there, hundred-dollar bills and note cards all around him, blood seeping from his forearm, snow filling the car. An important business term was eluding him. What was it? Something about . . . taking stock. That was it. Time to take stock. What did he have? He had this car, of course, but it wasn't his main asset. His main asset, his only important asset—yes, face facts—was the girl. He had to do something about that asset. There were two choices: protect the asset or destroy it. He tried to think of other options and could not. Protect or destroy, but it would be his choice, no one else's. He was in charge.

Freedy switched on the headlights, the only lights in town, and gunned the car up College Hill.

Nat and Izzie, lying on top of the Dumpster lid, heard the sound of the fading engine through the storm.

"Where's he going?" Izzie said.

"To get her," said Nat. His jaw was bad. He felt the side of his face: caved in.

"But where is she?"

Where was she? *A milion sounds nice.* It was somewhere in there, right in the open. Later would be no good. He had to figure it out now. He was supposed to be smart, supposed to be good at solving problems. Solve this one. A simple sentence. *A milion sounds nice.* What was the most important part of any sentence? The verb. *Sounds.* Nat said it aloud. "Sounds, sounds, sounds. For something to sound nice . . ." There had to be a listener to hear it. For something to sound nice, you had to hear it. To hear it, you had to be in a place to hear it. Freedy had a place. He'd been listening.

A convincing idea, especially since he had no others. "Let's go," Nat said.

They went, but it was slow. He was slow, not Izzie. He was slow lowering himself off the Dumpster, slow finding his way to the street. Izzie tugged him along, stooping once to pick something up, somehow sharp-eyed and surefooted in the darkness.

"If he does anything to her, my life is over," she said.

"That's not true."

"How can you be so stupid?"

His jaw hurt too much to argue.

They ran, or tried to run, up College Hill.

"What's that in your hand?"

"For killing him," Izzie said.

Crazy amount of duct tape. Took forever to get it all off, free her from the pipe. She fell to the dirt floor with a thump. The candle burned near her face. The other twin was a lot prettier now.

"Bad news," Freedy said. "They fucked me."

The gold eye, the one that would open, opened. "I need a doctor." So quiet he could hardly hear her, even with his super hearing.

"Say that again and you won't." He wasn't in the mood. What was he going to do with her? The simple solution was asset destruction, moving on. But moving on to what, exactly? And he'd invested a lot in her. Plus there was still the potential for a big payoff. He just needed a time-out, that was all, to rethink.

"Feel like a little spin?" he said to her.

She just lay there.

"Get up," he said, louder and not so friendly.

They heard him. On the other side of the wall, Izzie turned sideways, raised one foot high like a trained Thai kick boxer, precisely as Grace had done the night they found the tunnels, and kicked in the wooden paneling in the big room of the old social club. Nat shone his flash through the opening, and there they were in a little square room lit by a single tall candle balanced on the dirt floor, Grace on her back, hair matted with blood, Freedy crouched over her.

Izzie saw her sister's face and made a horrible sound. The next instant she was diving through the hole in the wall, switchblade glinting in the candlelight, so quick. But Freedy was quicker. Somehow he was already up, already slapping at her arm as though he'd known what was coming. The next moment, she was down. By that time, Nat was in the little room too, flashlight raised high, striking with all his strength at the back of Freedy's head.

He never connected. Without even looking, Freedy jabbed with his elbow, a pistonlike blow that caught Nat just under the rib cage, knocking the wind out of him, knocking him down. The candle fell, started rolling, rolled through the hole in the wall, dropped down into the big room on the other side. Then Freedy's fist started landing, although Nat couldn't see a thing, flashlight smashed, candle gone. He took a punch in the back, scrambled away, felt Grace. He found her hand, not warm, not cold, the same temperature as his.

Nat held on to her, would hold on to her at any cost; but then came that fist, and again, and he felt her slipping, slipping away, and gone.

Total darkness. Didn't bother Freedy. This was his territory. Freedy slung the girl over his shoulder and carried her out of the little square room and into F. Had he ever felt stronger? No. This kind of challenge or whatever it was brought out the best in him. He headed down F, the girl on his shoulder, at a fast walking pace, almost trotting in total darkness. Didn't bother him. He turned into Z, invisible Z, without breaking stride. Z, on the way to building 13: now came the beauty part.

* * *

Total darkness: until flames shot up on the other side of the wall. Nat felt heat flowing in through the hole. He rose. Izzie was already up, the knife, half the blade snapped off, in her hand. They stepped out into a tunnel they didn't know, heard a grunt in the distance, hurried after the sound. Flickering light followed them for a few yards, dwindled to nothing. They kept going, almost running in the darkness. Nat kept one hand on the wall; he didn't know how Izzie was doing it. She was a little ahead, then more so.

Suddenly his hand felt nothing but empty space. He froze. "This way," she called from somewhere on his right. "Another tunnel." He followed her. She moved so fast, almost as though she could see in the dark. He heard another grunt, Freedy's grunt, much closer now.

And another, closer still, followed by a moan, a female moan. Nat caught up with Izzie, brushed against her, took her hand: ice cold. He felt something else, a sort of breeze, a damp breeze, blowing in his face from the direction they were headed. "Wait," he said in Izzie's ear.

"Piss on that," she said, shook him off, kept going. He went after her, stumbled on something soft.

In the darkness, but very near, a few feet away, no more, Freedy said: "Come and get me."

Izzie made a savage noise.

Lights flashed on. Red ceiling lights, the color of exit signs, recessed behind mesh screens. In the light, Nat saw a sort of snapshot. They'd come to a sheer drop-off in the tunnel. Grace lay on the edge of it. Freedy clung to a ladder bolted to the brick wall, leading down, just his head and shoulders visible. And Izzie had stepped, or charged, right over his head, and was now turning to look back, poised in midair, the switchblade in her hand, her eyes wild. The piece of eight Grace had found in Professor Uzig's cake floated weightless around her neck.

No one can remain poised in midair. She fell out of sight, and it was far, far too long before the thud.

"The beauty part," said Freedy, and started up.

Nat kicked at him, kicked right at his head. An alarm started ringing, not far away, distracting Freedy for a moment, probably the only reason the kick landed at all. Not on his head, but his shoulder, the right shoulder.

Freedy cried out in pain. "Call that fair?" he said. "That's my bad shoulder." He lunged up the ladder, swiped at Nat with his left hand, got hold of one of Nat's legs. With his other leg, Nat kicked that bad shoulder again, hard as he could. Freedy lost his grip on the ladder, held nothing but Nat's leg. He dug his fingers into Nat's flesh, trying to somehow kill him that way. Nat kicked him one more time, without compunction.

Nat heard, or felt, a faint flicking sound: Freedy's fingernails, snapping off. Freedy looked surprised. Then he fell. Another expression, a vengeful one, was coming into his eyes when he disappeared from view.

Nat looked over the edge. A long drop to a brick floor. Freedy lay beside Izzie, both of them in postures the living can't adopt.

He turned to Grace, lying in the tunnel.

She opened her eye. "Nat?"

Her face was so bad he could hardly look at her. But he did. And when he did, he noticed something strange. Under the matted blood, her hair was the same light brown color as Izzie's.

He thought of things: body temperatures, raised eyebrows, Clairol bottles, Grand Central Station. How stupid could he be?

"Izzie?" he said.

She closed her eye.

Then came running feet, loud voices, people in uniform: firemen, police, maintenance workers. It was getting very hot. He saw flames behind them.

"There are lights here?" he said.

"In master control," said someone. "Think we wander around in the dark?"

Nat didn't know what to think, not then, not when dental records proved that the dead twin was Grace, not for a long time after.

32

What do we have in common with the rosebud, which trembles because a drop of dew lies on it?
—Friedrich Nietzsche, *Thus Spake Zarathustra*

Nat got two years for attempted extortion, all but four months suspended. His public defender was surprised that the case was prosecuted at all, then surprised at the verdict, and finally the sentence. She sensed some force working against them. Nat knew what it was. Mr. Zorn wanted someone to pay.

Nat paid. He wasn't the only one. Mr. Zorn never endowed a chair in philosophy at Inverness, but he did donate a new residence in Grace's name. The college accepted Professor Uzig's resignation the day before the announcement. Philosophy 322 was deleted from the catalog.

Nat served his sentence in a minimum-security prison not far from Boston. It wasn't too bad. His facial bones knit well after surgery. He had unlimited daytime access to the exercise yard with its basketball hoop. He started taking his foul shots again, hundreds and hundreds a day, sometimes thousands. Despite all this practice, he never exceeded 60 percent, not close to what he'd done in high school. He'd lost that soft touch, didn't even enjoy it anymore. The ball, which had always wanted to go in for him, no longer did. But Nat kept shooting: part of the sentence he was giving himself.

He wrote the clock poem, a few others, started sending

them to journals he found in the prison library. A review in Chicago accepted one of them. The payment was six free copies of the issue his poem appeared in. Nat showed it to Wags when he came to visit.

"Pretty cool," said Wags. Wags was feeling a lot better, had applied for transfer to the film program at a few schools, was waiting to hear. The TV movie shot at Inverness, the one about the fraternity brother and the bone marrow transplant, was broadcast during Nat's term. Wags had made the final cut, was visible for five or ten seconds, roasting marshmallows at a tailgate party.

Nat had other visitors. His mom came. She'd found a new job. It meant selling the house and moving to Denver, but the pay was better. Maybe not *but* but *and*, since she seemed to be looking forward to the move.

Patti came too, on the way to Fort Dix with her boyfriend, who'd been called up. The boyfriend was real, not a creation of Grace's—Nat could see him through the chain-link fence, waiting in the rental car. But the question of who the father had been remained open in Nat's mind. Patti didn't bring it up and Nat didn't ask. Did it even matter now? She brought him a present, a book of inspirational advice currently on the bestseller list. He donated it to the library, unread.

And Izzie.

She looked pretty good. Her eyes weren't quite symmetrical anymore and she walked with a limp, but less of one every day, she said.

Izzie explained the switch. It was about what Nat had thought. At the last minute, after Izzie had called her father saying Grace had been kidnapped, Grace decided she should be the one up top, dealing with him. She hadn't liked how Izzie handled the call. Izzie had gone down to the cave; Grace had dyed her hair, come up to Nat's room playing the role of her sister. It was just a question of Grace being more capable when it came to thinking on her feet.

"She was," Izzie said.

Nat was silent; he knew there was more to it than that.

"Better in every way," Izzie said. "She was the special one."

That saying people had when someone close to them died, the one about a part of them dying too: Nat realized it was true in Izzie's case, maybe even literally. He took her hand. He hadn't intended to do anything of the kind.

Izzie had rented an apartment in Paris for the year, was planning to take a few courses, maybe do some skiing when she felt stronger. She was leaving in a few weeks.

"There's lots of room," she said.

He didn't speak.

"Why don't you come?"

A dump near the prison attracted seagulls. Chased by a second gull, one flew over now, something shiny in its beak.

"I'll think about it."

"Say yes."

Past and present blur on a battlefield where it is always 1863.

In Peter Abrahams's new novel of suspense, Roy Hill finds his job dissolving, his marriage crumbling, his life falling apart. Then a chance encounter with a team of Confederate reenactors opens his eyes to a forgotten past, and puts him on the road to a bloody future....

LAST OF THE DIXIE HEROES

by Peter Abrahams